3/22
9/30

P9-CQX-547

Also by Andrea Dunlop

Losing the Light
Broken Bay (a novella)
She Regrets Nothing

We Came Here
to Forget

We Came Here to Forget

a novel

ANDREA DUNLOP

ATRIA BOOKS

New York   London   Toronto   Sydney   New Delhi

ATRIA
BOOKS

An Imprint of Simon & Schuster, Inc.
1230 Avenue of the Americas
New York, NY 10020

This book is a work of fiction. Any references to historical events, real people, or real places are used fictitiously. Other names, characters, places, and events are products of the author's imagination, and any resemblance to actual events or places or persons, living or dead, is entirely coincidental.

Copyright © 2019 by Andrea Dunlop

All rights reserved, including the right to reproduce this book or portions thereof in any form whatsoever. For information, address Atria Books Subsidiary Rights Department, 1230 Avenue of the Americas, New York, NY 10020.

First Atria Books hardcover edition July 2019

ATRIA BOOKS and colophon are trademarks of Simon & Schuster, Inc.

For information about special discounts for bulk purchases, please contact Simon & Schuster Special Sales at 1-866-506-1949 or business@simonandschuster.com.

The Simon & Schuster Speakers Bureau can bring authors to your live event. For more information or to book an event, contact the Simon & Schuster Speakers Bureau at 1-866-248-3049 or visit our website at www.simonspeakers.com.

Manufactured in the United States of America

10 9 8 7 6 5 4 3 2 1

Library of Congress Cataloging-in-Publication Data has been applied for.

ISBN 978-1-9821-0342-2
ISBN 978-1-9821-0344-6 (ebook)

For my mom and dad

We Came Here to Forget

"I WISH WE could have stayed longer," I told Blair. We were slap-happy from the fourteen-hour trek from Buenos Aires to Salt Lake City. Being on the long flight together had made us like little kids left unsupervised. We were stuck in coach, but fortunately we'd had an entire middle row to ourselves. We drank the complimentary booze and gorged on snacks as though none of it counted so long as we were in the air. We'd just finished a training camp in La Parva and were due for a bit of a break before World Cup season got going in November. If I felt any sense of foreboding leaving South America, it was only because the low-level buzz of it was constant by that point.

The trip had been Blair's idea; he'd suggested to me and Luke—his brother, my boyfriend—that we see another part of South America before heading back to Park City. Things had been tense between Luke and me, and I sensed Blair thought we all needed a vacation.

"You two can if you want," Luke had said, as though Blair had been asking his permission. "I need to chill at home before my Red Bull thing."

"We should," I'd said to Blair, straining to sound nonchalant about how testy Luke was being. "That would be a blast. What about Buenos Aires?"

I'd had more fun than I'd expected to. I wasn't often alone with Blair, and I'd forgotten how much I enjoyed his company. He was much more easygoing than his bullheaded, charismatic brother. For once, I saw this as a mark in his favor rather than something that made him the less exciting one.

"Me too," Blair said now as the flight attendants announced that we were preparing to land. "We'll go back sometime."

"Promise?"

"I promise."

I'd been anxious about the long flight, but as we came in to land, I felt a cold thud of dread. I suspected this had more to do with Luke than anything else. I knew we needed to have a serious, State of the Union conversation, and I knew that I'd have to initiate it. It was always me who had to do the emotional heavy lifting.

As we taxied to the gate in Salt Lake City, the cabin began to come back to life: people waking each other up, putting their shoes back on, and reassembling their carry-on luggage. Phones emerged from where they'd been stashed, and passengers scrolled through messages and called loved ones to let them know they'd landed.

I wasn't so anxious to check my own phone. It had brought me too much bad news in recent years, and I'd come to cherish being disconnected. On some level I knew that the worst was yet to come. I wouldn't say I'd had a premonition, only that some small part of me was always waiting for that call. Luke was picking us up from the airport, a peace offering. For two days I'd managed not to think about my problems with him, worry about my sister, or even think about skiing. But it was over now, and time to get back to real life.

I was vaguely aware of Blair beside me, pulling out his phone and watching it as it came to life. Then I felt his body stiffen next to mine and horror started creeping in.

"Blair," I said, hearing my own voice as though from the bottom of a well. The fear that lived at the edge of my every waking moment now consumed my mind. The worst possible thing. But it was too absurd; no one should hear that kind of news sitting on an airport tarmac surrounded by strangers.

Blair reached over and took my hand. "Oh, Katie."

Penny's Rabbit Is Sick

HOW DO you lose yourself? It is all at once, in a flash? Or is it as slow and irreversible as the melting of a glacier—so that by the time the once-solid core of you has diminished to a handful of fragile crystals, the chance to do anything about it is long past? It seems to me that you lose yourself quickly, and that you lose others little by little.

The question I keep trying to answer is, when exactly did we start to lose her?

❦

Penny was as constant a part of my childhood as the acres of forest behind our house in Coeur d'Alene, Idaho. We were born only twenty-two months apart, and like most siblings so close in age, we both discovered and created the reality of our childhood as a pair. I looked to Penny to help me make sense of things, to explain the world to me from her position just up ahead.

Penny was the prettier sister. From childhood on, girls understand that there will always be a prettier sister. Penny was delicate and fine-boned, taking after our mother's side, whereas I shot up like a weed long before puberty and had thick wrists and a solid frame. I was made with bones that wouldn't break no matter how much abuse I threw at them, taking after my athletic father. I fell out of trees, crashed on the mountain, and did all the things that had my peers showing off plaster casts for classmates to sign without managing to bust myself up. Penny was the opposite: forever getting hurt, forever breakable. But Penny was precocious and could talk circles around the kids her age by the time she was five. Our childhood was a series of incidents in which Penny would taunt me to the edge of a fit and then I would smack her or tackle her and the corridors or our little midcentury modern, four-bedroom home would ring out with "MOM! Katie's *hurting me*!"

"What a sweet child!" people said when they met Penny. She had strawberry-blond hair and freckles speckling her fair skin, which went nearly translucent in the winter and would burn at the mere suggestion of sunshine in the summer. She'd also gotten my dad's clear blue eyes, which mesmerized people even before she could talk. And Penny *was* sweet—just not to me, but that wasn't in the job description. As kids, we were close in that tumultuous I hate you, I love you way that siblings are. Together, we dug in the dirt, fished tadpoles from the streams, and built complicated forts out of scrap wood and mats of woven-together sword ferns. Penny organized games of capture the flag with the kids in our neighborhood, and her team always won. It seemed then that Penny was destined to be a leader; she was smart in a way that made her seem, in strange flashes, much older than she was, almost cunning. She was magnetic, convincing, and far more social than I was. I was a little ambivalent about people, more liable to get lost in my own dreamy thoughts or entranced by nature.

Sisters learn early on that everything you are will always be in relation to the other: you'll always be the pretty one, or the smart one, or the strong one as compared to your sister. It was especially acute because of our ages and the fact that our town was small. The Cleary sisters were like mismatched salt-and-pepper shakers: a pair that never quite made sense. Penelope and Katherine Cleary. Penny and Katie. P and K. Back then CDA was still tiny and undiscovered, far smaller than its less comely nearby cousin, Spokane, Washington.

My parents were strict about some things—swimming without adults around, being home when we said we'd be, lying, being cruel to other children—but lax on others. This was the 1980s and children—at least children in places like Coeur d'Alene—didn't have so much structure, so much expectation. My parents let us roam outside, climbing trees and eating wild huckleberries without worry. They never seemed to have any particular expectations about what their daughters ought to be. They accepted my tomboyish nature as much as Penny's girlieness. Title IX had come just in time, so they introduced us to every sport they could think of. They took us skiing for the first time when Penny was six and I was four, and I was immediately hooked. I don't actually remember this, or at least I don't think I do. I have a faint memory of looking out over the tips of my kiddie skis for the first time, of shooting out ahead of my sister on my second run so that my dad had to zoom after me, but it's probably only that I remember being told that this was how it went. Memory is an unreliable narrator.

I will always be grateful for my happy childhood. Trust me when I tell you that no one has gone over it in more forensic detail than I have, searching for any hint of darkness. There just isn't any.

If my destiny seemed clear from childhood, so in some ways did Penny's. In our long hours exploring among the pines and hemlocks behind our house, Penny was always finding wounded animals: a baby bird that had fallen out of its nest, a mouse with a mangled foot. So it was no wonder—everyone would say later—that she got into medicine. She would carefully transport the animals back to our house, where my mother would help her set up a triage station in our shed, create a habitat out of a shoebox, a feeding system with an eyedropper. My mom had been raised on a farm in the south end of the state and had a handy and expansive knowledge of animals. I tagged along in these moments, a little in awe of my mom and sister.

Penny *loved* animals. She was one of those girls who obsessed over horses: horse shirts, horse books, horse toys. We didn't have the land or the money for horses of our own, but my parents paid for Penny to ride at a nearby stable twice a week. At home, we had the usual spate of pets: a dog, a cat, rabbits, and the occasional pet rodent. Penny's were always getting sick; the rabbit alone ran up vet bills like you wouldn't believe. But those tiny pets often die one after the other, don't they? Who hasn't had a parade of hamsters that marched through their childhood? Poor Penny always chose the sick ones. Mine were robust, like me.

❧

My mom, Deborah, worked several days a week as a guidance counselor at the local junior high school, something she was well suited for with her inexhaustible capacity to listen and her preternatural calm. She was tall with a willowy prettiness that neither Penny nor I had inherited: me taking after my father and Penny after our grandmother: a firecracker of a woman who stood all of five foot one.

Our dad, John, was cheerful and practical. He worked as an accountant and was the most popular guy in the office. He was happy as long as he could ski most days in the winter. He'd bummed around various ski resorts throughout the 1970s before settling in Coeur d'Alene at a time when real estate was cheap as dirt. I might have inherited my love of skiing from him, but I likely got my drive from the grandfather who'd emigrated from Austria and was more or less present at the inception of Alpine skiing. He died when I was ten. I have a framed photo of the three of us at Silver Mountain that sat beside my bed for years.

His wife died shortly before he did, and my memories of her are scant. I know she was religious and made an attempt to get my sister and me into Sunday school. Penny was beloved there—so gentle and receptive—but I didn't fit in as well.

One afternoon, the dozen or so children gathered in the basement of the Heart of the City Church were given a photo that was meant to represent paradise. It featured a beatific-looking blond woman staring out from the porch of a lovely house as a towheaded toddler pushed a sailboat around a sparkling pond. We were told to first tear the pictures into pieces—paradise lost—then tape them back together—paradise restored!—in an emulation of God's love. I hadn't meant to thwart the lesson, I was simply an overzealous kid. When the Sunday school teacher saw my pile of shreds, she was dismayed. But, I pointed out, if I was representing God in this scenario, couldn't I do anything?

I didn't last long in Sunday school after that.

※

I don't have a clear memory of meeting Luke Duncan, nor do I have any memory of my life without him in it. According to our parents, who learned the story from our instructors, Luke and I instantly bonded over being the most daring six-year-olds in the ski school. We were literal fast friends who had our instructor convinced he'd be sued when one or both of us went over a cliff on his watch. Luke's older brother, Blair, was also a gifted skier and was tasked with keeping an eye on the two of us, meaning that, from then on, the three of us were always together.

Penny and I had our own rooms, but I would often sleep in the trundle bed that pulled out from under her twin bed. In the glow of Penny's night-light, we would have long meandering conversations about everything: the mysterious adult world, the secret lives of animals, the possibilities of heaven and hell, and our own far-off futures. Naturally I already had the Olympics in my sights. We'd watched hours and hours of the Calgary games that year, though my sister preferred watching the feminine and elegant Katarina Witt to the super-G and slalom.

"I want to live in a big house on the mountain and have eight husky dogs," I said. "I'll go skiing every day and I'll have a whole room in the house for my trophies."

"Don't you want to get married?" Penny asked.

I made a face. I was nine, Penny was eleven, already in her dreamy preadolescence. "Who would I marry?"

"What about Luke?" she asked.

"Gross. Luke's my friend."

"One day you'll want to be more than friends with boys. You'll probably want to marry Luke," Penny said matter-of-factly. "He's pretty cute, Katie, even if he's just a baby."

"Ick. Anyway, what about you?"

"Well, I'll marry either Sean," she said, name-checking a floppy-haired, blue-eyed boy in her sixth-grade class who was the subject of many hours of gossip between Penny and her best friend, Emily, "or Jonathan Taylor Thomas. It just depends on whether I decide to move to Hollywood to be an actress."

Penny's vision for her future was as malleable as most kids'. One day, she wanted to be an actress; the next, a veterinarian; the next, an airline stewardess.

"And I definitely want to have lots of kids."

"Like the Kimballs?" I asked.

We burst into a fit of giggles. The Kimballs lived four doors down from us. They had two girls our age, as well as eight additional kids ranging in age from toddlerhood to early twenties. Their father seemed to avoid being home as much as possible, and their mother was an enormous woman who'd long lost any control she might have once had over the household. She primarily seemed to focus on making sure none of the younger ones inadvertently killed themselves or each other. They ordered pizza for dinner almost every night, and their ramshackle house was a lawless empire of children. Luke and I *loved* it there.

"Not like that," Penny said, scrunching her nose.

Starting at age twelve, Penny began to rack up an impressive number of boyfriends. I remember her first date as vividly as if it were my own, partly because mine wouldn't come along for a long time. In sixth grade, Penny was "going out" with a boy in her class named Jake. This mostly meant passing notes back and forth via trusted emissaries and occasionally holding hands in the hallway between classes. No "going out" actually happened until Penny put the hard-core press on our mom and dad to let her go to the movies with Jake. Emily had a crush on his best friend, Ethan, so a double date was ideal. Being that it was a group thing and it seemed very unlikely that anything untoward could happen at the Riverstone Theatre during a matinee showing of *The Mask,* my parents relented. Penny and Emily were in a frenzy getting ready for their date: Penny's room with its pink vanity mirror was a haze of sugary body sprays and glittery Bonne Bell lip balms. They both wore baby tees and pulled their long hair away from their faces with butterfly clips.

"They're being like, really silly," I said to my mom, plopping down on the couch with her to watch *Kindergarten Cop* while my dad, who considered himself (wrongly) a menacing deterrent to adolescent boys, ferried the girls to their date. "I don't get it," I sniffed.

My mom smiled at me, probably knowing that I felt a little left out. "I was the same when I was Penny's age."

I scrunched my nose. "Are you serious?"

"Oh yeah." She laughed. "Completely boy crazy."

"Gross. I hope it's not genetic."

"Well, it's fine if you don't, but you may feel differently in a few years."

People, including Penny, were always telling me this, that I was going to feel differently about boys one day, and I dreaded it. It made me feel like a time bomb.

"It would be so much easier if I were a boy," I said.

"Maybe in some ways," my mom said, "but being a girl is great too."

My mom had cut back to part-time at the school so that she could take me to all my skiing stuff—I most certainly didn't adequately appreciate her sacrifice at the time, but we were uncommonly close, given our many hours alone in the car together driving up and down every mountain in the region.

The hullabaloo resumed when the girls arrived back at the house and changed into their pj's.

I lingered at the threshold of the doorway to Penny's bedroom.

"How was your date?" I asked. I was aiming for nonchalance, sarcasm even, but at ten I had the faculties for neither.

"Sissy!" Emily squealed. Emily's only sibling was an older brother, so she was keen to share big sister duty with Penny. Though Penny frequently enumerated the many ways in which little sisters were the worst, she usually tolerated me hanging around them.

Penny gave the most world-weary sigh a twelve-year-old could muster, but let a smile creep in and gave me a sideways nod, signaling I could enter. They were sitting cross-legged on the lower half of Penny's trundle bed with an open bag of Cheetos and a mound of Twizzlers and Whoppers between them.

"Ethan totally likes you," Penny continued as I settled in and reached for a Twizzler.

Emily squealed. "I almost had a cow when he put his arm around me." Penny nodded sagely.

"And *you* guys! Oh my god, you were making out like the *whole* time."

"Ew," I said, and Penny rolled her eyes.

"He's an *eighth* grader," she said, as though that explained everything, and it sort of did. Middle school was a treacherous place, throwing together all those children in their various stages of metamorphosis; some of the boys in eighth grade were nearly six feet tall and had begun to resemble impossibly awkward men. Penny smiled slyly and pushed the long curtain of her hair over her shoulder. Emily saw it first.

"Ahhhhh! You have a hickey!"

I craned my neck to see, and there it was, a quarter-size red-and-purple welt just underneath Penny's ear.

"Mom and Dad are going to kill you," I said.

"Not if they don't know about it," Penny said, walloping me with a pillow. "It's no big deal," she said, "I'll just wear a scarf."

I didn't want to admit how baffled I was by the hickey. How did you even get such a thing? It involved kissing, obviously, but the mechanics were unclear. I'd learn later that hickeys were a particular teenage phenomenon that was just exactly as stupid as it appeared.

Back then, the point of all the boy stuff seemed to be more about Emily and Penny than the actual boys themselves. Many hours were devoted to unpacking their crushes' most minute actions, reading each of the paper notes passed in the hallway—never mind that searching the missives of a fourteen-year-old boy for subtext was, to paraphrase Cher Horowitz, like looking for meaning in a Pauly Shore movie.

Many years later, I'd search through an old box of Penny's teenage journals and notes that she'd long ago abandoned in my parents' house. I was looking for some kind of clue, but the only shocking thing was how ordinary they were. Like generals, she and Emily would plot and strategize their next moves, their next notes, their next phone calls, as though the fate of civilization hung in the balance. But it was the time with each other that seemed to matter, and that I envied. Luke and I talked, but it was to plan adventures, recount adventures; and mostly there was just doing.

That same year, a girl in the grade between us—Jennifer Baker—died suddenly of meningitis. Neither Penny nor I knew her well, but her death sent shock waves through the school. There was a vigil for her in the school gymnasium, and I remember the drained and haunted faces of her parents, the bewildered grief of her older brother, the way a halo of tragedy seemed to surround them. Our experiences with death before then had been minimal—almost abstract—involving minor pets and other people's grandparents. Penny marshaled her class to do a fund-raiser for the family and to send them cards and flowers. Even young, she was good in a crisis.

⁕

Thinking back so many years later on Penny as a little girl would bring me both comfort and anguish. Some part of me believed if I could discover the exact moment her unraveling began, if I could just locate the thread, we could reverse what happened. As though we might even put back together what's come undone.

Liz Sullivan Is Out of Here

December 2009

A S FOR my own unraveling, it begins on a chilly December day that starts out perfectly ordinary and then spirals into something else. My only intention that morning is to quickly cross the state line to go to the Nordstrom in Spokane. I need to buy new pants because none of mine fit any longer. These days I need to give myself discrete, manageable tasks to hang each day on or I'm likely to only make it as far as the couch or not emerge from bed at all. Today: pants.

As I haul a pile of jeans two sizes bigger than what I used to wear into the dressing room, I try not to feel sad about the weight I've gained. It feels too stupid to be sad about. I walk by a row of supersoft T-shirts that are on sale and grab a handful. I get some new underwear and bras as well. I've been squeezing my newly voluptuous tits into my 34B bras, and it's getting obscene. I look at myself in the pallid light of the dressing room, which seemingly illuminates every pore of my tired skin. My hair looks like a neglected animal.

I leave with a bagful of clothes, and my plan is to go to the gym. I'm dressed for it, since my gym clothes are all that still fit me, and I'm actually going to go today.

I get in the car with every intention of heading to the mildly depressing big-box gym by my parents' house. I fucking hate that gym. Last week, a pudgy trainer sidled up to me and gave me some unsolicited (and incorrect) advice on squats in an attempt, I assume, to try to sell me one of the personal training packages they push on new members. It was all I could do not to punch him. But I'm supposed to be exercising regularly. It's supposed to help.

Instead of driving to the gym, however, I find myself on a route so familiar I'm practically on autopilot. The airport. I park and head to arrivals, like I'm picking someone up. This series of irrational actions gives me an odd thrill. Am I finally losing it? I've spent days—weeks, probably—of my life in airports all over the world, but I've never been as fascinated as I suddenly am by this ordinary terminal.

My therapist, Gena, has been working with me on a technique borrowed from yoga that she refers to as staying in "the witness mind." She encourages me to try to observe my feelings without judging them so as to avoid getting caught up in self-loathing and blame. But now I feel like I've somehow slipped from my body and am watching from above. I don't think this is what Gena meant. I wonder idly if I am suffering a psychotic break. People are staring at me, but it's not (necessarily) because I look any more deranged than usual. The white noise of whispers that fills a room when I walk in has become so constant that I hear it even when I'm alone.

Announcements play on a loop over the airport's sound system—*you must check in two hours prior to international flights, the gate will close ten minutes before departure, allow forty minutes for security*—in a robotic-sounding female voice as disembodied and ubiquitous as the voice of God. She repeats herself in Japanese, French, German. Airports seem to exist in a kind of purgatory outside of time and space. You have no control over when those you're expecting will arrive, or when you'll be allowed to continue on to your destination. Outside of security, I'm surrounded by people waiting. The travelers pass by me in a rush, off to go stand in a long line to remove their shoes and coats and electronics and three-ounce bottles of liquid from their carry-ons before they disappear on the other side, continuing on to wherever they're going.

The longer I stay, the more inconceivable it feels to leave and go to the gym, where rows of middle-aged people huff and puff, trying to stave off holiday weight gain, or to head back home, where my parents are trying so mightily to go on with their lives. I watch the reader boards as they flash the names of dozens of far-flung cities. Some, such as Zurich and Vienna, I've flown through many times in another life. Others—Dubai, Phnom Penh—I've never even thought about going to. Except now I do; suddenly any place feels preferable to here. Then I see Buenos Aires come up, and it hammers my heart.

Blair. I haven't returned his last several phone calls even though I miss him more than I can bear. I'm not sure that night in Buenos Aires would feel like the best night of my life if it hadn't also been the last night of my life as I knew it. I go to the ticket counter, thinking I'm somehow playing a joke on myself as I ask about the next available flight. But then, I'm pulling out my credit card and my passport. For a moment, I gaze at the latter in amazement, wondering why my passport is in my purse. Then I remember that I lost my driver's license the other night at Silver Fox. A mortifying sequence of events comes back to me—I'm laughing drunkenly, exuding the licorice smell of Jägermeister, and spilling the contents of my purse on the floor. The license clattering away, gone forever.

The flight doesn't leave until later that evening, so I have time to kill. I go back to the car to get the clothes I just purchased. Being outside of the airport makes the fog lift a bit: the crisp, cold, nonrecycled air hits me, and it occurs to me that as easily and senselessly as I arrived here and purchased a ticket, I could turn around, cancel the flight, and just go home. But standing at the airline counter made me realize how badly I need out of Coeur d'Alene, where everything reminds me of everything. Is that why I bought these clothes? Was I plotting my escape without even knowing it? *Dear Gena, my witness mind thinks she's witnessing a woman having a nervous breakdown.*

I schlep the Nordstrom bags through security past a series of blessedly apathetic TSA agents who seem not to care how I might board with these bags. I buy an overpriced suitcase inside the terminal and decide I'll just pretend I didn't know it was too big to carry on, play clueless. A very huffy gate attendant will check it for me as I pretend to be apologetic.

In the surreal hours between my unplanned arrival at the airport and my flight's departure, I sit at a lonely airport bar that serves cocktails in pint glasses and tap away at my phone. I send my parents an e-mail to tell them about the trip, attaching my flight info, and letting them know where I left my car, for which they have a spare set of keys at home. I do my best to keep the e-mail light and sane sounding—*Just decided to take a little trip last minute. Need to get away for a while. If anyone calls for me just tell them I'm traveling.* They'll be worried, but they're already worried. The three of us cooped up in our madness together isn't helping anything. *I'm thirty years old*, I think, holding up my end of an imaginary argument, *I don't need to ask permission.*

Next, I search Airbnb for a place to stay. I find an apartment in Palermo Soho—one of the nicer neighborhoods in the city, according to Google. My sensory memory of being in Buenos Aires is sharp and clear, but the details—where we stayed, what we visited—have all left me. It's the feeling that's indelible: of me before, of Blair, one of my oldest friends, coming into a new and sudden focus. I book the apartment for two weeks. The Internet has made everything so easy! I rarely booked my own travel before, and it's weirdly thrilling. I'm giddy, ratcheting up toward hysteria. I'm going to sit here at this bleak, nondescript bar, drinking a cocktail that is both too sweet and too strong, and tap, tap, tap my way into another life. Maybe I should take some Spanish classes. Booked. Maybe I will get myself a little job, so I can stay as long as I want. I answer an ad on Craigslist for English-speaking tour guides. Is it really this easy to start a new life? Maybe it is; I'm high on the prospect. From here on out, I'm someone new. I'm Elizabeth Sullivan—my middle name paired with my mom's maiden name—the fake name I use when I meet strangers in bars to throw them off the scent if they recognize me. Elizabeth? Liz. Liz Sullivan. Here I am.

⁓

As I'm landing in Buenos Aires in the late afternoon after the connecting flight from Lima, my luggage is arriving in São Paulo, Brazil. I don't know this, of course, until I've been standing at the baggage claim carousel at Ministro Pistarini for what feels like an eternity. The two girls who sat next to me on the flight from Lima get their bags right away. They're from LA—decked out in expensive workout gear, eyes hidden behind massive designer sunglasses—and they talked through the whole flight. Never to me, only to each other. They went through an extensive beauty routine en route, because you know being on a plane just *murders* your complexion. I'd hoped the wine they were drinking— complimentary on these international flights—might induce a nap, but it only made them louder. They were just so excited to be on their way to BA. WOOHOO! As they disappear into the terminal, I realize I could've just introduced myself. It would have been nice to know *someone* here. But off they go, and I remain, watching the luggage turn and turn until only a few solitary bags are left on the carousel. Who these lonely remaining bags belong to is a mystery; perhaps someone is currently waiting for them in São Paulo.

I'm third in line at the Aerolíneas counter. I used some of the flight time to brush up on the bit of Spanish I'd picked up from Jorge, a tech coach from Chile who'd worked with the team for years. *Equipaje.* Right, luggage. I should have gone LAN Argentina, but Aerolíneas was so much cheaper. I have money saved, but I don't know how long I'll be here.

I approach and mumble something in Spanish. The airline representative says something in Portuguese, then immediately switches to English when I don't respond.

"Hello, how can I help you, miss?"

"I've lost my luggage."

"Okay, excellent. Where you are flying from?"

"Spokane, Washington," I say. "I connected through Lima."

"Excellent." She returns to her computer with a great flurry of typing. "Flight number please? Name?" I give her my real name, hoping it's the last time I'll have to say it for a while.

"Excellent," she tells me. Apparently my name rings no bells. It probably wasn't a story here. I've lost any sense of proportion.

"Okay." She smiles, and I want to hug her for some reason. Perhaps because she's the first person I've spoken to in so many hours. "Your luggage was sent to São Paulo. But it's no problem. You write for me here the address where you are staying and we send it there, one day, two days, maybe, but no more."

I write it for her.

She nods approvingly. "Palermo Soho. Is nice. You know it?"

I shake my head.

"You will like it." She smiles.

I make my way to the buses heading to the city center. The air outside is pleasant, almost balmy. I've left behind winter too; it's spring in the Southern Hemisphere, soon to be summer. It dawns on me that I don't have so much as a change of underwear in the gym bag I used as my carry-on: a ghastly rookie mistake for someone as well traveled as I am. I don't know how to pack for this new life any more than I know how to live in it. I have only the minimal toiletries I bought for the flight and my wallet and passport. I have my Spanish classes and my tour guide orientation in two days and I have only the—surely ripe—travel clothes on my back.

I wearily file onto a bus, and at first I don't know what it is that feels so different, that washes me in relief. Then I realize: anonymity. No one's eyes are following me as I move, there's no ripple of alarmed whispers as people recognize me and point me out to their companions.

Buenos Aires was an impulsive choice, but as the bus hurtles toward the city, I feel sure it was a good one. I'm thousands of miles from anyone who knows me or knows *of* me. The last time I was here was the last time all my dreams for myself—along with any hopes of resolution, of a happy or normal life—felt possible. I can recognize how irrational it is to think there might be some sort of key here, some clue I've left for myself, some portal through which I might travel and obliterate what's happened in between, but it doesn't stop me from longing for it. I gaze out the window, trying to connect to what I'm seeing, to spark some nostalgia. But the urban sprawl outside the window gives me nothing. I'd forgotten how vast the city is, how one neighborhood tumbles into the next in a web that seems to go on forever. The city center, where the bus leaves off, is crowded with high-rises and clutches of palm trees sprouting between buildings to form little oases.

According to his bio on Airbnb, the owner of the apartment where I'll be staying is a fiftyish American expat who moved to the city a decade before with his partner. From the central bus station I take the green line to the Scalabrini Ortiz stop in Palermo as instructed. All the way there I study my map, trying and failing to remain inconspicuous; my height and my blondness attract attention everywhere other than the Nordic countries. But people are just gawking; they don't recognize me. I suppose I'm uniquely attuned to the difference.

I try to make sense of the steady stream of Spanish around me, but it washes over me. Everyone looks cheerful; they're laughing, or maybe it's simply that these are the only people I'm seeing clearly—my fellow miserables fading to gray in the background. I emerge in what feels like a completely different city, and at last I feel a stirring of familiarity. The afternoon sun is coming through the trees that canopy the wide cobblestone streets, and I pass stylish modern buildings with Spanish-style villas crammed in between. I couldn't be anywhere in the United States.

⁓§⁓

"Welcome! *Bienvenidos!*" Tom, my host, leans in and kisses me on the cheek. "This is the place." I find myself instinctively searching for signs that he knows—the startled look, the flash of horror—after all he has my real name and my credit card. But if he does recognize me, he betrays nothing. I chastise myself; the world doesn't revolve around what happened to us.

"The building is gorgeous," I say. There's a pool in the courtyard, and the gates that protect the building are heavy, fortified. Though the other neighborhood streets are teeming, Tom's apartment is on a quiet, posh-looking block.

"Isn't is precious? We got it for a song too. They were practically giving away real estate after the crisis in '01. Come in, come in." Tom beckons me from the foyer. The furniture is modern and sharp, and there's a narrow terrace with a view of the Rio de la Plata. I'm not sure I deserve to stay somewhere so beautiful. "I've just made tea, would you like some?" I nod and follow him into the narrow, gleaming kitchen. He pours me a cup, and we sit for a moment. I feel a sudden wave of exhaustion so intense I could collapse on the spot.

"You know this neighborhood got its nickname because it's meant to resemble SoHo in New York, but being from there I think that rather flatters New York. Maybe in its heyday. Anyway! This is the perfect neighborhood for a young person. The Argentines, they're very enterprising, very resilient. After the crash, all of these little artisan boutiques started sprouting up around here, with people converting warehouses into galleries and showrooms. Dreadfully hip. When we first started visiting twenty years ago, this was a rather nothing part of town, but it's undergone quite the *renaissance*." He says the word with its full, flamboyant French pronunciation. "How were your travels, my dear?"

"Not too bad. Although they've lost my luggage. Or, rather, they sent it to São Paulo."

"Oh dear. Aerolíneas, I presume? They always lose luggage."

I nod. "Actually," I continue, "I neglected to bring a change of clothes in my carry-on. Is there somewhere nearby I could go to pick up a few things?"

Tom sends me to a shopping mall, and just as I arrive there, a new wave of jet lag hits me hard. I feel adrift and disoriented. I've been all over the world, but it's a blur of mountain resorts and ski slopes, with only the occasional brief trip to a capital city where I was surrounded by the considerable buffer of my teammates. Buenos Aires feels more foreign than I expected. I've overheard no English. I'm both panicked and relieved by this.

I skim the racks but can't find anything in a 36D. All my adult life I'd been a sleek aerodynamic 34B. Being an athlete shielded me from some of the body anxiety that hounded other women my age. At just under six feet, my coaches were happy when I was between 165 and 170. Weight was just a number—like my resting heart rate, my CO_2 levels, box jump reps—but now it's another reason to loathe myself. After I stopped training, I packed on twenty pounds, giving me these never-before-seen knockers. I know I probably look fine, but I feel like the extra weight carries everything that happened, that it's an outward sign that I'll never again be what I once was.

A pretty, minuscule salesgirl appears at my elbow. "*¿Necesitas ayuda?*" I have to repeat myself twice to get across that I'm not finding anything in my size. My accent needs work. My conversations with Jorge have clearly given me misplaced confidence.

The salesgirl explains that they only carry B cups there. Later, I'll wonder about this—do all women in Buenos Aires have the same size breasts?—but for now, I just feel dejected as the kind-eyed salesgirl directs me to a department store. There, in a bleary haze, I buy a granny bra I'll never wear again, as well as a couple of sundresses, one of which I will later discover was meant to be a bathing suit cover-up. I was never one for fashion.

When I make it back to my apartment, I'm ravenous and exhausted. I order a trio of greasy empanadas from a bodega across the street, where two old men sit at a rickety table outside smoking and staring at me unabashedly. They're not exactly leering, but I'm a sore thumb. I see—or perhaps just imagine—some hint of disappointment in their stares, like if the universe were going to cough up a blond foreigner into their midst, couldn't it have done better than this?

The grease from my empanadas soaks through their little wax paper bag and the smell of them makes my stomach growl. I take the food and the strange, ugly clothes back to the apartment that's mine for the next two weeks. Its spotlessness is a reproach to my grubbiness. There's a laptop computer in the corner, which Tom told me I'm free to use. I log in and connect to the Wi-Fi. I have several e-mails from my parents. *Call when you can,* my dad writes, *your mother is worried.* I e-mail them back to tell them I've arrived and I'm fine. Don't worry about me. If only.

I e-mail Gena the therapist to cancel my next several appointments. *I'm taking a trip,* I say, *I'm in Buenos Aires and not sure how long I'm staying. I know it's probably a terrible idea, but I needed to get away.* I also tell Gena not to worry, though maybe it's narcissistic to think she would.

I take a long shower and crawl into the plush bed naked; it's 8:00 p.m. and I decide I can't stay awake any longer. Despite how far away I am, the time difference is only three hours. I've dealt with much worse jet lag many times, and in those days I had to get up and compete the next day. Now, I have nothing to wake up for. I could sleep for a hundred years.

I'm starving when I wake up. I spotted a McDonald's around the corner, and they have good breakfasts everywhere in the world. The Palermo Soho McDonald's is the chicest fast-food joint I've ever seen. The trim dark-eyed girls behind the counter wear smart blue uniforms, and there's a mini café on the inside that serves espresso and little pastries called *medialunas*. It's bustling. I get an egg sandwich and coffee, and it tastes the same as in the U.S. but different too. The smell makes me nostalgic. You know what I mean, that *McDonald's* smell. Penny and I are riding in the back of the station wagon, Dad is on dinner duty, which as often as not devolved into pizza or McDonald's. My sister and I knew how easily he could be swayed. The admonitions of "don't tell your mother"—who ate organic long before it was a thing—made it all the more delicious.

Even such a benign memory is not without its dark cloud. The question moves again to the front of my brain like a slide on one of those old-fashioned View-Masters clicking into place. Will I ever feel anything but sadness again? I feel tears coming up and quickly put my sunglasses on. I need to wake myself up, so I keep walking in the direction of the Plaza Serrano. When I reach the square, it's bustling and shaded by towering rosewood trees, and I'm nearly flattened by a wave of memory. Even though it's what I was looking for, once it hits me, I'm filled with a melancholy so intense my knees buckle. The place is familiar and distinctive, I've been here before. The cafés that line the plaza—their patios spilling out onto the cobblestones and blending into their neighbors—all look similar, and I'm imagining Blair and me sitting at any of them, at all of them. In an instant, my decision to come here feels like a mistake. I can never go back to who I was.

When I get back to the apartment, I check my e-mail again. One from my mom and one from Gena; two of the only people who have this e-mail address.

Katie, the e-mail from Gena reads, *I don't think it's a terrible idea for you to get away for a while, but you need to make sure you're taking care of yourself too. A change of scene can be a very good idea. You've been through a lot, so go easy on yourself, and be kind to yourself. Be careful about drinking. We can Skype if you need to. Love, Gena*

I'd created a new e-mail account that only my parents and therapist know about, and I resist the urge to check the other one. My old e-mail was made public when I was "doxed," to use the vernacular of the shadowy Internet world that's become painfully familiar to me. I've long since gone dark on social media.

The sheer number of messages I get—even this long after the fact—never fails to shock me. I would have expected the bizarre people who write hate mail to strangers to have moved on to a fresh kill by now. I'd like to think these people are lonely, angry trolls sitting in their parents' basements spewing invective because they have nothing better to do. But I once reverse searched a handful of the e-mail addresses on Facebook and they turned up normal-looking men and women smiling and laughing at Christmas parties and in vacation photos; people with friends, families, children of their own. I fought the urge to forward on the death threats and all-caps e-mails condemning me and my family to hell to these friends and family members. *Do you know about your husband's dark furtive habits?* I wanted to ask the wife of Joe Pinelli, one of my more dedicated digital tormentors. *Do you realize that after he tucks in Aiden, 7, and Hailey, 5, he opens up his laptop to write me pages-long e-mails full of hatred and scripture?*

The problem is, you cannot unsee this side of humanity, and it makes even the most benign-looking strangers appear to you as a potential threat.

I got some nice messages of support from ski fans, but those made me feel awful in their own way, like I'd let them down. They reminded me, uncomfortably, of who I'd been, a version of myself that had been hurtling away from me at an accelerating speed since that ghastly day. It also kicked back that terrible question: Had my singular focus blinded me? Was there something I could have done?

Everyone needs to believe they would have seen it sooner, that they would've been able to help her. People need this lie to feel certain that nothing like this could ever happen to them, that the Clearys are the stuff of horror movies, rather than ordinary life. The truth is, nothing can prepare you for something like Penny.

Penny on Christmas

I WAS ALWAYS especially happy to have a sister on Christmas. Like most siblings, we alternated frequently between being enemies and allies, but Christmas was sacred. Our parents weren't wealthy like the Duncans, but we always had plenty of presents at Christmas. As the holiday neared, no matter how badly we'd been squabbling, a Christmas truce fell on the Cleary sisters. It was easily my favorite time of year: my mom decorated every inch of the lower floor of our house; a resplendent fir tree we'd chosen as a family took over the living room; little Santas and reindeer and other yuletide knickknacks lined every windowsill; and my mom baked and baked. My dad was almost as excited as I was when Schweitzer opened in late November, and after that he would take me up every weekend. By the time I was ten, I could ski everything he skied. On weekdays when he was working, Blair and Luke's mom, Ann—who'd left her job after her eldest was born—would often take us up after school. She never liked to ski and so would wait for us in the lodge, reading a book.

In order to quench the over-the-top excitement of the holiday, my parents let Penny and me open one present on Christmas Eve. Once we were old enough to actually buy gifts with our allowances, we made a tradition of opening each other's. Penny was always a thoughtful gift giver.

Somewhere in the closets of my parents' house I still have a gorgeous forest-green scarf she gave me when we were teenagers. I remember thinking it was extremely sophisticated, like something I'd see one of the fancy ski bunnies wearing in the lodge.

After gifts, we'd leave cookies for Santa and carrots for Rudolph, and I'd sleep in the pullout trundle bed in Penny's room. We'd wake at the crack of dawn and count the minutes until 7:00 a.m., when we were officially allowed to go and wake up our parents. Penny, like all older siblings, discovered the truth about Santa Claus long before I did, so for a couple of years, she was complicit in the ruse along with my parents. Looking back, that seems like a very sweet lie in the midst of many others less benign.

We would always go skiing with the Duncans on Christmas. Even Penny would come when we were kids, before all of her injuries and ailments began. Blair was a year older than Penny, and, according to her, he was exceptionally cute. And, really, he never did seem to go through much of an awkward phase. Luke and I were already obsessed with skiing, spending hours at his house watching VHS ski videos on his big screen and using the giant trampoline in his backyard to practice tricks and flips in the summer, or doing them straight off their dock into Lake Coeur d'Alene. Normally we didn't like to ski with anyone other than Blair, but Christmas Day was always just for fun.

I remember clearly the last time we went as a group because it was days before Tad Duncan left his wife. Tad was trying to give his family one last holiday together, but at twelve, fifteen, and seventeen, respectively, the Duncan kids were old enough to know that something was up.

We started at the top of the hill together, but soon Luke had rocketed off through the trees by himself. There was no way Penny and the eldest Duncan sibling, Kristina, were going in there, but I nodded to Blair, and we followed him. We'd long been skiing off the runs at Silver Mountain, no matter how much trouble we got into for doing it. But that day Luke was barreling through the trees like a bat out of hell. I skied with Luke often enough to know the difference between him being daring and him being reckless. By the time we cleared the forest, all three of us were breathless.

"Hey," I said, clamping a gloved hand on Luke's shoulder, "you okay?" He was doubled over and breathing hard. He didn't answer me, and I looked over at Blair, who pulled his mask up, his brow furrowed. It was a rare bluebird December day, and from where we were you could see for miles in any direction. Suddenly, Luke let out a howl that rang out before being swallowed by the crush of snow and tree branches. He collapsed backward, his skis still bound to his feet and sticking straight up.

"Our parents are getting divorced," Luke said as I popped my skis off and sat beside him on the snow. I was already outgrowing my nearly new ski pants and I had to maneuver to be able to sit comfortably.

"What?" I looked to Blair for confirmation. He sighed and sat on the other side of Luke, putting a thick, ski-jacketed arm around his little brother.

"We don't know that for sure."

"Mom has been crying for two weeks straight! She thinks she's hiding it. She drank a whole bottle of wine last night at dinner. It's Bethany, just watch."

"Bethany from the company?"

Tad Duncan had been a lawyer when the kids were born but had for the past several years been developing a communications software system that had started to take off. Bethany was his head of marketing; she was twenty-seven. This detail seems more appalling in retrospect, now that I've passed twenty-seven myself and understand how young it actually is.

"We don't know anything yet," Blair said.

"Kris told me she heard them on the phone," Luke said. "Like, multiple times. You know she goes with him whenever he travels."

Between her rebellious older daughter and her talented sons, Ann never seemed to have a moment for herself. She often drove me to practice when my mom was working, and she always packed snacks for me just as she did for her own kids. I loved her. It seemed unfathomable that Tad would leave her.

"Kris shouldn't be telling you any of that, bud," Blair said.

"I'm not a kid!" Luke said. "And it's obvious anyway."

With that, he popped back up on his skis and tipped over the cliff more quickly than he should have. It didn't matter how well we all knew Silver Mountain, it was idiotic to plunge off like that. Luke was reckless then. He never really outgrew it.

Between Christmas and New Year's, Tad announced to his family that he was going to be moving to Sun Valley. He'd purchased a five-bedroom house at the base of Bald Mountain, where he would now be living with the soon-to-be Mrs. Duncan, née Bethany Little. From there, the family seemed to swiftly unravel. Kristina wanted nothing to do with him. She was in her senior year of high school and took the excuse to become the wildest girl in Coeur d'Alene before she left for college the next fall. The boys sided with their mother, but their lives were turned upside down. Tad wanted them to come to Sun Valley. There was a well-funded but relatively minor ski club there, and Tad saw his opportunity to be a big fish.

I remember Penny and me hiding at the top of the stairs, listening in on a conversation between my parents and Ann that spring. Our families had been close for years, and my mom in particular adored Ann; the two of them were forever trading recipes and gardening tips.

"I know I must seem like an idiot, but I didn't see it coming. I just never thought Tad would start fucking some twentysomething behind my back." Penny and I exchanged a horrified smile. The grown-ups in our orbit almost never swore, so this must be serious. "I was just so busy with the boys and their skiing and trying to keep Kristina under control. This was our deal, you know? I did *everything* at home so that he could focus on the company. I have my degree, I could have worked. I'm so stupid."

"You're not," I heard my dad say. "He is. I'm just disgusted with him."

This was about as harsh as my father got.

"And now he wants to take the boys away? What am I going to do?"

"That makes no sense," my mom said. "You do everything for them. How's Tad going to even have the time?"

"Well, he has *Bethany* now." Ann said her name as though it tasted bad.

"I'm sure the boys would rather be with you," my mom said.

"You know he has a trump card. Sun Valley is one of the best mountains in the country. Not to mention all Tad's new rich cronies who fancy themselves patrons of the sport." She groaned.

"Skiing isn't everything. Ann, I know they're talented but the chances of them going pro . . ." My dad trailed off. I was a little taken aback. My parents had always been so encouraging about my skiing dreams, did they know something I didn't? I thought uncharitably that this was because my dad had never chased the dream, had acquiesced to having a normal nine-to-five job and a life that didn't revolve around being on the mountain. I would never do that, I told myself.

"I know. But I'm afraid they'll resent me. Luke especially," she said.

They moved into the den, where we could no longer hear them, and I turned to my sister.

"You don't think they'll really move, do you?" I asked her.

She shrugged. "I have no idea."

I burst into tears. The thought of losing my two best friends was overwhelming. Other than Penny and my parents, I didn't really have anyone else. I was too advanced to ski with anyone else my age. Other girls my age were getting into makeup, talking about boys, passing intricately folded notes between classes, and cuffing one another's wrists with slap bracelets. I couldn't imagine where I would fit in.

Penny put her arms around me. Even as a kid, I almost never cried. "Don't worry, Katie. It will be okay. Let's just be glad Mom and Dad aren't like that."

At the time, it felt like our family was charmed. From what little information I later found out about other cases like Penny's, the women's terrible childhoods were offered as one possible explanation of their behavior. But I think it's a red herring, an attempt to explain the unexplainable. There is always a chance that something could have happened to Penny that I never knew about, but we had happy childhoods. I know. I was there. It's one of the only things I can still be certain of.

❧

I suppose anyone whose family has been blown apart feels it especially acutely around the holidays, but for me, Christmas is a particular touchstone. I always came home for it; no matter where I was in the world, I'd make the trip. And whatever else was going on with Penny, even in the later years, things always seemed to go back to being good between us, at least for a few days. Nowadays, most of the time my feelings about Penny are so complicated that I can't extract a single emotion from the morass, but on Christmas, I just miss my sister.

Liz Is an Expat

I MAKE IT through my first few days limpingly. My luggage arrives three days after I've landed, and I've already had to wash my hated new clothing once to get me through. I take long walks around my new neighborhood each day just to have something to do. Walking and being outside is meant to help and it does temporarily. It's late spring, and the city has the feeling of coming alive; there is no hour when the tables that spill out onto the sidewalks of the cafés are not occupied and the streets off the Plaza Serrano are not bursting with life; there are twentysomethings everywhere selling interesting clothes and artsy jewelry. I venture to the grocery store for staples and a small market stall for produce—an unexpectedly intimidating experience fraught with mysterious labels and arrangements. I return to the little bodega for the greasy empanadas, and the old men are still there—seemingly they have always been there and will always be there. When I get back to my building, it feels like a sterile and lonely fortress.

I study maps and landmarks to prepare for my tours, and in the evening I drink Malbec and watch American television with Spanish subtitles. How strange that they have all this American culture here; in the mall and in the McDonald's, every song I hear is American: Taylor

Swift or Justin Bieber, and on television it's all of our shows repackaged. Do they think this is what we are? What a rude awakening they must have if they visit.

I feel relieved three days in when I have my first day of Spanish classes in the morning and my meeting with the woman from the tour-guide company in the afternoon—it gives me some structure. The adrenaline of coming here has faded, and if I didn't have a reason to get out of bed today, I might not. My classes are on the third floor of a baroque shopping arcade where there are several classrooms surrounding a small interior courtyard. I eat my lunch alone in the courtyard, surreptitiously glancing at the other students, who all seem horribly young.

Late in the afternoon, I make my way to Tour Aventura for my guide initiation. I'd submitted an application and a photo online and have been accepted on a trial basis. I'll be paid a percentage of the bookings for each group.

The offices are a clean, blank little set of rooms in the Microcentro, one stop on the Subte from where my Spanish classes are. I go to the desk and ask for my contact. The person at the desk escorts me back to a small office in the back, where a slender black-haired woman around my age is sitting.

"Welcome," she says in English, "please sit."

I reach across the desk to shake her hand. *"Mucho gusto, soy Liz."*

"Bueno, Alejandra. I'm happy to see you weren't lying about speaking some Spanish," she continues in Spanish.

"Does that happen?"

She rolls her eyes. "We get a little bit of everything. Your accent," she says, looking a bit dismayed, "it needs work. It's very heavy. I'm used to it, but others will have trouble."

"I'm taking classes."

She waves her hand. "It will improve, your ear. Just being here. If you're staying. And you're blond," she says approvingly. She says nothing about the fact that I'm heavier than in the photo I sent her. I didn't mean to be dishonest, I simply don't have any recent photos. "Very American look, that's good. Some people specifically ask for an American to show them the city."

"They come to Buenos Aires and they want an American guide?"

She shrugged. "Just don't tell them you just got here, tell them you're an expat. We can start you in the first week of the New Year. You can be ready?" She hands me a thick notebook with information on the key points and a map with the route marked.

"I think so," I say, feeling fraudulent.

"It's really not so complicated. Here is the list," she says, flattening the map. "Plaza de Mayo, Caminito in La Boca, San Telmo, Recoleta Cemetery. It's three hours, mostly on foot with one short Subte ride. Yes?"

I nod at her.

⁂

Looking over my bank accounts, I realize I can afford to stay quite a while. It helps that the dollar is so strong against the peso, and though I rarely made good money while I was skiing, my living expenses were so minimal that I saved nearly all of it. Still, this condo is too pricey. At the language institute, I find a notice for an apartment opening in San Telmo: Casa de Volver. *What an odd name for a building*, I think, as my mind scrambles for the translation but knows something is likely lost: *the house of returns?*

I emerge from the Subte at Saint John and am hit with a jolt of recognition. Blair and I spent a lazy afternoon walking through the neighborhood's famous Sunday market, looking at the antiques and eating gelato in a café off the Plaza Dorrego. My eyes whirl around, looking for the café as though, if I find the right one, Blair might be sitting there waiting for me. But as quickly as it comes on, the feeling of recognition vanishes, and I'm returned to the excruciating present, alone.

San Telmo feels more contained than Palermo, with its converted warehouse and wide avenues, its fancy locked-down buildings with security guards posted outside. The Plaza Dorrego is shaded by leafy trees and dotted with intricate iron lampposts and café tables where people drink beer in the afternoon sunshine. The streets off the plaza are narrow,

31

and as I make my way to the apartment, I'm mesmerized by the faded, crumbling grandeur of the villas lining the streets.

The building is just south of the plaza, and the landlord—a sixty-something woman with a warm smile—meets me outside the entrance and leads me through wrought iron gates into a courtyard off of which are the entrances to the individual apartments.

"It's beautiful," I say, taking in the charming courtyard with its clutches of squat palms and monkey puzzle trees, the bougainvillea climbing in all directions. A faded fresco lines the walls, worn down in some places to the brick beneath it. A cherubic face, hauntingly disembodied, gazes heavenward.

"It has quite a history. It used to be the home of the Del Potro family, all of this," she says, gesturing to indicate the entire villa. "Just one family. But they fled north with all the other rich families in 1870 during the yellow fever epidemic. After that, it became a *conventillo* with dozens of families. It's been renovated since then, *por supuesto*." She smiles.

The building is grand, but the apartment is tiny. A studio with a half kitchen and a narrow rickety-looking shower. Nonetheless, I immediately imagine myself here, a place with a story. And the rent is dirt cheap. I could stay a long time on my savings. I love the idea of a space relinquished by the rich to the teaming immigrant masses and now, so many years later, to me.

"I'll take it."

⁓

That evening, I'm sorry to leave colorful San Telmo to return to my pristine apartment in Palermo Soho for my last few days there.

Being by myself so much is new for me. I've never traveled alone, much less lived alone. I realize now that, as much as it irritated me sometimes, having a posse of coaches, trainers, teammates, parents, and trustees surrounding me all the time was a comfort. It buffered all of us as we went from one place to another, reinforced the idea that we had something precious, that we *were* something precious. And now it feels like I've been drained of everything that once made me special. I've been leveled. In the United States, becoming famous is a pipe dream for a skier. But I became infamous instead, and now anonymity feels like the best I can hope for.

Being alone used to be thrilling because it meant I was on the mountain, my heart beating in my ears as I contemplated my line for a first descent. I used to enjoy my own company then, back when my instincts were finely honed and fear was a friend I could trust to tell me when something wasn't right, not a tyrant run amok in my brain. Time alone used to be fleeting and precious.

When I get back to the apartment, I'm tired but keyed up. The new sights and sounds and the novelty of the city seem to have temporarily tricked my mind out of its fugue. Now I feel it all seeping back in: that amorphous but persistent fear that those I love are in mortal danger, as though I've left them all in a house with a gas leak only I know about. The center of me feels weak, like I'm a cloud of a person. I was a skier, I was a beloved girlfriend, I was someone's little sister. I'm none of those things anymore.

Maybe a glass or two of wine would smother my nerves. The half bottle of Malbec left over fits snugly in one of the giant red wineglasses I find in the pantry; these are rich-people wineglasses, not meant to be filled to the brim. I take it to the balcony. The city lights sparkle, and I can see the dark waters of the river churning in the distance. There's a glimmer of nostalgia left over from walking through San Telmo, but the more I try to recapture it the more elusive it becomes: my mind is already comingling the memory with the present. It seems clear, looking back, that when I was in Buenos Aires the last time, Luke and I were already doomed. And Blair. Until that trip, it was as though I hadn't really let myself look at him in years. I realize now, too late, that I'd let so much of it pass me by because I was always hurtling forward in pursuit of glory, never simply standing still in the moment I was in. My old life was beautiful, and I'd raced right through it. I'd marched in Olympic ceremonies, stood on the medal podium, but it was never enough, because it wasn't gold. And now it's over.

I can only appreciate it in the rearview. Before, I found my peace and my euphoria in speed. If I had known I was speeding toward catastrophe, would I have done it differently? Could I have?

The wine gets me bleary enough to try to sleep. I've become wary of the bed; those quiet hours with no distractions have become my worst enemy. I try to read a novel I brought with me—something light and forgettable—but my mind is too wine drenched to string the words together. I close my eyes and feel the dizziness of sleep cloud my mind.

A few moments later, I'm awoken by an indistinct noise that sets my heart racing. I hear another sound, from the kitchen—it's muffled but chillingly human. Oh god, someone is in here. I grab the cordless phone from the nightstand without the slightest idea of who I might call. Tom told me the number for emergency services, but I've forgotten it. It's written down on a notepad. In the kitchen. As I pick my way softly along the plush carpet of the narrow living room, my nerves crackle like exposed wiring. Then I see it, a tiny hand stretched out on the kitchen floor, palm down and fingers slightly curled, as though the child had been trying to claw its way forward, but now the hand is still. A viscous pool of red is slowly advancing past it.

I jolt straight up in my bed. I'm drenched in sweat. Only dreaming. It takes me several minutes to catch my breath. I get out of bed and discard my sweat-soaked T-shirt. I douse my face with water, and with shaking hands, I riffle through my large cosmetic bag for the pills. A careless doctor had at first prescribed me Ambien, which put me into a flat, dreamless sleep that left me unrefreshed. Worse yet, I would occasionally do strange and humiliating things, like sleepwalk into the kitchen and plow through an entire box of granola bars. One evening, I even called Luke in the middle of the night and left him a long, unintelligible message. A different, better doctor—one Gena sent me to—told me to stop taking the Ambien. I didn't have a sleep disorder. She gave me Klonopin instead to help with the anxiety but told me to use it sparingly, as it could be addictive. I found myself turning to it more than I would have liked. I know I'm not supposed to take it when I've had this much to drink, but what is my body for anymore anyway?

༄

Two days later, I decamp to San Telmo, as planned. I'm not sorry to leave my Palermo building, and even the swimming pool doesn't feel like enough reason to stay; I haven't used it once. I've also had the dream again. The little girl in the kitchen, the blood, and while I know that the ghosts are products of my overwrought mind and will go where I go, I can't pretend these visions don't make me want to leave.

I move in on a Saturday afternoon and hang my things in the closet. That evening, as the sun is starting to go down, I venture into the beautiful little secret garden of the courtyard. I feel hidden away. Entombed.

༄

I'm intrigued by my dark-eyed, elegantly graying landlady, though beyond our first encounter, we only exchange a passing hello. She lives in the building in a unit just off the small lobby. I frequently see her in the courtyard with a woman who looks so much like her, I decide they must be sisters. I feel envious and heartbroken watching them drinking and laughing in the courtyard. Penny and I will never be old ladies together. I can't think of my childhood without heartache now, and so much of what had once felt promised in my future has now disintegrated too. I'd always thought my sister would be there when I got married, there when I had children, there when I won a gold medal. Her absence reverberates now in both directions—my memories of her suddenly untrustworthy, my future with her obliterated. My children, if I have them, won't grow up with cousins or an auntie. I will eventually face the death of my parents alone.

The approach of Christmas feels surreal. Decorations abound, but the weather is warm and the days are long, the opposite of the cozy white Christmases I'm used to. My parents are also celebrating the holiday somewhere warm, having decamped to Hawaii, as is their new tradition. I went with them last year. Once we no longer had Penny, it felt masochistic to simply sit at home and go through the same motions we always had. I know they wish I was with them, but we have plans to Skype on

Christmas morning. Like all of our family traditions, we're left with a sad facsimile of what was.

On Christmas Eve, I'm kept up late by the sound of fireworks, and eventually I go to sit in the courtyard, bringing the bottle of wine and the panettone that the landlady has sweetly left on all of our doorsteps. At midnight, the city releases thousands of paper lanterns into the sky, and I can't help but be moved; it feels like such a hopeful tradition.

On Christmas Day, I Skype with my parents, but my Internet is weak, and it makes a painful encounter even more so. It feels like some clumsy metaphor: my connection with my parents, once strong, is now strained. The screen freezes midconversation, their disembodied voices continuing on, and in their captured still, I think I can see all the anguish they're trying to keep from me beneath their suntans. I admire them now more than ever: they've stayed together in the face of everything, and they turned toward rather than against each other. I know I should be grateful for my family, now three. I try to make it sound like I'm having fun: I tell them about the plazas and the tango dancers I see everywhere on the sidewalks.

My landlady is traveling somewhere to see family. She's given us a friend's name and number in case of emergencies. Casa de Volver. I wonder who has come here before me. I wonder who will come here after.

Penny Has a Boyfriend

IT WOULD be hard to overstate how much the idea of Blair and Luke moving away rocked my world at thirteen. They were really the only friends I had, though Blair in those days was more of a big brother figure—tasked with keeping tabs on Luke and me as we crashed down mountains all winter and spring and took to those same trails on our mountain bikes in the summer. It wasn't that I disliked other girls; I just didn't get them.

I spent more time together with Penny and Emily in the summer: they would come and sunbathe by the lake and giggle over Blair, who was the only one allowed to drive Tad's boat. Blair, reserved and handsome, was three years older than Luke and me and felt impossibly far ahead of us at sixteen, on the precipice of manhood. This was heightened by his being especially adultlike for a teenager, particular about everything from his clothes to his cross-training workouts, destined even then to be a tech skier.

"You're such a dude," Penny said to me as she watched me horse around with Luke on the Duncans' dock that summer.

"I'll take that as a compliment," I said, giving her a crooked smile. Luke was sputtering in the water beneath me, after I'd pushed him in. I cannonballed into the water next to him as Penny rolled her eyes.

Penny and Emily wore floral bikinis from the Delia's catalog and slathered too-weak sunscreen on their fair freckled limbs. I never understood how they could waste the whole day there with their copies of *YM* and *Seventeen* and endless, meandering gossip. They'd both liked running around outdoors when they were kids, but in the past few years they'd moved into the mysterious girly world of adolescence.

My parents never gave me a hard time about not fitting in. They never wanted my sister and me to be anything in particular, only happy and safe. They were the opposite of so many sports parents I met—Tad included—who deposited the full weight of their own unrealized ambitions onto their children's young shoulders.

Tad Duncan believed in excellence with a religious fervor. He would do anything for his kids, but it was always conditional on them being the best. Kristina, their eldest, was a near-perfect student and champion volleyball player who only went off the rails once she'd decided it would be the best way to spite her father, after he abandoned their family to live in Sun Valley with a woman scarcely ten years her senior. The rebellion didn't land; by then, Tad was too focused on his boys. Luke and Blair were both at the top of their age group in juniors but were good for different reasons. Blair was quiet and precise, absorbing our coaches' feedback and fine-tuning his technique ever closer to perfection, whereas right from the start Luke couldn't be told anything. When we were younger, the coaches discouraged us from going too fast, wanting to hone our technique to protect us. But Luke defied both orders and physics by getting down the mountain faster than anyone else in spite of, not because of, his technique. Watching him, it seemed like there was no chance he actually had control of his skis, and sometimes he didn't: the only thing more spectacular than his wins were his crashes. The Duncans' divorce only stoked his rebelliousness.

"My dad wants us to move to Sun Valley," Luke told me one day when we were sitting at the lodge in Schweitzer the next winter, waiting for my mom to pick us up. It had been a grueling day on the hill; the slopes were icy, and we'd been pelted with rain on the bottom half of our runs. We'd been talking for twenty minutes about the rotten snow—a topic we could discuss endlessly but that bored anyone else in earshot almost immediately.

"Do you want to go?" I asked, feeling a lump in my throat. I'd been hoping—with thirteen-year-old magical thinking—that if I never mentioned the possibility of them leaving, it might not happen. For the year since the Duncans' split, Ann had been running herself ragged trying to manage the boys' schedules as she scrambled to get back into the job market and build a life for herself without her erstwhile husband. With Blair starting to compete in NorAms—meaning he was traveling outside the region to compete against adults—it was becoming impossible. It was alleviated only somewhat by the fact that Blair had turned sixteen and could drive himself to local races and take his brother out to Sun Valley to see their father twice a month. I frequently went along with them and couldn't help but be impressed by Tad's chalet, with its giant hot tub, which looked directly out onto the slopes of Baldy.

"Fuuuuck, I don't know," Luke said. "I mean the backcountry there is sick. The snow is better. My dad's all excited about the club there, he says we could quit school. Not like, quit, but get a tutor or whatever so we can just go big, you know? But my mom would be wrecked. And, Bomber, you'd obviously cry your eyes out." He smiled, and I punched his arm.

"You wish, loser," I said. "What does Blair say?" Luke had become wilder when their father left—cutting classes, getting caught with a joint on the way back from the Junior Olympics—while Blair had become more stalwart, turning himself inside out to help their mom cope with her sudden single-parent status and taking a more fatherly role with his brother.

Luke shrugged. "He says he'll go where I go, but I don't think he wants to leave Mom. God," he said, suddenly flinging his helmet to the ground. "My dad's such a dick."

I felt sick with several things at once: fear that Tad was going to win out and move my best friend eight hours away, dread at being on my own, and deep envy at the idea that Luke and Blair would get to turn their lives over to skiing.

It turned out Luke wouldn't have to choose. Ann was soon so exhausted that she herself urged them to go to Sun Valley. She went along, renting a condo nearby with Tad's help. He'd rearranged his life exactly as he'd wanted it. They left the summer before Luke and I would have started high school. I felt completely alone.

⁂

That summer, without Luke and Blair, I was adrift. A fourteen-year-old's idea of the worst-case scenario is pretty limited if she's lucky, and this was mine. I moped around, and Penny and Emily let me tag along to Sanders Beach and the occasional house party or bonfire, where I shamelessly clung to them.

By that time, Penny's life revolved around her two main interests: horses and boys. She volunteered three days a week at a local stables with an equine therapy program for children and adults with disabilities. The stables adored her so much, they let her ride the horses anytime she wanted to. Even as a teenager, Penny was a helper, someone whose life was about being there for others.

I visited Penny at the stables every now and then. I liked the horses: they were big and strong and graceful; I felt like they got me. One afternoon, my mom and I arrived early to pick Penny up. She was on the paddock with her favorite charge, Matthew, who suffered from severe cerebral palsy, and I watched as she chatted to him and he smiled sweetly back at her. I knew I'd never have the patience for what she was doing.

"You're so good with him," I said to her once she and Matthew had brushed out the pinto he'd been riding and returned her to her stall.

"Matthew's one of my best buds." Penny shrugged. I felt guilty that I didn't understand. But I never questioned Penny's goodness; it was so evident, ran so deep.

⁂

I got my first kiss at CDA High School during my freshman year, and it was a fiasco. As predicted, I'd started to feel differently about boys as adolescence took hold. There was one in particular who caught my eye, Matt Berman, a dreamboat and basketball star in my sister's year. The crush wouldn't have amounted to much if I hadn't gone to a house party with Penny that fall. After summer was over and all of us were back in school, the standing invitation to hang out with Emily and Penny had been rescinded, so whenever I was invited to something, I jumped. Being surrounded by my peers—with whom I had nothing in common—at school all day was only making me lonelier. The party in question was at a basketball player's house, meaning Matt would be there.

"What are you going to wear, Katie?" Penny wanted to know as I sat back on her bed while she and Emily crowded her vanity mirror, maneuvering their lip liners.

"Oh, um . . . this?" I was in my usual uniform of Dickies and a thermal.

They shook their heads and made me change into a baby tee that showed off my newly arrived bustline, made more impressive once Penny had replaced my sports bra with one of her push-up bras. They took my hair out of its ponytail and added a couple of strategic braids and pulled out tendrils to frame my face. They swiped my lips with gloss in a shade called Rum Raisin.

"I feel weird," I said, looking in the mirror afterward.

"You look pretty," Penny said. It was the first time she'd ever said anything like this to me.

"So pretty!" Emily echoed.

I figured I had no chance with Matt. I didn't know then that a girl's willingness is its own aphrodisiac. I'm sure I was mortifyingly obvious about my crush; nothing about me has ever been subtle.

We'd been at the party for a while, and I hadn't seen Penny for half an hour when Matt found me outside getting some air. It was nearly October but the weather was still warm.

"Hey," Matt said, strolling up to me and handing me a beer. I was stunned; it was as though he'd been looking for me. Had he?

"Hey, Matt," I said, willing my voice not to trill with excitement. His considerable height made me feel almost dainty. I wondered if this was how other girls felt all the time.

"How's skiing?" he asked. He knew who I was! I tried to remain calm. The only boys I'd ever really talked to were other skiers, and we talked about skiing, about which runs were good that day, how the snow was, the falls and epic runs. Matt was exotic, from this other high school world I wasn't really a part of.

"It's good. I'm hoping to make the U.S. Team next year." It would be the C Team if anything and it was a long shot, but he didn't need to know that.

"Damn, Cleary, that's dope. You're big-time." The jocks at my school had a habit of calling everyone by their last name; it would have put some girls off, but it made me feel at home. In my natural environment, I was also Cleary, or Bomber to Luke and Blair.

I asked him how basketball was going, and he rattled off a litany of things he was working on to improve his game and his hopes for college ball. He seemed impressed that I didn't glaze over. I was relieved; this was my comfort zone. I countered with my take on balance drills.

"It's hard to believe you're Penny's sister," he said, downing the rest of his beer in one long glug. "You're so much hotter."

With this he leaned in and kissed me, his huge hand moving inside my shirt in one swift motion. The thrill and horror hit me simultaneously. First there was the delirious fact of being kissed by Matt Berman, but then there was the insult to my sister, the aggressive grope. I shoved him off me. Hard. He was drunker than I realized, and he stumbled backward dumbly, toppling over. His face went quickly from embarrassment to rage to amusement.

"Oh! Damn," he said, "You hit like a dude, Cleary. Guys," he said, hollering to his friends who were several yards away by the firepit, deftly transferring his own embarrassment onto me, something boys like him become adept at early on. "Don't mess with Manly over here."

The nickname was neither clever nor accurate—my height had briskly outpaced my weight and, ironically, my main focus with my coach at that point was building muscle—but it didn't matter. Matt was popular and beloved, and the nickname had the advantage of being perfect for chanting whenever I walked into a room, ensuring that I was greeted with "Man-ly, Man-ly" wherever I went thereafter.

That night, all I wanted to do was leave. I searched the house for Penny, feeling disoriented. She'd be fine with leaving early, since her current boyfriend went to another school.

"Emily," I said, finding her in the kitchen talking to some other girls from her class. She'd always been well-liked, the perfect combination of pretty and nonthreatening, the girl next door.

"Little sis!" she said. Her voice was high and excitable, as it always was when she'd had a beer or two.

"Have you seen Penny? I want to get out of here." I was trying to hide the fact that I was on the verge of tears. "This party sucks."

Emily shook her head, "I haven't seen her in a while, but let me know when you find her and we'll go. Are you okay?"

I nodded, but the sympathy on her face made my tears spill over. "Fucking boys," was all I could manage.

"Oh, sissy," she said, launching herself into my side, under my arm. By that time Emily came up to my shoulder and fit perfectly into the nook of my armpit.

I scoured the house for my sister. No one had cell phones then, only Zack Morris on *Saved by the Bell* and the occasional city person out for a weekend in CDA.

The party had long since spilled out into the warm night, and I stalked the perimeter, looking for Penny. When I came around the side of the house, I saw two figures barely visible in the shadows. As my eyes adjusted to the darkness, I was able to make sense of the grotesque tableau. There was Brad Winkle—a senior at CDAH—with his back against the side of the house, head canted back in ecstasy, and, below him, my sister on her knees. I froze in horror for a moment that stretched an eternity before bolting back into the house.

I saw Emily, who had migrated onto the back porch.

"Did you find her?"

I shook my head, plunging my hand into a nearby cooler to retrieve a beer and drink it fast.

Sometime later, Penny appeared on the patio.

"Let's go," she said, nonchalantly. "This party sucks. Brad Winkle will *not* leave me alone tonight. He keeps trying to make out with me. Like, *Jesus,* I have a boyfriend."

I hadn't, thank god, told Emily what I'd seen Penny doing or with whom. In that excruciating moment I was flooded by several things at once: disgust at what I'd seen, confusion about Penny's lie, but also a deep protectiveness, a desire not to embarrass my sister, not to let her embarrass herself.

We left the party and never spoke of that night again.

Liz Meets
the Madman of Belgrano

THE WEEK between Christmas and New Year's Eve is maddeningly quiet in Buenos Aires. Many of the shops and restaurants are closed, and my Spanish school is on break. Everyone decamps to the beaches in Mar del Plata and Pinamar, or so I'm told. My tour guide duties won't begin for another week and a half. The normally bustling streets now have only the occasional couple or group of tourists passing by. The emptiness lets my mind fill with memories, and I feel myself hurtling toward a crisis. I call my mom in Idaho.

"Oh, honey, what's up?" she says, my voice giving me away immediately.

"I don't know what I'm doing here," I tell her.

"Do you want to come home?"

"No." My parents are a comfort, but I can't face coming home. At least not yet. "I feel like it's good that I'm here. I just . . . I don't know. I'm lonely, I guess. I really miss my friends."

She knows how complicated everything is with Luke and Blair. My mom has always been a chief confidante, but now she's my only one, which feels somehow unfair to her.

"What about the people in your Spanish classes?"

"They're all college kids," I say. "And like three random retirees."

"Well, I don't know, honey. I never would have gone to a foreign country by myself, I think you're so brave. Is there some other way you can meet people your age? What about taking some cooking classes or, I don't know . . . tango classes?" My mom has always been good at throwing herself into her hobbies, deciding she liked something and swiftly becoming an expert. Our garden had been the most beautiful in the neighborhood growing up, and when their now-ancient German shepherd, Barry, was young, she had trained him to be a search-and-rescue dog.

"Mom, tango?"

"I'm just trying to help."

"I know you are, I'm sorry. It's just hard," I say after a beat. "I feel like I don't know who I am anymore. And I keep thinking about Penny."

"I know, sweetie. But you can't let it define the rest of your life. And it won't. I promise."

"I know this sounds crazy, but I just want to call her sometimes. I still haven't taken her number out of my phone."

"It's not crazy," my mom says. "I feel that way sometimes too."

I imagine it for a moment, calling the number. Someone might answer, but it would not be my sister.

"Mom." My voice sounds small as I choke on the question, the one I've asked and she's answered so many times it's become a call and response, an incantation. My mom is made of steel; neither of us ever deserved her. "Did we do the right thing?"

"Yes, honey. We had no choice."

⤛⤜

The thing about tragedy is that it isn't about just getting through it, it's about getting on with your life when the dust has settled but the landscape is bombed out, smoke in the air, charred remains at your feet. On New Year's Eve, I decide I will take myself to dinner in Belgrano, a neighborhood I haven't explored yet. I even dress up a little, just a simple jersey dress and some earrings, but it's something.

Growing up, I'd been peripherally aware that other girls put untold energy into hating their bodies. Even watching Penny and Emily—both a perfectly normal size—I'd become aware that "fat" was not simply a physical state but a state of mind, a feeling, a lens through which all teenage girls seemed to at least occasionally see themselves. Being an athlete and spending most of my time with boys had shielded me—my body had always been a machine to fine-tune and optimize—but that was all gone now. Looking in the long mirror affixed to the wall of my apartment, I feel a mild disgust. All of my abilities, all of my strength, this was my armor, and now I feel gelatinous and weak: permeable. The old me hides in the more abundant shell of the new one: of Liz Sullivan.

Belgrano is one of the more expansive neighborhoods in the city and I take myself on a little walking tour before dinner. I'm still getting used to the fact that no one eats here until 9:00 p.m. In a lush stretch of park— the Barrancas de Belgrano—at the center of the neighborhood, a small band is playing beneath the pergola with people dancing tango around them. The dance really is everywhere in this city; maybe my mom's right and I should learn it.

I'd never eaten alone in a restaurant before arriving here and it makes me nervous. I find a little place called Aldonza Bar, make my way up a narrow flight of stairs, and take a seat at the bar. I order tapas and a Malbec and people-watch from my perch. There's a giddy, charged atmosphere; summer has begun, and the New Year approaches. 2010. It was supposed to be another chance at gold. Instead I'm here, marooned in my own life.

I'm conscious of a pair of guys two seats away from me at the bar. They've been conspiratorially casting glances at me for the better part of an hour. They look painfully young, and they're clearly on their way to getting happily shit-faced, but it's not like I have other plans. Eventually they order three shots instead of two and flag down the bartender.

"For you," he says in English, my accent having given me away, "from the, uh, gentlemen at the bar." We're sitting so close to one another, the whole thing is ridiculous.

"Thanks," I say. "Cheers!"

They seem thrilled that I've taken the bait and jostle over so that they're sitting right next to me.

"Welcome!" one says, his accent rough.

"*You* are welcome," the other one corrects. "We are please to meet you."

We clink our little shot glasses together and throw them back. The boys cheer and order another round. I suddenly decide I'm game. Their names are Alberto and Santiago. I don't remember which is which, and I don't ask their ages because, frankly, I don't want to know. They're going to a party and they tell me I should come.

"The host won't mind you showing up with someone who wasn't invited?"

"It's Edward's, no one is invited," says one.

"Which mean," the other adds, "everyone's invited!"

"Who is Edward?" I ask, a question that seems to open a Pandora's box of myth and nonsense. Edward is an aging matador, an American billionaire, an exiled British lord. It quickly becomes clear that my new friends have no idea who Edward is, but they do appear to have his home address. This is all a very dubious plan, but following them still feels like a better option than going home alone. And one of them—Santiago, I believe—is actually pretty cute. And he's sure to become more so the drunker I get, and what is New Year's Eve for but alcohol and bad decisions? What is there to stay sober for?

Santiago (I think) takes my hand as we walk the several blocks to Edward's alleged home. Okay! Santiago, mine for the moment. The sun has just gone down and around us people are dressed up and headed out into the night. There's a teeming sense of revelry in every direction, a liveliness I've been missing this past week. Alberto (I think) studies the piece of paper in his hand, seemingly annoyed that his friend is more interested in flirting than helping him find the place. The houses on the block are large and elegant, their numbers tastefully obscured. The boy hanging off of me is the one with the better English, and as we walk he asks me questions and I tell him a swift river of lies starting with the fake name, that I'm from Texas and a recently retired rodeo cowgirl. *Really?* Sure. Why not?

At last, Alberto seems to have found where we're going.

"Jeez Louise," I say, taking in the breathtaking town house with its ivy-covered facade. "This is it?"

The boys go into hysterics over "jeez Louise," but after a moment, Alberto checks the address and confirms. He rings the bell and a moment later, a man—much younger than I expected the mysterious Edward to be—answers the door.

Suddenly my boisterous companions have fallen silent, as though they're little boys waiting for their mother to speak for them. Christ.

"Hi," I say, "Edward? We were told"—mortifyingly, the man seems content to let me finish my sentence—"to come to the party," I manage.

"I'm not Edward." He smiles as though the very idea is hilarious. "But you're in the right place. Come with me."

He turns and we follow him. The boys look thrilled and the one puts a hand on my hip precariously close to my ass as we make our way inside. Soon, we're all distracted by our surroundings. The first wall is a lush garden leading up to the house's portico, a tangle of jungle plants split by the wooden esplanade we're now crossing. There are fairy lights strung through the foliage, giving the whole place an enchanted look. The festivities are already underway, and groups of glamorous partygoers are spilling out onto the patio and the small patches of grass that surround it. None of the ebullient din of the party could be heard from the street. It feels like we've gone through the looking glass.

"Some party," Alberto says, raising his eyebrows at us. The boys, I suddenly realize, look as underdressed as I do. I half expect some security personnel to appear and ask us to leave. I'm reminded of all of the parties the trustees threw us in Aspen and Vail where it always felt like a mistake that someone let a bunch of punk kids into a place this nice.

Inside, there is music playing and yet more beautiful people tumbling over one another. A jumble of languages emerges from the babble: Spanish, Italian, French. A handsome young man, his bow tie already undone, ambles by holding two overly full glasses of something clear. He says hello in Spanish to the three of us, and then offers me his extra shot.

"Might as well," I mumble to myself in English and toast my drinking buddy. "Bottoms up," I say and drink what turns out to be tequila.

We're carried along with a tide of people to a massive gleaming kitchen, where waiters bustle around efficiently and someone directs us to a bar in the corner. As we wait for drinks I take a moment to scan the crowd around me, and as I do, I notice that not all the guests are as young as the one who answered the door. People in their thirties and forties mingle with younger guests. There's an elegant octogenarian in a full-length black gown laughing gaily in a crowd of younger men; someone drapes a feather boa around her shoulders, and she smiles and plants a kiss on his cheek, leaving a gash of red lipstick behind.

Santiago (maybe) is getting handsier by the second. I'm feeling the booze and don't really care one way or the other. When we make it to the bar, I order a glass of champagne.

"*¡Vamos a bailar!*" Santiago says, pulling me back to the main room, where people have moved some of the furniture to make a dance floor and incorporated the rest. A skinny girl in a sequin dress has climbed on top of a thankfully formidable-looking coffee table.

The music—heaving house with a visceral beat—is not my taste, but it fits the mood of the party so well that I find myself getting into it. Santiago is a good dancer, and at first I enjoy being led along by him. But when he starts pulling me in, pressing his comically obvious erection into my leg, I start to feel a little claustrophobic. I down the rest of my champagne and use the excuse of needing another to get some space. He offers to come with me, but I tell him I'll be right back. He joins Alberto in trying to get a glimpse up the skirt of Coffee Table Girl.

I take my time making a slow lap around the party. The anxiety that has become my constant companion is both charged and released by the party's atmosphere and the booze. A middle-aged couple makes out with abandon next to a massive marble fireplace where a fire—which fortunately appears gas powered—roars beside them. The more I look into the faces of the guests, the more the mood starts to feel a little apocalyptic. Or maybe it's just me. I'm remembering the last New Year's Eve I spent with Luke and Blair two years ago. Red Bull, who sponsored all three of us, was throwing a giant party at the top of Whistler Mountain in Canada, and we, along with their other athletes, were guests of honor. The town had already begun to transform for the 2010 Olympics, and it all still felt possible for me. At midnight, a spectacular display of fireworks lit up the side of the mountain, and Blair and I watched from the deck. Luke was nowhere to be found, and when the countdown happened Blair and I kissed, just lightly, unthinkingly. Am I only remembering now that he looked at me for an oddly long moment after? Am I imagining it?

I grab another glass of champagne from a tray and head outside, where there is an expansive enclosed patio with a swimming pool and deck chairs. I lean up against the outer wall.

"Hi there." A foxy fortyish guy appears at my side. He has a full head of prematurely gray hair, a world-weary smile, and sparkling dark eyes. "You're American, aren't you?"

"That obvious, huh?" I ask. He smiles. "Well, so are you, right?"

"Sort of," he says. "I grew up partly in New York, partly elsewhere."

"So what's the tip-off?"

"Well, you're tall," he says, "for one thing. And there's an openness about Americans. I can always tell. I've never been wrong."

"About just that or about anything?"

He laughs. "So what's a nice girl like you doing in this den of iniquity?"

"Nice line."

"I thought so."

"Got picked up by a couple of young guys at a bar, they brought me here." I shrug.

"And you were free on New Year's, or were they just that charming?"

"God no," I say. "I'm new here, I didn't have any plans. I don't think the guys I came with actually know the host."

"I don't think very many people at this party do," he says.

I shake my head. "What kind of nut job lets a bunch of strangers into his home?"

At that moment, a boisterous blond woman about his age appears at his side and wraps herself around his arm.

"Darling! How many times have I told you, you've really got to lock the doors to the bedrooms. There was about to be an orgy back there, honestly! But don't worry, I've shooed them off. Oh, hello," she says, noticing me. "Who have we here?"

"Actually we haven't been properly introduced . . ."

Who am I again? "Liz Sullivan," I say.

"Gemma," the blond woman says, shaking my hand. Her eyes are a bright, inviting blue. Without knowing why, I like her instantly.

"Liz here was just wondering what kind of madman invites a bunch of strangers over to his house," the man says, and Gemma bursts out laughing.

"Liz Sullivan," she finally manages to spit out, "meet Edward White, the madman of Belgrano."

I feel myself blushing, though thankfully Edward looks more amused than annoyed.

"Actually," I say, shaking his proffered hand, "I said 'nut job.' Anyway, sorry."

"Oh Edward, I like her. I like you, do stick around." Thank goodness, she's shit-faced.

"I didn't realize," I say. "I thought you'd be surveying the party from a balcony somewhere. Keeping the high watch for Daisy Buchanan."

"Fitzgerald," Edward says, smiling. "Now you can stay."

"Spot on," Gemma says. "Edward is always picking up waifs and strays."

"I like colorful people."

"That's one word for them! So, Liz Sullivan, what brings you to Buenos Aires?"

It's the first time someone's really asked me this, and I don't have an answer ready. "I'm just doing some traveling. I needed to get away for a while. Bad breakup." That's true at least.

"Oh no!" Gemma says. "Another member of the Buenos Aires Lonely Hearts Society!"

"Breakups are one of the main things that bring people here," Edward says. "Anecdotally, anyway."

"We'll have to keep Gianluca away from you!"

"Gemma, don't be terrible."

She rolls her eyes and with a sly smile says, "Didn't I tell you? A soft spot for reprobates."

"I thought you liked him."

"I never said I didn't."

Have they forgotten I'm standing here? "Sorry, who's Gianluca?"

Gemma laughs. "It depends on who you ask! A Roman exile, a Grecian con man, the illegitimate son of Juan Perón."

Edward rolls his eyes. "Gossip and rumors. Gianluca is a very talented musician and dancer. I met him years ago in Saint-Tropez. He owns a tango studio here now."

"Oh, he owns it, does he?" Gemma is perhaps too drunk to notice that Edward looks irritated. "And do you want to tell her the story about the countess? It's really my favorite."

"That's about enough, thanks."

"So how do you two know each other?" I say, sensing that a subject change is in order. I can't tell if they're a couple or not.

"We've known each other since we were babies! Which was many decades ago."

"Out our age just like that, Gem?"

I try to get a read on Edward. He seems unlike those of his contemporaries that I know back home. There are the coaches and equipment guys who have wives and families and drive practical cars with room for offspring and gear, and then the eternal ski bums, who still live like twentysomethings despite the fact that they're more likely to shred their ligaments than anything else.

"We should embrace forty, Edward. We wear it well. Our fathers were dearest friends at Oxford," she continues, "but then Edward's father moved to New York City to seek his fortune. He married an Argentine who had decamped to Paris during the junta. It's all very Continental. Thank goodness they came back to England all the time. Edward was my first crush!"

"Still not quite over me, are you?" Edward sips his champagne and smiles, sending charming crinkles fanning out around his eyes.

"So you have family here?" I say.

"My aunt and uncle and a very beloved cousin, Camilla, though she travels so much she can scarcely be said to live here. She's here tonight though, home for the holiday."

I look out into crowd. The party is more densely packed every time I turn around, as though it's an organism whose cells are multiplying.

"I invite a few friends and they invite a few friends. I've been having these parties for a while now. What's the point in having a house like this otherwise?" he says, looking around as though only now noticing the ruckus. "I suppose the word is out."

"And you really don't mind having all these strangers in your house?" I ask.

Edward shrugs and looks at the bustle as though observing adored children in a sandbox. "I enjoy it. Think of me as a social anthropologist."

"Is *that* what the kids are calling it these days, Edward?" Gemma snorts.

He shakes his head. "Gemma will have you believe I'm an insufferable Don Juan, but my heart was shattered too. But that's more than enough about me. What foolish man broke your heart back in the U.S.?"

"I was with my boyfriend for about a decade. Then I had some family drama. I don't know, things got messy." I think I see something flicker in Edward's eyes, some recognition, but I know I'm probably being paranoid.

"That's a lifetime at your age," Gemma exclaims. "How old *are* you?"

"Thirty," I say. "And yeah. First love." This seems like a silly way to describe Luke, but it's as accurate as anything else I can think to call him. "We got together when we were nineteen and then broke up not long ago."

"Nineteen! I can't imagine," Gemma says.

"This is making me feel very ancient, but please, continue," says Edward.

"That's it, really. We tried to be friends." It feels surprisingly good to talk about Luke with these strangers; they don't know or even know of him. The narrative is mine. "Which turned out to be a stupid idea."

Edward nods and raises his glass to mine.

"Oh but that's terrible!" Gemma says. "How can you *not* at least be friends with someone you've loved? Are you just supposed to cut them off like a gangrenous limb?"

"Yes, Gemma," Edward says. "And if you can swing it, move to another hemisphere: which brings us here tonight."

Gemma looks exasperated. "For a time, I suppose some distance is healthy, but not indefinitely! Aren't we more civilized than that?"

"We're really not." Edward smiles. "At least I'm not. I don't want to see Amelia ever again, thank you very much. Or Rachel for that matter."

"That's the ex and her new girlfriend," Gemma says to us in a stage whisper. "*They* were all friends once as well. A very sordid business."

Just then, some friends of Edward's spot him and come to hug him. They ignore me entirely, and after a few moments of feeling awkward, I slink away. My head is swimming from all the champagne, and I think perhaps I should leave, but Alberto and Santiago intercept me with more shots and pull me back out onto the dance floor.

⁓❧⁓

As midnight approaches, everyone gets drunker and louder and more people arrive. Someone falls in the pool and then several more jump in. I'm worried on Edward's behalf about what these people might do to his beautiful house.

I've had so much champagne that my head feels pleasantly detached from my body. I let myself be carried along with Alberto and Santiago, who are now pawing at me alternately. Good grief! There are dozens of girls at this party, am I really such a novelty? After some mysterious conferring with a few fellow party guests, they head off to find cocaine. I tell them to find me later, not caring much whether or not they do.

I notice that someone has stopped the music and people are moving the furniture, shooing away an amorous couple who'd claimed the couch. Gemma pops back up next to me, her blue eyes shining, her expression bleary.

"Hello, darling, are you enjoying yourself? It's Liz, right? You'll have to forgive me, I'm just terrible with names." She clutches my forearm, in affection or maybe just to remain upright. "Better with faces."

I smile. "It's fine. Me too," I lie. I'm good with names. I've just realized that I want to be friends with this woman. "What's going on?" I ask.

"It's time for the dancing to begin!" she says with a mischievous grin.

"Everyone's been doing a pretty good imitation," I say.

She waves a hand. "Amateur hour. Gianluca is going to dance for us now," she explains.

Sure enough, on the makeshift dance floor that's emerged stands a man—is he thirty? Fifty?—and his beautiful young partner. Both have sparkling dark eyes and glossy black hair, fair skin, like many Argentines. This man is the cause of all the fuss? I can't decide if he's ugly or handsome. As he makes a series of movements to ready himself for the dance—his partner settling into his arms, her eyes shining and her face intent— he rapidly switches between one and the other: he is slender and wiry, a little taller than me maybe, with dramatic cheekbones and a long Roman nose. I decide he's more compelling than handsome. So unlike my golden boys, Luke and Blair. Luke with his thick sandy brown curls, his irreverent, crooked smile, and Blair's surfer boy locks, his blue eyes, his star quarterback smile. I'm convinced people thought I was better-looking because of my constant proximity to them.

The song begins and Gianluca holds his partner in a close embrace. There is a loaded moment where tension builds, and somehow the two of them there, scarcely moving, is breathtakingly intimate. Then they begin in a kind of walk across the floor, so deeply synchronized with each other that they almost appear to be one body. The drunken crowd is captivated into silence. A few bars in, the two of them up the drama, the space between them widening as she goes into a series of intricate patterns, swooping her long legs in tight figure eights and looping them around Gianluca's waist. He spins her and pulls her in, pushes her away. It's like watching a couple fight, or make love, or both, but more elegantly than any couple has ever done either of those things. The crowd murmurs exaltations—exploding into applause at the final move. When the song finishes, Gianluca and his partner are immediately swarmed with party-goers trying to get to them. The two gamely lead a few people through some moves.

"So that's the mysterious Gianluca?" I ask Gemma, trying not to sound as impressed as I feel.

Gemma laughs, and now Edward is with us again as well. I was so wrapped up in watching the dance, I didn't notice him.

"Ye-es, the one and only. Sometime when Edward isn't being so *boring*, he'll tell you all about how he met him, it's the stuff of legends! Edward was with his ex—a different ex, an Italian girl from a while back—and they'd been invited out on a superyacht owned by her aunt's husband, an Italian count. Gianluca had been working as a performer on some luxury European cruise line until he was sacked for sleeping with the guests. He was abandoned in Saint-Tropez and the countess discovered him busking outside a café. She invited him on the yacht to teach dance lessons, told her husband he was gay of course." She smiles and bites her lip as the man himself approaches, pulling Edward into a handshake that becomes a swift and hearty hug.

"Hey, man!" Edward says. "Glad you made it."

"I wouldn't have missed it. Hello, Gemma," Gianluca says, leaning in to kiss her cheeks. "Edward, you know she's the star student in my intermediate class."

"Naturally."

"This is our new friend Liz," Gemma says, and he turns to greet me with the customary two-cheek kiss and a smile of bottomless confidence. He's the star who's come down to earth. I know because I used to be on the other side of this divide. I used to wave to screaming throngs: feeling their energy, hearing their clattering cowbells, the roar of them as I came over the last rise, seeing the blur of their faces and the fluttering flags through the spray of white as I came to a stop. The fans. The moments you shared with them were both impersonal and addictive. People love watching sports because they feel like they're a part of something, and they are.

I know that everyone in the room has suddenly developed a burning desire to be able to dance like Gianluca and his partner. And in the drunken revelry, they reckon they could. This is what great athletes do: make it look, if not easy, at least possible. I'm not fooled, of course. I know the years and years of training that must have gone into making that spectacle look so effortless.

"That was beautiful to watch," I say. We're speaking English, thank goodness. I'm too drunk to try for much in Spanish. Though everything else about the two men is different, Gianluca has something Luke always had in spades: the warmth of star power radiating off him.

There's something else too. From a distance, Gianluca was compelling, but up close, he has such raw sexual energy I'm unsettled. He has a low, sonorous voice, and when he leans in to kiss me hello, I can smell him. He's wearing some sort of cologne, but there's something more to it; the scent of his sweat mixed with it is so intoxicating it gives me a contact high.

"Thank you," he says, clutching his hand to his heart as though I've just made his night. "How long are you in town? You should come take some lessons at my studio." His English is excellent, with only a faint, indeterminate accent.

"I'm here indefinitely."

"Well then. May I?"

I pause for what becomes an awkwardly long moment. I can move my body drunkenly to music like everyone, but I don't dance.

"Of course you may!" Gemma laughs and pushes me forward into his arms. "Don't be shy, darling, G is an excellent teacher."

He shows me a *basico*—the rudimentary walking step—then leads me through a few steps and turns encouragingly. Whatever I'd felt before is intensified once I'm in his arms. I'm swamped by an odd mix of desire and comfort: he is new and he is familiar. It's been a long time since I've just been held in someone's arms like this with no other agenda. He talks to me as we dance, which relieves some of the tension. I'm muted by everything racing through my mind. Edward catches my eye and gives me a knowing smile that I return with a nervous one. I can't help but feel my new friend has seen something I don't want him to see.

When I leave the dance floor, the boys have reappeared, and they hand me a drink. They're on either side of me on the dance floor when the countdown to the new year begins. One of them pulls my face in for a deep tongue kiss while the other kisses the back of my neck. Hands run all over my body, touching my breasts and creeping up my dress. They turn me around and I'm kissing the other one. I'm numb enough that all I feel is the sensations, and I keep chasing them. A wave of panic hits me that I'm in public until I glance around the dance floor and see that all around us, there's a similar sense of frenzy, of hands and flesh and tongues.

⁓𝒮ᵉ

I wake up several hours later on a narrow bed in a cramped and filthy apartment. I'm reminded of the crash pads of some of Luke's dirtbag friends in Ketchum: flats strewn with remnants of food and unwashed clothing that would only be tolerable to men under twenty-five and people with some kind of disorder. I'm sandwiched between Alberto and Santiago, and if anything I'm more uncertain who is who. I don't know what time it is, but it's still dark out. I realize with mounting horror—I'm still drunk but not enough to blot out my circumstances— that I'm naked, as are the boys next to me. And god, they're *boys,* I realize, looking at their sleeping baby faces. Jesus. I carefully search for my clothes and get dressed. Thankfully the two of them are out cold. Relief washes over me as soon as I'm on the other side of their door, out on the street. It's quiet so it must be very early. My mind is racing; the only saving grace is that I'm reasonably sure that everyone was too drunk for much more than a lot of messy fondling. I let myself laugh a little at the idea of them waking up next to each other.

As I make my way back to my apartment, exhaustion hits me and anxiety begins to creep in; darkness crowds the edges of my consciousness. I wait too long to take the pill and find myself curled in a ball on the floor of my small bathroom—it must be nearing morning but I'm divorced from time. Some part of me knows that all I need to do is stand up and go get the Ativan that's in a bottle on my nightstand. But crossing the tiny apartment feels like an insurmountable task. My breath is short and my throat is freezing cold, my chest in knots, my heart pounding, racing to keep up with the cycle of thoughts in my mind: *What are you doing here?*

Why did you come? You should be training. You gave up your dream. You've abandoned your parents. You failed Penny. Nothing will ever be right again. You will feel exactly like this forever. You are beyond redemption. You're a slut. You're worthless.

Finally the attack wears itself out and I'm able to drag myself up and over to my bed. I take an Ativan, not because it will help but because it will knock me out, and I can't bear to be conscious another second. As I drift off to sleep, I see the waxing blue light of the morning inching its way along the edges of my blinds. The first day of 2010 is dawning.

Penny's Hair

THE BALD patches on Penny's pretty head began appearing early in the second semester of her junior year.

"It's everywhere!" I overheard her say tearfully to my mother one evening as they sat at our kitchen table. She was finding hair on her pillow in the morning, clumps in the drain in the shower; it came out on her hairbrushes and when she ran her fingers through her hair. "I'm like a chemo patient in a movie."

"Oh, honey," my mom said. "We'll get to the bottom of it. It could just be stress." Stress could do strange things. Was Penny stressed? There was the matter of Ryan, the boyfriend from the other school, who my parents weren't so fond of. He seemed controlling. He had a lot of opinions about what Penny should and should not wear and do and say. Even easygoing Emily wasn't a fan.

At school, Penny's hair loss became the melodrama of the moment. There'd been a much-buzzed-about story in a recent issue of *Seventeen* magazine about a beautiful teenager who suffered from a disease called alopecia, and so the population of CDA High was surprisingly well-informed on the obscure condition. What could be more horrifying for a teenage girl than having her hair fall out? Worse still, alopecia had no known cause and no known cure. Penny was a sudden and tragic celebrity at school. One of the most popular girls in her class boldly offered to take her wig shopping when the time came. For the good-looking boys who also cared about seeming nice, she became the babe du jour: "Penny Cleary? Yeah, she's cute."

My parents were at their wits' end, and I'm sorry to say that I was no picnic during this time. For one thing, my competition schedule was getting more intense, with more out-of-state junior competitions. I still talked to Luke all the time on the phone and saw him at the bigger races, but I feared he was slipping away into a life that no longer included me. And I was wracked with envy of peers I was falling behind, like Sarah Sweeny, whose family had just relocated to Vail and who, at sixteen, was competing well at the FIS level with adults, while I had to continue to go to regular school.

During midwinter break near the end of February, my parents agreed to go to Sun Valley for a visit. They rented a condo on the hill—turning down Tad Duncan's offer to stay at the chalet. ("With the child bride?" my mom said. "No thanks!") But they said that it was okay if I stayed in the Duncans' guest room. Penny stayed home for a week of sleepovers at Emily's house and sneaking around with Ryan.

When we arrived at their house, my heart was hammering out of my chest. I'd seen Luke and Blair weeks before at a junior event in Jackson Hole, but we'd barely spent five minutes together. They both leaped on me in a giant group bear hug the moment I walked through the door of the chalet.

I was relieved at first that things felt the same with them. We settled back into our familiar grooves with one another as they showed me all of their new discoveries about the mountain. But soon the differences between us began to emerge. Blair was dating a snowboarder who'd been the junior champion the previous year, and Luke seemed to be testing out an entirely new identity. On the second day, he took me up to the snow park, and as we slid into the lift line, it was like I was suddenly seeing him for the first time. He'd gotten taller since the previous year and filled out.

He was dressing differently too, and not in a way I liked. He suddenly wore low-slung pants everywhere and T-shirts that went practically to his knees.

"I'm glad you're here, Bomber. It hasn't been the same without you," he said. The line was long and moving slowly, given the school holiday. Suddenly, a raucous group of guys appeared behind us, several of them leaning over to click their poles against Luke's.

"Bro!"

Luke turned delightedly. "Yoooo, it's the crew."

I felt myself become momentarily invisible in the cacophony as Luke's new friends overwhelmed the space around us. Looking at the ragtag group of them, I saw where Luke was getting his new fashion sense. They looked older than us, but it was hard to tell by how much.

"These lines are fucking gnarly, bro," one of them said, crunching a lit cigarette beneath his ski.

"Fucking *gapers*," another added.

"Guys," Luke finally said. "This is Katie. She's visiting from CDA."

The introduction seemed to have a cooling effect; had Luke never mentioned me?

"What's up, Katie? Brad," one said. Eric, said the other. Chad, said the third. I didn't think I'd be able to keep them straight, but it seemed unlikely to matter.

The three warmed up a bit after our first run in the park when I nailed a respectable 360. I was glad I could even still do it. Luke and I had always messed around in the park but I was more focused on my downhill.

⌘

Late in the afternoon, Tad caught up with me as I was raiding the fridge. Even with the new wife, I was plenty comfortable in the house.

"Hey, Katie. How was the hill today?"

"Not too bad, we were mostly in the park."

"So I take it you met some of Luke's new *friends*?" His tone left little doubt as to what Tad thought of them.

"Yeah. They're all right."

Tad looked at me askance. Somehow it felt like he was talking to me as an adult, something he'd never done before. I laughed.

"Okay, I don't really get it."

"They're absolute losers, and they're dragging him down. He's never going to qualify for FIS if he keeps this up. Now, he's going on about the X Games and wanting to shoot videos instead of train. There's no future in that, and those boys are reckless. They don't even wear helmets."

"I'll talk to him," I said. Tad nodded. This was why I was here, I suddenly understood.

We all went out to dinner on our last night in Sun Valley, and after Tad insisted on paying the bill, he asked my parents and me to hang back for a moment.

"I want to talk to you," he said, matter-of-factly, "about bringing Katie out to Sun Valley."

It probably would have been much more appropriate for Tad to approach my parents before he looped me into the conversation, regardless of how grown-up I thought I was at fifteen. But Tad knew how to persuade people to do what he wanted. He knew if my parents watched my eyes fill with hope at the opportunity he was presenting, that would outweigh any other misgivings. Given how close I was with his sons, he also likely knew that Penny was having trouble, though he made no mention of it now.

"Listen," Tad had said, a knowing look on his handsome face, which was so like Blair's, "Katie's done amazingly well as it is, but the opportunities the kids have in Sun Valley"—he shook his head—"are unmatched. Luke is doing great with his tutor, and Blair's already been accepted to Dartmouth—it will take him more than four years naturally, but that could eventually be a great place for Katie too; they're fantastic about working with skiers' schedules. For now, it would be easy to integrate Katie, she and Luke being the same age. They're all smart, disciplined kids. We're not going to let their education go by the wayside, we would never do that." The "we" he spoke of was always endlessly inclusive and open to interpretation: *we* were all on the same team. Team Katie, Team

Luke, Team Blair, Team U.S.A. "But if they're going to get where they want to go, the focus has got to be there. They need the right support and access to the right resources. And we could get you out here as much as you wanted. "

It would be hard to leave home, but the idea of a bigger mountain in my backyard—not to mention being able to leave school and having Luke and Blair back—was too much. Tad knew it. He was a man who got what he wanted. Tad was a pull-yourself-up-by-your-bootstraps Libertarian, a social Darwinist who felt that his own ascent in the world gave him permission to take anything he wanted. And what he wanted right now was for his sons to be surrounded by potential champions, in order to sharpen them into ones. He didn't want Luke to be distracted by the fact that his best friend lived elsewhere, didn't want him to fall in with the freeskiers, who he saw as burnouts. Defying his father was giving Luke no shortage of satisfaction. If Tad brought me here, he'd be the hero again. He had spent the year rallying the support of other rich local ski fans, and now he needed to deliver additional talent that was not his progeny.

"We'll think about it," my father said once Tad had laid out his offer.

"*Dad!*" I wailed, as though taking a night or two to consider sending your fifteen-year-old daughter to live with someone else was deeply unreasonable.

"It's a very generous offer," my mom added. "But it's a big decision."

"Of course you should think about it," Tad said. "Just so you know, the tutors can pick up wherever Katie leaves off. There will be no interruption in her studies whatsoever. And they'll work around the kids' training so that they're not having to squeeze everything in all the time. It will be so much less stressful for them."

I was relentless on the five-hour drive home the next day. I was half ready to divorce my parents as Macaulay Culkin had recently done—inspiring an entire generation into childish fantasies of freedom. Yes, I would *emancipate* myself! Of course I'd never have done it, I loved my parents too much, but I was so obsessed with glory, I was ready to bulldoze anything in my path. My parents tried to hold me off while they discussed it between themselves, but I thought the decision should be mine.

"Why don't you just let me go?" I hollered at them over dinner one night while Penny was out with Emily. "God! Why don't you worry about your other daughter?"

I wish I could bring myself to forget that I'd ever said such a thing, that I'd unintentionally cut to the quick the way only a teenager who both knows and doesn't know the impact of her words can.

So it was decided, and in the midst of everything, I prepared to move to Sun Valley. I felt sad about leaving Pen, but she'd be off to college with Emily after the next year anyway.

I wouldn't find out until years later that it was not alopecia that was making Penny go bald. My parents didn't tell me when they discovered she was shaving her hair off, and the revelation never spread. Either the kids at CDA High were credulous enough to believe she'd had a miraculous recovery, or they just moved on to something else. Penny's half-bald head: a harbinger of everything. Later, my mom would tell me that she'd tried to get Penny into counseling, but she was seventeen by then and resistant. And their friends had problems with their own daughters—cutting and eating disorders, underage drinking and boys—maybe it was all on a spectrum. A girl shaving her hair off—for attention? In an act of rage? Self-harm?—was a strange thing to do, but it wasn't so serious, was it?

I can't help but wonder what would have happened had my parents and I resisted the wealthy and formidable Tad Duncan. What if I'd been there that next year, living at home with my sister? Would I have seen other signs of her illness picking up speed? Do I blame Tad Duncan for intervening? I don't know. Some days I blame everyone, some days I blame no one. But always I blame myself.

Liz Learns Tango

WHEN I wake up for the second time around noon on New Year's Day, I expect to be devoured by shame. Sadly, drinking myself into oblivion and hooking up with strangers has become fairly routine and so has the spiral that follows. The last time I saw Blair he was in CDA for the weekend seeing his sister, but I'd left his messages unreturned. He'd spotted me at one of the local dives, surrounded by a true group of creepers, and nearly dragged me out.

"You never called me back, Katie, and what are you doing here?"

"Blowing off steam," I said, wrenching my arm out of his.

"This isn't like you."

"And it's not like *you* to be so patronizing. Since when are you my babysitter?"

"Since you started trying to annihilate yourself."

But this is different. No one knows me here, there's no one to hurt, no one to disappoint. The night will be just another secret swallowed by this sprawling city that has soaked up the lust and longing of so many before me. And it hadn't been a waste. I'd met Gemma and Edward; perhaps they'd become my friends. And then there was Gianluca. That dance.

Despite the alcohol and the sensory deluge of Edward's party, the memory of those few minutes, of Gianluca's arms holding me with such control and authority, is stunningly clear. It had released me for the briefest moment from myself, and I'd felt the dense knot of grief that lives in my chest breaking up. I want it again. I guess I'm taking tango classes.

Tango Fortunato occupies a glass storefront in the Microcentro, not far from where my Spanish classes are. The main studio is one large room, and students congregate on the periphery, lounging on the large L-shaped sofa that occupies one corner or sitting on the floor to change into dance shoes.

I've arrived early and the class before mine is still going on. I watch as a collection of adults of all ages pick their way through intricate combinations. A younger man and woman I assume are teaching assistants wander the room. They both wear T-shirts with the studio logo and periodically cut in on couples to demonstrate. They're both horribly beautiful. He looks typically *Porteño*—Mediterranean with dark hair and green eyes— while she looks like she's from somewhere else: Brazil maybe? She's tall and lean with large luminous dark eyes and dark skin, her hair cropped close to her head.

I walk in as the class wraps up, and the gorgeous male assistant comes by with a clipboard to check me in. The woman is standing in the corner, talking to Gianluca, along with a girl I recognize as his partner from the other night. I wonder if one of them is dating him. Are both of them?

I feel a pleasant jangle of nerves as I wait with the other students for class to start. I'm not sure how my general athleticism is going to translate here; I've never been especially graceful. The commentators loved to contrast me with my top rival, Kjersti Larsen of Norway. They would remark that I muscled my way down the runs while she appeared to glide down seamlessly, breaking the laws of gravity that constrain mere mortals. Kjersti. I miss her. There was always camaraderie between the Norwegians and the Americans on the circuit. I miss the odd intimacy of our rivalry: the way we would catch eyes on race day and smile at each other.

I don't expect Gianluca to remember me, but he spots me leaning against the doorway, trying to be inconspicuous.

"*Ciao,*" he says, walking over. Then, in English, "From Edward's party, right?"

"Right."

"I'm so glad you came," he says, "I enjoyed dancing with you." He kisses my cheeks. "Tell me your name once more."

"Liz," I say. My face feels like it's on fire and I pray it isn't noticeable.

"Liz!" he repeats, as though he'd just been on the verge of remembering it. "Welcome to my studio. It's humble but I'm proud of it. This is the main studio, there's a practice room and an office in the back. Come with me, I want to introduce you to some people."

He takes my hand, which startles me. He introduces me to his partner, Angelina, and his teaching assistants—also part of the studio's performance team, he explains—the gorgeous boy is Rodrigo. The girl is Calliope—Cali for short—and she's American.

"Where are you from?" I ask.

"New York," she says, her demeanor a little frosty.

"Edward," I say, "do you know him?"

"New York is a big city." She smiles. "I know him from here though."

I want to ask her more, but class is about to begin. As we disperse, I have the horrible thought that if Cali is American, she might recognize me.

The room has filled up with a motley mix: college students, thirty-something professionals still in work clothes, retirees, including one silver-haired woman in a full ballet costume.

"*Bienvenidos todos,*" Gianluca says. He continues in his slow, precisely enunciated Spanish, "Thank you for joining us here. It's an honor to welcome you to my studio. This is the beautiful Angelina, who will be helping me today." Angelina stands beside him with her hands clasped behind her back. In the lights of the studio she looks even more girlish, twenty at most. "And in the black shirts, Cali and Rodrigo. They're my advanced students, they'll be watching you and helping. We will start with a *basico,* which is going to be the foundation for the dance, along with the walks."

Gianluca and Angelina take us through the beginner moves, and we mirror them as instructed.

"Good, excellent. Now, first," Gianluca says, "tango is not about the steps. And you are going to hear a lot of nonsense about tango in Buenos Aires, so I want to get you off on the right foot, yes?" A small giggle ripples through the crowd at his pun, but we're all transfixed by him. "For one thing, what we learn here will have nothing to do with the stage tango, which is all melodrama. I teach *real* tango, which is all about connection. It's not about how a tango looks—though of course it's a beautiful dance—it matters how it *feels*. I will show you." With this, he nods to Angelina and she cues some music on the stereo system. A song crackles to life. Gianluca and Angelina face off like bullfighters and come dramatically toward one another; he sweeps her into his arms and takes her through a spectacular and dramatic series of flairs and dips. The class oohs and ahs.

"That," he says, "is for the stage. Now . . ." He glances again at his partner as she goes to the stereo to restart the song. This time they come together slowly, as though they're strangers meeting for the first time. He takes her in his arms and their movements are unchoreographed, and even more tightly entwined. They dance in a close embrace, with no space for dramatic flairs of Angelina's long, muscled legs. They move together not in synchronization as before, but more as one being. It's equally beautiful, but in miniature, as though the dance contains an entire world held firmly between the two partners. Watching them feels voyeuristic and tantalizing. "That," Gianluca says, floating away from Angelina after several minutes, "is the real tango. It's not a choreographed dance, it's a language two people speak. You will never dance the same tango twice, even with the same partner to the same song. Tango comes from the streets; it's a dance that's owned by the people of this city, the working class, *los inmigrantes*. You will no doubt hear about it being danced in brothels. At one time, Buenos Aires was a place of many lonely bachelors, but don't mistake it for being only about sex. It's infused with centuries"—he gestures dramatically with both hands—"of longing, of yearning for home, for the love of a good woman." He flashes a smile at Angelina. "And I want you to feel also its rebellious spirit. Tango is the dance of anarchists, revolutionaries; there is a longing not only to be sensual, but also to be free." He pauses for a moment, and the silence in the room tells me I am not the only one in the palm of his hand. "So that, my friends, is the spirit I want you to keep in your hearts as you learn tango."

With that, we go into combinations and move in a circle, trading partners every few minutes. Each time I dance with Gianluca, I feel my attraction deepening. It feels elemental: the way he smells, the way it feels to be carried along while I'm dancing with him. But it feels distant too, like an unattainable crush. It's the opposite of my feelings for Luke, which are so bound up in everything: in friendship, family, loss, loyalty, and betrayal.

After the hour, we're cast back out into the humid January night, and I'm counting the minutes until I can come back.

⁓

The tango classes add some much-needed structure to my life in Buenos Aires, and soon I'll also have my tours. I throw myself into preparing for my first outing with tourists by frantically studying the sites I'm showing and buying several guides and history books from the cozy bookstore around the corner from my apartment, which has a surprisingly large English-language section.

The history of the city is entrancing and overwhelming. From the waves of Italian and Spanish immigrants that flooded in throughout the nineteenth century to the artists and anarchists who organized in Buenos Aires's innumerable cafés, it was a place where people came to remake themselves, refashion the world itself. Tango. Borges. It's also brutal: the Polish Jewish slave trade that brought in thousands of young women and forced them into the brothels, the rise of fascism, the military junta that "disappeared" thousands of Argentine citizens, including many college students. I'd been vaguely aware of some of this history before I came but am shocked to learn that the junta only fell in 1984, during my lifetime. All of the reading had the opposite effect I was hoping for; I feel less prepared than ever to explain this city to anyone.

I make my way home from the café where I've spent hours over wine with my books, and find the streets of San Telmo have morphed. As I turn onto the side street off Defensa that leads to my doorstep, I feel I'm seeing this place for the first time as it truly is: choked with ghosts. As I look at the pools of light cast on the sidewalk by the streetlamps, I see not illuminated spaces but the depths of the darkness between and beyond them. It seems, walking these streets, you could pass through a patch of shadows and emerge on the other side an entirely different person. Or perhaps, never emerge at all.

Penny's Back Hurts

THE SUMMER before I moved to Sun Valley to live with the Duncans seemed to drag on forever. I worked as a counselor at a local camp, taking ten-year-olds on hikes and nature walks, green with envy that Luke and Blair were at a training camp in South America that my parents hadn't been able to afford. I was packing up the last of my things in my bedroom and beginning, for the first time, to feel nervous about leaving home.

Penny came in just as I was taking down my Picabo Street poster.

"All set to move in with your boyfriends?" she said, leaning on the doorframe. Her posture was made stiff by the new back brace she was wearing. She'd slipped a disk in her spine, and the doctor had her wearing a strange contraption that resembled a plastic corset. I was worried about her; the specter of back injuries haunted all skiers who'd been doing it long enough to see one of their peers be taken out of the sport permanently, as I had when fourteen-year-old Monica Friend had broken her spine at the Junior Alpine National Championships the previous year. Penny's injury wasn't that serious, but she'd been talking to the doctors about surgery, and it scared me. At least the bald patches on her head had filled in by then and were hardly noticeable when she wore her hair in a ponytail, as she did now.

I rolled my eyes at her. "You know we're just friends. Besides, Blair has a girlfriend."

"And Luke?"

"Who'd sign up for that?" I smiled.

"Um . . . you? Don't tell me you're not, like, saving yourself for him."

"Gross."

What I couldn't bring myself to tell even Penny was that somewhere in the year we'd lived away from each other my feelings *had* changed. The less I saw of Luke and Blair, the more I longed for them in a way that began to feel subtly, amorphously romantic. I still couldn't fathom that either of them would be interested in me; they'd had their own awakenings in my absence. Blair had Sabrina the snowboarder, and Luke's new friends seemed to come with a harem of heavily made-up groupies. At that moment, I was hoping that being near Luke every day once again would squash these flutterings of alien girlish feelings. It wouldn't, but it would be years before I did anything about it.

⁂

My first year in Sun Valley flew by. My skiing improved quickly and drastically, just as Tad had promised. I turned sixteen and joined Blair in FIS races, making it a year before Luke, which—as I'm certain Tad had hoped—lit a fire in him and refocused his efforts on downhill. Soon, all three of us were skiing NorAms all throughout the season and competing against people a decade older, skiers we idolized in some cases. Luke, accustomed to being dominant, loathed getting his ass kicked at the higher level, but I relished it. At last, I was surrounded by female skiers who gave me a new bar to rise to.

Tad swiftly took over my career, introducing me to his circle of wealthy ski fans, including a very impressive self-made female e-commerce millionaire who was dying to get her hands on a promising female skier. I felt no qualms about being her show pony. It wasn't long before my old rival from juniors, Sarah Sweeny, fired her team at Vail and, with her rich dad and their entourage, decamped to the burgeoning Sun Valley club. I'd hoped that with more time together Sarah and I might become friends, but I quickly learned that her nickname—Snow Queen—was well-earned.

Meanwhile, Penny started college at Boise State, sharing a room with Emily in a neobrutalist dorm on campus that she e-mailed me pictures of once the two of them had decorated with twin beds jacked up on blocks and fairy lights strung from the ceiling. My sister—who'd never been much of an academic—was suddenly talking about going premed. However, given the rotating cast of new college boys that otherwise dominated my phone calls with her, this scholarly turn felt unlikely to stick.

⁂

Maybe I always would have gravitated toward Luke, or maybe it was only that the chance presented itself. It was 1998, Luke and I were nineteen and Blair was twenty-two and, to the surprise of his father and our coaches, it was the older brother who made the Olympic team first. Both Luke and I missed out by a few slots, leaving us home to pout while Blair—suddenly the golden boy of his father and the Sun Valley trustees—went to Nagano with Tad, Ann, and Bethany in tow. They'd offered to take us along, but somehow it seemed like being there would be worse. I felt I might combust with envy. This was a decision I'd come to regret for many reasons.

The night before they left for Japan, I found Blair sitting by himself in the massive living room of the chalet, staring into the fireplace, a blanket over his knees.

"Hey, B," I said, coming over with a couple of mugs of hot chocolate I'd just made. "You want some or is it not on the *Olympic* regimen?"

He smiled at me and lifted the corner of the blanket so I could get under it with him.

"I'll make an exception."

"How are you doing?" I asked. "Are you excited?"

He nodded, though he looked preoccupied. "Of course. I don't know, this isn't how I pictured things, I guess."

"What do you mean?"

"Well, honestly, Bomber, if anything I thought it would be me going along as the third wheel to cheer for you and Luke."

I looked into the fire for a moment. I'd been so focused on how hard it was for Luke and me to be left behind, I hadn't thought about how it might feel for Blair to be out ahead, on his own.

"You know we're so proud of you, right?"

"Of course," he said, draping his long arm around my shoulders. "And, okay, this is going to sound really petty, but I kind of wish Bethany wasn't coming. I know it's probably not fair, but it feels like she's taking credit for something that's not hers. It's a big moment for my mom and I wish it was going to be just her and my dad. Or even just my mom, if I'm being honest."

I raised my eyebrows at him. Blair was usually circumspect about Tad. I'd never really heard him say a bad word about his father; he was always trying to keep the peace between him and his brother.

"I know, like I said: petty. And I appreciate what he's done for our skiing, but after everything he's put my mom through, I've never felt the same about him. I wish I did."

"That's heavy, Blair. But, I mean, it's fair." I was careful. As much as I was part of the family in one way, I didn't have the luxury of hating Tad, or even Bethany. I actually didn't mind her, I just didn't *get* her, the way she made her entire identity about her husband and two sons that weren't hers.

It occurred to me that maybe it was Luke and I who were being petty by not coming along to support.

"Blair, do you want me to come? I probably can't get on the flight tomorrow, but I bet I could get there in time for your first race."

He turned and looked at me for a long moment. He leaned over and brushed a piece of hair that had come loose from my ponytail over my ear.

"You know what? In four years, we'll all be there together, I'm sure of it. I'd love it if you were there, but I'm worried about Luke being alone. He'll do something stupid like ski off a cliff. Just keep an eye on him, will you?"

This may have been him giving me an out, but he wasn't wrong.

"I will. I promise. And seriously, no one will be yelling louder at the television than me."

～∽～

I wanted Luke to stay home and watch the opening ceremonies with me, to keep an eye out for Blair and drown our sorrows together.

"Can't. I'm going to watch it with Breanna," he said, smiling cheekily.

"Ugh, you traitor. And isn't she like twenty-four? What is she doing dating a nineteen-year-old? Gross." I didn't want to admit I was jealous of the flavor-of-the-week girlfriend, or maybe I was too wrapped up in my funk about Nagano to realize it.

"Guys do it all the time. Don't be sexist," Luke said as he headed for the shower.

I could see her appeal—she was comely with dark hair, long limbs, and breasts that seemed far too big for her slender frame—but I didn't want to think that this was the kind of girl Luke was into. The kind whose hair was always perfect and makeup piled on. I suddenly realized what kind of girl I wanted him to like: me. I also didn't see how he could be interested in anyone who wasn't a skier.

"Whatever, I guess I'm the only one who cares about seeing Blair."

"Bomber, don't be a pain about this, we're just watching it at her place. I'd invite you but . . ."

I rolled my eyes and huffed dramatically.

"Can you just get to know her at some point? Please? For me?" He threw his arm around me and my heartbeat quickened. God, when had that happened? We'd all been friends for so long. "Come on."

"Fine," I said, smiling and nestling into his armpit—we'd always been physically close, the three of us, our lives being so hyperfocused on our bodies. "Bring her up with us then, tomorrow. I'll be nice, I promise."

"Atta girl," he said, ruffling my hair. He wasn't much taller than me, though at six foot three he towered over most girls. Blair was a hair over six feet, meaning we were almost exactly the same height.

Was I planning it? Subconsciously I must have been. *Bring her up with us.* I was challenging her on my own turf, after all. And I knew that she was an intermediate snowboarder at best.

Predictably, Breanna spent the day tumbling over even the most unimpressive of moguls and generally slowing us all down. Luke has never been patient, and he certainly wasn't when he was nineteen. I could practically feel his attraction to her leaking out of him on each successive run.

"Jesus," Luke said, stopping to laboriously backtrack up the hill to make sure she was okay after her tenth fall of the day.

I could have predicted he'd dump her, but I wasn't ready to imagine what came next.

⁓ঠ⁓

A few days later, as we were finishing up at the gym, he said, "Hey, let's ski backcountry tomorrow. There's supposed to be fresh pow."

The snow was perfect—the kind of airy powder that makes us all better skiers than we'd otherwise be. I took my training seriously, but there was nothing like just being on the mountain with my friends. It returned me to my primal love for the sport: the brisk air, the spray of snow, the connectedness with the natural world, the spikes of fear and adrenaline and joy that pumped through my veins. I don't remember learning to ski; I only remember that my life was always divided into skiing and everything else, which naturally faded into the background.

Leaving Luke and me alone in the massive chalet was either a sign of trust or obliviousness on Tad's part. Luke was always indulged, given a long leash, since he would have snapped anything shorter in half. Because Luke had appeared to have taken the divorce the hardest, Tad had done the most to win him back. It was Blair who had to be perfect, not just on the slopes but also in school and in life. He was also expected to somehow keep his brother out of trouble, which was no small feat.

After we got back, Luke and I split up to shower, then met on the deck, where the hot tub was. This part of the house had a majestic view, especially on a sparkling day like this one. I stayed in my room for a long time, suddenly feeling too aware of my body in the black bikini that I'd bought for a trip we were planning to Hawaii that summer. I'd never worn it. I put it on now and told myself that this was just my friend Luke, so who cared how I looked in a swimsuit?

Luke was in the hot tub already and had pilfered a bottle of red wine from his dad's cellar. As I dropped my towel to join him in the tub, I could feel him staring. I'd never had a damn thing against my small breasts until that very moment, when I unhelpfully pictured the top-heavy Breanna and how she might have looked in my new bikini.

"What?" I finally said, scrambling up the steps to submerge myself in the water.

Luke shook his head, snapping out of his apparent trance. "Nothing. I mean, not nothing. You look good, Bomber, that's all."

He poured me a glass of wine and we fell into our normal conversation: rehashing our best runs of the day and talking about the final races of the World Cup season, which would resume after Nagano. It wasn't until the bottle was halfway gone that Luke finally kissed me.

Liz after Dark

"**Y**OU'RE COMING tomorrow, right?" Gianluca stops me and takes me by the shoulders as class is dispersing. I feel embarrassingly thrilled by his attention.

It's my third class that week and we've moved gratifyingly quickly. We learn walks, rock steps, crosses, and *ochos*. Gianluca's partner, Angelina, teaches most of his classes alongside him, walking around the class with the teaching assistants correcting our form, often stepping in to follow or lead. She's a good lead, but it feels bizarre to be in an embrace with her, held by her delicate, bird-boned arms. The moves are simple enough: there's no quick, explosive choreography, no hard-to-remember patterns. The difficulty comes, I soon realize, when you're not given instructions on *which* moves to do. Turned loose, you had to rely on your ability to pick up the directions from your partner's body, the signals translated to you via their embrace. When you manage it, it feels like witchcraft; when it goes badly, it feels as discordant as bad sex.

"What's tomorrow?"

"The social!"

"Oh yes," I say, now remembering from the website. "Social" brings to mind grandparents and Dixie cups of ice cream. "Should I come?"

"Of course! You need to practice. It will be fun, and you can meet the rest of the team."

I've learned about "the team" by now—in every class, we're joined by teaching assistants who are also team members, dancers handpicked by Gianluca to represent the studio locally and internationally at dance conferences.

"I'll be there."

❧

I begin my new job and quickly realize that I'm plenty prepared. The job is a cakewalk. Most of my tourists are from the United States; some are from Japan or Canada. On my first tour, all eight tourists are from the States, and I feel a trill of fear that they'll recognize me, but I learn quickly that people mostly see what they're expecting to see. I needn't have worried about my shallow knowledge of the city: people want to see the beautiful Spanish-style facades, the elegant ramshackle villas, the faded Belle Epoque glamour of the place; they don't want to look closely enough to see the bullet holes that mark the side of the Casa Rosada, the bloodstains on the sidewalks, the ghosts of young people that linger outside the cafés they were snatched from. On my second tour, I have a backpacker kid who is fresh out of the Peace Corps. He wears his manky hair in a preposterous bun that bobs in time as he explains the city to me, even though, according to him, this is his first visit. After that, if ever I'm feeling self-conscious about leading a tour, I try to embody his know-it-all energy.

Between classes I think about Gianluca more than I'd like to admit. It's a greedy crush, and he's more an idea than a man: a living embodiment of tango and this beautiful dark city, the hope for something beyond the wreckage of my old life.

On Friday night, I arrive at the social right at ten, just as a drop-in class is finishing. I take a seat on one of the couches, already feeling a little more at home in the studio. I change out of street shoes and into my dance shoes. All around me, I watch people doing the same. Observing this little ritual of people stretching and getting ready to take the floor is oddly comforting. The setting and accoutrements couldn't be more different from the start shack at the top of a mountain, but there's a feeling that's familiar, a coiled readiness. We're preparing to drop in.

The first two hours are all tango, for beginners like me who've come to practice what they've been paying Gianluca to teach them. Feet nervously find purchase, uncertain hands seek tenuous connection, occasionally a daring leg slides up the side of a partner's. Gianluca asks me to dance three times, and each time it feels like dismounting an old bicycle and stepping into a top-of-the-line sports car—all smoothness and control and plush, delicious-smelling leather. I feel drugged when he steps away.

As the hour creeps toward midnight, more of the advanced dancers—all of whom seem to know each other—arrive, and I become increasingly intimidated. The team members are all lean and fit, athletes, my people, even if they don't realize it. They glide and swivel and turn effortlessly, and the music appears to move straight through them. Their upper bodies remain fixed and still while their legs swoop beneath them, frictionless. Eventually I move to the sidelines, realizing I don't really belong on this run. I shake my head a bit at the clueless beginners who still clumsily pick their way across the floor, occasionally colliding with the better dancers.

Cali, the beautiful assistant from the first class, arrives around eleven thirty.

"Hi. Liz, right?" I'm flattered she recognizes me, even though I have been here a lot.

I nod. "How are you?"

"Good." She smiles. "Glad you came. Are you having fun?" The way she asks is almost proprietary, and I wonder how she came to feel so at home here.

"I am. It's a little scary to actually dance in the real world."

She laughs. "This studio is very far from the real world. But I know what you mean. Are you staying nearby?"

"I'm renting an apartment in San Telmo."

"I work over there, a few nights a week. A bar called Red Door," she says. "You should come by."

I smile and am about to say something when I'm interrupted.

"Ca-leeeeeee!" Gemma, the British woman from the New Year's party, tumbles in behind her, along with Edward. I've been hoping to see them again.

"Oh hello!" Gemma says when she sees me. "From New Year's Eve, Edward! Our American friend."

"Liz," I say, in case she's forgotten. "Good to see you. You take classes here too, right?"

"Gemma just finished the level three class," Cali says. "We're very proud."

"And I'm just here for the pretty girls," Edward says.

"That's complete nonsense," Gemma says. "Well, he *is* here for the girls, but Edward's an excellent dancer as well."

"None of the pretty girls would dance with me otherwise."

Gemma rolls her eyes and they go to change their shoes, leaving me alone until a moment later when Edward comes back and asks me to dance.

At midnight, Gianluca turns the lights off, and at first I think the social is over. I feel an immediate letdown, the specter of my empty apartment rising up. But then I see people heading back onto the floor and notice that the music hasn't stopped, just changed. All of the other beginners—with the exception of one or two confused stragglers—have left now, and I wonder if I should too. But I watch Cali and one of the other team dancers going out on the floor in the now-low light, and I'm so mesmerized that I'm frozen where I am. A pop song with a throbbing bass beat plays, and Cali's body is languid, released from the stiff frame of tango, and she undulates and rolls her hips, tosses her head as she spins. She and her partner dance first in an open frame and then he pulls her in close, and the way their hips are moving together, it seems like something I shouldn't be watching.

Gemma appears beside me.

"Well, that's not tango," I say.

Gemma laughs. "They're dancing zouk, it's very popular down here. Quite hot, isn't it?"

"I'll say. I feel like I should leave."

"Why do you think we dim the lights? After midnight, we get into the hard stuff: zouk, some *kizomba,* some sexy freestyle. Have you had a good night? Got some good dances in?"

"I did. This place is incredible."

"Careful," Gemma says with a laugh, "you'll get addicted."

Penny Finds God

BY THE time I was nineteen, we were traveling so much that it had ceased to feel as though I lived anywhere other than in a never-ending series of hotels. I'd podiumed in my first World Cup race that season, but I wasn't yet a star on the team the way Blair and Luke were, so I was usually stuck rooming with a teammate. For the first time in my life, I had an entire gaggle of girlfriends: gutsy, outspoken women who understood me. Still, they were minor players, I was never as close with anyone as I was with Luke and Blair. Even before we'd hooked up, Luke had been greedy with my time and Blair's, and there was always the fear that he'd go off the rails without us, especially during the off-season, when he was without the structure of his competition schedule.

Unless you were at the very top of the sport, there wasn't much money to be made in skiing. Once I'd made the U.S. Ski Team, I attracted more attention from sponsors, who matched my winnings and supplied all of my gear, but the team dues were hefty, and travel expenses were not always covered. I still relied heavily on the support of the trustees, leaving me endlessly indebted to Tad. Being on the road was exciting at first—the world-class resorts, the downtime in towns all over Europe, but it wore on me too. I felt like I never had enough clean laundry, like the bed was always either too hard or too soft, like I would never be free of jet lag for as long as I lived. In retrospect, these complaints could not possibly feel more petty; I'd give anything to have those happy years back.

I treasured the chances to come home to see my parents or visit Penny at the bachelorette pad she shared in Boise with Emily. I often felt like I'd been in space when I came to see them, as though time progressed more quickly for her and Emily than it did for me. There wasn't anything I'd rather be doing than skiing, but there was an undeniable monotony to it. The repetitive hours of training and dryland workouts, the spectacular views from the various start houses that nonetheless began to blur together: from Lake Louise to Sölden, it became one long glittering stretch of Alpine. Meanwhile, Penny's and Emily's lives progressed as they made their way through school, observing more ordinary coming-of-age rituals, such as living on their own for the first time, figuring out how to budget for groceries, and how to hold their liquor.

Penny's health troubles had continued to get worse. She'd needed surgery on her back, but it did not get rid of her pain entirely, and worse yet, the surgery had messed up some of the nerves in her bladder, meaning that for a time she had to use a catheter. She'd also been diagnosed with lupus, which caused swelling in her joints, fatigue, and sometimes horrible unsightly rashes. It seemed like such bad luck, and here I'd hardly been sick a day in my life. I was still invincible then. I'd had my share of tumbles into the giant safety nets that lined the race courses, but I'd sustained nothing more serious than some spectacular bruises. Maybe it was this sense of bad luck, of being marked for suffering, that caused Penny to seek out religion.

Though the chasm between my sister's life and mine was growing ever more vast, she still reminded me of home and I missed her when I was traveling. Penny even came to visit me in Sun Valley once. I remember being so touched that she'd made the effort, I fell all over myself to introduce her to everyone as though she were a visiting dignitary. I showed off the house as though it were my own, showed her the special home gym Tad had installed on the lower floor.

Neither Luke nor I had gotten into Dartmouth, but I'd belatedly started at Arizona State University, which offered a bachelor's in communication that could be completed online. Luke eschewed the idea altogether. I would study between training sessions, reading my textbooks while the ice bath percolated around my exhausted legs. I had the vague notion that I might someday work as a sports correspondent or a brand rep, but any future that lay beyond skiing wasn't one I wanted to think much about.

By her junior year of college, Penny had abandoned the idea of medical school and was instead pursuing a combined bachelor's and master's program that would put her on the fast track to becoming a physician's assistant. Despite this intensive course of study, that year she seemed mostly consumed by her studies of Brandon—a hunky, milk-fed white boy from southern Idaho. She couldn't wait for me to meet him! He wasn't her boyfriend—at least not yet—but they'd kissed once after a Young Life party.

"Brandon doesn't drink," she said proudly, "which is just, like, *so* refreshing compared to the rest of the boys my age."

Religious zealousness was an odd addition to Penny's personality; suddenly, she was quoting scripture during my phone calls with her and telling me that my body was a temple of the Holy Spirit. Despite our many differences, Penny and I possessed a similar capacity for obsession. But where mine was single-minded, Penny's was ever shifting—usually from one boy to the next. In the moment, however, it was every bit as laser focused as mine. And in that period of Penny's life, it had found a home in the cuddly, inclusive Christianity peddled by the Young Life campus ministry. And, of course, by Brandon.

I asked Emily what she thought of all this.

"You know how she is when she has a crush. And she's been having such a hard time with the lupus and everything," she said, sounding unconcerned. Penny's constant health troubles could make it hard to criticize her decisions; it automatically felt unfair.

My parents and I were a bit dismayed when Penny told us that she wanted us to come bear witness to her baptism. Those were her words:

bear witness. This was especially confusing because we'd both *been* baptized, christened in those strange, old-fashioned little baby gowns that look as though they're meant to accommodate an infant with alarmingly long legs.

"This is different," Penny said. "This time *I'm* making the choice, I'm accepting Jesus Christ as my personal lord and savior. Being sprinkled with holy water when you're a baby doesn't count. If I want to walk with the Lord, I need to receive Christ on my own terms."

These did not sound like Penny's words but someone else's. Brandon's, I guessed.

On a Sunday in early June, we watched Penny and Brandon's goatee'd cool guy minister walk with Penny, her petite frame engulfed in a white gown, into the chilly waters of a lake at the edge of Lucky Point State Park. He said some blessings and then Penny crossed her arms over her chest as he guided her backward into the water. When he lifted her up again, her face was full of wonder. Her Young Life friends cheered madly from the shore while my parents and I smiled, bemusedly.

Nothing ever developed with Brandon. I wondered what sort of half-bit Christian Romeo this kid was. Did he go around college parties making out with girls and then abandoning them post baptism? Didn't seem very Christlike to me, and I was pissed on Penny's behalf.

Penny was so sensitive that her happiness always seemed precarious. She was easily thrown off course, so vulnerable to illness and injury and heartbreak. Even though my skiing took up no small amount of my family's time and resources—something I didn't fully appreciate until much later—I was the easier child in many ways. I was simple: I just wanted to ski. There was a burgeoning chaos to Penny, a deep unpredictability.

Despite the brief, strange foray into religion, I talked to Penny whenever I could that year: she and Emily were the only ones I could talk to about Luke. I didn't dare share it with any of my ski friends while it was this nascent.

It seemed simple at first. Luke and I already spent so much time together; now we would just do so as a couple. Nothing definitive had been said, but we'd kissed passionately that first night in the hot tub. We'd moved inside after a while and into bed, where hands had wandered, and we eventually fell asleep exhausted by our own churning, circling desires.

Luke and I had been friends since we were five; if he was going to cross that Rubicon with me, it *must* mean he wanted to be with me, right? It wasn't as though he had any trouble getting girls. Despite spending all my time with boys, there were many things about their inner lives I didn't understand: in this case, the gulf between their immediate desires and any thought of the future.

One morning, shortly after everyone had returned from Nagano, we overslept, and I woke in a panic that we'd be found out.

"You've got to get out of here," I whispered, laughing and tossing Luke's swim trunks at him. He caught them and pulled me in for a quick kiss.

"The wine bottle!" he said with a mock horrified face—we'd left an empty one by the fireplace—and winked at me as he crept out the door to hide the evidence.

I wasn't really worried about being blamed if Tad did find it. Luke was the designated troublemaker in the household. Tad traveled frequently and had to know Luke brought girls around; this definitely wasn't his first foray into his father's wine cellar. The only time I'd really seen Tad get angry was when he'd busted Luke with cocaine; drugs were different—drugs showed up on tests. I also knew, though, that the rules were different for me. However much Tad talked about my being family, I wasn't.

As I was coming down the hallway, I heard Luke nearly collide with Blair in the kitchen.

"Hey, man," Blair said.

"Oh hey, bro." I could practically hear his nervous heartbeat.

"What were *you* doing last night? You were gone when I came in."

"What do you think?" Luke said with a laugh, both avoiding and implying the answer. The last place Blair would expect Luke to be was in bed with me. I suddenly felt the grip of nerves; how would we tell him? How would he take it? It felt like we'd violated some unspoken pact.

"You dog," Blair said, and then the two proceeded to go into their training schedules like nothing was out of the ordinary.

Dismayingly, at first, it seemed that nothing *was* out of the ordinary, at least not when we were around other people. At night, Luke would sneak into my bedroom, where we'd make out for hours. We'd let ourselves get down to our underwear but no further, burning ourselves up with unsated desire. In retrospect, I'm glad I had this time with Luke. Making out is best done by the young, where the fear of going too far adds an extra kick of adrenaline; and we were both junkies for that.

But when we were with Blair or our teammates or Luke's freeskier buddies, it was the same as always, which left me feeling confused and isolated. I couldn't very well talk to my best friends about it, since one was Luke and the other was Blair. My mom and I were close, but we didn't have the kind of relationship that some girls have with their moms, where they can talk about things like love and sex, and I *certainly* wasn't going to talk to my dad about it. This left me with Penny, weird religious phase or no. I called her one evening to break the news about Luke, and she was delighted.

"I *knew* it!" she said. "Emily, my sister hooked up with Luke!"

"Jesus Christ, Pen, really?"

"Emily is dancing around our apartment right now, just so you know."

I laughed despite myself. It felt like such a relief to tell the two of them: my two big sisters.

"I'm putting you on speaker. Tell us everything!"

They were thrilled that we'd broken through the friendship barrier, but clucked knowingly at his confusing behavior around everyone else.

"He wants to have his cake and eat it too," Emily said. "I hate it!"

"Katie," Penny asked, her voice serious, "do you want Luke to be your actual boyfriend?"

I paused; it felt strange to put it in those terms.

"I don't know . . ." I said. "I mean, he's my best friend."

"But you're into him!" Emily crowed. "I called this, by the way, I forgot to mention that. Penny had her money on Blair."

"I'm glad my love life is so hilarious to you two."

"Of course, it is," Penny said. "Listen, you obviously like Luke as more than a friend. I know you're in a committed relationship with your skis and all, but I think you want him to be your boyfriend."

"Definitely," Emily chimed in.

I knew that I didn't want to go back to being just friends and watch Luke chase after every cute liftie who landed in town on a work visa. The desire I felt for him now was both reassuringly comfortable and thrillingly new at once: it was intoxicating. And I definitely knew that I didn't appreciate him treating me like a buddy when we were around other people. But what I couldn't quite explain to Penny and Emily was that it felt a little unfair to expect him to make the leap on his own. All these years, especially with Luke, I'd never wanted to be treated like a girl, and now I suddenly did.

"Time for a DTR," Emily said.

"A what now?"

Penny and Emily both groaned and laughed.

"You're hopeless." Penny sighed. "It means *define the relationship*. What are you to each other? Friends with benefits or boyfriend and girlfriend?"

"And what if we have different answers to that question?"

"Nope!" Emily said.

"Either get on the same page or be done with it, go back to being just friends. I know how close you guys are," Penny said. "It's not worth it unless he's serious about you." I was moved to know that Penny still felt a little protective of me; she'd always claimed to find my friendship with Luke weird.

"Exactly," Emily jumped in. "There're other boys you can mess around with down there."

"DTR," Penny said. "Do it. And report back."

Liz Is a Tiger

CALI, THE beautiful teaching assistant, has become like a celebrity in my mind, and so I can't help taking her up on the invitation to Red Door, however casually she'd thrown it out. She's behind the bar when I show up around nine on Wednesday.

"Oh hey," she says, putting down the glass she's polishing. The place is almost empty. "Nice to see you, Liz."

"Hey, Cali." I feel my cheeks burning; I wonder if my loneliness is obvious.

"What can I get you?"

I pull myself up onto a stool. I'm wearing my now-uniform of T-shirt and jeans. I've chosen a T-shirt with a V-neck, trying to appreciate my new body as best I can. It's worked maybe a little too well; I felt the eyes of every man I passed between the Subte stop and the bar. I've noticed that men are more open with their admiration here than in the States. A woman brings a kind of disruptive energy when she walks down the street: it's uncomfortable and, if I'm being honest, a little thrilling.

"What's popular here?"

Cali considers. "Fernet and Coke, do you want to try one?"

"I've never had Fernet."

"It's bitter. Kind of like Campari."

My tastes when it comes to cocktails are hopelessly unsophisticated; I've only ever been into beer and wine.

"Doesn't sound like my thing," I venture.

"Tell you what, I'll make you a caipirinha. I've gotten really good at them, and I *hate* making them when it's packed but it's my favorite cocktail."

I watch as she muddles the mint and measures the drink expertly and quickly.

I take a sip. "Oh wow, this is delicious."

"Hat-cha," she says. "I knew it. Franco!" she calls out to the other bartender polishing glasses and tending to the sole patron at the other end of the bar. "*Mi caipirinha está perfecta ahora, yo te lo dije.*"

He smiles warmly and rolls his eyes. His gaze lingers on her, and I'm certain he has a crush on Cali; I am certain everyone who comes near her has a crush on Cali.

"Can I ask you something?"

"Shoot, Shirley." She looks up from the lime wedges.

"What brought you to Buenos Aires? Other than perfecting your caipirinha."

She smiles a Cheshire cat smile at me, and it occurs to me that, as much as I want to know, maybe I shouldn't have asked her this.

"If I wanted to do that, I'd go to Brazil, honey, it's their cocktail. But as to why I left New York, that's a very long story. I couldn't stay in my job anymore. I had to go somewhere, so I came here a year ago. I guess I had a vague notion that I'd like it here and I turned out to be right."

Before it happened, I never considered other roads my life might've taken, and now I think of them all the time. Specifically, I think about how my choices might have altered Penny's. We were so close in age that, growing up, our lives seemed calibrated to each other's, like the one wouldn't exist in the same way without the other.

"Nice," I say. So Cali is a free spirit. She came on a whim rather than as a last resort, depending, I suppose, on what the rest of that long story contains. "And how did you meet Gianluca?"

"Here," she says. "It's one of his regular haunts."

"Huh, I thought this place was a bit of an expat bar."

"It is. Haven't you noticed that he collects them? Us. He comes in here all the time to play pool and *recruit*."

"Try to get pretty girls to come to his studio?"

"Precisely."

"And somehow he convinced you."

She smiles and shrugs. "I ignored him for a while, since I just thought he was trying to sleep with me."

"Wasn't he?"

"Well, sure, but I started hearing from other people how good the studio was, so I gave it a try and I was hooked. Anyway, Gianluca is pretty easily distracted by shiny new things, so we're friends now. I got to know Edward, and then Gemma when she came here a few months back, and yeah. It's been a blast, actually."

"So have you heard this story then, about how he and Edward know one another?"

She laughs. "I've heard about eighteen different versions of it. I'm sure none of them are true. Something about a countess on a yacht and a jealous husband. In some versions the countess is young and beautiful, in others she's old and rich. In all of them, the husband ends up dead." She laughs at the alarm on my face. "Like I said, I'm sure it's not true. I've also heard that Gianluca is a disgraced matador and the illegitimate son of General Pinochet."

"I heard it was Perón."

"Well, there you have it. And what about you?" she asks. "What brought you here?"

"Also a long story. But part of it was a really bad breakup." I guess if Cali hasn't recognized me yet, she isn't going to.

"Buenos Aires Lonely Hearts Society." She smiles.

"Hey." I smile and take another sip of my drink, which is going down fast. "That's Gemma's joke."

"Busted. She's right, though."

A memory of Blair comes back to me as Cali goes off for a moment to tend to a new set of customers. He and I walking down a wide street, near the Plaza Serrano maybe?

"I love it here," I said to him. "Wouldn't this be a fun place to live?"

He nodded, smiling at me in a way I hope I remember forever as clearly as I do now. I was so happy that night, all the sweeter because it felt like I hadn't been happy in a while. I hadn't spoken to Penny in over a year by then, and the worry over her and Ava felt like a stone lodged permanently under my heel. It was unimaginable then that the worst was yet to come, that a reconciliation would never happen. But a new season was about to start, and I was healthier than I'd been in a while. Our country was on a hopeful precipice of history: poised to elect an inspiring young senator from Illinois.

"We could," Blair said. "It's close to the Andes."

"We could be tango dancers!" I said to him, grabbing his hand and marching him down the street singing "Dum, dum, duhhh dum," dramatically.

"All that, Katie, all that," he said, laughing. "Whatever you want."

Would it have been better or worse to know then that it was all about to end?

I swear I feel Gianluca walk into the room. God, I'm crushing hard. Though maybe I'm mixed up between the appeal of the dancing itself and the man who's brought it to me. I know Luke would find this man ridiculous. Luke was narrow-minded about masculinity: he felt that his way—athletic, dominant, his whole body and being just screaming "I'm a *man*!"—was the only way to be male. He dismissed anything that diverged from that: the flabby, the weak, the effeminate, the artsy. At least Blair and I had gotten him to drop his habit of saying "Dude, that's gay" whenever he found something unimpressive. Gianluca, with his flair, was an entirely other kind of masculine.

He calls out to Cali before he notices me, and she glides across the bar to kiss his cheeks and give him a long hug as though it's been weeks rather than days since they've seen each other. I wonder still if Cali has slept with him, realizing now that she sort of glossed over it. Gianluca has a friend with him: handsome but rough-looking with a thick neck and tattoos up his muscled arms.

"You remember my friend Mauro," he says in Spanish as they order a round of drinks. Cali goes to find another bottle of Fernet, and I feel the unsettling weight of Gianluca's eyes landing on me.

"Oh, hello."

"Hi, Gianluca."

"G, please. My name is a mouthful."

The way he says *mouthful* sounds obscene, and I think, from the way he's smiling, that he means it that way.

Mauro nods a hello and tells G he's going to get them a pool table, leaving us alone for a minute while G waits for their drinks. He's standing so close to me, leaning forward on the bar with one hand, unnervingly in my space.

"*Che*, I have a nickname for you," he says, smiling.

"Excuse me?" His eyes are sparkling. I have the stomach-dropping anticipation of impending humiliation.

"I. Have. A. Nickname," he says, cocking his head at me, "for you."

"You barely know me."

He puts a hand on my shoulder, laughing off my defensiveness. "Relax," he says, squeezing it. I've absorbed everything from the past two years into the space between my shoulders. "I have nicknames for all of my favorites. And you need a nickname if you're going to live here, you know. Your Buenos Aires name."

Is he flirting? Is this how people flirt?

"Well," I finally say.

He raises his eyebrows at me.

"What is it? What's my nickname?" I turn my stool to face him, trying to get my bearings. I feel myself leaning in, close enough that I can smell him.

He seems delighted that I'm taking the bait.

"Tiger," he says.

"Why Tiger?"

96

He shrugs. "Fierce feline. Tiger, tiger burning bright. Eye of the tiger."

I flush. "Because I remind you so much of Rocky?" My childhood nickname comes back to me with a jolt. Manly Cleary. In a thousand ways big and small, I've gotten this message since I was a kid: don't be so strong, so big, so fast, so aggressive, so *you*. When people referred to me as a big, strong girl—which I always was—it wasn't always meant as a compliment. I didn't care so much when I was an athlete, but now I'm just a woman.

"Yes!" G says. "Exactly. It's your eyes. You look so intense in class, like you *must* learn tango. It's adorable."

I nod, bemused. Adorable? Fuck him. Well, fuck me. The armor is gone and he sees a fleshy, ordinary girl.

"Actually, it's mesmerizing." He leans in. "I can tell your heart is in it. But we've got to get you to loosen up a little. To tell you the truth, you're my special little project." Just then, Cali returns with his drinks. The bar's gotten busier, so I just ask for a glass of wine when she asks if I want another. I tell her she can choose.

Is my heart in it? I realize that I *want* to become a good tango dancer while I'm here; it would be nice to stop feeling so useless. I want more of whatever it is I've been feeling on the dance floor. Perhaps if I had that focal point, that goal to work incrementally toward each day, it would give me some relief. Perhaps it would make me feel that my body was my own again. Right now, it's a padded cell that houses my addled brain.

"G," I say, as he is getting ready to take his drinks to his friends.

"Tiger."

"I'm wondering about . . . that is, if you offer private lessons." I don't mean this to sound suggestive, but once the words are out of my mouth, they're absorbed by the air of sex that surrounds him and transformed. "I'd like a coach," I continue, trying to anchor myself in that familiar, anodyne word. "I'm not happy with my progress."

He is smiling at me in that maddening way, as if I am just *too* amusing. As if I am not a fucking former world champion. And I find myself nearly saying this out loud. Do you know who I am? What I was?

"Is that right? That's funny because you're one of my best students, but those are always the ones who want to work harder. And, as a matter of fact, Tiger, I do teach privates. But only for very special students. Only if I know I'm going to enjoy it."

I feel my face twisting with incredulousness, as if to say, *I don't have the time for this nonsense.* Except I have all the time in the world for this nonsense.

"It's a yes, for you, Tiger. Of course. When do you want to begin?"

I want to be irritated that he calls me Tiger, but I can't be. It reminds me of the nickname that Luke gave me when we were kids, one later adopted by the rest of the team—Bomber. So *Tiger* it is. It gives me comfort that maybe this man, however improbably, sees something of what I was. He sees Katie Cleary. He sees Bomber, wrapped in the unimpressive shell of Liz Sullivan.

"Tomorrow," I say, not caring how he interprets my urgency. "Does tomorrow work?"

"Tomorrow," he says. "Four p.m. is my only time."

I nod. I have a tour from two to four, but I will cut it short to be there in time. I will reroute it to end at Casa Rosada. I am filled with heady anticipation at the idea of slotting back into the familiar role of protégée, of being coached, especially by him.

"I'm looking forward to it."

Penny Is a Good Big Sister

SHORTLY AFTER my sister moved back to Coeur d'Alene to start her new job at the Kootenai Health Clinic, she called me to complain about our parents. Penny had gotten herself into a bit of money trouble and thought they were overreacting.

"Mom and Dad are freaking out, they're being total jerks about it," Penny told me over the phone. "I just overspent a little. They're acting like I'm a criminal over a couple hundred bucks."

There was a subtext to the accusation, something that always simmered just beneath the surface of our relationship: *Mom and Dad spent so much on you growing up, Mom and Dad love you best, and now, you owe me, you need to take my side.* So I agreed with her that they were blowing things out of proportion; I told her I'd talk to them.

I called my dad to try to get him to see reason. I knew this was why Penny had told me, to recruit me—in her eyes, the favored child—to be her ally. And she had a point, after all. A few hundred bucks? Not even enough for a pair of ski boots.

As a rule, my parents didn't discuss Penny's issues with me. They wanted to preserve their relationship with her, and our relationship with each other. Looking back, I see that they wanted to avoid her becoming the "bad" one.

"Dad, I just got off the phone with Penny. What's going on with you guys?"

"She shouldn't be putting you in the middle of it, Katie." My dad sounded exasperated.

"It just seems like you guys are being really hard on her over a few hundred bucks."

"A few hundred dollars?" My dad's voice was uncharacteristically angry. "Your sister ran up *eight thousand dollars* on five different cards! We only found out because we started getting calls from debt collectors!"

I was horrified not just that my sister could do something so stupid, but also that she'd lied to me about it so coolly and deliberately. I called her on it, and instead of being embarrassed, she immediately went on the defensive.

"You know what, Katie? Screw you. You have *no idea* what real life is like. I'm sorry I don't have a rich benefactor like Tad Duncan to pay for all my expenses. But, of course, side with Mom and Dad. Always the golden child!"

She hung up on me and ignored my calls for the next two months.

I was only able to get back in her good graces by needing her. I caught my arm on a gate and tore my rotator cuff. I was terrified that it could be serious and called her crying. She was working as physician's assistant by then, so I habitually presented her with any and all medical queries. For Penny, to be needed was to be loved, to be valued, to exist. She calmed me down about my injury, reiterated what the team doctors had told me. And, like that, I was forgiven. But the brief period of not having my sister in my life shook me. Regardless of how little we might have had in common, she was my only sibling, my touchstone. Without her, I was unmoored.

❧

I had to hand it to Penny. I didn't necessarily see the appeal of most of her boyfriends, but the one thing they all had in common—with the exception of the scripture-peddling Brandon, who evidently only had eyes for

Jesus—was their boundless devotion to her. She wrapped men around her finger, and though she often wasn't terribly nice to them, they showered her with gifts, and praise, and seemingly did whatever she wanted. I can't pretend I wasn't slightly in awe of it, and all of a sudden I wanted some of that for myself.

Penny's beau of the moment was Jon—he worked as a plumber and drove a truck jacked up to the hilt. Penny had broken up with her last boyfriend mere weeks before meeting him. As always, the moment one man disappeared, another came immediately to take his place. This was extraordinary to me. Other than the horrible kiss with Matt, there'd only ever been Luke. The idea of the parade of men who came through Penny's life made me feel faint.

It was good advice that Emily and Penny had given me to be direct with Luke, to make him choose. The stakes were too high. If he really broke my heart—and I was somehow certain that it would be him and not me doing the breaking—what then? I'd seen it happen with other skiing couples, and it was a mess. We lived together and trained together, we were best friends, and what about poor Blair, who would be caught in the middle? A week after my conversation with Emily and Penny, when Luke crept in my room, rather than open the covers up to let him in, I sat up in bed and pulled my knees to my chest protectively.

"What's wrong?"

"We have to stop," I said.

The moonlight was refracted by the blankets of snow outside my window, and as my eyes adjusted to the darkness, Luke's features became clearer. My heart surged. Maybe we *could* go on forever like this. Didn't I want, in some ways, to keep these ecstatic nights but maintain our friendship in the light of day too?

"Why?" Luke seemed baffled and a little bit pissed off. He reached out and put his hand on my knee, and I smacked it away. I meant to do so playfully but it felt aggressive.

"You know why, Luke. You're my best friend, we train together, we *live* together. How could this possibly be a good idea? What if Blair finds out? What if Tad or Coach finds out?"

"How is *Coach* going to find out?" Luke asked, smiling.

"It doesn't matter," I said. "We're stopping. You can find some other girl to mess around with, you've had no trouble with that before."

He looked hurt, and I felt him retreat from me on the bed. I hadn't meant to come off quite so harsh; I realized only as he was sitting there that it was already too late for me. I had feelings for Luke—I didn't quite want to put a name to them just yet—but knew I was on dangerous ground. And messing with my head was going to mess with my performance, and I couldn't risk that.

"Jesus, Katie."

I shrugged. "What, Luke? Don't act like you're all heartbroken. You don't care."

And this was the root of it, I realized, the way he'd dropped my hand when we saw our teammates on the street. If Luke was going to reject me, I would beat him to it. We were always racing each other, it was our whole thing.

"How do you know?" he said softly. "How do you know what I'm feeling?"

Slowly, he looked back up at me, and by now his face was clearly illuminated in the blue light of my bedroom. My heart was in my throat. Mortifyingly, I felt tears coming to my eyes: I was overcome. Fear—my old friend, my wonder drug—but so different now with no place to go.

"Katie." He reached out and took my hand, which was clammy in his. "Do you want to be with me?"

Instead of waiting for an answer, he kissed me.

After a long moment, I pulled away. "But . . . what about . . . everything?" I was furious at myself for losing my composure. "I'm scared," I said.

"It's okay," he said with a laugh. He'd seen through my tough talk, and maybe that's what I'd been counting on. If he'd wanted the out, I'd given it to him. If he stayed, it meant he didn't want it. "I am too."

I felt frozen in place.

"What does this mean?"

He chuckled. "I have to spell it out for you, don't I, Bomber?"

I forced a smile. "It wouldn't hurt."

"Katie Cleary, I'm in love with you. I don't know exactly when that happened, but here we are."

With the words in the air between us, Luke's leonine confidence faltered at last.

"Look, maybe you just need some time to absorb all of this, so I'm going to just let you . . ." He started to get up off of the bed, and I grabbed his arm and pulled him back to me with all of my strength.

"Me too," I managed.

He shook his head. "Say it."

It was sweet, unexpected that he'd need to hear the words. It was the most vulnerable I would ever see him.

"I love you too, Luke."

Liz with Her Eyes Closed

THE SUN is shining and the tourists are cheerful as I walk them through the sprawling necropolis of Recoleta's famous cemetery. From here, we take a quick trip on the Subte to Puerto Madero, and from there, everything is in walking distance. I'll show them the Plaza Dorrego in San Telmo—stopping for gelato, which I know will delight them—and then to the Caminito in La Boca and on to the Plaza de Mayo and the Casa Rosada. My group today consists of three middle-aged couples: two from the States and one from Vancouver, B.C. It hurts to think of Vancouver; the opening ceremonies are only a few weeks away. There's some tiny part of me that still thinks I'll be there, that can't accept that it's over. I keep dreaming about missing my flight, running for the plane in my travel uniform only to watch it taking off. I shake it off and let myself get reabsorbed in my role as tour guide, explaining some of the notable people who are buried in Recoleta. Evita, of course, several Nobel Prize winners and Argentine presidents, Napoleon's granddaughter. I gain my bearings once again and the tour goes smoothly until we reach the Plaza de Mayo, our final stop.

As we make our way up from the Avenida de Mayo, I see their white head scarves bobbing together, their banner with its family photos unfurled at the helm of their sad parade. I'd forgotten it was Thursday, when each week for the past thirty years the Madres de la Plaza—mothers of young people who were disappeared by the military junta—march here. They've been coming here seeking answers and justice since the junta was still in power, though at first they marched in pairs to avoid being arrested. I feel my stomach drop at the sight of them. What could be more sympathetic than a mother who has lost her child? Whose grief could ever be more potent? They are the living embodiment of every parent's worst nightmare: both terrifying and sainted in their grief. I can barely look at them. What must it be like to be here still, after all these decades? They're hollow-eyed, carrying signs that read *NIÑOS DESAPARECIDOS*; some of them old women now, wheelchair-bound. It occurs to me that Argentina is a bit like the United States in that it's forever trampling its own history in the name of relentless forward momentum. Is it admirable or pitiable, the way these women refuse to move on?

"What are they protesting?" one of the Americans asks me. It seems unfathomable that the atrocities that happened here so recently aren't more well known. And yet, I didn't know either until I came here. A regime that killed thirty thousand of its own, and yet the story lacks the grandeur of World War II, so it doesn't register with us. The United States was not the hero, so we don't care.

I give my tourists the rundown but see by their faces that even the little I tell them is too much to absorb in this moment. *Here*? I can feel them thinking, *in this civilized friendly city*?

At last one of the men says, "Sad," and it's as though it gives everyone permission to move past this uncomfortable digression. They are on vacation, and it's not as if they've come to Berlin; they were not expecting to have heavy hearts, and I don't imagine they'll think about any of this again. We circumnavigate the plaza and I pause to look at the map. I can't imagine why they'd take any notice of me, but I feel that if one of the *Madres* looks directly at me, I might burst into flames.

"So," I say, stopping in front of the Casa Rosada. We're back in safer territory now, beneath the iconic balcony that's the one part of Argentina's history Americans *do* know, the chapter in which Evita asked the country not to cry for her. "As we reach the edge of the Plaza de Mayo, you'll see one of the most famous buildings in Argentina. Does anyone know this one?" People become like schoolchildren when they're on a tour: anxious to share the right answer.

"That's the Evita building!" the woman from California exclaims.

"Correct!" I say, and it is, sort of. "Many of you will recognize the Casa Rosada from the famous film scene where Madonna sings 'Don't Cry for Me, Argentina' from the balcony." I go into my speech about the building's historical significance, and, all the while, I see from the corner of my eye that the male half of the couple from Vancouver has a strange look on his face. I wonder if the *Madres* have unsettled him and feel a sudden flash of kinship for him. When we walk away from the site, back across the Plaza de Mayo, he falls in next to me.

"Hi, Steve." Thankfully, I've always been good at remembering names; a small thing that leads to happier tourists.

"Hi, Liz, listen," he says. "I don't suppose you follow ski racing?"

I feel the blood drain from my face. I glance down at my map to hide my expression. "Oh, not really. Why?" I hear my own voice as though from the bottom of a well.

"It's been bugging me all afternoon, trying to figure out who you look like, and it just hit me. You're a dead ringer for that gal, Katie Cleary. Do people ever tell you that? She was a silver medalist last Olympics, I think."

Bronze, I think, *and it was the Olympics before.*

"Oh," I say, turning my face away, as though checking a landmark. I fear that if he looks at me close up right now, he'll know. It isn't rational. Katie Cleary is a minor figure in this man's life. "What happened to her?" It's masochistic, but I can't resist.

"You didn't hear about it? It was a huge news story in the U.S. Canada too for a bit."

"Well, I'm so disconnected down here, you know." I tell tourists I've been here for five years, playing the role of a full-on expat.

"I don't remember all the details. Georgia, you followed that story like it was a soap opera. What happened to that poor skier girl?" he asks as his wife sidles up to us. "Don't you think Liz looks just like Katie Cleary?"

"Oh goodness, but you do! Yes, the Penny Cleary-Granger trial. So awful!"

"That's right. I gather it ruined her career, suppose it would have anyone's."

I nod my head, for a moment unable to speak. I take a deep breath, forcing my eyes to be bright. I notice that even when asked directly, this nice Canadian couple can't say out loud what Penny did.

"Well," I say, clasping my hands together, bringing us all back to the moment: far removed from the tragedy of a stranger they think they'll never meet. "That brings us to the end of our tour. Are there any questions I can answer for you all?"

There are so many questions, today of all days.

At last, I wrap up, telling them I have an appointment to get to and that I enjoyed meeting them all and hope they have a fantastic rest of their stay.

I should never have scheduled the lesson with Gianluca back-to-back with a tour, I realize as I haul ass to the studio. By the time I arrive, I'm a sweaty mess and my nerves are frayed.

"I'm so sorry, my tour ran late," I say, crashing into a chair to change my shoes.

"Relax," he says. "I'll let it go this once. Only once though, Tiger. Tango takes discipline. And my time is valuable."

I feel a hard stab of shame. There's nothing I hate more than being late for a coach. I nod and furiously fumble with the ankle strap on my shoes. It's hard to believe that G, the debauched bon vivant, has anything on me when it comes to discipline.

"Now," he says, getting down to business once my shoes are on and I'm standing at the ready, "let's see what we're working with."

He puts music on and leads me through a few basic moves. Both he and the studio seem to change every time I see them. First, there is the studio during class, when the place is full of strangers all feeling the same thing at once, hanging on G's every charming, authoritative word. At the social, when the didactic energy has cleared and the place has become a *milonga*, everyone revolving around G like lost planets. And now, I'm alone with him for the first time, and, undiluted, his presence, the weight of his focus, is almost unbearable.

"Okay," he says after a few moments, turning the music off and standing back from me. "You've got the basic steps down, that we knew, but tango is not about steps, it's about connection. And, Liz, being a follow requires patience, receptiveness. You need to open yourself to what your partner is doing, rather than trying to *anticipate* it."

I make a face. I don't like the idea of being a passive partner, someone to be moved around by an external force. The idea of a partner is already outside my comfort zone. The solitude of my sport is what I loved about it. I only had to rely on myself: it made me brave and strong, whereas the idea of opening up enough to let G—or anyone else—lead me, makes me vulnerable.

"Come here," he says, pulling me in so that there's only a sliver of space between our chests. "When you follow me, it's not your feet following my feet. The communication is translated from here." He rests his hand on my sternum; the touch feels startlingly intimate. I hear myself make something like a gasp, and he lets it pass without acknowledgment. "The heart. If you don't learn to feel it here, you're not really dancing."

To be taken apart in this way feels comforting and familiar. I want to be dismantled. I was always eminently coachable; I could always convert instruction into action. The opposite of Luke, who barreled down the hill in his hell-bent way, reckless and reliant on his extraordinary instincts, tucking in ever closer to the fall line. Blair was more like me: the good and eager student. We were patient and willing to learn someone else's way well enough to make it our own.

"Okay, *un momentito*," G says and walks away, leaving me feeling exposed.

He returns a moment later, having fetched Angelina from wherever she was, and leading her to the middle of the floor. My stomach drops at the sight of her. She and I exchange a weak smile.

"*Hola, Leez.*" I'm surprised she knows my name, though G certainly reminded her.

"Now, as Angelina and I dance this song," G says, "I want you to watch our chests, rather than our feet. That's where the dance is really happening, that's where we communicate and connect."

Angelina trots to the stereo to put the music on. She looks so at home here, so at home next to him. It's like her connection with G remains even when they're not dancing. He smiles at her approvingly, and jealousy constricts my throat.

They settle into each other's arms, and I watch them exchange a glance that feels intimate. The lurid thought crosses my mind that Angelina follows G so well because he's been inside her.

As instructed, I watch their chests. Through the fog of my envy at watching G with this girl—who I already assume he loves, and who's a far better dancer than I'll ever be—I see it. Though it appears Angelina is moving in many different directions, they remain connected as though by an invisible tether, locked into each other's orbit as though they couldn't move from it if they wanted to. They start simple with some basic walks and *ochos,* then add some crosses. Then, they ramp it up dramatically and spin around the tight axis they've created, her feet hooking around his legs and vice versa; they move into and out of the other's space with precision and ease. I'm mesmerized by the depth of their connection.

"Thank you, Angelina," G says, and she smiles, nods at me, and goes back to the practice room, where she's working with a student.

"That sets the bar pretty high," I say. I feel like he's shown me this to put me in my place.

"Angelina has been dancing her whole life," he says.

"All sixteen years, huh?"

He smiles. "Nineteen. And she's originally from Russia. They're more grown up than most at that age."

I raise my eyebrows. "Oh, I bet. How long have you two been dancing together?"

"A year," he says, and this strikes me as rather convenient. I try to muster up some disgust. G must be at least in his midthirties, and he's way too old for her. But still, all I feel is admiration and envy.

"The point is," he continues, "I don't expect you to emulate that exactly, but you can learn to have that connection with a great number of partners."

"Kinky," I say, smiling.

G laughs. "It's not about sex. Well, not exactly. It's an intimacy between you, your partner, and the music. Without the music, this dance means nothing. This is why tango is so precious to *Porteños*. Our entire history—the beautiful and the brutal parts—is encoded in the music. It brings us all together."

"I thought it was the dance of anarchists and immigrants." Did I say that to show I'm listening or to be contrary? Both.

"It began in the *conventillos,* was created by the poor, by the children of slaves, like most art forms worth anything. But then the rich boys who liked to go to the brothels on the wrong side of town got a yen for it and took it with them on their European tours. Once it became the rage in Paris, the high-class *Porteños* wanted their export back, this freshly laundered version of it. But its heart remains the same, and if you don't hear the heartbeat, Liz"—he closes the space between us in one swift movement so that his breath is in my ear—"you can't dance it."

G goes to find a song on his playlist. It has the regular elements: violin, flutes, bandoneóns, but it's jazzed up with unexpected drums and rhythms overlaying the classical strains. It's still dramatic, but more playful too. G is rolling his shoulders back and forth as he walks back to me. I pull my frame up, ready to be taken back into his capable arms. He shakes his head at me. "You see, I like this because it's a 'new' style, but in reality it's a throwback to the origins, when tango was fused with *Candombe* still, with the echoes of African drums. Now, close your eyes."

I look at him, confused.

"Close. Your. Eyes."

I do as I'm told.

"Don't worry about steps, just move to the music for a few minutes."

I open my eyes. What am I doing here? I'm in one of the bad dance movies that Penny and Emily used to watch over and over in high school.

"Closed," he says. "Move. Feel."

I want to laugh. I feel silly. I tentatively start into a tango step.

"No steps," G says, grasping my shoulders and holding me in place. "Just stay there and move. You need to give yourself over to the music, get out of your head."

I feel like I'm naked and being examined by a roomful of strangers.

"Relax," he says.

I start to sway my shoulders back and forth.

"I don't think I can do this." My heart is hammering.

"You can, just let go. Don't think. Be in your body: your hips, your shoulders, your hands," he says, his hands brushing first my hips, then my shoulders. "Don't think about tango, don't think about dancing at all. Just move, find something to connect to." I still have my eyes closed, but I can hear that he's close to me, only inches away.

"Good, good. There we go," he says.

I give myself over to the tonic of his approval, the warmth of his nearness, the many layers of the music that I can both hear and feel coming up from the floor. But halfway through the song, I lose my nerve and stop. I open my eyes. He smiles at me.

"This is making me really nervous," I confess.

He nods. "You don't feel good about your body." His voice is completely neutral, his statement a diagnosis.

I blush furiously. I don't want this to be true; it feels tired. I want to defend myself, tell him it wasn't always this way. My body used to be my job and I respected it. Now it feels like the extra layers of flesh carry everything that's happened to me.

"No," I say at last, "not especially."

"This is my biggest challenge, when I'm teaching people to dance. Before you can connect with a partner, you need to be able to be in your own skin. Watching you right now, I see you let go for a second and it's beautiful, but then you catch yourself. You're fighting it."

I'm flushed and fear I might start crying. As the next song begins, G pulls me in to lead me. "Relax, relax," he says into my ear. "Open, open."

111

I'm relieved to be back as the follow, and I feel myself dancing more smoothly. It's what a good coach does: pinpoints the little fix that will open you to the next level of yourself. But this feels like something else too. It's addicting to be near someone who sees potential in you and can cultivate it. Even if I end up paying for it.

Penny Knows All about Love

LUKE AND I didn't sleep together right away. He would be my first, and I knew I would not be his. It was palpable how much we both wanted it, but he was careful not to push. After we'd made it official, I felt relieved that Luke was still Luke. I'd feared that being together would change everything between us, that Luke would somehow no longer see me as his equal. And when I was stupid enough to ask him how many girls had come before me, he was stupid enough to answer honestly: five.

Of course five is not so many—not, frankly, as many as I'd feared. I'd had plenty of firsthand experience watching girls throw themselves at Luke, something that unfortunately continued long into our relationship. But at that age, when Luke was only the second boy I'd so much as kissed, five was an army. I began flipping through my mental index of the girls I'd seen him with: the petite girl with the giant tits who did promo for Red Bull, the tall, elegant Rossignol rep in her late twenties who'd come through for the season the year before. Since I didn't know *which* of them Luke had actually slept with, I pictured him with all of them. I envisioned them performing impossible sexual pyrotechnics.

I hated the idea of being awkward and fumbling, of being vulnerable. I wanted to be prepared, but I couldn't exactly get experience ahead of time. Instead, I did research. I tried watching some porn, but even as a virgin I knew that this couldn't be what real sex looked like: the hair flipping, the squealing, the vociferous enjoyment of giving a blow job. I decided to step it back and just grab a *Cosmo*. I sneaked it in with my groceries and shuffled off to one of the new grocery clerks who didn't know me by name. Not only was I buying the girliest magazine in the world, but I was also buying it *because* I wanted to read the section teased on the cover as "50 Sexy Moves That Will Make Him Your Slave."

At home, I squirreled it away to my bedroom, as if it were no less illicit than porn, and flipped straight to the dirty stuff.

"Eat him for dessert. Literally, spread your favorite yummy treats like whipped cream and chocolate sauce all over his manhood and chow down!"

That sounded both messy and not nutritionist-approved. Next.

> If you're not in the mood for the whole enchilada, why not give him a mind-blowing hand job? Start by running your index finger up the seam of his member, then trace circles around the head with the tip of your finger going first clockwise, then counterclockwise. Get your other hand in on the action by gripping and twisting the shaft in the opposite direction your finger is moving. Trust us, this will bring new heat to *holding hands*!

This one seemed like it would take a week at a specialized clinic to be able to execute. I needed to talk to Penny. Being with Luke gave me some common ground with my sister—I was in boyfriend land, where she'd long had a permanent residence. The credit card incident lingered in my mind, but I wove a safety net of justifications around it. Penny was right; after all, I *did* live in a bubble. Maybe the debt was just a normal part of being out on your own for the first time. And she'd lied only because she was embarrassed.

Sometimes, I envied my sister her quiet life back in our hometown:

her straightforward job, her eternal, uncomplicated relationship with Emily. I relished finally having something in my life that she could relate to: a boyfriend. She'd long made it clear that she had no interest in hearing about my skiing. I knew that from the outside, the life I wanted seemed insane. As talented as I was, as much potential as I had, the chances of turning it into a sustainable career were minuscule. Even if I started racking up World Cup wins this season, as I planned to, there was always someone faster, gutsier, and more talented waiting in the wings. In Austria and Norway, being a ski racer was a real career, but in the United States no one other than diehard ski fans cared about it for more than five minutes every four years during the Olympics. And the threat of injury lurked around every gate on the course. We'd all seen it a dozen times: a skier having the run of their lives and, in an instant, their season—maybe their entire career—was extinguished. It was unreasonable to expect Penny to understand why I wanted this madness. But boyfriends were Penny's gold-medal event. I took the chance to pick her brain about it when I was home for Thanksgiving.

I took the short flight home Wednesday night. I was nursing a sore hip flexor, and my coach had put me on R & R for the long weekend. I was relieved to get out of the gym for a few days. Penny came into my bedroom that night. Being in there always filled me with nostalgia.

"Are you sure you don't want to come to Turkey Bowl with us tomorrow?" she asked, referring to the annual game of touch football she and Emily played with their high school friends to celebrate them all being home from college. After the botched back surgery, Penny had become a bit heavier than she used to be, but she wore it well; it made her softer, more feminine. She'd been trying to get back to exercising, she told me, but then had gotten an infection in her ankle joint—a complication of her lupus—and it had sidelined her. She was designated cheerleader for the big game the next day.

I shook my head and smiled, scrunching up my feet to make room for her to sit at the foot of my bed.

"Coach would kill me."

"You could come cheer with me?"

"I'll bring my pompoms," I said with a smile. "When's Jon getting in?"

She beamed at the mention of her boyfriend. "Tomorrow afternoon. He'll be here for dinner. I'm so glad I get to spend some time with him before he has to go back to Arizona; this long-distance thing is killing me."

"I bet. So no Turkey Bowl for him either, huh?"

Penny made a face and shook her head. "He would take it too seriously anyway. He's so competitive."

This squared with my experience of him. Jon was shorter than me by several inches and, perhaps because of this, seemed doubly intent on broadcasting his masculinity whenever I saw him. He was the sort of man who went to the gym every day and got too invested in the outcome of sporting events he wasn't participating in. His shoulders were broad and his chin square, his countenance that of a grouchy bulldog.

"Hey," I said, "can I ask you something?"

"Of course!" She leaned back on her hand. Penny was pretty in that all-American kind of way, with her green eyes and the smattering of freckles on the bridge of her nose and cheeks. Men had always liked her, and she'd always returned the favor. She would never have been so nervous her first time, which I assumed had gone down with a high school boyfriend, though she hadn't confided in me about it.

"So Luke . . ."

"Ye-es? How goes it with the new *boyfriend*?"

"It's fine. But we haven't slept together yet."

Penny shrugged. "Well that's fine, no reason to rush things."

"It's just . . ."

She looked at me expectantly.

"It's my first time so . . ."

Penny smiled. "I know, honey."

"How do you know?" I asked indignantly. Was it that obvious?

"Relax," she said with a little laugh. "I just guessed. You've never had a boyfriend before, and I didn't really think you would have just given it up to some random. It's a good thing. It should be someone you love."

"Right." I was suddenly mortified; my sister and I didn't talk about sex. I wondered suddenly if Blair and Luke did, or if they had ever appealed to Kristina for her advice on women.

"So *do* you love Luke? Is he the one?"

"The one what? You mean like *the one*?"

Penny dealt in romantic absolutes: there were no half measures. She was always deeply in love and planning the rest of her life with whomever she was with, spinning off a fantasy outcome—wedding, babies, a rooted existence on some cul-de-sac somewhere, a kind of future I couldn't even wrap my head around. It wasn't that I didn't ever want these things, but they existed in a far-off universe beyond the glory of gold medals and World Cup globes.

"Whatever," Penny said. "Don't have a heart attack. Is he the one you want right now? Do you love him?"

I knew I did. After all, I'd told him so. But saying it out loud to another person was different. I nodded.

"Well, there you go," she said. "I don't think you'll have regrets."

"But how . . ." I began. Penny's brow furrowed. "That is, how do I . . . do it?"

She smiled at me sympathetically.

"Luke's been with other girls." *Five*, I thought, as the image of the miniharem came back into my mind. "And I'm afraid that he's going to expect me to . . . and I won't know what to do. Like, are there techniques or . . . ?"

With this, Penny lost her composure and giggled.

"Ugh, forget I asked!" I pulled a pillow over my head to hide my furiously blushing face.

"No, no, no," Penny said. "Come on, I'm sorry." She pulled the pillow away from me and I narrowed my eyes at her. "It's sweet. I didn't mean to tease you. It's just that I've never seen you like this! My little sister is intimidated by something! Finally! Let me revel in the fact that you need my advice for just a second, won't you?"

"Revel away," I said.

"Okay look, Katie, it's not like a super-G. You don't need to, like, plot your turns or whatever. Just take it slow and do what feels good and try to tell Luke how you're feeling, let him in. Don't make that face at me, I know being vulnerable is not your forte. It's a different kind of brave. You'll get the hang of it."

"But what if I'm terrible?"

"First of all, there are only two ways for a girl to be terrible at sex: one is to lie there like a dead fish, the other is to do something truly weird that ends up hurting his dick. So, you know, don't do either of those things and you'll be fine. Are you on the pill?"

"I'm not stupid," I said.

"Just checking. Anyway, the first time with someone new, especially the *first* first time, is a little awkward. Think about your first time on skis."

"I don't remember my first time on skis," I said, thinking that my dad had told me that even the first time, I was pretty good.

"Okay, bad analogy. But you'll be fine, I promise. And if Luke loves you—which, duh, he always has and I *always* knew that, just saying—he'll be patient."

So instead of going in protected by preparedness, I did something much harder: I dropped my armor.

It seemed, somehow, that as soon as I'd made the decision to sleep with Luke, he knew. He came into my bedroom as he did every night, and yet everything felt different this time. He kissed me, and I told him I was nervous. He replied that he was too.

"Why are you nervous? You've done this before," I said, trying not to let any bitterness creep into my voice.

"Because this is different."

"How?"

"My first time wasn't with someone I loved. It wasn't you. I wish . . ." He trailed off and his voice faltered. He *was* nervous. My fearless friend. He'd had to lay down his armor as well.

"What do you wish?" I whispered.

"I wish I'd waited. For you," he said.

Somehow, hearing this allowed me to let go of whatever else was holding me back. Luke ran his lips down my torso, but this time when he reached the edge of my underwear—our fail-safe—he slowly removed them. He kept kissing and went down between my legs. I think he registered my surprise because he looked up at me.

"I'm just going to . . ." He smiled and spread my legs apart. I felt his tongue and experienced a ratcheting of nerves, a thundering of blood. I wasn't entirely naive. I'd had an orgasm before, but only on my own, furtively alone in bed thinking of someone—usually Luke—or in my dreams when I'd be taken by some faceless man. This was something new and breathtakingly intimate. This was my best friend, his tongue, his lips, his hands. What came next was painful in a way that was not unpleasant. Sex would get better, cease to be painful, become a path to discovery of new things the two of us could do with the finely honed machines of our bodies. But even that first time, it was like a miracle to be that close to him.

⁓

After that, it all felt much more serious, and we knew we had to tell Blair. The day we decided to come clean, there was fresh powder, so first, we skied. It was a perfect day: the sun was out and beaming down, and soon our jackets were unzipped. I wondered as I watched the two most important men in my life: Was this the last time we would be like this? What if telling Blair about Luke and me was the end of the three of us?

We ate in the lodge after a spectacular morning on the hill, and as we sat across from Blair exchanging glances, he finally burst out laughing.

"You guys are ridiculous, you know that?"

We both stared at him.

"You're not that subtle. So are you guys hooking up or what?"

Luke got defensive. "We're not just hooking up."

"We're . . ." I began, uncertain of the exact words I was looking for: Together? An item? Boyfriend-girlfriend?

"Shit," Blair said. "You guys are in love. I knew there was something up, but I didn't know it was as serious as all that." A thousand things raced across his eyes, and I tried to catch hold of at least one—was there sadness, shock?—but then he obliterated it with a smile. "Well, congrats, guys. Just no weird PDA, okay? I still have to live with you."

And that, at least for many years to come, was that.

Liz Is New Here

O N THE first Sunday in February, the dancers of Tango Fortunado are performing in the Plaza Dorrego, practicing a new routine they've put together for an upcoming festival. Unlike many of the street performers—who wear tuxes and sequined dresses even in the middle of the sweltering summer—the girls are in tight, tiny black shorts and the men in dark pants, both with their signature T-shirts broadcasting their allegiance to Gianluca Fortunado.

I see Gemma sitting with Edward at the edge of a space that's been cleared for the four couples who make up the performance team, and she waves me over.

"Edward, darling, look who it is!" Gemma quickly procures an extra wineglass from the waiter and tips the last of their rosé into my glass.

I kiss their cheeks. Edward smiles at me but looks a bit pained; his sunglasses are pulled down over his eyes.

"Someone," Gemma says, "is feeling a little rough after last night. Really, darling, I'm disappointed in you. If a night out with me at La Brigada is going to level you, I don't know how you're going to keep up your reputation."

"Gemma, an *hour* out with you would level lesser men."

"I'll take that as a compliment. By the way, Liz, you should come over tonight. Just a small get-together. They'll be there." She gestures at the team.

"Yes." Edward smiles. "Please come. I cannot promise I won't be in the back bedroom with a cold pack, but Gemma will look after you."

"You're going soft!"

"Three bottles of Malbec with this one last night," Edwards says. "Plus cocktails before and after."

"Jesus," I say.

"It was over the course of *many* hours. And the steaks at La Brigada absorb at least half of that. The only way," she says, gesturing to the waiter to bring another bottle, "is to keep drinking now, just something light. This rosé is practically water!"

I notice the crowd growing quiet as Gianluca appears.

"*Bienvenidos todos,*" he says. "I am so pleased to present the elite dance team of Tango Fortunado. This is their first time showing off the new choreography that they'll be performing at the Festival of Dance in Rosario next month. For those who don't know me, I am Gianluca Fortunado, owner of Tango Fortunado. We have classes Monday through Friday, including drop-in classes each Friday followed by the best student *milonga* in Buenos Aires. Now, please welcome my dancers." As he speaks, people wander over—pulled in by that voice—and by the time he makes way for the dancers, a decent-size crowd has formed.

The performance, though shaky in a few sections, is impressive overall. Cali's partner is the tall blonde I saw her dancing zouk with at the social. Each pair of partners are good physical complements to one another, and the four couples dance in near-perfect synchronization and, halfway through, each lead dramatically releases his partner to the man next to them, repeating this every few bars until everyone is back with their original partner. Then, suddenly, all the couples break loose and two men dance with each other in the center in a way that looks like a highly choreographed knife fight. Then, two of the women do the same. The gender bending seems to surprise and delight the crowd. It's all over too quickly.

The dancers come our way when they've finished, and I notice that the crowd parts for them seamlessly. I'm struck by the expressions of the onlookers; the awed stares remind me of my old life, the way the performers become the focal point and the watchers become the background. Gemma introduces everyone almost too quickly for me to follow: Cali I know; her partner is Anders from Norway, Rodrigo and Valentina from Buenos Aires, Ada from Germany, Mateo from Brazil, Beau from France, and Sandra from Shanghai by way of London.

"And, everyone, this is Liz. She's new."

Cali comes over, kisses my cheeks, and pulls up a chair between Gemma and me.

"Nice job, Cali."

She scrunches her face. "Thanks, but I completely fucked up my dip. Luckily, Anders compensated for me." I smile. This too feels familiar; I was never satisfied with anything but perfection.

"How was your lesson with G?" she asks. Had I told her about that?

"Oh," I say, "great. Intense, but he's a good teacher."

"Ohhhh, you're taking private lessons with Gianluca. You minx, you're blushing!" Gemma says, laughing.

"Am not." I am, of course.

Cali smiles knowingly. "It's fine. Everyone has a crush on him at first."

"Gemma, I'm going," Edward says. "See you all tonight."

"Boo," Gemma says as Edward leans in and kisses her lightly on the lips. "I hope you've a better showing tonight, Edward."

He nods and waves at the rest of us.

"He okay?" Cali asks.

"I think he's having trouble sleeping again. Edward has terrible insomnia," Gemma explains to me. "He used to take Ambien, but at some point it just stopped working. I think he did too much blow in his twenties. So now he's like a vampire."

"You two are close, huh?" I ask.

"Oh, Edward? Yes, he's like a brother. But nothing like my actual brother, who's a bit of a shit, if I'm being honest. To say nothing of my sister, who isn't even speaking to me at the moment. I know it's odd to have a man as such a close mate, but Edward's just always been in my life. People never believe me that there was never anything romantic between us."

I nod. "My best friend back home, well, *both* of my best friends, were guys. Brothers, actually, we practically grew up together." I can scarcely remember my life without them, and now I have no idea how to have them in it anymore.

"Your ex didn't mind you being so close with them?" Gemma asks. "I've had some boyfriends who did *not* fancy my being so close with Edward."

"Well, the ex is . . . was . . . the oldest friend."

"*Damn,*" Cali says, "that's brutal.

"That's heartbreaking! Is there any hope of you being friends again?"

"We tried, but . . ." I trail off; there's far too much to explain. Luke and I might have survived our failed romance, but not the *way* it failed. I never felt the loss of myself more keenly than I did when I was with him. And I knew he couldn't bear to watch me fall apart, to watch me unbecome myself. He pulled away slowly, incrementally, breaking my already shattered heart a little bit at a time until I couldn't bear it and made him end things. I could feel his revulsion at the tragedy and chaos that descended on me, as though what had happened to me might be contagious. He loved who I'd been before, not this sad, needy doppelgänger who'd taken her place.

"This is why Edward and I could never go there. Who would I run to with my boy troubles? Not to mention that I would crush him beneath my Amazonian heft! Besides, I believe in being friends with exes, but he does not. He moves thousands of miles away so he doesn't have to run into them."

"Every time?" Cali says wryly. "That seems unmanageable."

Out of the corner of my eye, I watch for Gianluca and see him standing under one of the giant jacaranda trees with Angelina. Her face is tense and he appears to be placating her. My heart sinks a little with the certainty they're a couple.

"Well, Edward's never had much use—or need, I might add—for

practicality," Gemma continues. "In case you hadn't gathered this, his family is minted on the British and the *Porteño* side. He ostensibly works for the family biz but can more or less come and go as he pleases. I'm not sure he's even bothering with the ruse of work at the moment. Other than his artistic patronage. Edward never stays anywhere long enough for moss to grow, let alone roots to take hold. In that, Buenos Aires suits him perfectly: we're all on the run from something here."

I nod. "My friends back home are all so tight-knit. I didn't want people to feel like they had to take sides." This is true, I didn't want people to choose sides, mostly because I knew they'd choose Luke. Who wouldn't? Luke is still the golden boy, whereas I'm no one now. I realize that without the additional context, disappearing into a foreign country following a breakup seems dramatic. But for all they know, I'm a big old drama queen and this is just the sort of thing I do. Maybe I am now. Maybe that's who Liz is.

"What about the other one, the brother?" Cali asks. I can't help but smile when I think of him. He'd been so much braver in the end. I see him so clearly now, now that it's all too late.

"Blair. We're still friends. But he doesn't know I'm here. I told my parents where I was going, that's about it," I say.

"There's more to that story," Gemma says knowingly, "and we'll get it out of you eventually."

Penny Is Having a Baby

THEY WERE always so focused on Katie, they must not have seen it.
   She really was probably neglected.
Something must have happened to her when she was a kid.

I don't pretend to know the shape or the depths of what went wrong with Penny, but I do know that it's not my parents' fault. I think anyone close to us knows this too. The public is a different matter. People *need* there to be a root cause, some defining incident or an entire brutal history that drove Penny to do what she did. If there's nothing to pin it on, if Penny is just a random aberration, it means it could happen to anyone. It means that their daughters or sisters might also grow up to be monsters.

If anyone really tortured my parents about Penny, it was my parents. Every incident—every bad boyfriend, every lie she told, every strange overly emotional moment—was reopened like a cold case and examined down to the tiniest detail. As though it might lead us to what? An opportunity to go back and change it? And yes, my skiing, the unevenness of having such different daughters, how that affected their parenting; that's occurred to them, I know it has, though they're careful about how they discuss it whenever I'm around. They don't want me to feel guilty,

126

as though there's any way they could save me from that. But a look at my cohort shows that this has nothing to do with it; no one else's siblings turned out like Penny.

Still, there's no moment we've obsessed over more than Penny's first pregnancy.

The year Penny got pregnant was the best year of my life, but the thing about the best year of your life is that when you're in it, you can only imagine that things will keep getting better. Not only did all three of us make the 2002 Olympics in Salt Lake City, but we all podiumed—Blair with a silver in slalom, Luke with a gold in super-G and a silver in downhill, me with a bronze in super-G. My parents came to watch, along with Penny and Emily. Somewhere in an archive of old television footage, there exists several seconds of them—along with the blended Duncan clan—jumping up and down with signs near the bottom of the course. For once, it felt like Penny was proud of me.

She'd recently turned twenty-six and was getting rather anxious for Jon, who'd turned out to have some staying power, to propose. Twenty-six wasn't so young to be getting married in Coeur d'Alene; plenty of people got hitched to their high school or college sweethearts even earlier, and Penny always had dreams of the domestic life that I couldn't fathom. When she called me to tell me she was engaged, this wasn't even her biggest piece of news.

"I haven't even told Mom and Dad yet," she said excitedly. "I'm due in March!"

I was in the midst of gearing up for the beginning of the new season in November, and I was on my way to dryland training when she called.

"One sec, Pen," I said. Luke was looking at me expectantly. "Tell Coach I'll be there when I can."

Luke raised his eyebrows at me.

"Family emergency," I said helplessly. If I cut Penny short on this call, she'd hold it against me for months. Things were good between us, but her moods were mercurial, and it forever felt like she might just slip through my fingers if I did or said the wrong thing.

Luke shook his head.

"Sorry, Pen, go on," I said.

"Jon is over the moon. It was so sweet, Katie. I was so nervous when I told him, just because, you never know, right? Obviously we'd *talked* about marriage and babies and all of that, but it's totally different when one is on the way. So I tell him at the kitchen table and he, like, jumps up and runs upstairs. I'm thinking: What the hell? He looks excited but I'm also freaking out, and I mean, he *ran* out of the room. So he sprints back downstairs and basically throws himself at my feet. Suddenly, he's on one knee with a ring box, and I can't even tell you what happened after that, I kind of blacked out for a minute. I said yes, obviously."

"Wow, the whole package," I said. I loved Luke, but I couldn't imagine doing either of these things yet.

"The great thing is," Penny continued, "he already had the ring, so I'm not worried that it was a case of, like, *Oh, she's pregnant, I have to propose.* It's the prettiest ring, Katie! A diamond solitaire with a white gold band."

"I'm so happy for you, Penny. I know Mom and Dad will be too."

"Will they?"

"Yes."

I knew they worried about Penny's tendency to rush ahead with things. But she seemed more stable now; she'd worked in the family medicine clinic at Kootenai for almost four years. I often came to visit her at her office when I was home, and I loved seeing her in her element. She was clearly beloved in the office; she moved with such confidence there and was so competent and warm with the patients.

And my parents would make the most adoring grandparents. Their philosophy had always been that, as long as we were happy and safe, they wanted for us only what we wanted for ourselves. I knew they had some misgivings about Jon. He'd been out of work for a while and he and Penny had always seemed like a bit of a mismatch. But when they'd tried to address any of their concerns about Jon with Penny, she collapsed into floods of tears. Whatever issues we had about Jon, it appeared we were stuck with him now.

With the baby due in March, by the time I came home for Christmas, Penny was obviously, exuberantly pregnant. I was on a very brief visit back from Europe, where I was having the best World Cup season of my career; with wins in Lake Louise and Val d'Isère under my belt, as well as a strong performance on my home turf of Park City, I had a real shot at adding my very first World Cup globe to my collection. I dreamed of the iconic crystalline globe at night, as, I was certain, did Luke, who himself was having an unparalleled hot streak. The general public, when they cared at all, cared only about the Olympics, but for skiers, World Cup racing was an even higher distinction.

Penny and I had been enjoying a renewed closeness over the previous few months. Many of the other skiers I knew had siblings who were also athletes, the sport being a family tradition. Sarah Sweeny's older sister had been an even stronger skier than she was, up until a back injury had sidelined her. Now she was part of Sarah's training team, and I saw them together in Park City—where we all currently lived—constantly. The older Penny and I got, the more we struggled for common ground. But now we were having a parallel experience of hope and excitement, me for my first World Cup title, her for the life growing inside of her. Even though we didn't understand the shape of one another's ambitions, we understood the depths of them, the feeling of wanting something so badly that it eclipsed all the minor annoyances of daily life.

Penny was luminous that year at Christmas, her pert little beach ball of a belly constantly cradled by her hand, her skin glowing, her eyes shining. My parents were happy to have both of their girls home, ecstatic about becoming grandparents. I was more excited to be an auntie than I ever imagined I'd be. I focused so much on what the muscle and sinew of my body could be shaped to do, but here was Penny's producing life! Pregnancy is only an ordinary kind of miracle when it's happening to someone else: when it's your own flesh and blood, it feels like everything.

The prospect of fatherhood seemed to have brought out the best in Jon; his normally taciturn manner had loosened. He was gregarious with us and solicitous of Penny, fussing over her and running to deliver her anything she asked for.

As we were preparing for Christmas dinner, Penny said she had something to tell us.

"I wanted to wait until Katie was here," she said.

My parents froze in the kitchen, my mother's oven-mitted hands halted in midair. We all turned to Penny, who was nursing her one allotted glass of wine—her colleagues from the clinic had assured her that a little bit was fine—and beaming.

"I'm having twins," she said in a stage whisper. "Two girls!"

There was delirious excitement all around, and Jon, who of course already knew, gamely endured an onslaught of good-natured jokes about him being outnumbered.

Penny produced a sonogram pic and we marveled at the sight of the two tiny beings cuddled into one another. Suddenly, I got tears in my eyes: the realness of seeing their little bodies in the picture. My nieces! I threw my arms around my sister.

"Emma and Abby," she whispered.

"Their names?"

She nodded, her eyes welling up now too. "Ugh, hormones," she said, laughing. "Oops!" She looked startled. "One of them is kicking! Oof, little girl, I think you're going to be an athlete like your auntie."

Penny took her hand in mine and laid it gently on the bulge of her stomach. And to this day, I swear to you, I felt that baby kick.

⁓⧖⁓

I was in St. Moritz for the FIS World Championships six weeks later when we got the call. In anticipation of this being my big season, my parents had decided to take some time off from work and follow me on the final leg of the tour. It was a huge trip for them; they didn't take extravagant vacations and had been saving up for it. I was having an early breakfast with them in their room at the Grand Hotel des Bains when the phone rang. In my memory, the moment slows and every tiny detail crystalizes: my mom picking at a flakey pastry from the room service tray, my dad's unkempt bedhead, the fact that no one was alarmed when the phone rang. I thought it must be one of my coaches calling, so I picked it up. It took me a moment to realize that I was hearing the terrified voice of my sister. A dizzying array of facts came next. Penny had gone into labor, but it was far too early, so they were doing everything they could to keep the babies where they were. Jon was out of town on a job—wrapping up a final project in Arizona—and he was on his way back. Penny also mentioned the terrifying complication of preeclampsia—meaning her life, as well as those of the babies—could very well be at risk. Emily had taken her to the hospital and was there with her now.

I went directly back to my room and began packing in a mad fury. Luke and Blair appeared at the doorway, ready to head to the base together; their downhill race was that afternoon.

"Hey," Luke said, alarmed at my tornado of movements, "whoa, what's going on?"

My voice sounded strangely calm and hard. "I have to go home."

Luke let out a disbelieving laugh. "Katie, *what*? Are you crazy? You have downhill in three days."

It was Blair who came to my side, made me put down the handful of clothes I'd torn from the hotel dresser and sit.

"What's going on? Are your parents okay? I thought you were with them this morning."

"It's Penny," I said, and at that moment, a huge sob came up. "She's gone into labor."

Blair gasped, and Luke—never much for listening to the details of anyone else's personal life, including mine—looked perplexed. He was agitated, thinking about his race, irritated by the intrusion.

"Well, the babies will still be there later, you have plenty of time to go meet them before Innsbruck."

I looked at Luke aghast and Blair spoke for me. "It's too early, Luke."

"I have to go home," I said, my eyes dancing back and forth between the two of them. I was looking for their approval. I was mad with worry, but the idea of missing the race felt surreal—the race was tight, between

Sarah Sweeny, Kjersti Larsen, one of the Austrians, and me, and a scratch would easily put me out of the running for a World Cup globe—and I needed them to tell me I was doing the right thing, that I had to go home. I didn't *want* to leave, but the need I felt to get to my sister's side was primal. "My parents are booking flights right now."

"Is Coach helping?" Blair asked. I nodded.

"Katie! You can't *leave,* you have races!"

"Luke," Blair said.

"Penny will understand. And your parents are going, what are you going to do anyway?! Come on, Katie, this is too important."

Luke wasn't wrong, just insensitive, and it wasn't as though I didn't know this about him. Luke was invincible and invulnerable. Luke pushed me to be my best, and usually, it was what I needed.

"Luke, a word," Blair said, practically shoving his brother out into the wide, plush hallway. I carried on packing, and a few moments later, Luke came back through the door and pulled me into his arms.

"I'm so sorry, babe, I was being a dick, you know how I get during competition. I just don't want you to miss your downhill, but there's always next season." He pulled back and kissed me, brushed a piece of hair that was stuck to my clammy cheek away from my face. "You do what you gotta do, okay?"

I wish I could say I didn't feel I needed Luke's permission to go home, but his blessing helped me walk out the door. We all thought I was doing the right thing.

"I can stay," Blair said, "and help you and your folks get everything sorted out. Just say the word."

"No," I said. "Oh my god, I'll never forgive myself if you two miss your race, go on, get out of here. I'll be fine, I'll call from the States." As I hugged them both and sent them on their way, the fact lodged itself deep in my heart that only one had actually offered to miss his race. I told myself it was because Blair was a tech skier, and downhill meant everything to Luke.

The last-minute flights we were able to get were a nightmare of layovers and nonsensical way stations. Zurich to Paris, Paris to Amsterdam, on to Houston, and then finally to Spokane. At every stop, we called Penny for updates.

Penny told us Emily had driven her to the hospital. Thank god she'd been there; the fact that this happened when not only her fiancé but also her parents—who rarely traveled—were far away seemed particularly cruel.

When I spoke to her, Penny sounded shaken. "They've got me upside down, Katie," she said with a little laugh at the absurdity of it all, "just trying to keep my little ones in there." By the time we reached Houston, her water had broken, her blood pressure was skyrocketing, and the situation was growing more precarious by the moment. My parents' faces were ashen as we boarded our final flight. I pulled up the hood of my sweatshirt and quietly sobbed through a movie during the final leg. Because of the last-minute booking, my parents and I couldn't get seats anywhere near each other. Thankfully, the stranger I was sitting next to handed me a tissue wordlessly. I suppose a person crying on a plane isn't so strange. On every flight everywhere in the world, someone is likely to be on their way to or from a tragedy.

By the time we touched down, it was all over. The babies didn't survive. Emily had picked Penny up, and she was resting at home. Jon was still trying to make his way home, waylaid by his truck having broken down somewhere outside of Salt Lake City. It didn't hit me until that moment quite how clearly I'd been envisioning those two little girls as a part of our family. I'd had to miss the baby shower but had wrung up a monstrous bill buying up half of Penny's registry on Babies "R" Us. Babies make you project into the future, and without even meaning to I'd imagined twins—one like me, boisterous and physical, one like Pen, quiet and kind—running through the halls of our parents' house, flinging themselves at me when I came through the door for visits. I imagined their girlish ringlets and their missing teeth, I wove them into my own visions of the future, imagining them one day wanting to try on my gold medal. Children of my own were still an abstract, distant thought, but the idea of being an auntie filled me with a kind of love I'd never experienced. I'd embraced it with my whole heart, and I felt the loss acutely now.

Once we arrived, we went straight to Penny and Jon's creaky little two-bedroom house in Hayden to pick Penny up and look after her until Jon returned. I'd last been here over the holidays, right before Jon had left for his new job. The place had been in a state of half-finished disarray: the scraggly yard untouched; a restoration of the kitchen cabinets underway but not yet completed; the second bedroom half-painted a calming shade of periwinkle, a roller still in its foil bin, the drop cloth spread over the carpet. I was surprised as we came in through the front door, calling Penny's name, to find that the house was exactly as it had been, but with an additional few layers of squalor, including the overflowing litter box of Penny's cat, Noodles. It seemed every surface was covered with debris and clutter, and the kitchen smelled of neglect and spoiled food. Even as I took in the disturbing tableau I made excuses for it. Penny worked hard at her clinic job and she'd had a difficult pregnancy; suddenly, I was livid with Jon. How could he be so useless? What was wrong with him that he could only find work in Arizona? He'd abandoned her.

That night, I slept beside Penny in the old trundle bed in her room. My mom had outfitted them with their old unicorn sheets, worn soft with age and replete with the homey, indelible smells of childhood. Penny was exhausted and a little wonked out on painkillers. My mom made us grilled cheese sandwiches and soup for dinner and we tucked ourselves into bed at 9:00 p.m.

"I'm sorry you missed your race," Penny said, her voice cracking. Noodles, who'd come with her from her house, pawed concernedly at her. "And you never even got to meet your nieces."

My eyes filled with tears, but I tried to be strong for my big sister, grasping her hand. "I don't want to be anywhere but here right now. I'm glad I came. There will be other races, it doesn't matter."

I had no idea what to say to Penny; the horror of what she'd been through was too immense. There was nothing to do but be there, and I was glad I was. Terrible as the circumstances were, I hadn't felt so close to my sister in years. Back here with her, lying in the trundle bed that I'd spent so many childhood nights in, I remembered that though skiing often felt like the only thing that mattered, it wasn't. True, the other things that mattered to me could be counted on one hand—my folks, Penny, Luke, and Blair—but they mattered more than anything, and maybe I needed to be reminded. I'd always been allowed to be self-centered because it was what I needed to make myself a champion, but this would not always be true. And I owed so much to my family, Penny too. I felt a rightness being there with her that night. Strange as it seems, I treasure this memory even now. It was a sad moment, but everything seemed so clear. Right and wrong still meant something.

I called Luke and Blair at the hotel the next day, hoping to catch them between training runs. I'd sent them both an e-mail update already with the worst of it, but I was longing to hear their voices.

Blair picked up.

"Bomber, I'm so sorry. We've been thinking about you nonstop."

"Thanks," I said. "I'm glad I'm here. Kjersti won the downhill, I see."

"She skied well," Blair said, "but you would have been better."

"I would have skied like shit, I would have been so distracted. Probably better this way. And congrats on rocking the giant slalom, B."

We all knew that going out on the course if your head wasn't in it could lead to a catastrophic crash. Even on the best day, a tiny bobble could lead to disaster; we were always on the knife's edge.

"It's never the same without you here," Blair said. "But you did the right thing and I'm proud of you. You're a good sister."

I heard Luke in the background.

"Luke wants to talk to you. Take care, okay? Lots of love to the fam."

"Yeah."

"Babe!" Luke's exuberant voice broke through the fuzzy connection. "Did you see?"

He'd won his race, meaning his first World Cup globe was more or less a lock. "I did," I said. "I'm so proud of you."

"Oh man, it was turny as shit, I almost blew out after the first gate." He rattled off a recount of the race. Normally, I'd be happy to hear every detail, but my mind was a blur. After a few minutes, he seemed to suddenly remember the circumstances.

"I'm sorry about your sis, Bomber," he said. "It sucks. But she can probably have more kids though, right?"

"Yeah probably. I hope so."

"Ah, Bomber, we gotta go. I love you, babe. I'll see you soon."

❧

Penny sweetly insisted that I didn't need to stay very long, and my coaches wanted me back in time for Innsbruck. But I stayed for a couple of days, curled up watching bad movies with my sister while my parents were at work. We didn't talk about what had happened; we were just quiet together. One afternoon while Penny was sleeping on the sofa, the landline rang.

"Hello?" I said, picking up the old phone with its long cord that let my mom migrate from the kitchen to the living room while she was on it.

There was a distinct pause at the other end of the line.

"Sissy? Is that you?" The surprised voice was Emily's, and the sound of it flooded me with warmth. "What are you doing at your parents' house?"

"Em! Yes, it's me. I'm home with Pen today, didn't she tell you I was coming?" I wandered toward the living room, leaning up against the little archway that separated the two spaces. I gazed at my sister sleeping on the couch, Noodles curled in the crook of her legs. Penny already looked younger than me—with her baby face—and when she slept, additional years seemed to melt away.

"No!" Emily said. "I didn't know Penny was over there. I was just calling to check on her. I only tried here because no one answered at her place. How is she?"

"She's doing okay. I mean, she's exhausted obviously. And the pain pills are making her a bit loopy, but that might be for the best. God, Em, it's so good to hear your voice." Between the jet lag, the multiple flights, and the stress, I wasn't much less exhausted than my poor sister.

"You too! I miss you. You're such a good sister to come all the way home from Europe. Aren't you in the middle of your season?"

"Yeah, and my parents were with me in St. Moritz, as you know. The first time they've ever been to Europe and this happens! They'll probably

136

never get on another transatlantic flight as long as they live. But there was no way we weren't going to come home right away, especially with Jon not here."

There was a heavy pause on the other end of the line. "Where did Jon go?"

"He's still on his way back from Arizona. His truck broke down outside Salt Lake. Didn't Penny tell you?" Where on earth did Emily *think* Penny's fiancé had been while she was taking her to the hospital in preterm labor?

Another pause, so long it was eerie this time. "I haven't talked to her in a few days, the last I heard she was headed home from the hospital. But wait . . . wait. Jon took her, he was there with her, she told me. She said he held her hand through the whole thing, that they said goodbye to the twins together."

Now I was silent. I peered again at my sister's serene face, her eyelids fluttering in sleep. I felt a chill run through my body. At the time, I would have told you it was exhaustion, overwhelm, and confusion all happening at once. But looking back, I know. That feeling was the devil walking into the room.

Liz Is Losing It

PENNY AND I never looked much alike, with our different coloring and opposite body types. When we were kids, we'd often ask strangers to choose who among she and Emily and me were sisters, and people chose Penny and Emily every time. Emily—according to my mom, who still checks in on her Facebook periodically—appears to be doing well, is dating someone new, looks happy. Despite how different we look, every once in a while—like now, as I finish my makeup in the tiny, dimly lit bathroom of my little San Telmo apartment—I'll be looking at my own face and feel a flash of recognition so intense it stops me cold, an unwelcome reminder that, no matter our differences, Penny and I are made of the same stuff.

Tonight, I'm going to Edward's Belgrano mansion as an invited guest rather than a party crasher. Gemma tells me to come early to hang out with her while she helps get ready for guests. She answers the door, and I follow her into the main room, where I only now notice a stunning portrait of a dark-eyed woman hanging above the massive fireplace; it's flecked with gold and seems to shimmer before my eyes. Gemma notices that I'm transfixed.

"Do you like it? It's new. Or it's new here at any rate. I convinced Edward to have his family buy it four years ago when it came up at Christie's; Klimts are so rare."

"It's beautiful," I say dumbly, an understatement.

"Edward does enjoy having me around to help him spend his money. Come on back, let's have some champagne before everyone else gets here. Do you know about Klimt?"

I shake my head. I'd been in plenty of rich peoples' homes before—a perk of being connected with the trustees and the Duncans—but I still felt like a kid in a museum. None of the ski fans in our milieu were particularly into art though; back then, I was the prize commodity.

"He was an odd duck," Gemma continues, opening the vast gleaming fridge in Edward's kitchen and pulling out a bottle of Veuve Clicquot. "Viennese. And quite the pervert actually, obsessed with the female body—naturally—and something of a recluse. No café society for that one. He had dozens of extramarital affairs, but he rarely left the house or even put pants on."

"Living the dream."

Gemma laughs. "Indeed! I'm only hoping to save Edward from the same fate. He spends entirely too much time in his bathrobe if I'm not here."

We wander back into the living room and stand near the fireplace. For a moment, we both stare at the Klimt.

"Edward has the right house to pull it off too. *Sadly* I've never owned any property that would support something as flashy as a Klimt."

"Your knowledge of art is impressive," I venture.

"Well, yes, I specialize in impressive. Pedigree, credentials, lineage. All of the things I was raised to believe in. But it's all useless in the end isn't it? Or rather, its usefulness is limited to a very small radius. And I assure you, I'm currently very far outside of that radius. And the irony is, I thought I *wanted* out."

"Buenos Aires seems like a good place for an . . . art dealer?"

She smiles, throwing back the rest of her champagne.

"Curator."

She slips back into the kitchen and returns with the bottle.

"And what goes on in your radius, Liz? Tell me about your life. What would you be doing right now if you weren't here?"

For a moment, my mind reels. If I weren't here, I'd be preparing for the Olympics in Vancouver, but only if my life had gone very differently. Only if . . .

"Well, it's winter there now, of course," I say, plastering a smile on my face to hide my discomfort, "so lots of skiing, some snowshoeing maybe. Hot tubbing, drinking hot chocolate with peppermint schnapps. Simple stuff."

"Sounds divine. You're very sporty, aren't you? You remind me of my friend Katherine, she's always going hunting and horseback riding. Her cheeks are forever this ruddy outdoorsy shade of pink, it's very fetching."

I startle at the name, but it's just a coincidence.

"Hello, ladies."

Edward emerges from the back of the house. He looks livelier than he did earlier, but a bit off-kilter too. His eyes are shining.

"Edward, I was just bragging about your art collection."

"Ah, so bragging about your own taste then."

"Credit where credit is due. And we were talking about skiing! Edward is quite a good skier," Gemma says. "We used to go to Chamonix every year—why don't we do that anymore?"

"Because you're a terrible skier, among other reasons."

"I'm hopeless at all sports as a rule, but I'll get a couple of runs in as an excuse for the après ski. Have you been to Chamonix, Liz?"

"I have. I've skied all over the world, actually." Why am I saying this? The champagne has gone straight to my head. I drank the first glass quickly and Gemma stealthily refilled it. I suppose I want them to know that I'm not as boring as the fake backstory that I've concocted: that I work on the administrative side at the resort. The truth is, unless I'm bull-shitting with a stranger in a bar for five minutes, I'm not creative enough to imagine any life but the one I've lost.

"Have you?" Gemma says, her interest piqued.

"One of the many benefits of being the fifth wife of the Sultan of Brunei."

Edward guffaws just as the doorbell sounds.

"Camilla!"

Edward is beaming when he walks back into the room with his beautiful dark-haired cousin. At first, I think she looks nothing like him with her olive skin and her mountain of thick curly hair, but then there is something similar too, something in the mannerisms. She and Gemma kiss hello, but there is a strange note of discomfort that I'm left wondering about.

Edward introduces us and we kiss hello too.

"Where are you from, Liz?"

"I'm American," I say.

"You're *North* American," she corrects, and I'm momentarily stunned. "We're both Americans, after all." She smiles in a way that leaves little doubt as to what she thinks of my country.

"So you're from here then?"

"One hundred percent *Porteño*. And what brings you to Buenos Aires?"

"Just visiting, I suppose. Learning some Spanish, leading tours."

"You're leading *tours*?" She raises her eyebrows.

"Just the main tourist sites. I guess they like having guides who speak English."

She looks as though she might burst out laughing.

"And tango!" Gemma attempts a rescue. "She's taking classes with Gianluca."

"Of course," Camilla says with a pointed look at Edward. "G loves his *extranjeros*."

"Let's get you a drink, Camilla," Edward says, and Camilla flashes me a look that confirms that she finds me quite hilarious.

"Well, that went well," I say to Gemma, feeling mortified.

"Don't worry about it, she'll warm up."

"Will she?" I ask.

"Surely," Gemma says. "Any day now!"

141

The dance team shows up around midnight and immediately takes over the couches. They have a physical intimacy with one another that reminds me of the drama kids from my high school, who were always draped all over one another, giving each other back rubs in the hallways, holding hands, and hugging. But that group felt like a union of outcasts whereas this one feels like something else, like a group anyone would want to be a part of. Or perhaps it's just me who wants to be one of them. And in the center of it all is Gianluca, like a sultan in the midst of his harem.

I watch out of the corner of my eye as he extricates himself from one of the girls—it's Sandra from Shanghai—and goes to speak to Edward. The two of them go out onto the empty patio where it's drizzling softly, and I watch their faces become strangely serious in the eerie glow of the pool lights.

Gemma catches me spying and leans her head on my shoulder.

"What do you suppose they're talking about?" I ask.

"Oh, probably just discussing some studio business."

I look at her confused.

"I thought Edward wasn't on the team."

Gemma smiles. "Edward's an investor. As I said, he likes to buy art."

"Oh." Gianluca's owned by a rich man, just like I once was.

As we watch them, the mood appears to lighten and Gianluca pulls Edward into a handshake that becomes a hug.

"I reckon he's got what he wanted," Gemma says. "He usually does."

"How did Edward come to be a part of his studio?"

Gemma gives me a little sideways smile, as though gauging how much she should tell me. "I told you about that summer in Saint-Tropez—gosh, it must have been a decade ago now—how Gianluca ended up on the yacht with all of them?"

"Sure, the Italian countess, right?"

"Exactly! Oh, I was so blotto on New Year's I couldn't remember what all I'd said. But we're friends now, so I can tell you. So Edward, his girlfriend, her aunt, and Gianluca, they spend this whole summer on the Riviera, having a grand old time. The count himself isn't around much, has a mistress stashed elsewhere, you know the drill; lets his wife have the run of the boat. But he comes back at the end of the summer and discovers that Gianluca is perhaps not . . . inclined the way his wife led him to believe."

"They're having an affair?"

"Naturally. Anyway, there's some kind of confrontation on one of the upper decks involving the three of them. No one knows for sure what happened but the count ends up plummeting over the railing to his death four flights below. Of course, Gianluca is completely innocent in the version the countess tells, he's only protecting her, and she's backed up by the staff, who adored her and loathed the count. I don't think her niece, Edward's ex, ever believed the story, but it's so like Edward to fall for someone like G. My darling Edward, he grew up everywhere and nowhere, so he always feels a kinship for wanderers. Wouldn't be the first time it's gotten him into trouble."

"And has it? Gotten him into trouble, I mean."

"Depends on what you believe, I suppose. All I know is Edward came back here with a new 'investment,' a new friend, and a rather unbelievable story about Gianluca's heroics on the high seas. In their version, Gianluca stepped in to protect the countess when her husband tried to attack her."

I raise my eyebrows at her. "You don't believe it?"

"I've been here for a few months. He's not the only one with a conveniently heroic origin myth. Come on," she says, taking my arm, "let's go in."

I squeeze in on the couch next to Cali and she kisses me hello, lets her long leg drape over mine. "Where's Angelina tonight?" I ask.

"Oh god," she says. "Those two are a hot mess. Don't get G started. He'll either be ranting or crying."

"Crying?" I'm surprised.

"Oh, you don't know the half."

When Gianluca comes back in, it quickly becomes his party again. He commandeers the music and asks me to dance a tango with him.

I can't help the hope from burbling up through the cracks of my heart. Angelina gone, and I'm his first dance of the night. Tonight, I feel more perfectly in sync with him than I ever have; I'm dropped into my body in a way that's so sharp it's almost painful, in that it reminds me how numb I've otherwise become. When the song ends and Gianluca steps away, it feels like someone has shoved me out into the cold.

I'm not alone for long though. Everyone asks me to dance after that. No one is exactly like him, but his team members are created in his image. He taught them to dance, certainly, but it's also as though he taught them how to feel and touch, as though they've all become his proxies. Cali's partner, the Norwegian whose name eludes me at the moment, even teaches me some zouk.

The night becomes a blur of sensations. And late, late in the evening when most of the nondancers have left, I feel galvanized. I go to find Gianluca.

I see Sandra first: she's facing outward, the light from the main room catching her face in the darkened hallway. She bends at the waist, dropping like a stripper and grinding her hips into the man behind her: who I now see is Gianluca. He has one hand on her hip, the tips of his fingers hidden beneath the waistband of her tight pants, his other hand is in her hair, fingers wrapped around the silky black strands.

This is how it starts. My heart is racing and I am trying to convince myself that none of it matters. Aren't I having so much fun? But then, the loop, the loop. *Of course he doesn't want you, no one wants you, you're nothing next to these people, you're fat now and broken and a sorry excuse for a woman, you lost Luke, you lost Penny and Blair, you lost . . . you lost . . . you're lost.*

I make my way to a back bathroom and close the door before curling myself up on the floor. The cool marble of the immaculate floor is a comfort against my cheek, but it's not enough. I feel my throat go cold and tight, my hummingbird heart feels as though it will explode, and my chest is a giant knot being pulled tighter and tighter. The adrenaline cancels the depressive effects of the alcohol, and time stands still. I have been here forever and I will be here forever.

☙

I wake up the next morning in a plush, unfamiliar bed, my mind muddy and my limbs heavy. I feel a flicker of panic but I'm too exhausted for it to take hold. I glance at the bedside table to find a half-full glass of water and a prescription bottle on its side. Lorazepam 4 mg tablets. Now I remember and I'm flushed with embarrassment. Edward found me lying on my side. He was so kind, he helped me to bed and gave me the drugs. "Take one, take two," he'd said. "The best thing now is to sleep."

What had I said in response? Had I told him anything?

It didn't used to be like this. I was tough once, resilient. But now it's as though I live in the attic of a towering house where parts of the floor have rotted away. At any moment, I could make a wrong move and I'll fall forever.

I get out of bed gingerly. I'm wearing a pair of Edward's pajamas. I find my clothes folded neatly on a chair. I change and walk out into the kitchen.

"Good morning," Gemma says. "Oh you poor darling, come sit. I'll make you some toast."

Edward is by the pool but hears us and comes in, giving me a sanguine smile.

"How are you this morning, my dear?"

"Tired," I say, "and mortified."

"Oh don't be," Gemma says. "Panic attacks are the absolute worst. Edward told me, but don't worry, we've all been there."

"Well, I'm grateful. Some party guest I am."

"Oh, every good party ends with sedatives," Edward says. "Trust me." He takes his sunglasses off and it occurs to me that perhaps he hasn't slept at all. "You're not the only one who needs some help to make it to morning."

"Goodness yes," Gemma says, returning to the table with toast. "I spent most of my first week in Buenos Aires on the floor of Edward's bathroom."

"Really?" This comes as a surprise from the lighthearted Gemma.

"Oh yes. I didn't leave London because things were going *well*."

"What happened?"

"I had a nervous breakdown, or I suppose that's an old-fashioned term, isn't it?"

145

"Psychotic break," Edward says.

"That's the one. Oh, that sounds rather less romantic though. Anyway, I had one. I'd been depressed for a while before that, I realize now. *Very* depressed."

Edward leans over to squeeze Gemma's hand. I realize that her cheerful demeanor might be as much smoke screen as anything.

"How did it happen?" I ask.

"The strangest thing. It was this completely ordinary morning. I was making tea for my husband, Thomas, and I had this deep moment of"—she searches for the word—"dissociation. I had this sudden realization that all my life was making tea for my husband—dash of milk, heaping scoop of sugar like a child would want—and everything else was a mirage. I was in hell, and hell was standing forever at the counter of our Mayfair town house stirring sugar into tea. I began screaming all of these delusions at my husband."

"Whoa. What did he do?"

"He told me to pull myself together and left for work. British men, at least the ones of Thomas's ilk and age, don't really 'do' mental health. All things can be solved by a stiff upper lip and—irony!—a cup of tea."

"So what did you do?"

"It only got worse from there. When Thomas dismissed me, I decided he was the devil—the actual devil, remember, I thought I was in hell—and became extremely paranoid and obsessed with escaping. I didn't sleep or eat for almost a week. I crashed my car and ended up in hospital."

Gemma looks into her cup of tea as though to add something but thinks better of it.

"Sometimes," Edward says when the silence becomes heavy, "there's no way out but *out*."

Penny Is in Love for Real

HOW COULD we not have known? I look back now and it's a question I can circle and examine from every angle and still not find an answer to. One answer is that we *did* know that something was wrong, but we had no context for it. We were reassured that young women struggled, did strange things, went through rough patches. And it was so much easier to find ways to blame Jon. Jon—with his shifty friends and his perpetual snarl—had been a bad influence. And Penny had always been susceptible to influence, her heart so big and soft and porous.

In retrospect, I can see the mental gymnastics my parents and I went through to explain it to ourselves. A woman lies about how she lost a pregnancy because she is ashamed that her fiancé has left her, abandoned her in a precarious state. And she's so humiliated by this and so mad with grief when she loses her babies that she invents another narrative where he is coming to her rescue: he's on his way and will get there as soon as his uncooperative truck will allow him. She convinces herself that he too is grieving and is desperate to be by her side *just as soon as he can*. Or, there is the version Emily hears, that Jon *has* made it back in time to be by her side, to squeeze her hand and cry with her through the devastation, to say goodbye to the two little girls, tiny and blue and gone from this world.

Not one lie, but two separate lies, perhaps more. Perhaps one in which my parents were there, I was there. It was around this time, we'd later find out, that Penny's virtual online life began to grow tentacles. There were hidden Facebook groups and secret pages that no one who knew Penny in real life would see until much later. In these dark corners of Penny's invented identity, she would live out alternate realities: that the twins had lived but were in the NICU, balanced between life and death; that one had died but the other had survived, leaving her with one beautiful living baby and one set of tiny footprints in plaster to remember the other; that both babies had lived but her fiancé had died trying to get home to them. For now, all of this remained in the shadows.

When my parents and I pressed her to explain after my call with Emily, Penny cried, collapsed, shut down. How could we do this to her when she was in so much pain? And we didn't want to grill her any more than she wanted to explain herself. No, it was Jon's fault, we decided, Jon who was not on his way back from anywhere but gone for good. It's the oldest story in the book: man knocks woman up, panics, flees the scene. Tragically, the woman is so distraught she loses the pregnancy. The simplest explanation is usually the truth, so why wouldn't that be it?

Because Penny *had* been pregnant. Hadn't she? She'd looked pregnant, shown us ultrasound pictures, *and I had felt the baby kick*. I'd felt its tiny living foot collide with my hand from inside of my sister, it's not something you imagine. It had to have been real.

Much later, when it was clear that this incident was not the ending of a sad chapter but the beginning of a much more harrowing one, my parents would confess that they suspected something more disturbing, even though I would not let myself. *Pseudocyesis.* False pregnancy, a condition in which all the symptoms of the pregnancy are there—weight gain, nausea, swelling, even the sensation that a baby is moving inside of you—but the fetus is not. But even this left more questions than answers. Hysteria might make a woman believe she felt a baby kicking inside of her, but could it make her sister believe the same? And had Penny known the ultrasound picture wasn't hers? Which parts of the lie were real to her and which did she knowingly manufacture?

This is where my parents' experience of Penny and mine began to truly diverge. I finished my season third in the World Cup standings after I podiumed in Innsbruck and won in Lillehammer, mollifying my sponsors after I'd missed my big race in St. Moritz. Luke and I were now a bona fide power couple. Two top skiers from the same birth year. It was a rare phenomenon to have two top skiers from the same birth year, and the fact that we were a couple made us a favorite among the small cadre of American journalists and fans who cared about the sport.

It wasn't so much that my parents hid from me what was going on back home. It was more that they were selective, hoping that none of it would ever be anything I needed to know about. Several months after the incident with the babies, Penny was evicted from the house she'd shared with Jon after not paying the rent for months. My mom went to help her clean the place and pack and discovered a horrifying scene. My sister's house had become the house of a crazy person: the electricity had been shut off weeks before and food had rotted in the fridge, there were baby clothes and toys everywhere, and—worst of all—there was no sign of Noodles.

The only explanation I can offer for how we moved on so swiftly was that shortly after Penny lost the babies, she met Stewart.

Stewart Granger. He was thirty years old, originally from Hayden and now a captain in the U.S. Air Force, stationed out of Mountain Home Air Force Base. He was visiting friends for the weekend in his hometown when he met Penny.

Stewart was a cut above Penny's other boyfriends in every way. He was tall and even a bit handsome in his sleek airman's suit. He had the polite reserve of a military man: yes ma'am-ing my mother and yes sir-ing my father in a way that made him seem both older and younger than he was.

Most importantly for us, Penny just seemed better when she was with him. The cloud of melancholy that had settled on her after she'd lost the babies lifted, and the whole incident seemed to quickly fade into a terrible but remote memory. It was because of Jon, I was more convinced than ever.

"You know," my mother told me on the phone right after they'd met

Stewart for the first time, "I had a dreadful boyfriend right before I met you father."

"You did?" I was surprised. Both because it's always surprising that your parents were young once, and because it was hard to imagine my sensible mother choosing the wrong man.

"Yes. I was young and stupid. He was not nice at all," she said in a way that made me understand that she meant abusive. He'd even convinced her to steal some money from her boss and lie to her own parents. She was ashamed of all of it but said it gave her perspective too; she'd never done anything like it before or since. Maybe that's what Jon had been for Penny: just an aberration.

But now, there was Stewart, disciplined, solid, straight-and-narrow Stewart, a massive upgrade from the dreadful Jon, on whom we placed all of our grief and anger. This time when my sister said she was getting married, I hoped she meant it.

Liz Came Here to Forget

A T FIRST I'm ashamed of my meltdown, but later it feels as though I've passed some initiation rite, and now I talk to Gemma almost every day. The next week, Edward is having Gianluca and the team over for dinner, and Gemma insists I come. She worries about him, she says, rattling around in that mansion by himself. And she loves the team, but the team is trouble; it goes without saying that Gianluca is doubly so.

"I know Ed's all charm and polish on the surface, but he's really quite a mess underneath. I feel it's my duty to keep an eye on him. Otherwise, he'll just drink too much and sleep with floozies."

Edward is an exotic species for me. I knew plenty of people who partied their faces off, especially in the off-season. Even Luke—with his impossible drive—was always having to be pulled back from the edge. But the skiers who were wild were *wild* in every sense of the word, and Edward is so polished, so self-contained. And though the two could hardly be more different physically, there's a recklessness in Edward that reminds me of Luke, though it seems self-destructive rather than what Luke's is: a cocky, shortsighted invincibility. If he has the successful run he's meant to in Vancouver, he'll be unstoppable. I have to remember that he's no longer my problem.

The night of the dinner party, Edward is cooking and Gemma and I put place settings around the massive walnut dining table. Edward is a phenomenal cook. He loves Mexican food, which he's making tonight. I can't imagine where he's learned this. But this is special, he explains, because it's impossible to get down here.

"Try this," he says, offering some of the mole he's making to Cali, who's just come into the kitchen to investigate. The team is drinking wine by the fireplace with Gemma, but Gianluca has not yet appeared. He's on his way, almost an hour late. No one seems too invested in punctuality here.

"Oh god that's good." Cali smiles.

"You have no idea how difficult it is to find ancho chilis down here, they are absolute wimps about spice. It's maddening, you can't find them anywhere."

A melodious cello tune begins, and Edward smiles.

"Ahhh . . . the Bach. Yo-Yo Ma. Perhaps it's a bit of a cliché, but I love it," he says.

"It's pretty," I agree.

In the sitting room, someone groans. "We can't dance to this!"

"You can dance later, you heathens!" Edward says, turning back to the stove where something is ready to be taken off the burner and something else is ready to be added. I lean from the doorway and see that Valentina has gotten off the couch and is up on her toes, doing ballet moves as the others cheer. Anders from Norway gets up and lifts her tiny frame.

It takes me a moment to realize that Cali has frozen in place, her eyes staring into the middle distance. I put my wineglass down carefully, as though she might shatter if I make any sudden moves.

"Cali? Are you okay?" I put my fingertips lightly on her shoulder, and she jolts back to life.

"Yeah." She shakes her head and tries to smile, but it slips from her. "I'm sorry, I . . . excuse me."

Edward looks up from the stove as Cali pushes off and heads abruptly to the patio. "What happened?"

I shrug. "I don't know."

He looks anxiously at some delicately caramelizing onions. "Well, is she all right?"

Why is he asking me? I barely know Cali. Should I have some intuition here?

"I'll go check on her."

Cali is sitting on one of the pool chaises, staring into the glowing blue of the water beneath her.

"Cali?" I say. She turns to me and her eyes are shining. "I'm sorry," I say. I hate it when someone catches me crying. "I can leave you alone. Or not."

Her fingers meet her cheek and quickly whisk away a tear. She shrugs but smiles in a way that makes me think she'd like me to stay. I gingerly take a seat on the chaise next to her.

"You must think I'm a weirdo," she says after a few moments.

"No."

"That piece. I freaked out, I just . . ." Her voice catches.

"Well," I say, feeling like I have to give her something if this is the moment we're going to become friends. "Will it make you feel better to know that I had a panic attack when I was here on Saturday? I slept in the guest room after Edward gave me a horse tranquilizer. So whatever it is, no judgment."

"That does actually make me feel better."

"Do you want to tell me what's going on? If you don't, that's okay."

"I might as well. I keep trying to convince myself that I'm over it, but if I'm falling apart at a cello suite, then clearly I'm not. I know I didn't tell you much about New York. I spent two years as a cellist with the Philharmonic and was on my way to becoming a principal. Truthfully, it was the only thing I ever wanted since I was a little girl." For a moment, she's lost in a reverie.

"What happened?"

"The director was—still is—Francesco Bellini, this venerable Italian who was known for being a kingmaker. It felt like he took special notice of me right away—but then, it was hard to know if that was because of my talent or because I stuck out. It will probably not shock you to know

I was the only black woman in my section. To be honest, I didn't even care why. He was so charming, incredibly charismatic. He felt like a father figure. I trusted him. In the beginning, he brought out the best in me, I was improving so fast. The better I got, the more attention he paid me, and it was honestly addictive. Eventually, he started wanting to work with me privately. I'm sure you're worldly enough to imagine where this story is headed. I was so naive, he'd been married for thirty years to this stunning woman. Evidently, there were all kinds of rumors about him, but no one thought to warn me.

"It started with rubbing my shoulders, you know, loosening them up to help my strokes," she continues, rolling her eyes, "then it was pushing my legs apart to adjust my stance. And it just escalated . . . He would touch himself while I played." I'm frozen in horror, listening to her. "It was awful. At first, it was just a major distraction and my playing got worse. But then he lost his goddamn mind and told his wife he was going to leave her for me. Mind you, I never cosigned any of this! But the story becomes that we're having an *affair.*"

"That's ludicrous."

"Well, the media didn't care so much about the facts. I was one of the youngest cellists there, so it seemed like I stood to gain from his attentions. Oh, the irony! He was the one who ruined *my* career. *He's* doing fine, mind you. His wife took him back; apparently, this is something he just *does* every few years. He never follows through with it, it's just some little temper tantrum. He has to keep his wife on her toes or something? For the sadistic pleasure of it? I don't know. It just doesn't usually get out to the press."

"How *did* it get out to the press?" I ask.

"Oh, that's the worst part," says Cali. "Well, one of the worst parts. There was only one other young cellist, Brian. I thought we were friends. There was never proof and of course he denies it, but he's the only one I told about what Bellini was doing. I was so worried and I felt that if something really awful happened . . ." There was no need for Cali to elaborate on what that something really awful was. "And I'd never told anyone else about his creepy advances. I thought no one would believe me. And Brian benefitted, certainly, from getting me out of the way."

"How has this man not gotten sued?" I ask.

"He's a revered, wealthy white man. Does that not answer your question?"

"Yeah," I say, "I guess it does."

"The arts community is so insular and New York is such a small town at the end of the day. It's one of those stupid things: the more you try to defend yourself, the guiltier you seem. People were all too ready to believe that I wanted to take advantage."

"But even if you *had* had an affair with him, he's the one who's married, he's the one who is in a position of power," I say.

"Yes, if this were being tried in the court of women's studies, I'd definitely win. Sadly, in the court of public opinion, the woman loses every time."

I exhale. "Yeah, isn't that the truth."

For a moment, we're both quiet.

"Sorry," she says, "that was a lot."

"No," I say. "Don't worry. I . . . well, not to make any of this about me. But I do understand. It's a long story, but my career got fucked by a drama I didn't create, so yeah, I get it."

"I'm sorry to hear it, but it's nice to know I'm not the only one. I'm playing hard at being the carefree expat. Some days I almost believe it. Other days . . ."

"Don't you miss playing?" I ask. I suddenly see more clearly why I was so drawn to Cali, even though neither of us had been forthcoming about our pasts. She has the sheen of the extraordinary. She knew what it was like to give her life over to a singular goal, only to see it swept away in one catastrophic incident. I feel something similar to what I'd felt with Luke and Blair all those years, like I was with my same animal. "You must have worked your whole life to get where you were."

"Hell yes, I miss it. Why do you think I fell apart over a little bit of Bach? That was my audition piece for the Philharmonic. I practiced it so much it's probably imprinted on my DNA at this point. My life used to revolve around the cello. I just lived in this bubble where nothing else mattered. I guess that probably made me kind of oblivious to anything

155

else. I'd barely even dated when it happened. But yes. I miss being onstage. I miss the crowds and the other musicians. I miss the long black skirts and the smell of resin, all of it. But being here, with the team, it helps. And dancing. There's no cello in tango music, so it feels safe. And I'm obsessed with practicing. I need something to practice every day or I fall apart."

"I hear that," I say.

"Yeah?" She looks up at me for the first time in a while. For a moment, I think I might take the opening. But then I think about Luke. I think about how many times I called Emily, how eventually she just stopped answering.

"You know, I can picture you as a musician," I say instead.

"You'd barely recognize me," Cali says.

"Really?" I ask.

"Oh yeah. Here, I'll show you," she says, picking up her phone and scrolling through a photo album. She hands it to me. It's a sleek professional photo of Cali onstage with her cello. She's wearing an ankle-length black skirt and a conservative white blouse with a pussy bow. Her hair is longer and coiled tightly at the nape of her neck in a wide chignon.

"It's like you in a parallel universe," I say. I've only ever seen Cali in bright colors, short shorts, with her short hair that shows the shape of her uncannily perfect head.

"I know," Cali says, "it's been quite the hair journey. I felt like I had to wear it straight all the time, it was so much work. It literally took me hours and about a half-dozen products."

"I like it now," I say. "I mean both are pretty but . . ."

"I like it now too," she says, smiling wistfully and running her fingers over her scalp. "And it's a good thing, I don't think I could have made it through TSA with my hair arsenal."

"What are you girls doing out here? Dinner's ready *and* Gianluca finally decided to grace us with his presence and . . . oh dear, serious faces! Everything okay?"

"Yes! I was . . ." I say, manically trying to cover for Cali in Gemma's sudden presence. "Just feeling a little out of it."

Cali smiles. "Gemma knows," she tells me. "and Edward. They're the only ones."

"That dreadful old bastard," Gemma says, coming to Cali's side and rubbing her back.

"I'm fine," Cali insists. "I just wish I could stop walking around feeling like I'm made of glass."

"You will," Gemma says. "Someday it will fade, I promise."

"I know you're right," Cali says, leaning her head on Gemma's shoulder. "I just wonder where to go from here."

"That's what we're *all* trying to figure out. It's what everyone comes to this city for: to forget who they were, become someone new. God knows I can't stay forever though."

"Poor Anders," Cali says, smiling at her.

"Anders? Like Cali's Anders?" I ask.

"Not exactly. Didn't you know? We're strictly forbidden to sleep with our dance partners," Cali says.

"That seems like a really good way to get everyone to sleep with their dance partners."

Gemma and Cali laugh.

"Nah," Cali says, "getting on the outs with G isn't worth it. I love him, but he can be . . ."

"Mind-bendingly petty," Gemma finishes.

"Loyalty is important to him," Cali adds diplomatically. "Besides, it's just our partners; no one else is verboten."

"And Gianluca is allowed to sleep with anyone, of course."

"Doesn't he have a girlfriend?" I ask.

"Oh, Angelina? *Girlfriend* is a strong word. Depends on the day," Cali says.

"You will be surprised to learn that Gianluca is quite lovelorn."

"You're right," I say. "That is surprising. And what about you, Cali? Any on-team dalliances?"

Cali cringes. "Maybe Rodrigo."

"Oh, he's so beautiful. Was it amazing?" Gemma asks.

"I've seen you two dancing," I say, thinking of the party that weekend. "Looked hot."

Cali shakes her head.

"*No*. Why?!" Gemma asks.

"Well," Cali says, smiling, glancing inside to make sure Rodrigo isn't about to walk in on this conversation. "It turns out his dancing skills do not translate as well as I had hoped."

"Oh nooooo," Gemma says.

"I mean, he's so beautiful!" Cali says. "And trust me, it only gets better when the clothes come off."

"So far, so good," Gemma says. "Tell us! And when was this?"

"Oh, months ago. We were at the social and we danced until like three a.m., and it was amazing. Just . . . erotic. But then, okay, first weird thing. He lives with his parents, so we obviously can't go to his house. So instead, he takes me to a *telo*."

"A what now?" I ask.

"You haven't heard of these yet? The 'love' hotels?"

I look at her, baffled. Gemma is beside herself with laughter. "A telo!" she squeals. "Oh it's too good."

"Let me educate you," Cali says. "You know people here live with their parents until they're like thirty, so when they need to go smash their boyfriends or girlfriends, they go to a *telo* and rent rooms by the hour."

"Yikes!"

"It's a fact of life here," Gemma says. "They think it's absolutely no big deal. Of course, people use them to have affairs as well, but that's for the married crowd. I gather the lunch rush at telos is all people shagging their coworkers."

"Right. So, anyway," Cali continues, "I hadn't been to one yet, but I'm not *so* shocked, and some of them are actually pretty nice, I've heard."

"And the one our fair Rodrigo took you to?"

"Ye-ah. I think it must be the student discount version. So, so bad. Like red velvet, heart-shaped bed, shag carpet, the works. I half expected Austin Powers to burst out of the closet. The worst part of it is, I think it's funny, but the kid is in full seduction mode."

"Oh dear," Gemma says.

"Indeed. Anyway, you know how it is, once you've decided to bone, it's hard to turn back. And it's been a while, so I'm willing to get past the bad decor, and at this point I've had some wine and we've been dancing this amazing tango all night. I'm still in the place. So I decide to just forge on and be relieved that he's not suggesting we break open the costume closet."

"Costume closet? You're joking," I say.

"I'm absolutely not. Anyway, I forge on. And you guys, it's bad."

"Bad how?" I say.

"Yes, please dish," Gemma says.

"In about every way that sex can be bad. It was as though I were a machine that he had no idea how to operate. He tried to go down on me . . ."

"Wait, *tried?*" I ask.

"He was down there but there was this tongue darting and . . . oh, I can't, it was too awful. I wanted to pull him back up and interrogate him: like, whoever told you to do that to a vagina, they must be stopped."

"What did you *do?*" Gemma asks.

"I pulled him up and kept going."

"And??"

"Jackrabbit hammering for about three minutes and then it was over. The worst part is, we have the room for an hour, and at that point we're like ten minutes in."

"Was he mortified?" Gemma asks.

"No!" Cali says, slamming her hand on the armrest of the chaise. "He didn't even have the sense to be embarrassed. He just *dozed off.*"

"What did you do?!" I ask.

"I'm alone in the tackiest hotel room in the universe, with my failed little Don Juan taking a nap. I raided the minibar obviously. Then he wakes up and wants to go again. At this point, I've downed two minibottles of tequila so I figure why not, everyone deserves a second chance."

"And?"

"I've now revised that maxim to: *Bad sex once, shame on you. Bad sex twice, shame on me.*"

"Oh, Cali, I'm so sorry," I say.

"Poor love! That is the worst," Gemma says.

She rolls her eyes and shrugs. "I mean, it's *fine*. No lasting harm done, I suppose, but there's just something so"—she wrinkles her nose—"soul-sucking about bad sex. I remember my brothers used to make this joke when they were teenagers that sex was like pizza, still pretty good even when it's terrible. I disagree. Sex is like . . . I don't know, a soufflé, if you botch it, it's just a big mess!"

"Have you made a soufflé before?" Gemma asks, seeming distracted and impressed by this detail.

"No, what do I look like, a midcentury housewife? But you know what I mean, it's like why bother if it's bad? You just think: Why am I even here? Meanwhile, he's completely unaware that he was terrible. It's just ignorant to be with a woman and not be able to read any of the signs that she's not enjoying herself, you know?"

We both nod.

"I guess he needs a good teacher?" Gemma says.

"Yeah, well, it's not going to be me."

"I think every man needs that first girlfriend to learn with. Someone who they actually have a bond with who can communicate with them and be honest with them." I'm thinking of Luke now, irritatingly. Even though he'd been with other girls, we were different, he told me—with me it was all new again. "Not that that should be your job, obviously."

"Yeah. To tell you the truth," Cali says, "he was only the third person I've ever been with. Is that dismal or what?"

Quite the opposite. I was struck with envy, because at one point I'd been able to count my lovers on one hand as well. After my breakup, my breakdown, I decided I might as well give casual sex a try. I wasn't some girly girl, I wasn't going to get *all emotional* about some guy I didn't know. Wasn't this just another use for the body? But whatever I was looking for, it wasn't to be found in sex with strangers. For one thing, I was always wasted. I would find myself floating in and out of my body while it was happening, alternately grasping at transcendence that was nowhere within reach and trying to escape from the too-closeness of the stranger inside of me.

"Wow! I feel like a proper harlot now," Gemma says. "But you're right that every man needs a great teacher. Good thing Edward and I had each other."

My jaw drops. "I thought things weren't romantic with you two!"

Gemma waves it off. "Oh they're not, this was twenty years ago! At any rate, Cali, if you've only been with three people, Buenos Aires is the perfect place to expand your horizons."

"Maybe I'll just stick to dancing. It's like you get all the good parts of sex without the disappointment, without the inevitable letdown, the shame spiral, whatever."

"Oh, honey. Let's not give up on the whole enterprise, shall we?"

I consider this. Do I not owe it to myself to explore beyond Luke? To have some sort of awakening? I need someone real—someone who moves me a little—to put between me and Luke. After all, he had lovers before me and—I realize with stomach-dropping dread—has almost certainly had lovers since. That's what I came here to do, isn't it? To disappear. To forget.

Penny Is Getting Married!

T HE WEEKEND Penny and Captain Stewart Granger got married at the historic downtown Roosevelt Inn in Coeur d'Alene is my last truly good memory of her.

To the surprise of no one, Penny had a big wedding. She invited all of her high school friends and all of her coworkers from the clinic, as well as just about everyone else she'd ever known. Penny had been the kind of little girl who dreamed of her wedding day, who dressed up as a bride for Halloween when she was eight *and* when she was ten, who married off her Barbie dolls at every opportunity. She wanted the big dress, the bridesmaids, the tiered cakes, the whole shebang. My parents, having seen worse than I had, were happy to indulge her: as though the maelstrom of taffeta and buttercream could wash away all of the darkness that preceded it.

She was getting married in August, so fortunately I was able to come see her more frequently leading up to the wedding. Other than a handful of training camps, summers for me meant rehabbing whatever was injured, time in the gym, and cross-training on my mountain bike. I came up one weekend to go with Penny and my mother to Marcella's bridal boutique in Spokane to look for a dress. My mother and I sat on plush white couches, drinking glasses of champagne while the attendant wrestled Penny into the complicated gowns.

The first dress Penny came out in was a strapless ballroom gown with a voluminous tulle skirt. The dress engulfed her petite, busty frame, but Penny was beaming.

"Well?" she asked us.

"Oh . . . well, do you like it?" my mom said diplomatically.

"I feel like a princess," Penny said, gazing at herself in the three-way mirror. "Katie, what do you think?"

"You kind of look like a cupcake."

Her face fell.

"I mean you look like a *beautiful* cupcake. But, Penny, it's a lot."

"You just don't want to have a dress that wears you," my mom added.

Penny huffed. "Sorry we can't all be six feet tall."

I knew I wasn't the best pick for something like wedding dress shopping, but Emily hadn't been able to make it. I was also the maid of honor. I'd always expected it to be Emily, but something had shifted between them. Penny didn't talk about her as much as she once had, and when I'd called Emily to see if she could come today, she'd made excuses and hurried off the phone. I'd asked Penny if something had happened, but she said of course not, they were both just busier now and didn't see each other as much since they weren't roommates anymore.

I wouldn't find out until years later what my parents already knew: during the final year they'd lived together, before she moved in with Jon, Penny had been taking Emily's half of the rent and then, for whatever reason, not using it to pay their rent. It wasn't until they received an eviction notice that it came to a head, and then Penny denied everything. The girls had such a history that they remained friends after, but they were never the same.

"Well, this is only the first dress," the attendant said now, saving the day. "Let's keep moving! It always takes a little while to find the right silhouette."

Penny gave her a brave smile and nodded. I feared this would be added to Penny's list of ways in which I'd let her down; she'd always had a knack for keeping score. As she headed back to the dressing room, I looked at my mom helplessly and she smiled. "It's fine," she whispered, "there are better dresses for her. She just had to get the Cinderella one out of her system."

There was no talking her out of a ball gown, but we found her one with a straighter skirt that nipped in at her natural waist and flattered her figure. Seeing her in the dress, my mom and I both choked up. My sister, getting married. It was a new beginning.

Because Penny never spoke about the pregnancy, it was easy enough to pretend the whole incident had never happened. It was a strange paradox with my sister: she could hold a grudge like crazy, but her own mistakes seemed to evaporate from her mind almost immediately.

Luke came with me to the wedding and seemed a bit agitated. Normally, he was super relaxed in the summertime, and he was flying high after his back-to-back gold medal and world championship wins; I couldn't imagine what his deal was. The morning before the rehearsal dinner, we splurged on pancakes at Benny's, a diner we'd both loved as kids, and I brought it up.

"Hey," I asked him. "What's going on with you, you're acting strange."

"No I'm not," he said defensively, plunging his fork into a many layered bite of pancakes and downing it.

I cocked my eyebrow at him, and he relented.

"I dunno . . . weddings are weird."

"They're weird?"

He looked like he wanted to crawl out of his skin. We'd been together for years by then, and on the rare occasions when Luke decided he needed to discuss how he felt about something, he squirmed like a convict with a bad rash. The first few times, I was sure he was breaking up with me; now I knew better. Our mutual successes—though mine were a bit more modest—had brought us closer.

"Spit it out, Luke."

He scratched the back of his head. "Blair was asking me when I thought we might get married."

Now it was my turn to squirm. "Blair asked you *what*? Why would he ask you that?"

"He just said, you know, we've been together a long time. You probably like, wanted me to put a ring on it at some point, you know?"

"Blair said that?"

"Those weren't his exact words. But girls get weird at weddings, so. . ."

"Oh yeah?" I smiled now. "Girls get weird?"

"You know what I mean!" He laughed. "I don't want you to think . . . I mean someday obviously but . . ."

"Oh god, please stop," I said. "I mean, yes, someday. But I want a matching gold medal before we start talking about matching gold bands, okay?"

A wide smile took over his face. "This is why I love you, Bomber. Well, one of many reasons."

Luke wasn't great about expressing himself, but I thought I understood. It was why I loved him too. His focus sharpened mine. We were skiing's golden couple. Glory before anything else.

"What the hell, Blair?" I said, thinking out loud.

"It's fine, he's just being protective. He doesn't want me wasting your time. Which, I'm not. Katie, you know that, right?" He turned momentarily serious again.

"Luke, of course I know that. Do you think I'm wasting yours?" Marriage was something I couldn't wrap my head around yet at twenty-four. I wanted to make my own life mean something before joining it with someone else's in such an official way.

Now, he laughed, and, at last, the tension dispersed. "I love you."

"I love you too."

⸙

The night before Penny's wedding is one I'll remember forever. I try to hold on to it because in some ways, it was my last glimpse of Penny as she was, the Penny I remember from my childhood.

We were all staying at the Roosevelt for three nights during the wedding festivities. After the rehearsal dinner, five of us—Penny, Stewart, Emily, Luke, and me—went to the hotel bar to have another drink that turned into several. We laughed as Penny and Emily begged the piano player to play "Sweet Caroline" and "Tiny Dancer" and we all sang along off-key. Stewart was the most cheerful I'd ever seen him, the top buttons of his shirt undone. He and Luke—both guy's guys—got along well. Stewart's upbringing had been a bit hardscrabble, and this, I'd learned upon meeting his very sweet family, was the reason for his drive and discipline. His family was proud of him and they adored Penny, the smart, pretty girl from the nice, middle-class family. I got the sense they were a little overwhelmed by the wedding, even though it wasn't especially lavish.

That night, Stewart stayed in another room—holding to tradition—and Emily and I stayed over in the bridal suite with Penny, poring over the old photo albums that Emily had brought along with her. Emily and I had never spoken about the pregnancy after our one strange conversation, but no one wanted to think of that now. That night, it felt like we'd gone back to a time before Penny lied about strange things or pilfered rent checks. We were girls again.

The next day my father would walk Penny down the aisle with tears in his eyes, a cousin's toddler would make everyone laugh when she hammed it up as the flower girl, the nurses from Penny's office would get roaring drunk and tackle one another to catch the bouquet, and Penny and Stewart would dance their first dance to Billie Holiday's "I'm Yours"—which had been my grandparents' song—making everyone cry. The next day, as we watched her, it was impossible to believe that everything was not going to get better from here. Seeing her get married, it was as though my parents and I let out a collective sigh of relief, a breath we'd been holding for years. This wedding would fix things.

But the night before belonged to Penny and Emily and me—the three sisters. Whatever came next, that night was real. I hold on to it because, in some sense, I would never see my sister again.

Liz Finds a Wonder Drug

"OKAY," HE says as the long melancholic tango comes to an end. "That's probably enough for tonight." It's only now that I realize that the hour slated for my lesson with Gianluca has long since passed. Ordinarily, he plays a bit of a song and then stops the music to break down what we've just done, go over additional technicalities, and such. But tonight, at some point, he'd just let the music play and we kept dancing. I feel drugged from dancing with him, high off the elemental relief I get from it.

There was a feeling I lived for during races, a brief few moments when my mind and body felt perfectly fused, when my body was working as hard as it possibly could and my mind was fully engaged—taking in the terrain, calculating where I needed to be on the next turn, preparing for the jump I knew was coming at the end of the course. There was no space for anything other than the moment I was in. I never expected to find that feeling again, and, impossibly, I've found an echo of it here. When G steps away from me for a moment, I feel the jarring sense of leaving it.

"Okay," I say. I feel the effects of the dance leeching from my veins too quickly. G smiles at me and turns back toward the office. For a moment, I stand there, uncertain about what I'm meant to do now. Everyone else has long since left; our lesson started late to begin with, at nine o'clock. Because G is working these lessons into an already full schedule, we squeeze them in when we can, as frequently as we can—I'd be here every day if I could, running through my savings like a junkie. I like the idea that he is making room for me, though for all I know, he needs the cash. How much does Edward put in to keep this place afloat? What does their mysterious bargain entail?

"Come on," he says without turning around. My feet take me along like we're still dancing and I'm simply following. Tango, it seems, is a wonder drug: a way of being close to someone without the messiness of sex or love, a potent but temporary hit of both. A place you can go with a stranger but leave unscathed by shame and heartache.

I've never seen the back office before and I don't think students are normally allowed in. It's shabby and cozy with an exciting air of secrecy. There are scraps of costumes and extra pairs of worn practice shoes piled in the corner, a box of the T-shirts the team wears. G sits on the carpet with his back resting against a large, overstuffed, ramshackle sofa. There's a bottle of whiskey and two glasses beside him. I gingerly sit down next to him, slipping my heels off of my pleasantly aching feet. He pours me a glass without asking.

We've just spent over an hour with our cheeks pressed up against one another's, but that was with the veil of the dance shrouding us. Sitting here with him now feels nearly postcoital, a fog of intimacy hanging over us still. Sometimes after Luke and I had sex, he would lie there on his back and, without warning, all of his fears would come tumbling out in a steady stream: he'd be a failure, he'd let everyone down, underneath everything, he was a fraud who'd convinced everyone he was a champion, and that sooner or later the truth would come out. These confessions were notable in their rarity; on the slope and in the start house and at the foot of the hill and the bar and the gym and on television, Luke was cocksure and brash. He was always the only thing that stood between him and being the best: he'd never quite shaken off the rebellious streak he'd developed after his parents' divorce. I remembered Blair and me physically dragging him from bars in Park City when he started looking for someone to fight. But once I'd seen the soft underside of his arrogant veneer, I knew it was there all the time. Fragments would suddenly reveal themselves to me, even in a roomful of people. I knew too that I was the only one who could see it. I could never only be his friend after that.

I sip the whiskey. G stares down into his glass.

"You were good tonight," he says quietly, turning toward me with a hint of a smile. "You've had a breakthrough."

I try not to let how thrilled I am show. "It felt different tonight."

"Tell me," G says, letting his head fall back. His eyelids always look a little heavy, like he's being lulled by some music only he can hear.

"It's hard to put into words."

"Try," he says, "for me." He puts his hand on my bare knee.

"Well . . ." What can I say that won't make me sound like I'm in love with him? Because, though I know I'm not, I feel elements of it when we're dancing: the closeness, the opening, the freedom of it, without all of the doubt and comedown. "At first, I was thinking about the steps, but then I wasn't, it just . . . we were moving together and it felt, not like we were one body exactly, but like we were in this perfect tandem. It felt freeing, it took me out of my head, like suddenly I had no past and no future. Just here and now with you and the music connecting us at a thousand tiny points."

"Liz," he says, a departure from my nickname, but still not, of course, my name, "that's beautiful."

"I've never felt anything quite like that." I'm breathless now, it's been so long since I spoke to anyone like this. I say the words before I can get self-conscious about how it all sounds. "Not with another person, any-way. Only on the mountain."

I let it hang there for a moment, as though it might explain itself, deciding he might just take it as some sort of metaphor. His hand moves from my knee, his fingers trace the inside of my thigh.

"What mountain?" he finally asks.

"Before I came here. In my old life, that is, I was really into skiing," I say, telling him, not telling him.

"Yeah? I've never been skiing. I bet you were great at it."

"Pretty much." I nod, and he laughs.

Before I came here, I didn't exist outside of skiing, and not talking about it is more difficult than I'd imagined. And if I could in this moment, I'd fold myself into G. He feels safe. He's stroking my thigh, but it feels more affectionate than sexual, or it feels both. It feels intimate. He's my coach, and coaches are our confessors, the holders of safe spaces and secrets.

"Tiger, that explains a lot about you," he says. "I should have known I was in the presence of greatness." I feel something that's been deadened in my chest come back to life a little. I do want him to know I'm great, or at least that I was. "Why'd you quit?"

"I got injured."

"I'm sorry to hear that. So when you say dancing reminds you of the mountain, I'm curious, what does that mean?"

I shrug. The panacea of dancing with him is wearing off and I am suddenly aware that I have made myself vulnerable by telling him so much already. My sweat has turned cold on my skin. I refill my whiskey glass without asking and take a long sip. He smiles.

"Back in the vault, huh?"

"What?"

"Since I've met you, you've been on the defensive, and tonight, for the first time, you were different." He takes his hand away from my leg, and I wish he wouldn't.

"I'm not defensive," I say, sounding defensive. "I'm just private. What's wrong with that? I know putting the intimate details of your life on Facebook or whatever is all the rage right now, so pardon me."

"Is that what you think I do?" He's amused.

"Well, no, not *you*, just . . . people," I say. What I want to say is *women*, women are expected to be vulnerable. When men are tough, we call them masculine, and when they're vulnerable we practically throw them a fucking parade. But women are just expected to go around with our hearts hanging out like it's the natural way of things.

"Can I tell you the real meaning of your nickname?"

I feel the blood draining from my face. I shrug, as if to say, you can't hurt me, even though it's clear to both of us that he can.

"It was this image that came to mind the first time I danced with you. I thought: this big, strong, beautiful girl will tear you to shreds if you try to get too close to her."

I nod slowly. Am I insulted by this or kind of impressed with myself? I can't decide. A tiger sounds like someone who could protect herself.

"And what was I tonight, a kitten?"

"No, Liz," he says, "tonight you were a woman."

I want to blow it off, but how can I? Tonight was the first time I have felt human in so long.

"And what about you?" I say, letting myself smile. "What animal are you?"

He laughs. "I don't know, an aging stallion?"

"You still strut like a prize stud."

"The important thing is that I still have my balls, Liz. I haven't let the world make a gelding of me."

"Have a thing for horses then?" I say.

He shrugs. "I grew up around them," he says. "My father owned an estancia in Chascomús."

I wouldn't have pegged him as having grown up a rich kid. But the estancias, as least as I understand them, are fancy, like the vast ranches in Montana or Wyoming not far from where I grew up. This is definitely true of the ones that are as close to Buenos Aires as Chascomús.

"You know I've heard some pretty colorful stories about you," I say.

"I'm sure. Do tell."

"Let's see: That you're secretly a disgraced Spanish matador. That you're the illegitimate son of Juan Perón. That your father was a Nazi general." I realize as the words come out of my mouth that the last one, if it's true, would be devastating and I'm sorry I said it. "But I'm guessing none of those are true." I nearly throw in the story about the yacht, but I don't want to betray Gemma.

He laughs and shrugs.

"You're just the son of some perfectly nice rancheros," I say.

"I am the son," he says, downing the rest of his glass, "of ghosts. It's late." He gets to his feet. "*Escucha,* there's a *milonga* we all go to the first

Sunday of each month, it's off the Caminito on Pinzón. It's a little café—Calle Roja—and the owner likes to sing tango standards when he closes up in the evening. We get there around one a.m. The team will be there, of course, but if you tell any of the other students, I'll have to kill you," he says, smiling.

I put my hands up. "Not a word. It's been fun getting to know everyone on the team."

"They're my family," he says.

"Do you ever think of growing the team or . . ." I say, trying to sound casual.

He smiles. "Maybe. Why? Are you interested?"

I shrug, knowing how obvious I am. He nods, considering it.

"You could be good," he says. "We could get your dancing up to speed. You'd need to lose some weight though."

He says it so casually. Mortifyingly, I get tears in my eyes almost immediately. I nod, trying and failing to take this as I would have when I was an athlete. But I'm not an athlete anymore, I'm not anything anymore.

"Hey," he says, reaching for my hand. "Hey, don't take it personally. Listen, you're gorgeous. There's just a difference between what I think is sexy and what looks good onstage."

The bitter with the sweet. My head is spinning.

"Yeah, of course. Listen, I've got to get going. I'll see you Sunday, okay?"

Penny Is Going to Be Fine

I T WASN'T surprising that Penny started trying to get pregnant so fast—she'd always wanted to be a mom—but when it became her single-minded obsession immediately after the wedding, the past began to feel like prelude. The ghosts of the two little girls, shrouded in mystery, wouldn't leave me. I couldn't find a way to tell these fears to Luke or anyone else. I couldn't say it aloud, but I was scared to death of her getting pregnant again.

"I just don't think it's healthy to be *so* focused on it," was all I could manage to express to Luke and Blair.

"Well, she's a newlywed," Blair said, smiling. "And her husband is great, right? You like him?"

"Sure. I mean yeah, she seems more stable with him." We were still all clinging to the idea that Jon had been the source of Penny's troubles and that Stewart represented the solution. "I just don't see what the hurry is. She's only twenty-seven!"

"She wants that baby like you want a gold medal," Luke said, not knowing quite how right he was. Penny and I shared a capacity for obsessiveness. She would try and try again until she got a child. We would both keep pushing our bodies until they gave us what we wanted.

"I have to have surgery," Penny told me on the phone one night, choking back tears. After months of trying, she'd been to a fertility specialist. "They have to remove scar tissue, from last time."

How can I explain the mental gymnastics I did then? Scar tissue, surgery, more proof that her lies about the babies had been in the details, not about their actual existence. They'd been there at some point, they'd left her with wounds. I held on to the delusion that Penny's lies were discrete, rather than a vein of poison that ran through her. Because the most mysterious of all was *why* she would lie about any of it.

After Penny's surgery, she immediately started fertility treatments, a monstrous-sounding process that she documented in prolific social media posts about injecting hormones into her belly, the hormonal and mood swings that mimicked pregnancy without any of the payoff, and, all the while, negative pregnancy test after negative pregnancy test. It was all made worse by her lupus, which was causing horrible bouts of insomnia and fatigue, swelling in her joints, and inexplicable nausea.

I worried about where she was getting the money to cover the fertility treatments. I offered to help out. After my bronze in Salt Lake and the hullabaloo around Luke and me, Red Bull had signed on as a sponsor and I had more cash than I'd ever had. She told me I didn't need to, but I wired the money.

After my initial unease, I'd become desperate for Penny to have a baby as well. A healthy baby would wipe the slate clean. The marriage had felt like a new beginning, but we were never going to be able to forget what happened until Penny had a living, breathing, healthy child. And Penny's need for a child seemed depthless. Nothing else could be enough.

When I was home visiting one week, I decided to surprise Penny at her office at the Kootenai Health Clinic to take her out to lunch. I hadn't seen her in months. I'd texted her that morning, so I knew she'd be at work. We hadn't planned to see one another until that evening.

"Hey, Beth," I said to the receptionist I'd known for years, one who'd danced at Penny's wedding.

"Hey, Katie!" She got up and gave me a hug. "It's so great to see you. What are you doing here?"

"I'm in town for a few days, I thought I'd come by and take Penny to lunch. Is she in with patients now?"

Beth looked confused.

"Penny's . . . not in."

"She isn't? I texted her earlier and she said she was on her way here."

"You'd better talk to Penny," Beth said, growing more uncomfortable by the moment.

"Beth . . ." I began, but the phone rang, and Beth put her finger up, her face apologetic. I gave her a meek wave and walked out, bewildered.

My heart was racing. Was this beginning all over again? Once you know someone is capable of lying, you're never on solid ground again.

That night, Penny and Stewart came to my parents' house for dinner. I meant to pull her aside and ask her about the office, but she preempted me. She was pregnant!

It felt like a buzzkill saying anything, but at last I mentioned it gingerly.

"Penny, I stopped by Kootenai this afternoon to take you to lunch."

"Oh," she said serenely, her face already beatific in pregnancy, "I went home early, I was having horrible joint pain. With the baby and my lupus, I have to be extra careful."

I nodded. Later, much later, I'd remember the look on Beth's face. Oh how powerful it is: the desire not to see the truth.

Liz Is Not Your Little Project

I TELL MYSELF I just need new clothes as I duck into a San Telmo boutique that I've peered into the windows of a dozen times. But, really, I'm dressing up for G. I'm hopeless at shopping for clothes and spend an hour parsing through the racks of the small shop before choosing a handful of things to try on. I buy a floaty, feminine skirt with a pattern of red flowers, something Katie never would have worn.

Embarrassingly, I'm imagining a movie sequence in which the heroine removes her eyeglasses, shakes down her hair from its topknot, and is revealed to have been beautiful all along. I can't go five minutes without replaying his comments from the other night: *You would need to lose some weight.* And instead of being mad, I just want to please him. I'm disgusted with myself.

Cali picks me up in a cab to take me with her to Calle Roja.

"Hey, you look great," she says. "I'm excited for you to come to the *milonga*. It's the only thing I look forward to more than the social."

Since the dinner party at Edward's, I've been spending a lot more time with Cali—filling the space between dancing and tours. Seeing how relieved she clearly feels having opened up, I wonder if I shouldn't as well. But then, Cali's story is nothing like mine. Cali and I mostly talk about

176

dance and Buenos Aires and gossip about Gianluca. She tells me how being here has saved her, how dancing has given her something she never thought she'd have again: a way to not just listen to music, but also to be right inside of it, to let it come through her. And the team itself—along with the studio and Gianluca—has given her community, a sense of being part of something bigger than herself. It's let her come back to life, to re-become herself.

We grow silent as we turn off into the entrance of La Boca. Caminito is a tourist trap, and during the day it's packed with people taking in the iconic multicolored houses, the tango dancers on every block, and the cheerful, cheeseball cafés and taverns. The neighborhood's Italian roots run deep and it even briefly seceded from Argentina and raised the Genoese flag in the late nineteenth century. But beyond the tiny area that's been sanitized for tourists, La Boca is a rough neighborhood: packed with shanties made from colorful corrugated iron and parts of old ships, the aroma of the neglected port assaulting anyone who gets too close.

"I've never been here at night," I say.

"We'll make sure the cab stays put until the door opens."

"Now I feel much better."

"Relax, it's so much fun. You just have to be smart in this neighborhood. Tourists don't come here at night, why do you think G loves it so much?"

"*Ocho-siete-seis Pinzón, ay está.*"

The driver is grandfatherly and seems reluctant to leave us. I assure him we're meeting friends, but secretly I'm relieved that he's obviously going to stand by while we get let in.

We knock twice and, after a moment of waiting, a beautiful dark-haired woman in her forties answers the door, cocking an eyebrow at us. I can hear the music from the street: the low growl of a burned-out voice carrying a melody in a way that makes the hair on the back of my neck stand up.

"*Sí?*"

Cali tells her we're with Gianluca. The woman widens the door, mak-

177

ing no other gesture of welcome. I turn and wave to our cabdriver, who shakes his head and drives away.

Calle Roja at any other time would look like an ordinary, slightly shabby Argentine café. The floorboards are smooth with wear, and the photographs on the wall are aged and yellow with cigar smoke. But at this moment, with the tables piled high and haphazard in the corner and the chairs pushed to the edges to create a dance floor, it's like something from an old film. The lighting is low, with giant candelabras blazing from the corners. The dancers are expert: there are some oldies who look like they've been at it for a century mixed in with young, impossibly sleek-looking couples who move with the precision and barely constrained drama of professionals. I spot several team members locked in with one another.

"There's G," Cali says, and I look to where he's standing in the corner, talking to a rotund older man. The sleeves of his shirt are rolled to his elbows, he has a glass of Fernet in his hand, a day's worth of scruff on his chin, and a smile on his face. My stomach lurches with a mix of desire and humiliation. Cali pulls me along.

"Ah good, you brought Liz," he says. He kisses Cali's cheek and then puts his arm around my neck in a proprietary way. I stiffen at his touch, but it makes him pull me closer.

"Oh," says the old-timer, "*qué bonitas*. Young ladies, I must insist that you dance with me this evening."

"You don't want to say no," G says exuberantly. "Horatio was practically there at the invention of tango."

"It's my bar, so I get to dance with the most beautiful women first. *Droit du seigneur*," says Horatio. "Also, I have to show cocky young *bailadors* like Gianluca how it's done, it's a service."

"Well that's the first time anyone has called me young in a while, *Viejo*, but I'll take it. You know"—Gianluca leans in, and I can smell the anise of the Fernet, feel the heat of his breath— "Horatio started this *milonga* when the junta was in power and tango was forbidden. He has an outlaw soul."

The song ends and the next one begins. Horatio extends a hand to Cali, which she delightedly accepts.

"We'll dance in a bit, Tiger," he says, leaning back against the bar top on his elbows. "What's your poison?"

"What's on offer?"

He glances over his shoulder. "Looks like Malbec and Fernet."

"Malbec."

He nods, pours me a paper cup, and hands it to me; as he does he studies me. I'm avoiding eye contact.

"You're not mad at me, are you?"

"Of course not," I say too quickly.

"Oh," he says, putting down his glass and looping his arms around my shoulders. "You are. I've hurt your feelings. *Cariño!* I forget how sensitive Americans are."

I feel at once unwieldy and yet at the same time so flimsy. I don't have anything to hang my self-worth on anymore. I'm a ghost of myself.

"I think you're beautiful," he says, but now I think I hear pity in his voice, and it makes me squirm. I take his arms off my neck.

"I'm *fine.* Anyway, tell me about Horatio."

"His father was a dock worker, like a lot of the people around here. But Horatio always had an artistic soul. He loves to sing; he'll do a set for us later. When the neighborhood became a tourist attraction during the day, he started his café, and he hired some of the best dancers around to lure people away from the Caminito. The man has vision, I'll tell you." G pivots to face me and leans in closer. I take what I hope is an inconspicuous deep breath to take in the smell of him. "During the day, he covers his little patch of sidewalk with a specially made temporary dance floor, much nicer than most of the ones on the main street. And so many great dancers love him: they'll come perform. So," he says, leaning in a fraction closer, "the wide-eyed tourists will be wandering down the Caminito, with all of these hucksters in their faces saying 'Sir! Madame! Come, come, best lunch special on the Caminito, best tango in Buenos Aires!' And these cheesy dancers doing bullfighter impressions, and then, they glance down an alley and what do they see but Horatio's little oasis? The canny son of a bitch. Of course, then it got listed as 'the best kept secret' on the Caminito in a half-dozen guidebooks, so now there's usually a long wait during the day. But his *milongas* are the soul of the place."

The next set begins and while Cali is scooped up by a younger dancer, G leads me to the floor and pulls me into a close embrace. The breaks between songs barely exist and when the set ends, G pulls back from me and looks into my eyes. I'm shocked by his expression because he looks as drugged as I feel. He puts both hands on my face and pulls my ear to his lips.

"Oh Tiger, Tiger. You're my special little project, you know? The way we dance, it makes me so badly want to fuck you, but I want to keep you too."

I feel my jaw drop but I have been so caught up with him that I don't see Angelina circling like a shark. Before I can respond, she pulls him away and unleashes a stream of Spanish too angry and fast for me to decipher. First, he's rolling his eyes but then he's trying to placate her. I realize I've been standing frozen on the dance floor, my eyes wide and my mouth gaping. Before long, the new set starts, and Horatio asks me to dance.

Two things are true at once that night: I never want to leave and I am longing to be away from the excruciating sight of G with another woman, someone young and beautiful and delicate. I grab a glass of wine with Cali and tell her what happened. The words are out of my mouth before I can worry about the fact that she's probably closer to him than to me.

"Are you surprised?" she asks. "You've met him."

"What does he mean he wants to keep me?"

Cali rolls her eyes. "Oh, well, that's a bit of a familiar refrain. For a lot of people, Buenos Aires is a stopover, and that makes G a stopover too. He gets very attached to the people in the studio. And then, he's always having a dramatic falling-out with someone. Not just the women either."

"Is he . . . ?"

"Oh no, I mean, not that I know of. I don't know, nothing about G would really surprise me. He never talks about his past in anything other than riddles. Rumors abound, as I'm sure you can imagine. People gossip about him all the time. Especially in the dance community, which is pretty tight-knit."

"Ugh, how awful." My skin crawls with the idea of people talking about me behind my back, the whispers I came thousands of miles to escape.

"Are you kidding?" Cali says. "He lives for it."

Penny Has a Daughter

FAILURE TO thrive. That's what they called it when Ava—out of NICU and home at last—still wasn't gaining weight or hitting her developmental milestones. It seemed like such a gentle term for something so terrible, a catchall phrase that encompassed none of the visceral stress and fear of having an unhealthy baby. *Failure to thrive,* as though she were a houseplant who'd been potted in the wrong soil. Health is, ultimately, what all new parents wish for their children, and it eluded poor, tiny Ava.

For the many months—though not quite nine, since Ava came early—of Penny's pregnancy, I felt as though I were holding my breath. I tried as best I could to put the last time out of my head. I envied Stewart and his family their uncomplicated anticipatory joy. For me, there was a nightmarish déjà vu to it all: I flew home (thankfully only from Park City this time) when Ava came unexpectedly early. At the hospital, I sat next to Penny, squeezing her hand. I kissed her forehead when they wheeled her away for a C-section. Penny returned from that other room on a gurney, tiny Ava with her tiny hands grasping at nothing behind the thick plastic of her incubator. Seeing them, I felt a strange cloud of doubt, like I couldn't be sure this baby was truly Penny's. I recognized that this was completely illogical, but when it came to my sister, I could no longer trust even what I saw with my own eyes. It wasn't that I thought of her as a liar, nothing that simple. It was more that I felt that reality itself became distorted when Penny was involved. This time, I hadn't dared to love Ava in anticipation of her arrival, so when I finally saw her, when I reached into the incubator to touch her tiny hand, a blinding rush of love hit me all at once.

Ava was born in March. My season had ended early when I'd caught an edge during one of my final races in San Sicario. I'd gone careening into the nets and shattered my left shinbone. I'd had to be airlifted off the hill and had undergone major surgery. I was still walking with crutches when Ava arrived early, so I moved back to Coeur d'Alene to rehab and be with my sister. For one thing, I needed to be away from the team; it was too hard to watch my healthy teammates moving around me, past me. As long as I came back for regular checkups, my coach was fine with me going home. Not being in Park City would help me resist pushing through the injury too soon, as my coaches knew I might otherwise do.

Luke didn't make much of a nurse, acting as though my injury might be catching. It was more than that too. Perhaps I was only projecting onto him, but it was as though he started to worry that I might not blossom into the greatness that everyone had predicted, that my bronze in Salt Lake was going to be the pinnacle of my career rather than the beginning. This made it impossible for me to discuss my fears about the injury or anything else with him. I talked to Blair instead. He came over as I was packing to head back to Coeur d'Alene.

"The doctors said you'll be fine in a few months, Katie," he said when I told him I was worried. "You've got time, you're going to come back and kill it in Turin."

"What if I don't though?"

The question hung. Blair had continued to have success as a tech skier but, just as I was, was more known for his relationship to Luke than anything. I knew he wanted to do well in Turin as much as I did.

"You know I believe in you, but you can't control for everything. None of us can. We'll all survive."

It was a kind of a sacrilege to admit that anything but the best could ever be enough. But it was a relief too. Skiers fell into two camps when it came to thinking about the future: there were those who squeezed in an education so they'd have something to fall back on, and those who so passionately disbelieved in life after skiing that they refused to make any other plans, some declaring they'd prefer to die on the mountain than work a nine-to-five and meaning it with every fiber of their being. Blair was majoring in quantitative social science at Dartmouth, focusing on the relationship between organized sports and low-income communities. He wanted to pass along his love for the sport, a love that was not so tied up with winning as Luke's was.

❧

I knew in my heart why I was nervous around Penny and the baby, but I refused to peel back the layers of my fear. We had all moved past it, I told myself. Penny was better, she was married to Captain Stewart now. She was stable and happy and it would all be fine. If only little Ava could make it through the next few weeks.

The NICU is a liminal space that feels like the worst kind of purgatory. Babies too small and fragile to be in the world take labored breaths and look out with shocked, uncertain eyes from their plastic enclaves. Terrified parents roam the halls like zombies. We made sure Penny was never alone: when Stewart wasn't there, my parents or I would be, holding Ava when we were allowed to and trying to remain cheerful in the air of the NICU, which was thick with worry and fear. We brought meals for Penny and books to read to Ava. Penny was admirably calm and seemed to have tapped into some deep reserves of resilience. It didn't occur to me then that she was perhaps *eerily* calm, considering the circumstances. Penny had always been at her best when she was in the center of a crisis; it's what made her so good at her job.

A month after her birth, to everyone's infinite relief, Ava was released from the hospital. Despite her sickliness, Ava was an adorable baby, and soon she was starting to smile back at us. Even in the face of all that worry, I loved being an auntie even more than I'd imagined I would. The smell of her head, the warmth of her delicate little body, brought out a primal love in me. One afternoon, my mom and I babysat while Penny ran some errands. Ava fell asleep on my chest and my mom snapped a photo of her there. I lay still, marveling at her, a deep joy coursing through me.

When my parents were with her, I saw a cautious happiness seeping through. The road had been long, Penny's pregnancy had been difficult, and the NICU had been hellish, but she was home now. She was safe.

But "failure to thrive" encompassed a great many small, interwoven evils: she wasn't gaining weight, her eyes weren't tracking properly, she wasn't able to absorb nutrients, so they'd had to attach a feeding tube, a fixture that remained on her even when they weren't using it. Penny told us she had to cut back to quarter time at work so that she could take her back and forth to all of her various doctor's appointments. She obsessed over her care, ceased to talk or, seemingly, think of anything else. Penny's Facebook page was a steady stream of updates about Ava's condition; the comments below were a tidal wave of support and sympathy from both friends and family and a great many people I'd never heard of from Penny's ballooning list of friends.

I hoped that Ava would be on the mend by the time I went back to Park City in the fall, but it felt like medical Whac-A-Mole. New, unrelated issues kept popping up: ear infections, for which she needed tubes, a surgery to implant a different kind of feeding tube. Penny explained that her compromised immune system just exacerbated everything. Everyone told her how strong she was to stay so calm for Ava.

When I arrived back in Park City in the fall, my shin was healed but I was emotionally exhausted and ready to be absorbed in my training. On the one hand, I had loved being at home with Penny and Ava. I'd always thought it was odd that people talked about the way babies' heads smelled—until I'd held Ava for the first time. To feel her tiny hand curl around my finger, to absorb the warmth of her as she slept on my chest, leant being human a new and unexpected beauty. But the constant tide of worry was almost unbearable; when would she move on from this place to become a healthy little girl? Because in all the reports from the doctors, there was never any "why"—it was just one of those tragic mysteries.

"Sorry the little lady isn't doing well," Luke said the night I got back to Park City. "I'm sure she'll turn around. One of my cousins had a preemie and it was rough for the first year but you should see the kid now, he's a bruiser!"

Luke knew I was upset with him that he'd only visited me once while I was in CDA, and he was a little upset with *me* that I was upset with him. This was our deal, we were stronger together than we were apart because we never asked the other to sacrifice any career opportunities. While I'd been with Penny that summer, Luke had been traveling with Red Bull in between training camps, shooting videos of him cross-training, mountain biking, surfing, and interviewing other pro athletes. I was breaking with our pact by expecting him to be by my side. And, as he kept pointing out, there was nothing he could *do,* as though *doing* were even the point. When he did visit, he shuffled anxiously around the periphery of my family's house. Luke had no capacity to give me the kind of calm, tacit support that I needed. Blair, on the other hand, had risen to the occasion during his more frequent visits that summer, spending quiet hours watching movies with my sister and me while Ava slept. Going to the gym with me for my long, tedious rehab workouts. Helping me clean Penny's kitchen when it got beyond the pale, once even going to the gun range with Stewart to help him blow off steam. Penny was bearing up better than her husband in the face of their child's setbacks—Stewart's eyes were purple-rimmed and he looked constantly haunted, while Penny was beatific and brave, tireless in her quest to help her daughter.

When Blair was with me, he did not see what I saw. Or perhaps it was that he could not feel it: the wrongness that crept in sometimes when Penny was holding Ava or watching her. She said and did all the right things, cooed and cuddled her and smiled at her, but there was a note of discord. But if I was the only one who felt it, maybe I was inventing it.

I tried to let Luke's absence that summer go. I knew on some level that it was unfair to expect Luke to morph into someone else in the face of my personal crisis. Loving people meant accepting them as they were.

"I'm sure she'll be fine," I said to Luke that night as I was unpacking and settling back into our condo after the summer away. I could feel how deeply uncomfortable he was talking about Ava, so honestly I didn't really want to talk to him about it either. I wanted my life to go back to normal, and in that moment, this still felt possible. We were years out of the Duncans' house at that point and sharing a spacious, rented condo in the heart of Park City. Since we spent so little time here, we kept the neutral anonymous furniture and tasteful ski-themed art that the place had come with. Neither of us felt any urge to nest beyond putting some family photos up here and there, along with some of us as a couple and with our third musketeer, Blair. We framed the *SKI* magazine cover that had run just prior to the Salt Lake City Olympics. They'd posed us on Baldy on a glorious sunny day. We were in our racing suits, and I was wearing more makeup than I'd ever worn in the rest of my life combined. They'd blown my hair out and it hung down my shoulders in loose waves, a pair of ski goggles pushed perfectly up into my hair. Blair and I stood proudly, holding our sponsored skis to show the logo like we'd been told to do so many times. Luke posed between the two of us, lounging on the glittering snow, looking like he was at the beach. The headline that ran with the piece was: THE HOPEFULS: ARE THREE YOUNG SMALL-TOWN IDAHOANS THE FUTURE OF THE U.S. SKI TEAM? They loved the fact that we'd known each other since we were kids, that we lived together, that Luke and I were a couple. We'd made a running joke of shouting out our answer to the cover's rhetorical question each time we passed the photo: *Hell yes!* we'd say, sometimes thumping the wall next to the photo. It had become part of our pregame ritual.

I wanted to believe that I could come back to the condo, my shin fully healed after a gold-star rehab effort, and just resume my life as it had been before. But I think some part of me was already dislodged and knew nothing would go back to the way it had been.

Liz at High Tea

THE DAY comes and I feel the weight of it from the moment I wake up. February 12. The opening ceremonies. I lie in my bed, trying to let the late summer sunshine coming through the cracks in the blinds and the humid February air distract me from the fact that on this very day, many thousands of miles away, nearly everyone I cared about in my old life is gathering for the opening ceremonies of the Vancouver Olympic Games. Whistler was one of my favorite mountains to ski, and it would have been close enough that my family could have easily come to cheer me on. At thirty, I'd be at the peak of my career, with several World Cup globes in my collection, as well as a handful of medals. Speed skiers like me take time to develop and, so long as they can avoid catastrophic injury, get an edge from the extra years of experience and peak later. This was supposed to be my moment.

I manage to drag myself to my Spanish class, and by the time I'm finished, I have several messages from Gemma, who has decided that we *must* go to the Alvear Palace for tea that afternoon. I rush back to my apartment to change into a sundress.

I've not yet been to the Alvear, though I've suggested it to many a tourist. The hotel is a stunning mass of marble and gold gilt, like the children's book version of a fancy hotel. The staff wear tuxedos, and the carpets are bloodred. I arrive a few minutes late—after changing my outfit three times—and everyone else has arrived. Gemma, Edward, Cali, Anders, and Gianluca stand on the sunny street outside the hotel; their attention is drawn in a tight circle around a petite woman animatedly telling a story. I find with a stab of dismay that Edward's cousin Camilla is in the center of the group. When she sees me, curiously, she greets me like I'm a long-lost friend.

"This place is really something," I say to Gemma, who takes my arm as we head into the Alvear. She pushes her sunglasses back into her hair and shivers with delight.

"Isn't it? I hope you're ready for the tour."

"Please!" I say as we make our way through the massive gilt columns, the chandeliers, the mirrored sconces.

"Well!" Gemma says, turning her voice toward the whole group, showing off a bit. "It was opened in 1932, and as you can *see*, the decor is reminiscent of the Louis XV and Louis XVI style. It was originally owned by a Buenos Aires businessman and socialite who'd spent time in Europe and wanted to bring a bit of that Belle Epoque glamour back to his hometown. This was around the time lots of Europeans were coming to visit, and you know how we Europeans just love to take home with us wherever we go. *Oh hello, we're taking your country away from you, but we've brought some lovely tea and some fabulous decor!* So yes, one of the original designers was French."

As Gemma talks, I notice Edward giving his cousin an indulgent little eye roll; Camilla returns a bemused smile. I feel a flash of tender embarrassment for Gemma, who, fortunately, appears oblivious.

"Oh wait until you see the L'Orangerie," Gemma says as we approach the hostess desk, where she asks in English about seating for seven.

"I am afraid," the hostess says, her tone frosty, "that there is no room on the patio at the moment, but I can seat you near the window."

Gemma looks utterly deflated. I realize suddenly that this outing must have been her idea.

Before any of us see what's happening, Camilla emerges from behind her and is suddenly in a rapid-fire exchange with the hostess, who moments ago looked like she'd bitten into a lemon and is now laughing merrily at something Camilla says. In the next instant, we're following the hostess to L'Orangerie, where a table has magically appeared. I can instantly appreciate what a shame it would have been to sit elsewhere. Sun streams in from the large windows on all sides of the glass-enclosed atrium. There are potted and hanging plants everywhere, creating a Babylonian enclave.

"*Well,*" Gemma says as she sits and smooths her napkin on her lap, "thank goodness we have some *Porteños* with us today!" Anders sits next to her and reaches out to take her hand.

Camilla smiles and shrugs, sitting down between Edward and Gianluca. She talks to both of them in Spanish throughout the tea—which is a succession of sumptuous sandwiches and cakes, along with numerous bottles of champagne. I try not to stare at Gianluca, who is paying far too close attention to Camilla for my taste, with his body turned almost entirely toward her. Do they know each other? They're talking like old friends, old flames even.

I focus instead on Anders. I have a special affection for Norwegians; they were always some of my favorite people on the tour. I ask how he ended up in Buenos Aires, and Anders explains that he had been traveling through South America, and on a stopover in Buenos Aires, he'd taken a class with Gianluca and gotten hooked. That was eight months ago, and he'd been here ever since, working at a local café to supplement his income. He'd been a software engineer back home in Norway, but he'd been traveling for a little over a year.

"That's so cool. What made you decide to take off?" I ask.

There's a heavy moment of silence, and Gemma, who'd been half paying attention, reaches to squeeze Anders's knee. "Anders's sister passed away," she explains.

"I'm so sorry," I say.

"Thank you," Anders says stiffly. "She would have been twenty-seven next week. Two years older than me."

Later as we're leaving the hotel, I fall back with him.

"Anders?"

He looks down at me, seeming to try to relax a bit. I put my hand on his forearm.

"I just want to say that I'm so sorry about your sister." He nods and looks at the ground. "I lost my sister too."

"You did?"

I nod. And it's true. Penny is lost to me. I'm taken aback when Anders sweeps me into a consuming hug. But then I let myself be hugged and it's a relief; it's not half the story but it feels good to tell someone something.

"Everything all right over here?" Gemma asks, her voice inscrutable.

"Everything is splendid," Anders says. His English is good, if almost too sharp and sprinkled with the occasional anachronistic vocabulary word. "We'd better sober up before it's time to dance!"

Later, we go to the social, and Gianluca has eyes only for Camilla.

"So what," I say to Gemma. "She's the shiny new thing?"

"Camilla? Oh no, she and Gianluca have some . . . history."

"Ah. Who *doesn't* he have history with?"

Gemma laughs. "She's really something, isn't she? To be honest, I think she finds me ridiculous. Edward doesn't see it."

"Why's that?" I don't want to say that actually, I think he does see it, and that I'm certain Camilla would feel the same about me if she thought about me at all, which I'm sure she hasn't.

"I think she has *feelings* about foreigners coming here and insinuating themselves."

"What about Edward?"

"He's her family. And you know how that goes." She sighs. "We'll forgive our family almost anything."

Penny Is the Best
Mom in the World

As I was back in Park City trying to get in fighting shape for World Cup season and, hopefully, the Turin Olympics, Ava was becoming something of a social media celebrity. Every time I looked on Facebook, there were more comments on Penny's posts, more names I didn't recognize on her ever-expanding friends list. The frequent pictures of Ava featured updates on what Penny called her "healing journey." They would sometimes be written in Penny's voice, but more often in Ava's.

> Boy am I giving Mommy lots of laundry to do today, I puked on
> her three times this morning! I'm sad because we had to put my
> NG tube back in. But I'm being very brave and giving Mommy lots
> of snuggles.

Beneath was a picture of Ava looking forlornly at the camera, her feeding tube snaking out of one of her tiny nostrils. Was this what Ava was really thinking? There seemed no question that Penny could rely on the depth of their connection to speak for her, to be her proxy to the world. The likes on each of Penny's posts soared into the hundreds with dozens of comments from well-wishers below, mostly other moms. *Ava has the best mommy ever! Ava says be brave, Mommy, I'm going to be better soon.* Sometimes there were pictures of other infants: *Riley is sending Ava big, big hugs. Parker sends kisses to his girlfriend, Ava!*

I was getting the updates directly from Penny, but I still couldn't tear myself away from her posts. I was searching for something between the lines, though I couldn't say exactly what. It felt unseemly that Penny was sharing such personal stuff with people who, increasingly, appeared to be strangers. Some of the posts were blatant in their self-pity.

> I love being Ava's mommy and wouldn't trade it for the world but it is just SO hard sometimes. I just want her to be healthy. That's ALL!!!! Is that so much to ask for? I worry about her nonstop and some days I can barely sleep or eat (that's one way to lose the baby weight LOL. Sigh). But she's my little angel and I know God has made her a warrior.

Ava's problems were endless. She would conquer one milestone: she was sitting up! Only to fall behind in others: she wasn't reaching for objects as she should be, still wasn't absorbing enough nutrients, was having trouble keeping food down. She was in a brutal sort of race to claim the basic functions of her humanity. When I saw healthy babies and toddlers on the streets of Park City, it gutted me. Even with all her troubles, Ava was so cute, with sparkling eyes and a smile that made my knees weak; she seemed destined to grow into a beautiful child, if only she could make it there. Eventually, the NG tube was gone from her tiny face and replaced with a G-tube that went through directly into her stomach, giving Penny a way to make sure she was getting enough nutrients and circumventing the problem of her acid reflux.

"I just don't understand it," my mom confessed to me on the phone shortly after the surgery. "Whenever she's here she seems to eat just fine."

I came home to celebrate my twenty-fifth birthday in October with my family, and Ava—seven months old by then—ended up in the hospital for dehydration and a spiking fever. I remember seeing her lying limply on my sister's lap and being struck with a deep terror. I told myself it was the surroundings—being in a children's hospital was upsetting— and nothing to do with the oddly serene expression on Penny's face. Later that day, a picture of Ava hooked up to the IV appeared on Penny's Facebook.

> Rough day for my little girl today! She's still having trouble with eating and it's caused her to get dehydrated. Most of the nurses at Children's are amazing but today Ava's nurse was grouchy and couldn't find her vein! I know I should be patient but it's just so hard when we're in the hospital all the time. I'm a mess today, bursting into tears every five minutes.

This was not the Penny I'd seen in the hospital, looking as calm and ma-jestic holding her daughter as a pietà in a classical painting. But maybe she'd been putting on a brave face for me.

Back in Park City, I thought about Ava and Penny all the time. I scrolled through Penny's Facebook like a zombie, my stomach a snarl of guilt, worry, and suspicion I couldn't yet put a name to.

Luke tried to bring me around by telling me that Penny wouldn't want me to be worrying about her. This only showed how little he understood my sister; her only comfort these days seemed to be other people worry-ing about her. Why else would she share all these details online? But then again, it was something new moms just did, right? Isolated at home, they sought out community online. Nothing wrong with that. There'd been a time when Penny had cared about other things—when she'd had hobbies and friends—but those other things had been swept away by Ava's illness. But what mother wouldn't be consumed by the constant unexplained illness of her infant daughter? At that point, I still imagined that we were moving toward a future in which Ava was a happy, healthy little girl and Penny would resemble herself again. Some days, I felt like I was holding my breath until that future arrived.

Penny existed in a constant state of emergency and I would abandon whatever I was doing to pick up her frequent calls, which were dominated by the minutiae of Ava's health. Given her line of work, there seemed no end to the various treatments, therapies, and courses of action Penny could find to experiment with. She often seemed to know more than the doctors treating her, and several times lost patience with her pediatrician and moved on to another one.

To the outside world, Penny's determination was admirable. The Greek chorus of Penny's Facebook page was in agreement that she was a good mom, the *best* mom, her little Ava was lucky to have her. And these moms in the chorus, they understood. Many of them seemed to have sick kids themselves, and Penny appeared to spend no small amount of time giving them the benefit of her medical expertise.

They never would have said anything at the time, but my parents were uncomfortable about Penny sharing all of the details so constantly. Every time they ran into someone they knew—which was all the time in our small town—they were full of concern over Penny's latest post. Whenever I was home, I had a similar experience. People seemed both horrified by the circumstances and yet oddly ravenous for the details. These were followed by the platitudes about people they'd known with sick kids who'd had stunning turnarounds. According to these stories, the more imperiled the child was in babyhood, the more boisterous, robust, and brilliant they were later on, as though being a sickly child were somehow a harbinger of good things.

And in this sea of concerned strangers and acquaintances, where was Emily? Where were Penny's other friends, the ones I'd last seen dancing at her wedding, full of joy?

My life continued back in Park City but I was only half in it. I'd always felt out of place around my nonathlete peers, but now I felt out of place around my teammates too. Everyone was sympathetic, but athletes are naturally self-centered and mostly very young, and my family's drama was remote. And there was something I couldn't articulate to anyone, even if they had been able to hear it, the dark cloud of fear that was creeping in, a nagging sense that there was something we were not saying.

For a while, my desire not to think too hard about anything else gave me an edge. I threw myself into my training, and somewhat to my surprise, I qualified for the team going to Turin. My focus had been shot for months and I came in twenty-fifth in super-G and eighteenth in downhill, miles away from the medal podium. Blair came home with a bronze medal in slalom and Luke with three silvers and a chip on his shoulder about not getting another gold.

In March, as the season was winding down, I came home for the weekend to celebrate Ava's first birthday. My parents hosted the party at their house and the forced joviality of it all was excruciating. Ava looked exhausted and spent much of the time sleeping in Penny's arms or in my mom's. Her skin had a yellowish tint, and when one of Penny's old buddies from the clinic asked about it, I heard her go into a lengthy explanation about some mysterious kidney issues Ava had been having.

A half hour into the party, I saw a very welcome face coming through the door: Emily. I went straight for her and wrapped my arms around her. I hadn't seen her since Ava was first born.

"Sissy! I watched you in the Olympics. I was so proud."

"I didn't do as well as I hoped but . . ."

"Even to make it though!" she said. I nodded, though of course, being an also-ran didn't count for much, not for the sponsors, and not for me. It felt like every year, every season went by faster than the last. I'd been mercifully spared any catastrophic injuries, but the wear and tear added up over the years: tendonitis, torn muscles. I was twenty-five: young in the world but getting up there in the skiing world. Every year, there was a new crop of seventeen- and eighteen-year-olds coming up. There was a time when I would have been able to say all of this to Emily, but without knowing when or how, the window on that intimacy had closed. So instead I simply said, "Thank you." She excused herself to go find Penny. I figured I'd catch up to her later. We'd planned the party to stretch on as long as needed into the early spring afternoon. I wanted to find a way to ask her about Penny, to see if she'd been feeling any of the disquiet I could no longer ignore. But before I could get the chance, she was on her way out.

"You're leaving already?" I asked, catching her arm.

"Yeah, sorry, sissy. I just have so many papers to grade this afternoon." Emily was now a seventh-grade English teacher, a challenging job for which her sweet and patient nature seemed uniquely well suited. "We'll talk soon though, okay?"

She'd always felt like our third sister, but as I watched her head up the driveway to her car, I saw the truth: she wasn't actually family. She could walk away. Maybe they always would have drifted apart; after all, even in small towns not everyone stays close with their childhood friends. But Emily had known Penny all her life, and maybe she felt it too, the wrongness. Emily and I had talked once and only once about the discrepancies in the stories Penny had told us about her previous pregnancy, and then, as if by mutual agreement, we'd closed the door on the incident. But now I couldn't stop thinking about it. It hovered on the periphery of my mind no matter how hard I tried to push it away. I knew there was a line between Ava and those phantom babies, but I couldn't bring myself to draw it.

How fierce is denial when acceptance means losing so much?

⌘

The final day of my visit was a sunny one, and Penny and I took a long walk along the lakeshore, Ava bundled up to protect her from the bracing air. She was livelier that day and when Penny and I stopped to rest for a while on a bench, she squirmed ferociously in my sister's lap, making us both laugh as she reached for and burbled at the geese who strutted along nearby. The moment of normalcy was like a sliver of light. Maybe everything would be okay.

On the way home, I stopped by the grocery store to pick up protein bars and tried my mom's cell to see if she needed anything. She didn't answer. I tried my dad. Nothing.

But when I arrived home, both cars were there. In the middle of the day.

"Mom? Dad?" I called through the foyer. "Hi, buddy," I said, leaning down to scratch Barry's ears.

"In here, Katie."

I came down the hallway and was greeted with the strange sight of my mom and dad sitting side by side at the ancient dining set. I noticed with alarm that my father's eyes were red-rimmed.

"Hi, honey," my mom said. "Can you sit with us for a minute? We need to talk to you about Penny."

I lowered myself numbly into the chair next to my mom and could feel the dam I'd been patching over for months—years—to forestall this very moment finally bursting. I felt tears springing to my eyes, my breath quickening. That afternoon while I'd walked with Penny and Ava in the park, my parents had been to see Doctor Anderson, our family practitioner of over two decades. They'd laid out for the kind doctor all of the many moments that I'd been trying for years to convince myself were isolated incidents, the products of growing pains and bad boyfriends. Taken together, they added up to a horrible, unspeakable truth. Penny wasn't simply unlucky, she wasn't just a worrier or a hypochondriac. She likely suffered from a mysterious disorder known as Munchausen syndrome by proxy, a grotesque and terrifying disorder that had been a subplot in a popular late 1990s horror film. Her unfortunate health history hadn't been some bizarre curse; it had been her creation. And when Ava was born, her focus had shifted to the baby. There wasn't a great deal known about the disorder, but Penny fit the profile: female, white, middle class, with a job in the medical profession.

"What the hell are we going to do?" I asked my parents. Without realizing it, I'd clasped my mother's hand and was squeezing it so hard my knuckles had gone white.

"We'll get her help," my dad said, trying to sound certain. "We'll stick together. We'll get through it."

In our minds, Penny was a victim as well as Ava. Her own mind had turned on her; we just needed to make her see.

"I can't go back to Park City," I said. "I shouldn't go back."

"Honey, it's fine," my mom said. "We'll keep you posted. You don't need to stay."

I went to take a shower and found myself screaming, the echoes ricocheting off the walls and bringing my poor parents running to the bathroom door. This syndrome was the only thing that made the last ten years of life with Penny make any sense at all, and yet, *how* could this be true? Where did we go from here?

⋙

The next day, in what I now recognize as a stunning act of bravery, my mother went to speak to Ava's pediatrician, her third in as many months. My mom filled him in on Penny's troubling history with illness, and most crucially, the pregnancy, which, my parents at last explained to me, had likely never been real. The doctor appeared to calmly absorb the information, and my mom left his office frustrated and fearful that he didn't believe her. What she didn't know was that he legally *couldn't* tell my mother how deeply alarmed he was and that once she'd left his office, he'd alerted a hospital authority called the SCAN team—a task force of doctors at Children's that handled suspected child abuse and neglect—who'd subsequently called Child Protective Services. But this would all come out later.

It was Stewart who called me in Park City, his voice hysterical. "Katie, they took Ava, they took Ava. Oh my god, oh my god."

At first, Penny cried to us too, but as the details burbled forth, she quickly turned. My mother's name was all over the paperwork as the person who'd alerted the doctors. And for all of us, there was no going back.

Liz Says Yes

THE NEXT day, Cali and I plan to meet after my Spanish class to grab some lunch and walk through the botanical garden. A group that includes a few Americans and Germans who seem to have become friends are packed in on the small couch in the lounge killing time between classes, and whatever they're watching is on commercial. I get out early and linger idly there with one eye on the door for Cali. The programming resumes and the familiar image of the start house comes into view. For a moment, I'm transfixed by the sight of one of my old teammates, Andrew Weibrecht, getting prepped by the team's hype man, Rudy, a bodybuilder Luke brought on as a trainer. His energy became so invaluable that the coaches made him an official part of the staff two years ago. Rudy's not mic'd up, but I can still hear him, and the memory of his voice reverberates in my brain. I've been trying so hard to avoid seeing any footage of the races, but now that it's in front of me, I can't take my eyes off it.

"Hey, there you are! I was waiting downstairs but figured I'd just come up. Oh man, the Olympics! I'd totally forgotten they were happening right now," Cali says, turning to look at what I'm staring at. "Whoa, earth to Liz? Hel-lo."

I turn to her slowly, trying to force a smile, but given her reaction, I guess it emerges as a grimace.

"Hi, Cali," I say. I'm trying and failing to regain my composure; my voice sounds as though it's coming from the bottom of a well.

"Are you okay? Jesus, what's wrong?"

"Can we just . . . I need to go home."

"Yeah, of course, come on."

Cali bustles me out and we're suddenly in the teeming streets of the Microcentro, with what feels in that moment to be all of humanity: tourists, office workers heading home, little kids. Cali puts her arm in mine and guides me to the subway and to my stop in San Telmo. Mercifully, she doesn't say anything, just keeps her arm tightly wound around mine.

Back in the courtyard, I try to recenter myself: I'm in Buenos Aires, where I'm having a not bad time. It's been a week since I've had to take an Ativan.

Cali waits for me to say something.

"I'm sorry about that."

"There's nothing to be sorry about." She gives me a sad smile. "I just wish you could tell me what's going on."

"I want to," I say. And it's true. I know it would be a relief, just to have one person in my new life see me in context. But when I think of telling her, I'm almost immediately engulfed in shame. I don't want to watch that look of horror widening her eyes.

"For what it's worth, it was a relief to tell you about what happened to me in New York. I mean, I know your story might be way worse, but I would understand. I promise."

I nod but say nothing.

"Something with the Olympics?" she tries.

I nod. This part Cali would understand. She trained to do one thing her entire life, built her life around one singular ambition, and in an instant, it was taken away from her. She was cast out. "I used to be a skier," I manage. "I got injured."

Cali raises her eyebrows. "Oh. Man, I'm sorry to hear that." For a

201

moment, we're both quiet. I feel that if I say one more thing, the whole story will come bursting forth and I'm not ready. "Is that everything?"

I shake my head, thinking that my expression must look desperate because she relents.

"Whenever you're ready, Liz, I'm here."

⊷

I have a lesson with Gianluca that night, and for the first time since I've met him, I don't want to see him. I don't want to be swept away by his touch and his scent. I just want to wallow in my sorrows and mourn my lost self. He reminds me too much that I'm not who I was: *you would need to lose some weight.* The words echo in my mind, and it makes me want to be released from my own skin, though I can't imagine how I became so invested in the opinion of this man, this fabulist who weaves a net of myths around himself—I think nastily that perhaps the thing he's really trying to hide is how perfectly ordinary he is.

He senses that something is off right away but I tell him I'm fine, just tired, and we forge ahead with the lesson. But he won't let it lie.

"Hey," he says, taking my shoulders in his hands, arresting our movements mid-dance. We're halfway through our time and I've been counting the minutes—there is a bottle of Malbec and a box of *alfajores* waiting for me at my apartment and I'm anxious to indulge in my misery. "Where are you?"

"Right here," I say. "I'm just tired."

I was a champion once and it suddenly infuriates me that he's never seen this side of me. All he sees is this weakened flabby version of me who's been leaning into him, practically offering herself up as a sacrifice, giving him whatever of her he'll take—and somehow right now I feel like she is *his fault* and all I want is to destroy her.

G drops his hands from my shoulders. "You're wasting my time," he says, turning defensive now. "If you're going to stonewall me, Liz, there's no point."

"Why? You're my dance teacher, so teach me how to dance. Why do you need to know all the intimate details of my life? You keep acting

like it's all so much more and it's just really"—I'm on a roll now—
"melodramatic, you know?" *He is ridiculous,* I think. *Look at him.* "I'm
not part of your little cult."

He smiles now. He's gotten to me and it was all he wanted. "You're
really cute when you're mad."

"I am not *fucking cute.* Goddamn it, Gianluca, you know nothing
about me."

"Okay," he says, smiling smugly, like he's already won the argument.
"Whatever you say, Tiger. You've told me plenty whether you realize it
or not."

I can't take it. "I haven't told you the half. I am . . . was one of the best
downhill ski racers in the world. I spent my entire life training. I should
be at the Olympics right now, and instead my career is fucked and I'm
here pretending any of *this* matters. God, you know what? Forget it." I
stomp off in the direction of the door. I reach the edge of the studio floor
and come to a halt, remembering that if I don't take my shoes off, I'll
wreck them.

But then G's got my arm. I turn and look at him, that infuriating
smile. I shove him away. He laughs. "There she is."

I lose it. I burst into tears. There are many people who've known me
most of my life and have never seen me cry. Most of them.

"Come here," he says. All the fury has gone out of me in a rush, and
I let myself be folded into G's arms.

"I'm sorry," I say, not exactly sure what I'm apologizing for except that
I'm mortified to be crying on this man, who will now pity me when that's
the last thing I want from anyone, but especially from him. He shakes his
head, holding me tightly, with one hand around my waist, one stroking
my hair.

"Come on," he says. "Change your shoes."

Suddenly, I just want to be told what to do next. *Put your shoes on,
there you go. Come with me, take my hand, that's it. Here, put the helmet
on, and I know it's warm but take my jacket, I'm not letting you ride with
bare arms.* Dreamlike, I follow his cues and before I really process what's
happening, I'm straddling the back of his Ducati.

His flat is the upper floor of an old house, a crumbling grand stucco structure at the edge of Caballito. His sprawling studio apartment is in homey, artsy disarray. In one corner, there's a galley kitchen with mismatched plates, in the other, a bed with rumpled sheets. In between, there is a couch, no television. G continues his soft, persistent instructions. *Take your shoes off, sit down.* I sink into the old sofa as he pours wine into two small blue glasses and hands me one. "Thanks," I say, my voice gravelly and strange; it's the first word I've said since we left the studio.

He sits next to me, placing his own wineglass on the crate that serves as a coffee table. He watches me take a long sip of the wine. When I put my glass down, he says, "Come here," and pulls me into his lap. He strokes my hair and it feels like my blood rushes to meet his fingertips wherever they land on my skin.

"Something else happened," he says, his voice low. "It's not just the skiing."

I nod.

"Do you want to tell me?" he asks.

I shake my head. To recount the whole gruesome story right now is the last thing I want.

"What do you want?"

"I don't know." Tears are coming to my eyes again.

Gianluca's hand tightens in my hair and he pulls my head forward and kisses me, and I feel my heartbeat in my stomach, now lower. He pulls me up so that I'm straddling him. He runs his fingers under my shirt, trailing the bare skin of my ribs. I'm so much softer there than I once was, and it strikes me that no one has touched me like this in a long time.

"What do you want?" he asks again. I feel him hardening beneath me.

"I want," I say, my voice suddenly clear, "to feel something."

He nods. He takes my shirt off, pausing to look me in the eyes. My heart is racing. He reaches around and unclasps my bra, slips the straps off, and pulls it away. I curl forward a bit, feeling exposed even in the low light of the flat. He pulls my hands to my sides and puts his mouth to my breast.

"But you think I'm . . ." The words, the words.

"I think you're beautiful. I want to make you feel," he says. "Is that what you want from me? I need you to tell me you want it."

"Yes."

He flips us around, so that I'm sitting and he's kneeling between my legs.

"Yes what?" he asks as he unbuttons the top of my jeans, unzips them, and begins to slide them down over my hips. My underwear catches on them and I try to reach for them but he gently moves my hand away. He pauses to remove his own shirt, and now I can feel the heat of his skin near mine. He leans forward, resting his chin on my stomach and looking up at me; I can barely catch my breath.

"Tell me what you want," he says.

"I want . . . I want you," I manage.

He kisses my stomach, runs his tongue down beneath my navel. "Do you want me to put my mouth on you?"

"Yes." I feel like I'll pass out when he does it.

A moment later, he pulls back. "Is that good for you?"

I say yes and my voice sounds guttural, unlike my own.

"I'm going to make you feel," he says. He puts his mouth back on me and slides first one and then two fingers inside me.

When I'm right on the edge, he stops and stands up. He pulls my hand up and puts it on him, huge and hard in his jeans.

"Do you want me inside of you?"

I nod.

He unbuttons his jeans and the sight of him is sudden and looming. "Tell me. Say the words."

"I want you inside of me." I've never said words like this aloud; it was never like this with Luke.

He sits down, pulls his pants all the way off. "I want you on top," he says. "I want to watch your face while I'm inside you."

Suddenly, I feel too exposed and I feel unsightly and sure this is a mistake.

"I don't . . ." I curl inward and cover my face with my hand. "I can't . . ." I'm breathless, confused, feeling a thousand things.

"Don't think, feel," G says, pulling my hand away from my face. "Like we're dancing. Just follow me."

I let myself unfurl and he pulls my hips over him. Asking me one last time, "Do you want me? I want you so much right now."

And yes, of course, I say yes.

Penny Is Not a Criminal

ONCE PENNY'S illness had a name, the depth of its roots became suddenly and irrevocably visible. It wasn't just now with Ava, it was always with everything. It was a lifetime of inexplicable illnesses and injuries, a draw to the sick that masqueraded as compassion, a vast knowledge and infinite obsession with medical details that far exceeded professional usefulness. It was the ghosts of the two little girls who had never been, who lingered now like bad omens, two tiny Cassandras.

Having a name for Penny's affliction brought scant relief as the treatment possibilities were vague and the outcomes bleak. Most of the cases I read about in my frantic Googling of the disease made headlines because the children in question had died. There seemed to be no stories of people triumphing over the disease to be found anywhere, no kernel of hope to hold on to. Even the notion that Munchausen syndrome by proxy was a treatable disease at all was up for debate; afflicted women were child abusers and monsters, rather than victims themselves suffering from their own dark delusions. We didn't want Penny punished, we wanted her helped. We wanted her to be protected from herself and Ava to be protected from her.

The only way I could think of the disease was as something entirely separate from my sister, as though it were a parasite that—if we could some-how remove it—she would recover from. Even though I could see now how far the tentacles reached into Penny's past, my conviction remained that there was still a Penny in there to be saved: the Penny I'd known as a girl, and even as a teenager, the one who was sweet and sensitive and silly. I had so many memories of her laughing and gossiping with Emily, going bonkers over some boy, or prattling on in their shared made-up language—a conflagration of gibberish and the first-year German they'd taken together their freshman year. It occurred to me that I hadn't seen her really laugh in what felt like years. But surely there was a way to bring her back.

Penny called me about my mother's betrayal nearly as soon she discovered it. I was back in the Park City condo then with Luke and Blair had come for dinner; thankfully, it was only the three of us. I took the phone call in the bedroom.

"Katie, Mom is *crazy*, can you believe her? She called the doctors and told them all these lies about me! What the hell?" Penny was sobbing. The two days since CPS had come had been like a car accident happening in slow motion, the severity of what was taking place deepening by the second. Ava had been returned to her parents quickly, with a court order that required they stay with Penny's bewildered in-laws under strict supervision.

"All I've *done* this past year is try to help my daughter, and now we have to go stay with Stew's parents because the court won't let Ava be with me unless I'm supervised, like I'm some *criminal*. We're all crammed in on each other and now I feel like my in-laws are always watching me. It's so humiliating!"

I thought about Stewart's retired parents and their tiny two-bedroom house in Hayden. Adding two adults and a baby would be close quarters indeed. My parents had reached out to the Grangers, but they'd seemed wary and hadn't returned their calls. And who knew what Penny was telling them? The Grangers were simple, unsophisticated people who treasured their quiet, small-town life. Penny was smarter than all of them put together.

"You could stay with Mom and Dad, couldn't you? At least they have more space." I wanted Penny to be with my parents; the Grangers had no idea what they were dealing with. I was fantasizing about some scenario in which my sister was forced to retreat to my parents, who seemed like the only ones who could help Penny understand that she was sick, who could help her and in turn help Ava.

"After what Mom did? Are you kidding me?"

"She didn't know they were going to call CPS, Pen, she was just worried. We've all been worried."

Penny's sobs abated suddenly.

"Worried about Ava or worried about *me* with Ava?"

Into the eerie silence that opened came a rush of all the small moments that had built up over a lifetime with Penny, releasing themselves all at once into my bloodstream. I stared at the wall. I was in our third bedroom, where Blair sometimes crashed, where my parents stayed when they came to visit. For some reason, the generic vintage prints of Park City advertisements struck me as absurd, like I couldn't believe that this was what I was looking at in this moment. I suppose I knew it was a point of no return. Penny had never come visit me in Park City, despite my many offers to send her a plane ticket. She'd been drifting away for years.

"Penny, I think you need help."

"What the fuck does that mean, Katie?" Her voice was calm and sharp, the tears from moments ago long gone.

I burst into my own tears of desperation. "Penny, I love you, we all love you. But you need help. We're so worried about you." Even then, I couldn't say the words themselves; I couldn't name it.

"You knew," she said, her voice turning to ice. "You knew Mom was going to the doctors. You probably all sat around and talked about it. Goddamn it, it's always been like this, the three of you against me."

"Penny, it is *not* like that. We're just worried. After everything that happened with the babies three years ago . . . it just . . . we want to help!"

"What the hell does that have to do with anything?" she said.

Now I started to get angry. She acted as though faking a pregnancy were some normal youthful blunder, an ordinary and irrelevant chapter in her past. Penny lived in the moment in the most terrible way: apathetic to the burning wreckage she'd left in her wake. "Penny!" I said. "Do you have any idea what you've put me through? I thought I had two nieces on the way! I bought them toys and books! I *mourned them,* Penny, when they died." I couldn't even say the rest of it: that they never existed. They'd been a delusion at best, a cold-blooded, manipulative lie at worst. She created them and then she killed them. Was my sister crazy or evil? I still don't know.

"Stop pretending to care about me," she said dismissively, landing a gut punch and avoiding the accusation in one swift moment.

"Of course I care about you. I love you, you're my sister!"

"Like that's ever mattered to you. The only thing you care about is skiing, and being Mom and Dad's golden child. So just stop it, okay? It's not like we're close."

"Penny, how can you say that?" My mind raced. *Weren't* we close? Hadn't I done what I could to be a good sister? Yes, I'd been focused on my skiing, but I'd tried to be there for Penny, hadn't I? I'd listened to her as she obsessed endlessly over her health, over Ava's. I'd tried to carry some of her pain for her, not that it ever worked. "I love you. Mom and Dad love you. We just want to help."

"I don't have time for this bullshit," Penny said with venomous efficiency, as though she were a customer-service rep at the end of her rope. "I have my own family, and they're in crisis right now, thanks to you three."

"Penny, don't do this."

"I have to go." Just before she hung up, I heard Ava in the background, not crying but just making some sort of baby exclamation, the last time I'd hear her voice.

I sat there for a long moment after we'd hung up. I could hear Blair and Luke laughing in the next room. I'd told them both about Penny, and they'd been alarmed but had remained positive and reassured me that things would work out. It meant something coming from them; they knew my family, knew Penny, who—according to them—was just kind of weird and dramatic. But in that moment, I realized that they didn't have any idea what I was dealing with. I was alone in this.

༄

The next six months, as the CPS investigation into Penny wound its way through the courts, were a miserable but somehow galvanizing time. Until it was all put out in the open, I hadn't quite recognized the toll that Penny's illness and the constant worry about Ava had taken on me, how isolating it had been to know so deeply that something was very wrong but not be able to articulate it. Luke was better at supporting me during this time; the fact of the court case gave him a way to wrap his head around what was happening. I pushed down the thought that perhaps he hadn't entirely believed me before. But then, I hadn't entirely believed it myself. However alarming it was to have the doctors at Children's, social workers, and Ava's court-appointed special advocate involved, it validated what had previously felt like paranoia. Something *was* wrong, and all these people knew it. Surely, something would be done.

CPS called me frequently as they put their case together and one such phone call made me late to training. I usually loved off-season. After months on the road and the grueling race schedule that ran November through March, it was fun to be back in Park City with all of the other Alpine athletes, training during the day and drinking beers in the evening with the snowboarders and ski jumpers, trading good-natured insults with the freeskiers. But this year was different. As I slipped into the gym as unobtrusively as possible, the phone call with the caseworker replayed in my head, and it felt as though I was looking at my teammates through a telescope, their world unreachable even as I walked among them. I'd been asked to come home for a "family meeting," something the social worker assigned to the case had conceived of. I would see my sister for the first time in months, albeit from across a courtroom.

My father, we decided, wouldn't come to the meeting. He would get too angry and it wouldn't be productive. My mom and I met with the social worker, Quinn, and I nearly gasped when I saw her. She was twenty-three at most with wide blue eyes and a pixie cut, hemp jewelry on her wrists and neck. I knew it was unfair to judge her on sight and that she was probably doing the best she could, but I couldn't imagine that she was prepared for anything like my sister. Her office—its every surface covered by stacks of file folders—did nothing to assuage my fears. Family court is as desolate a place as you can imagine. The horrible truth is that most people end up there because of deep and systemic issues related to poverty. My sister with her shiny hair and her designer handbag did not look the part.

Penny arrived with Stewart, his parents, his sister Pamela, and an entourage of people I'd either briefly or never met. There was Stewart's best friend, Tim, and his wife, Samantha, and a slew of Stewart's multitudinous rotund aunties whom I vaguely recognized from the wedding, which now felt like a far-off dream. Why had they let her bring *so* many people? Why should these strangers have any say in my family's fate? At least they would finally have to listen to us explain all of Penny's history: the lying, the obsessions, the mysterious medical ailments. But Penny hadn't just brought an army, she'd brought a cult. For reasons I couldn't fathom, the social worker let each of them have their say, and they talked about how outrageous the idea of Penny abusing Ava was. She had thoroughly and systematically turned every last one of them against us. From their mouths we heard not only how wonderful Penny was but how *awful* we were: that Penny had been neglected by my parents, that my mother and I were plotting to get Ava away from her out of spite. It was so outlandish it was hard to figure out how to even defend ourselves. In their minds, they were on the righteous side of a young mother who'd been victimized by those meant to love and protect her. According to them, Penny had had a lifetime of bad health, and her needs had always come last, neglected in favor of the younger sibling, whose glory my parents were allegedly obsessed with to the exclusion of anything else. She'd woven a compelling fiction, and I could see in their eyes that they *hated* us.

By the time it was my mother's turn to speak, it felt like we were the ones on trial.

"I love my daughter," she said, barely keeping it together, "and I love my granddaughter. We don't want to hurt Penny, but she needs help."

Out of the corner of my eye, I watched as one auntie leaned over to another and whispered something in her ear—she let out a loud scoff that morphed into a laugh. My mother halted for a moment and I could hear her taking a deep breath.

"Don't laugh at my mother. Don't you dare," I burst out, staring daggers at the aunties, who rolled their eyes and held their hands up as though to say, *Oh, pardon* us. My mom took my hand.

"It's okay, honey." She carried on and explained everything about how she had come to the decision to speak to Ava's doctor. I tried my best to appeal to their empathy when it was my turn to speak. I reiterated that we loved my sister and only want to help—what other motivation could we possibly have? I told them I understood that they thought they were doing the right thing but that we'd known Penny her whole life, and we saw this all in a context they couldn't. I was begging them to listen to us, but I could see their implacable expressions. Penny didn't look us in the eyes even once.

The whole ordeal was messy and complicated. The wheels of the court kept turning; Ava's court-appointed special advocate filed a motion to try to have Penny and Ava placed with my parents, but it was denied. A psychologist evaluated Penny and found her to be deeply disturbed. Given his limited exposure to her, he told us, it was impossible for him to diagnose something as complex as Munchausen syndrome by proxy, which is mostly defined by a series of actions rather than traits, but that she certainly fit the profile, as well as showing strong indications of narcissistic personality disorder, something often paired with the MSP. Initially, his diagnosis felt like a win. After all, the psychologist was a neutral party, agreed to by both sides. I realized just how deeply I'd begun to doubt reality itself by then. On an intellectual level, I knew Penny lied, I had plenty of evidence. But on a visceral level, it still felt hard to reconcile. She didn't *seem* to be lying much of the time, and it was unclear—even with the psychologist's diagnosis—whether or not *she* knew she was lying, or if she had genuinely lost track of the truth.

Of all the things I cannot reconcile about this time, one is my strange nostalgia for it. As murky and complex as the legal proceedings were, at least we had forward momentum after all the years of inertia and worry. It was impossible to imagine that all of this would lead to nothing.

I imagined then that the summit of this awful climb was just beyond the horizon, that my life could soon go back to its normal trajectory. Having this finish line in sight let me compartmentalize and focus on my training, even enjoying a couple of the training camps in Mammoth and New Zealand. Whenever I tried to talk to Luke about Penny, he said, "Babe, don't think about it. Focus on the good, okay? It'll all work out."

Maybe he thought he was reassuring me, but the message was clear: he was done hearing about this.

I flew home for the judge's decision on a Thursday and held my mom's hand with white knuckles as we waited. There was no jury in a dependency case such as this one: just one man who held our fate in his hands. As I listened to his words, I felt like I was in a vehicle that was being submerged, water rushing in from all sides. He'd considered all of the evidence and testimony and was recommending the child stay with her mother.

After all that, nothing changed.

After all that we'd been through, after drawing the line in the sand that cut Penny and Ava out of our lives, nothing changed.

Back in Park City, I was a mess. Luke tried to be supportive, but it was clear he was losing patience with the whole thing.

"I know it's been rough," he'd say, "but it's over. Gotta move on, right?"

He was wrong. It wasn't over.

Liz Is in It Now

FOR THE next two weeks, I'm barely present in my life when I'm not with Gianluca. My world has been sharply divided into being with him, when I sink into a primal kind of ecstasy that makes me forget I even have a mind or a past, and without him, when I'm replaying moments with him, when my body is remembering his.

The rest of the time I'm with Gemma and Edward and the dance team. I realize that they have given me what I'd missed most about my old life: the easy, uncomplicated friendship of my teammates. And, one by one, it comes out that it was not only Cali and Anders who had gone through something that turned their lives upside down before coming to Buenos Aires. Breakups, death, ruined careers—it seems everyone came here to forget something.

One day, I run into Beau and Valentina while I'm leading a tour through the Plaza de Mayo; Beau plays a song on his phone and they do part of their routine right there in the street, delighting my tour group.

Mostly, I see Gianluca alone late at night, and after the first time, we're never at his place, always at mine. He never spends the night and I pretend that it doesn't bother me. He says he can't sleep in unfamiliar beds. Then why meet here and not at his apartment? I don't ask because I don't really want to know the answer.

When we're alone together, G makes me feel like I am the only woman who's ever existed. Physically, being with him is like a drug, and it makes me grateful to have a body.

At first, Cali and Gemma are thrilled, but a couple of weeks in, when we're at Edward's and I'm counting the moments until I can leave to meet G at my apartment, Cali asks about us.

I shrug and smile. Nearly every night of the past week I've seen him, let him come over, fuck my brains out, and leave like a thief in the night. I tell myself I'm being modern.

"Yes, you've been seeing a lot of him, haven't you? Judging from the dark circles under your eyes," Gemma says. It's just the four of us tonight. I catch Edward gazing at Cali slightly dreamily and wonder what he's up to.

"Well, what does one come to Buenos Aires for if not for a romance?" Edward says, smiling.

"Is that what it is?" Cali asks. "Has he taken you on a date or anything?"

I laugh like she's just said something ridiculous. "A date?"

"Come on," she says, looking to Edward for backup. "You know what G is like. And what about Angelina?"

"Over. It was never anything serious according to him." I'd asked him about this as well, the morning after our first night, panicked that I was in for a showdown I'd lose. But he said they'd cooled off, that it had only ever been a little fling, the natural consequence of their dance partnership—why did I think he forbade this sort of thing on the team?—but now they'd gotten it out of their system and they were back to being partners, just friends.

"You could have fooled me," Cali says.

"Cali! You're being a terrible spoilsport," Gemma says.

"I'm being protective."

"You're sweet. But I'm having fun. Speaking of romance," I say, "Gemma, how are things with Anders?"

"Oh god. He's having a rough go of it."

"Sister stuff?" Cali asks.

"Yes," Gemma says. "I don't mean to sound unsympathetic, but it just doesn't seem healthy. I came over the other night and found him watching old videos of her on his laptop, shit-faced on aquavit and sobbing. He punched a hole in the wall!"

"While you were there?" I ask.

"Oh no, the carnage was there when I arrived. It was her birthday last week and it's sent him into a death spiral."

"How long ago did this all happen?" I ask.

"Three years ago," Gemma says. I'm struck by this; the way he talks about it is as though it was yesterday—three years out and he's punching holes in the wall. What if I'm the same, what if I never actually feel better? "At least he's here now. I think it was worse in Norway. His parents got divorced after Berit died, and his mom was so devastated that she's left her room at their house exactly as it was. Anders told me it's like a shrine. I know there's no wrong way to grieve, but constantly reliving it does not seem helpful. There must be a better way. Anders is in so much pain and I just don't know what to do with him sometimes."

For a moment, we're all quiet, everyone bearing their own cross, considering each other's.

"Well, if you don't mind a subject change," Edward says, and I think, *please.* "Cali, I have something for you." He gets up and leaves the room, smiling at Cali and putting a hand on her shoulder. She glances at him and I see something sparkle briefly in the air between them.

We wait in giddy silence until Edward returns from the long dark hallway. Only Gemma looks relaxed and smug, and I think she must already know about whatever's coming.

Edward rolls something tall and obscured by a black bag forward. Cali gets to her feet. Of course, a cello. For a moment, I wonder how it will go, presenting her with a cello like this. I'm remembering the night of the Mexican dinner.

As Edward pulls the covering off and Cali steps forward gingerly, her eyes grow wide and her hands come to her mouth.

"Edward, why do you *have* this?" She's examining the instrument in awe, running her fingers along its spine, the curves of the body. The three of us are mesmerized watching her.

"I play a little," he says, smiling serenely. Cali is enraptured, and he knows he's done the right thing bringing out the cello.

"Edward is quite the renaissance man," Gemma says. "He's got whole caches of instruments back there."

"That is a nice way of saying that I'm a dabbler. But I do love instruments, and it's always nice to have them around—you never know when you might have a virtuoso in your midst. This one actually belongs to my mother. It was in New York, but I sent for it."

"It's a Goffriller. Gorgeous," Cali says. "One of the best, along with the Strad and the Montagnana. Though I've always preferred the Goff, to be honest. It's brighter." I realize the instrument must have cost a fortune.

She looks at Edward, and for an instant I feel like Gemma and I should leave the two of them alone. Or rather, the three of them.

"Cali, play something for us!" Gemma booms.

She looks at us uncertainly. "I haven't even looked at a cello in ages."

Edward reaches for her hand. "No pressure. It's here for you anytime."

"How can I not play it though?" she says, looking surprised at her own words. "I can't insult the Goff." She looks down at the beautiful instrument with reverence and a bit of trepidation, as though approaching a majestic, unpredictable horse.

Edward moves swiftly from the room and returns with a chair from the dining area. "Will this one do?" he asks. Cali nods, suddenly businesslike. He pulls a resin block from his pocket; Edward is like a stage director. Cali takes a seat, pulls the cello between her long legs, and begins to adjust the stand. Edward quietly joins us on the couch. We're hushed watching her. Even Gemma is utterly still for the first time since I've met her. Cali is wearing a tank top and shorts and so as she positions herself with the cello, only her bare limbs are visible, making it seem as though the cello almost disappears into her, and she into it. She resins the bow, and then begins a little warm-up routine, making a series of minute adjustments, nimbly turning the pegs and rolling her shoulders, stretching her neck from side to side. When she's ready, she looks back up at us.

"I'm playing you my favorite piece. It's a Brahms. Often paired with a piano, but I like it on its own."

We nod.

For some reason, I worry that watching someone play the cello alone in a room might be uncomfortable. I fear she'll make odd movements or ridiculous faces. But watching Cali play is grace itself. Her beautiful, slender arms are a ballet of movement, and her face is lost in some otherworldly ecstasy. Her eyes remain closed, but a thousand emotions seem to pass over her lovely features. The music surrounds me and I think of Penny in her religious phase, talking about hearing the voice of God, and I wonder if I still believe there might be a God. I did before, in a vague, unexamined way. But now? After? I don't know. This is one of many questions left unanswered: What does any of it mean? Why did it happen? Who the hell am I now?

But if there *is* a God, would he not speak in a language that all could understand? One that moved you on a level deeper than words could? Would he not sound, I think, just like Cali's cello? She moves on from the Brahms to Mozart, then Beethoven. She tells us this later; as she plays, she simply floats from one piece to the next, with only a deep breath and a pause to delineate the pieces. At last, she stops, spent. She looks up at us, as though only now remembering that we're in the room. I can't tell if the expression on her face is grief or joy. She excuses herself, setting the cello gingerly against the chair. She disappears into the courtyard. Edward suddenly doesn't look so sure of himself.

"I'll go," I say.

Cali is sitting by the pool with one leg hugged to her chest and the other dangling into the water. I fear she'll be upset, but as I settle myself down next to her, pulling up the edge of my skirt and letting my own calves slide into the cool water, her face looks serene, even happy. For a moment, we sit together in companionable silence.

"I've always loved the cello, you know," she begins, "but after New York, I started to worry that I was getting jaded, that it had become about what it meant to my identity rather than the music itself, about *being* part of the Philharmonic, about *being* a principal. Not about the music."

"And now?"

She turns to face me. She's smiling, but her eyes are sad.

"Now I know it wasn't just the status, the job, the dream. It was always the music. Always me and my cello."

"Then you have to go back," I say. As I say this, I am thinking of the mountain. Certainly, I too had become wrapped up in the glory, the pursuit of crystal globes and gold medals, sponsorships and deal making. But in the end, it was always me and the mountain. My first and truest love. What if it didn't all have to be over? As Blair said, there was always going to be an after.

"Yeah," Cali says. "Maybe I'll go find some little orchestra in Texas or something, move back home. I could always teach."

"No. Just because it's not *about* the glory doesn't mean you have to give up the glory. Hearing you play tonight . . ." Words escape me for a moment. "I've never heard anything like it. I was so moved."

"Thank you."

"I'm envious, you can do what you love until you're old. You don't belong on some dinky little stage, you belong in the spotlight, at like . . . I don't know." We both laugh. I so obviously know nothing about classical music, and I don't need to in order to see how talented Cali is. "Carnegie Hall? That's all I got, but you know what I mean."

"You're very convincing," Cali says, "but what about you? I mean, I know you got injured but . . ."

I'm still not ready to go into it. Especially not tonight, in this beautiful, crisp evening air, in the afterglow of the music, the prelude to another night with Gianluca.

"There is a very long story," I say, "that I'm not quite ready to tell. But I will tell you, I promise. Is that okay?"

"You take your time," she says. "I'll be here."

❧

I send G a text message when I'm back in my apartment and he's at my door in a half hour.

"Hello, beautiful," he says, and the familiar way he kisses me when he walks through my door is comforting. I'm not nothing to him. Am I?

"You took the bike," I say as he sheds his moto jacket, placing his helmet gingerly on my narrow kitchen counter.

"Every chance I get before the weather turns," he says. "Wasn't sure I'd be able to make it tonight, I can't stay long."

"Well, I'm glad you're here," I say, hoping I don't sound as pathetically grateful as I feel. He makes himself at home, pouring himself a glass of Fernet, which I keep here only for him.

"Me too. How was your night?"

"Good. Cali played the cello for us."

"Cali plays the cello?"

"You didn't know?" This is the thing about G: even though he wants me to tell him everything, to bear my soul as well as my body—intimacy distilled down to its elements—I'm not sure he remembers the details of my life or anyone else's. "She used to be in the New York Philharmonic."

"*Che,* really?" He whistles, impressed. "That gorgeous and talented too?"

I nod, suddenly wishing I hadn't brought it up. I feel a sharp stab of jealousy. I know Cali is beautiful but I don't need to be reminded by the man I am about to take my clothes off in front of. I don't need to think of myself being measured against her.

"Is she seeing anyone?" G asks, making it worse.

I shrug. "I suspect she and Edward might be into each other." Edward, I want to add, who is wealthier than you, and more powerful, whose money helps you and your studio keep going.

"Lucky bastard," he says, shaking his head. He drinks the rest of his Fernet. Smiles at me. "Come here you."

Idaho Journal Sentinel

October 12, 2008

MOMMY DEAREST: DID THIS IDAHO MOTHER MURDER HER DAUGHTER?

Ava Granger had a brief and difficult life up until her death on September 10. Her mother, Penny Cleary-Granger—Hayden resident and older sister of ski racer Katie Cleary—seemed like a paragon of motherhood to most who knew her. By all appearances, she'd gone to heroic lengths to care for her daughter, Ava, who was born premature and had been diagnosed with failure to thrive. But now, the *Journal Sentinel* has learned, Penny Cleary-Granger is under investigation for the murder of her three-year-old daughter. What happened?

"Penny was such a good mom," a family friend of the Grangers, Samantha Perkins, told us. "I don't know how I would cope if my child was sick, and now she's under suspicion of hurting her? I can't even imagine. I don't know how she's still standing."

A look at her extensive social media history paints Penny, 29, as a devoted mother who would go to any lengths for her daughter, and a loving military spouse who kept the home fires burning for her husband, Air Force Captain Stewart Granger, while he was away on multiple tours of duty in Iraq and Afghanistan. A *Journal Sentinel* investigation has discovered five separate Facebook pages for Cleary-Granger, with the followers totaling over 7,000. Many are "friends" who had never met Ava or Penny in person, but have followed Penny's extensive chronicles of her daughter's illnesses for years from such far-flung locations as New York, London, and Perth.

Neighbors of the Grangers in their small town of Hayden, ID, remember Ava as a happy little girl, despite her many trips to the hospital. "She was cute as a button," Nadine Frost, who lived next door to the Grangers, said. "And with Stewart having to be gone so much, there was a lot for Penny to deal with, you know? But she never complained. Even though she was working part-time and being a full-time mom, she was always offering to watch our grandkids. And she was so good with them! We always felt so secure since she was a doctor and all. She was constantly taking them in for earaches, fevers, all that stuff kids get."

Though records show that Penny Cleary-Granger holds a nursing degree from Boise State, a *Journal Sentinel* investigation into her employment history shows that she falsified documents in order to work as a physician's assistant, a job she left voluntarily before her daughter was born. She appears to have told friends and acquaintances that she was still working as a physician's assistant or, in some cases, a doctor.

Asked whether she remembers anything strange, Frost recalls that Penny seemed a bit paranoid about Ava's health, in particular her claims about her daughter needing to be fed via her NG tube. "The little munchkin always ate fine when I watched her. And she was with me a couple of times a week while Penny was at work," Frost said. "Seemed like maybe she was worrying a bit too much. So I guess I thought that was a little strange."

The combination of her sick daughter and the fact that Penny's husband was on a tour of duty in Afghanistan garnered plenty of sympathy for the young mother among peers who knew her, but according to a separate Facebook page Penny created called "Ava's Rainbow: A community of support for my little soldier!" Stewart Granger had died in the line of duty. No one who knew the Grangers in person—and would therefore know that Stewart was very much alive—was in the Facebook group, which was set to private.

The community of Hayden, already shaken by the death of Ava Granger, has been rocked to its core as news has spread that Penny is a suspect in her murder. The Hayden Police are currently investigating whether Ava's mysterious death in Shriner's Hospital for Children in Spokane, WA, was caused by a lethal amount of sodium, fed to the child via her G-tube. Her mother had access, as she was constantly by her side in the hospital and left unsupervised for long stretches; it's the motive that remains baffling. Why would a mother—especially one who appeared to the outside world to be so devoted—harm her child?

The bizarre case has raised the specter of Munchausen syndrome by proxy, a psychiatric disorder that causes a parent—usually a mother—to invent, or even inflict, medical aliments in their child in order to receive attention and sympathy. Cases in this day and age are amplified by the ubiquity of social media outlets where mothers of children suffering from illnesses—real and imagined—can gather in previously unheard of numbers.

As the investigation into Ava's death continues, the residents of Hayden struggle to make sense of the charges.

Samantha Perkins counts herself as a stalwart supporter.

"There's just no way she'd ever hurt her. I'm a mom too, and moms just know," she said, her eyes tearing up. "We just know."

Liz Crosses the River

THAT SATURDAY, Gemma knocks on my door early.

"Good morning!"

I blink at her bleary eyed in the morning sunshine. It's 9:00 a.m. and the summer is fleeting, the sun coming up a little later each day.

"Hi," I say.

"Another late night of *tango*?"

I smile, though I'm smarting because most of the night was spent arguing with G, who'd come over an hour later than he said he would. I called him on it and it had caused a big fight, which ended up being the prelude to several rounds of sex. This had begun to feel like a pattern.

"What's up?" I ask.

"We're going on a visa run, come with us!" As a condition of our respective tourist visas, we're required to leave the country every three months. The easiest way to do so is to take the ferry from Buenos Aires to Colonia, a tiny, charming Uruguayan city just across the Rio de la Plata.

"Oh okay, sure. Give me a sec."

I'm hungover and exhausted, but I rally, and soon we're aboard the high-speed ferry—the Buquebus—and rocketing across the churning brown waves of the river. The Rio de la Plata is an unlovely body of water.

At 140 miles, it's the widest river in the world, and being in the middle of it feels like being at sea. The river is an estuary, a meeting of the Uruguay and Paraná Rivers that empties into the Atlantic, meaning it's never anything but the color of mud, obscuring everything below the surface.

We dock in Colonia and have our passports stamped.

"Let's show Liz the historic district and grab some lunch down there," Edward says, taking Cali's arm. I'm the only one who's never been here.

"Oh yes! It's only a short walk, and there are some incredible ruins. They dug a whole little slice of the seventeenth century out of the hillside."

We take photos by the Portón de Campo and continue on to the Calle de los Suspiros.

"Ah, this is my favorite street in the district," Gemma says. "The 'street of sighs.' People mistake it for a romantic reference—that the sighs are lovers' sighs—but really it was named for the sighs of the slaves hauling stones up from the wharf to build the town."

As we walk, Gemma continues on her historical tour of Colonia with Cali, and I fall back with Edward. We walk in easy quiet, but at some point I realize he's looking at me from the corner of his eye, smiling curiously.

"You know," he says, picking his way carefully through the uneven cobblestones, "you don't really look like a 'Liz.' What made you choose it?"

I stop in my tracks and meet his gaze for a moment that unfolds into an eternity. Possibilities race through my mind, that I've misheard him or that he means something other than what I think he does.

"It's my middle name. Elizabeth," I say finally, looking out at the harbor. The sunshine is sparkling off the river and the outlines of our friends are thrown into sharp relief.

"And Sullivan?"

"My mom's maiden name."

"Ah."

"How did you find out?" I finally ask.

"I knew the night I met you. I Googled it to confirm, but I was fairly certain. My ex followed the story obsessively. She was heartbroken for your family. For you, in particular. She and her own sister are insepa-rable."

I nod, taking this in. "I don't really know what to say."

"I'm not trying to put you on the spot. I won't say anything. But for what it's worth, I don't think anyone would judge you, if that's what you're worried about."

I laugh, but it's heavy as a stone. "Well, that was definitely *not* my experience back home." As the shock of Edward's revelation recedes, I realize it's a relief that someone knows.

Edward shrugs. "Maybe, but it's different here. Everyone came here for a reason. Everyone's life is a mess back home."

"Not quite like mine though."

"Well no," he acknowledges, "and I'm not trying to minimize what's happened to you. I just thought an outside perspective might be helpful."

"It is," I say. "I'm not ready to talk about it. But thank you. For not saying anything."

He shrugs. "It's not my story to tell, Liz."

⁂

We have a wine-soaked lunch in Colonia's Plaza de Mayo.

"God," Gemma says. "I could eat a fucking horse. I'm a monster when I'm on the rag."

"Gemma." Edward rolls his eyes.

"Oh I'm sorry, darling, does my healthy, functioning female body offend you? Don't be prissy."

I laugh and it occurs to me that I can't remember when I last got my own period. Before the past year it was like clockwork, but the stress has made my cycle erratic. I guess it still hasn't gone back to normal yet.

We take a languorous walk around the small, picturesque city. We stroll through the artisanal market and Gemma buys up an armful of leather goods. We buy ice cream at the edge of a park where children are running around and people are walking dogs of all sizes.

If Cali hadn't seen him, we might have missed him altogether. He could have so easily disappeared into the idyllic tableau of the park on a sunny Saturday.

"Dude," Cali says, clutching my arm and gesturing to a couple in the park who are playing with their two small children. The mother, who looks about Gemma's age, catches my eye first. She's attractive and slim with black hair and light eyes. As I look more closely at her, I realize that she looks exhausted and maybe a little melancholy watching her children. Then her eyes meet her son's and she lights up. I glance across the field at the father and feel the gut punch of recognition. Gianluca is playfully chasing a toddler who runs in circles, squealing with delight. Seeing him here is so out of context that my mind struggles to make sense of it.

"Maybe it's his niece and nephew?" I say, trying to keep my voice even.

"Does he have siblings?" Cali asks.

"I don't know."

"Do you want to go say hi?" Cali asks softly.

"Nah," I say. "Anyway, we have to get going to catch the Buquebus. Right, Gemma?" I say, turning to find her.

"Oh, we have a few minutes. Why . . ." And then she sees what we're looking at. I'm half surprised that G doesn't notice the four of us there, but then again, he's not expecting us, and he's focused on . . . his kids. We're only an hour away from Buenos Aires, and yet we're in another country where Gianluca, evidently, has another life.

Both Edward and Gemma are quiet for a moment as we all watch the little family convening near a bench. The boy and girl climb all over G, clinging to him as he sips a thermos of what I assume is maté and has a tense-looking conversation with the woman.

"You didn't know?" Edward says, making me realize that he did. Perhaps it's how he pled his case to get Edward to invest: *I have a family to support.*

"No," I say. "No."

"Well, he's not *with* her, is he?" Gemma asks.

"I honestly have no idea. I don't know what's going on. Edward?" I ask.

Edward shakes his head. "They've been split up for a long time."

"Let's go," Cali says finally. "Do you want to go, Liz?"

We make our way silently back to the ferry terminal and board the Buquebus to head back to where we came from.

"Maybe," Gemma says, sitting down gingerly next to me on the upper deck, "there is a good explanation."

"For why Gianluca has a secret family that he's never mentioned to me?"

"But maybe there is more to the story. Maybe he's not the bad guy. It's so much more complicated when there are children involved." I'm surprised that Gemma is defending him.

"So complicated that you can't mention their existence to the person you're dating?" Cali asks. And I wonder, *Am I dating G?* It feels like less than that, and more, all at once.

I nod. There is no way to explain to them what I'm feeling without telling them all much more than I'm willing to. For one thing, I cannot bear to look at children who are the age that Ava would have been. And the sight of the youngest one—with his dark eyes and ruddy cheeks, so healthy and cheerful—has cut me to the quick. The fact that he belongs to G is too much. Then, it's as though an alarm had been tripped and my mind rockets back to my missed period. But it's been this late before, hasn't it?

"I should end it," I say woodenly, knowing as the words come out that I'm right but also that I won't do any such thing.

Edward says, "That seems hasty."

"Hey," Cali says, "whose side are you on here?"

"Gianluca has had a difficult life. Much more so than he lets on; most people who know him have no idea what he's been through."

"Maybe Edward's right. I can see you're crazy about him," Gemma adds.

Yes, I think, considering the lack of sleep and the way that G has expanded in my mind to captivate my every thought, *crazy* is exactly the word. And it's not sustainable, but the idea of never being with him again makes me feel faint. And what if I am pregnant? What am I doing? Am I really so incapable of balance? Does everything have to be an obsession? Does everything have to be a drug?

"Edward," I say. "What really happened in Saint-Tropez? Did he really kill someone?"

He lets out a long sigh. "It's complicated. Her husband tried to attack her, he stepped in."

"And you saw this with your own eyes?" Cali asks. "Or this is according to him?"

"I really don't think," Edward replies haughtily, "that the countess—whom I'd known for over a decade by the way—would have vouched for him if that hadn't been the case. It was she who asked me to help him get back to Buenos Aires. Do you really believe," he said, looking at me now, "that someone would lie about a thing like that?"

The After

IT WAS hard to imagine anything worse than what we'd gone through with Penny's dependency case until I experienced what came after. If I'd known then how very dysfunctional our child welfare system is, perhaps I would have expected it. Penny's case was complex; she was an aberration that the medical community was not built to withstand. She did not look or act the part of an abusive mother. For those whose interactions with her were brief, nothing about her read "unstable"—to the contrary, she seemed utterly competent and likable. It's a mark of just how privileged and sheltered I'd been until that moment that I expected the justice system to work, that I couldn't fathom it failing us as utterly as it did.

I tried to bury myself in skiing. Blair and Luke knew everything, but most of my coaches and teammates knew only the broad stokes, which was all I could bear to tell them. I learned quickly that most people don't have the stomach to hear about something like Munchausen syndrome by proxy, so I kept it simpler than that, telling people that my family had been through a big drama that had left me estranged from my sister. On the upside, it meant I didn't have to relive the details or withstand the looks of horror; on the downside, not knowing how serious it all was lead people to offer me platitudes. *I'm sure you'll work it out, my sister and I fight all the time! You should resolve it, family is the most important thing.*

My beloved tech Bartek chatted with me as he adjusted my skis before the final race of the World Cup season.

"You are sad, Katie Bomber," he said, his eyes meeting mine for a moment before returning to my bindings. He always called me this, as though Bomber was a last name instead of a nickname. Bartek was Czech, fortysomething I guessed, though he never shared his actual age; he was relatively sparse on the details of his personal life. He was gruff and I adored him. Techs were our lifelines—they helped us succeed and kept us safe on the course, or as safe as anyone could keep us. "I hear you have problem with family. Is hard."

Being that he wasn't exactly warm and fuzzy normally, I was touched by his efforts.

"My sister is very troubled. I don't know if I will ever talk to her again," I said. "I don't know what to do."

"I have little brother in Ostrava," he said. "Has drug problem. My family we try and try but he lie and steal from my mother. I love him very much but"—he shrugged—"what can I do? Sometimes nothing."

I nodded, grateful that for once someone was not immediately trying to make me feel better.

He made one last adjustment to the binding and then rattled it and made a satisfied grunt.

"Some people are like drowning man. If you try to save them, they only pull you down too. Sometimes you need save yourself, Katie Bomber." He put his hand on my shoulder and gave me a paternal smile.

⁓ॐ⁓

That season was abysmal, and by the end of it, I was starting to feel the pressure from my sponsors. If I fell any further away from the top ten, I knew some would drop me. Red Bull—by far my most lucrative contract—was already looking itchy. I started seeing Gena the therapist, and for a while things got better. By the time the 2007–2008 season began, I was back on the podium again in my first two races.

My relationship with Luke was still shaky. I could feel him beginning to inch away from me, and the more he retreated, the harder I clung. After all that I'd lost, adding Luke to the list of casualties just wasn't an option.

He'd encouraged me to go to therapy, but as for talking to me about Penny, he'd act sympathetic but shut the conversation down almost instantly. He seemed relieved when I started feeling better.

"Glad you're getting back to your old self, Bomber," he said after my first solid finish of the season. "You were really hard to be around for a while."

I feigned a smile, gutted.

⁓

Luke wasn't skiing well during our final training camp of the off-season in La Parva, and when Blair suggested a side trip to Buenos Aires, Luke shrugged it off.

Blair and I spent a delirious two days in Buenos Aires. He'd had his best season yet and had nearly taken home the World Cup globe. On our last night, we walked back to our little bed-and-breakfast in Palermo after a good steak and a lot of wine. It was nearly 2:00 a.m. and plenty of people around us seemed to be just starting their night; we hadn't even closed down the restaurant we'd been in. We got gelato and strolled around the plaza. It was the beginning of fall in Buenos Aires, but they were having an upside-down Indian summer and it was unseasonably warm.

"Bomber, you seem like you're doing so much better," he said, putting his arm around my shoulders. "I'm so glad. I really admire you and your parents, you know? You guys really stuck by each other and it can't have been easy. I'm proud of you, you're a tough cookie."

"I know I wasn't easy to be around for a while," I said, parroting Luke without meaning to.

"I wouldn't say that. It was hard to watch you go through all of that, sure, but being around you is always good."

"I wasn't exactly at my best," I said, unsure why I was doubling down.

"So? I'll take you at your worst over most people at their best. You know that, Bomber. You know I love ya."

"Aw." I took his arm. "You're a big softie. Jesus, I thought my career was going to be over last year," I said. "It was terrifying."

"We're all going to have to face it sometime," Blair said.

"I know, I know. Ugh, I hate thinking about it though! It's like, everyone else our age is just getting going on their careers and ours are going to be over. Skiing is the only thing I ever wanted to do."

"Aren't you a little bit excited for the next part though? I mean, there are some things I won't miss. The injuries, the constant travel. I want to be in one place for a while. I want to get married and have some kids. I want to be able to own a *dog* for Christ's sake."

I had a sudden and deep flash of envy for whomever the eventual woman in this scenario would be. Blair had been dating a snowboarder named Kelly for a while—I'd liked her—but they'd broken up midseason. Relationships weren't easy to maintain in our world. Sometimes, it felt like Luke and I were coasting on our long history until we could reach some better place where we could reconnect.

"Okay, yeah, I'll give you that. A little stability probably wouldn't kill me either. But what are we going to *do*?"

"I have this idea," Blair said, his voice suddenly a little bashful. "I mean, I love skiing so much and I feel like it's this sport that only a small number of people ever get to try. I want to start a ski school that's also a nonprofit. We could get kids who normally wouldn't have access to it up there on the mountain. Kind of like those adventure courses, you know?"

"Outward Bound?" We softened our voices as we made our way into the hotel.

"Yes! Exactly. Outward Bound on the snow. If I pitch it the right way, I know I could get Tad's rich buddies on board. What looks better in a brochure than smiling kids?"

"That's a great idea. I don't have anything anywhere near that cool up my sleeve."

"Maybe you could do it with me," he said softly.

"Maybe." I smiled. We'd reached the door of my room. "For now, I don't want to think about the after."

A moment of quiet descended, and out of nowhere there was an energy between us that hadn't been there before. Or maybe I was like a radio dial that had finally hit the right frequency and was only now picking up on something that had been there all along. Blair leaned forward and brushed his thumb against the corner of my mouth.

"You eat ice cream like a little kid, Bomber."

Then he kissed me. Just briefly, just lightly enough to pass as brotherly but yet decidedly not.

"You shouldn't be afraid of the future." He pulled back, as though just realizing what he'd done. "There was always going to be an after."

Liz Wants the Truth

AT THE social the next Friday, Edward makes a rare appearance. Watching him, I'm surprised anew at what a graceful dancer he is.

"It's funny with dancing," Cali says, settling in next to me on the cozy, voluminous couch. "Men go one way or the other the moment they're on the floor. If they're good, they become a thousand times sexier, if they're awkward, their appeal just leeches right out of them. There's no neutral ground."

"You're right. That said, I'm surprised Edward isn't out here all the time."

Cali smiles to herself.

"Hi, girls," Gianluca says, stopping by between dances. He gives us each an equally brief kiss on the cheek. I've been warned that he won't be overly affectionate when we're with the dance crowd. It's just business, he tells me, he can't appear taken. Maybe that's what did Angelina in. How can I not wonder if there's some other girl, some other "special project" he's dancing with, whispering in her ear that he wants to fuck her? My anxiety isn't helped by the fact that my period still hasn't arrived. In the back of my head a tiny voice replays the damning question over and over: *Am I pregnant, am I pregnant, am I pregnant?*

"Save me a dance?" he says as he goes back off to the floor. "Both of you?" he adds.

Cali gives me a hard look as he walks away.

"It's fine," I say, not feeling fine. "It's work."

"Okay, Liz. Okay."

⁂

That night, G is sweet and soft with me. I know he won't stay the night, but he lingers after we've had sex for an unusually long time. We lie side by side in my narrow bed and he stares into my eyes, unraveling the knot in my chest. We're in the between space where the postcoital chemicals are still coursing through our veins and my tilting endorphin high hasn't yet been eclipsed by the anxiety that he'll leave. Soon, I'll start watching for signs that he's on the move: his eyes flickering in the direction of the door, his hand reaching for his pants, his eyes clouding back over with his own separate thoughts, the channel that opens between us closing until next time. A next time that is never promised. I'll be left here in sheets covered with the scent of him, bereft, and wondering if I'm in love with him because what else could be this potent? How is it this strong if it's just sex? It's as though being with him has altered my brain chemistry. But for now he's here, the connection between us clear and present. I'm searching for a way to ask him about Colonia, but I don't want to ruin the moment.

"You're an incredible woman, do you know that?" he says.

I smile at him and close my eyes.

"I don't want you to ever be with anyone who doesn't see that."

I sigh. This feels like a warning that he has no intention of making this permanent. He looks at me for a long moment, combing my hair behind my ear, his eyes searching my face for something.

"What happened to you, Tiger?"

I swallow, propping myself up on my elbow and letting the sheet fall away. Over the last few weeks, I've lost some weight, and there is no one I want to notice this more than him. "What do you mean?"

He cocks his head at me and gives me a patient smile, because I know what he's asking. I let myself drop back down flat on the bed and stare up at the ceiling.

"Did you lose someone close to you?"

I nod.

"My sister . . ." I begin, but it's as far as I can get.

"You lost your sister?"

"In a way. She's not dead." It's so much worse than that. "We're es-tranged. Probably forever."

"Oh, Tiger, I'm sorry," he says. I wonder if he isn't a little unimpressed. It's not as dramatic as he's expecting maybe. "I'd taken you for an only child. You know," he says, pulling me close to him now, "I had a sibling growing up. A brother, but we don't speak now."

I consider this for a moment, if this is part of our bond, having en-dured these living deaths.

"What happened with him?"

He sighs. "It's complicated. We never had much in common. To be honest, it always felt strange that he was my brother. And then I discov-ered that, in fact, he wasn't."

"One of you was adopted?"

G let out a bitter laugh. "In a manner of speaking."

"What does that mean?" I find I'm suddenly desperate to know just *one* true thing about him. Something that isn't legend and rumor and bluster.

G shakes his head and the subtle movement away from me begins: next, he'll roll onto his side and then with alarming efficiency and speed, he'll be dressed and gone.

"G, tell me." My voice is more insistent than I mean it to be.

He laughs ruefully, kisses my forehead in a way that means goodbye. "You don't want to know, Tiger, just trust me."

"I do want to know." His back is to me. His feet hit the floor, and he grabs his pants. I clutch his shoulder and he turns to me, looking annoyed. He smiles as he stands up, but it isn't a kind smile. He puts his hands on his hips, still shirtless.

"You're like a little girl right now."

"Fuck you, G," I mutter, curling my knees to my chest. "Like it's so wrong to want to know you a little bit."

"You want to *know* me?" he says, crouching down and glaring at me until I have no choice but to look him in the eye. "Ha, okay, Liz, okay. Go ahead, ask whatever you want."

"When you first met Edward in Saint-Tropez, the woman on the boat, her husband . . . were you really only trying to protect her?"

He gives me a look that makes my blood run cold. "This is a very boring question, try again." In not answering the question, he has. I know him well enough by now to know that if he were really the hero of this story, he'd have answered me.

"Fine," I say. "What's the deal with your family? I'm assuming that you're not really the illegitimate son of Juan Perón."

He steps back and looks at me appraisingly, as though deciding whether I am worthy of knowing.

"When I was twenty-three, an old woman showed up at my door saying she was my grandmother. I didn't believe her until she showed me pictures of my parents—who were only a little older than I was when she lost them—I was the spitting image of my father, there was no question."

I'd read stories like this. Some of the women who marched in the Plaza de Mayo were grandmothers searching for grandchildren who were lost to them when their adult children were disappeared. Just as with my own parents, the sacred link between generations had been brutally severed.

"Your real parents were disappeared," I say, and then I ask the wrong question, "Do you know why?"

G laughs a horrible laugh. "They didn't need a reason, being a university student made you automatically suspicious, you could be getting subversive ideas. They were both studying architecture."

"How did you end up with your adopted family?"

"I was one of hundreds of babies who was 'reappropriated' to military families while the junta was in power. Meaning that the people I'd grown up calling my parents murdered my real parents; maybe not with their own hands but close enough. I'd always known something was off. I was only eighteen months old when they took them, but I still had memories that I could never explain. My 'parents' sent me to a child psychologist to convince me otherwise."

Since I'd met him, Gianluca had never seemed quite real. He deliberately made himself larger than life with the web of mysteries and exaggerations he'd woven, more a beautiful, thrilling idea than a person. But for the first time I saw him as he was, an all-too-human man. He wasn't trying to create a cult with his studio, he was trying to create a family. He was forever reaching for the nearest stranger because he was an eternal stranger to himself.

"Did you ever find out what happened to them?" I ask, holding his gaze.

"No," he says. "Likely they were drugged, blindfolded, and shoved off a helicopter somewhere over the Rio de la Plata. But just like the rest, we'll never really know. Thirty thousand civilians were 'disappeared.' There's a reason we stick with that romantic term—the truth is too ugly to bear."

"G, I'm sorry." I try to reach for him and he yanks his arm away.

"Americans," he says bitterly. "You come for the steak and the exchange rate, and you don't even know what this country is."

He's out the door before I can say anything else.

Where Has Penny Gone?

URING THE horrific eight months between Penny's arrest for Ava's murder and the beginning of her trial, a thousand emotions consumed me, each one fighting for center stage. First, a bottomless well of grief: Ava was gone, and I didn't need a judge and jury to tell me who'd been responsible. I was angry at Penny, I had been for a long time now. But I felt scared for her too, and the longing I'd felt for her only increased as her absence began to feel permanent. I see from the outside how it all appears unforgivable, but the desire to forgive someone you love blocks out the sun, and I convinced myself that she hadn't actually meant to kill her daughter, she'd just miscalculated. Because we'd had no contact with Penny or Ava in two years, the whole situation felt surreal. I kept waiting for someone to tell me that they'd been wrong, as though this were all just some kind of nightmarish prank.

I always figured that Penny would come back to us, if not because she wanted to than because she needed to. The credit card debt of her early twenties had turned out to be the tip of the iceberg. She'd made about every bad financial decision a person could make: she owed back rent, had defaulted on payday loans, had written bad checks. How long until Stewart ran out of resources to support her?

I knew there was nothing to be gained from reaching out to her, but there were times I ached for her so much, I couldn't sleep, couldn't stop thinking about her. I wrote her a letter and mailed it to her house. I told her that it was my love for her that wouldn't let me pretend that nothing was wrong. I told her I hoped she'd be standing next to me on my wedding day, as I'd been on hers. I told her I hoped she'd be by my side when I gave birth to my first child as I was when she gave birth to Ava. I told her I'd always love her. And I'd meant it. What a miserable fate.

Up until the news broke, I'd been holding on to hope that, if nothing else, Ava would eventually come of age and we'd all get another chance. We could help her then and perhaps we could help Penny too. By that point, her fertility—her weapon of choice—would be obsolete. Until then, I would have to reconcile myself to the fact that I would not get to see Ava grow up. As it turned out, no one would.

When the worst thing you can imagine—the thing you've been obsessively imagining—happens, it's worse than the anticipation of it, but not by as much as you'd think. An unspeakable aspect of the worst-case scenario is that it brings with it some relief, because you're no longer waiting for it.

Because of our estrangement from Penny, we heard what happened from the news like everyone else. The story broke while I was flying home from the two-day trip to Buenos Aires with Blair. By the time we landed, my voice mail was full with messages. When we met Luke at baggage claim, his face was ashen; he'd known for several hours. I know he flew home with me to Idaho to make sure I got there in one piece, but I have no memory of the trip.

The media attention ratcheted up fast, and what began as a local horror story quickly got picked up by the wire services, then by the morning shows and evening news magazines. Soon, my voice mail was filling up so fast I had to change my number. The U.S. Ski Team recommended a crisis PR agent and swiftly distanced themselves from the story with an anodyne statement about being sorry for our loss.

I could tell my sponsors were spooked—the story of a murdered child is too horrific to touch—and it didn't help that my previous season hadn't been stellar. I could barely sleep and was having panic attacks.

"Don't worry," Tad Duncan said, clapping his hand on my shoulder. "This will all blow over after the trial and you can focus on skiing again." But the look in his eye as he spoke was one I now recognized: I was bad for his brand too, and his sons'. I was toxic by association.

As the trial drew nearer, as the press became more relentless and my e-mail in-box filled with hate mail, it sunk in just how much there was to lose. No less than everything.

Liz at the End of the World

FALL IS coming on and before the weather turns, Cali and I decide to visit Ushuaia, the southernmost city in the world, portal to the Antarctic. I need to put several hundred miles between Gianluca and me while I figure out what the hell I'm going to do. I Google all of the many reasons I might not be getting my period: stress, change in diet, the moon. My search leads me down a rabbit hole that begins with legitimate medical advice and quickly devolves into homeopathy, folklore, myth, and sheer batshit mommy blogger nonsense. I know I need to just take a pregnancy test, but I've never taken one and I'm terrified, as though the act of taking the test might make it so. Luke and I were always careful with birth control, back when my body was for something. I know I haven't been as good about taking my pills; I've missed a day here and there, but is that really enough? Much of what I read is instructive on how to get pregnant, and makes it sound as complicated as a space shuttle launch. *How could this happen to anyone by accident?* I wonder.

The plane ride to Patagonia takes us over the vast alien landscape that lies between Buenos Aires and the tip of the continent. There are miles of arid, windswept plains with no sign of humanity. The Andes appear in their sudden glory. I've seen them before, but they always take my breath away; there is no mountain range that looks quite so steep and forbidding from above.

The mountains drop off precipitously into the sea as the tiny port city of Ushuaia comes into view. The landing strip is a short runway that ends right in the Drake Passage, which leads out into the southern Atlantic.

Cali and I rent a funky little condo near the water that's covered in the tacky nautical decor of every seaside town everywhere. The town itself is an unlovely, utilitarian port with some touristy shops and mediocre restaurants haphazardly added for visitors. But the town is beside the point; it's the location that matters. The steep Andean cliffs surrounding it and plunging into the ocean, the lush lakes and forests just outside the city, the bay with its perpetual, eerie fog, and beyond it, only Antarctica. The weather moves in and out swiftly, changing from sun to rain to clouds in the space of an hour, so that watching the sky here feels like looking at time-lapse photography. My body feels haywire: I'm in a giddy space between knowing and not knowing.

On our first full day, we take a Jeep tour through tangled forests and sparkling lakes, which send an unexpected flash of longing for home through me. There's a couple on our tour—half Argentine, half American, one speaking Spanish, the other speaking English with our guide, and Cali and I pivoting between the two. The couple has been together two years; he'd just been to visit her family in one of the northern provinces. "Good thing I speak some Spanish now," he tells us in English. "He doesn't speak any Spanish," she tells us later in Spanish. I ask how they talk to each other. She flicks the cigarette she's smoking. "We don't!" she says cheerfully, and the three of us laugh and laugh. Lunch is served in a tiny tent that we come across, seemingly by magic, in the forest where there's a burly cook who serves us bloody, delicious steak and quotes Borges.

On our second day, we take a cruise through the accessible parts of the bay and spot sea lions and penguins on the harsh, barren shores of the island.

Though there isn't much to the town itself, the views from the bay are spectacular, and we spend a long afternoon wandering around. There is a large sign in the classic Argentine *fileteado* that reads USHUAIA: FIN DEL MUNDO. The end of the earth.

"Liz, go hop in there and I'll take a picture!" Cali says.

I'm standing next to the sign smiling broadly when I hear her.

"Katie?"

The sound of my name, which I haven't heard in months now, is immediately disorienting. I turn in the direction of the woman who says it. Cali is watching, bemused, thinking that this stranger has mistaken me for someone else.

"Katie Cleary!" Now she's only a few feet from me and I process her face.

"Kjersti!"

I wrap my arms around her: my rival, my friend. Fresh off her gold medal win.

"What are you *doing* here?" she says. "Where have you been? You dropped off the face of the earth, and now I find you at the end of the earth!" I'm not sure if Kjersti is as adorably corny in Norwegian as she is in English, but if not, the Norwegians are missing out.

"Oh, um . . . I'm living in Buenos Aires right now. I'm just here visiting with my friend, Cali." I look over to see Cali standing apart from us, looking confused and reticent. I wave her over with a look that I hope says that I'll explain later.

"Kjersti Larsen, Calliope Ford. Cali, meet Kjersti, my old friend and newly minted gold medal downhill racer."

"Oh shit," Cali says as the two shake hands. "That's incredible, congrats!"

"Thank you, and nice to meet you. I love Buenos Aires. San Telmo," she says, clutching her heart, "my favorite."

"That's where we live," Cali says. I would have preferred to avoid specifics, but what difference does it make if Kjersti knows what neighborhood I live in? The cat's out of the bag. I would feel ridiculous asking her to keep it a secret.

"Seriously though, Kjersti, congrats on Vancouver," I add.

"You know the medal, it doesn't count, Katie, because you weren't there. You know I don't just say this."

Kjersti doesn't *just* say anything. I know she means it. I would feel the same. Wins against her were always more meaningful, and the losses too; for years, we'd pushed each other to be better, and I miss her more than I'd let myself realize until now.

"I'm so proud of you, Kjersti. I'm really happy for you. If it wasn't going to be me, I'm glad it was you. I mean that from the bottom of my heart."

"Not that bitch Sarah Sweeny, huh? I take care of her for you."

At this, I laugh out loud, and indeed, I'm glad it wasn't Sarah Sweeny. She didn't medal, small mercies.

"Shit," Kjersti says. "I wish I could stay and go have a drink with you girls. But I got to get my gear ready to head to Antarctica tomorrow."

"What are you doing out there?"

"BMW is sending me and Hans," she said, name-checking one of her teammates. "We're shooting a video."

"Damn! Can't let the freeskiers have all of the fun. Nice."

"When will I see you, Bomber? When are you coming back?"

Standing with Kjersti is like going back in time for a moment, and I can almost believe that none of it ever happened. She's talking to me as though it could be so, like she hasn't noticed that I'm clearly out of shape, like I haven't pulled a complete disappearing act. I wonder if I could even still have reps, a team, a future, even if I could get over my fear and get my head back together enough to face the mountain at all. Even if I'm not pregnant. Or if I decide not to be.

"I'm not sure," I say, "but I'll be in touch, okay? I promise."

"You better promise! I come find you!"

"You'll be too busy kicking Sarah's ass all over the Alps."

This gets a full-throated laugh.

"I promise though," I say, pulling her in for a hug. My voice catches in my throat, and I need her to leave before I start bawling.

"Okay, I better go," she says, pulling back to hold my shoulders and give me a long look. "Nice to meet you, Cali. Bye, Bomber. We'll see you soon, yes?"

All I can do is nod.

For a moment, Cali and I stand there silently, watching Kjersti walk away, her sleek panther-like form striding down the sidewalk and catching glances from men and women alike. Professional athletes are like beautiful aliens, similar to humans but perhaps one stage further along in their evolution. I realize too late that I never fully appreciated the beauty of the body I had; I was too obsessed with its mechanics.

"So, uh, Katie? *Bomber*?" Cali says finally.

I give her a sheepish look, but at least she's smiling, taking it in with cheerful grace. Dread is pooling in my stomach. I know she thinks she can handle it, whatever it is. I'll forgive her if she can't. I'm new in her life, I tell myself, and she's new in mine, it will only be a surface wound if I lose her.

"Ye-ah," I say.

"I mean, I know I wasn't exactly forthcoming about my past, but an alias is kind of next level."

There's really no choice now, I think. We can't be friends any longer with this hanging between us. I can't pile another lie on the ones I've already told her—the fake name, the altered backstory. After all, before Penny was a killer she was a liar. I can't keep this up.

"I want to tell you, but it's hard to know where to start," I say as we make our way to a bench that looks out onto the Drake Passage. The bay is both eerie and beautiful: the clouds above it are constantly churning, and the water, the light, the sky are never still. Beyond it, there's only the forbidding Antarctic.

"Well, how about we start with why you told me your name was Liz?"

"Liz, well Elizabeth, is my middle name. My actual name is Katie Cleary." I realize that this piece of information might save me from having to explain the rest. "Does that ring any bells?" My voice gets soft.

She thinks about it. "I mean, yeah, vaguely. But, to be honest, I don't really follow ski racing."

I smile sadly. That's not why she recognizes my name.

"How about Penny Cleary-Granger?" I say.

Cali's eyes grow wide with recognition. I can't be sorry that I didn't tell her until now; at least now she's less likely to jump to every horrible conclusion in the book, now that she knows me. Maybe.

"She's my older sister."

I hear the sharp intake of Cali's breath and my heart races. I envision her backing away from me or screaming for help. The weight of not having told anyone, of finally telling her, is crushing me.

"So, honey. That long story you were going to tell me at some point?" she says, looping her arm through mine as we sit on the bench. "If you're ready, I think I'd like to hear it."

Penny's Sister Takes the Stand

THERE ARE many more parents tried for the murders of their children than anyone would like to think about, and the sad reality is that most of these cases are no more than a blip on the local news. But the particular elements of our story combined for a perfect media maelstrom. First, there was Penny herself: a middle-class, conventionally attractive white woman. I'd now spent enough time around social workers and at family court to discover that this made her wildly unusual as a suspect of any kind of child neglect or abuse, let alone murder. These weren't the usual depressing systemic circumstances—poverty, addiction, prison time, child neglect as a result of parents whose lives were in tragic disarray. My sister—with her nice clothes, her professional background, her shiny hair—slipped right under the radar. A pretty, white female murderer is a beast that hides in plain sight because no one believes she exists. I suppose it would have been different if she'd killed her cheating husband or something—after all, *Chicago* was a hit—but pretty ladies only kill for sexy reasons in the public's imagination. Second, there was the sheer horror of the crime itself and the immense backlog of social media for speculators to parse. Third, there was me. No one other than skiing fans and Luke Duncan groupies knew who I was before the trial, but even the most minor level of celebrity mixed with a murder case turns the wattage up to a million. Suddenly, I was recognized everywhere. I got messages of support, hate mail, rape and death threats, marriage proposals, the gambit.

The narrative Penny's defense team tried to advance was that my parents had favored me in such a way that it amounted to neglect and deprivation of my sister. Trial watchers obsessed over our relationship; rating women against one another is America's favorite pastime, after all. Who was the sweet one? Who was the bitch? Who was the smart one? But most importantly, who was the *hot* one? Was it Penny, with her curves, or me, with my lean physique? Penny was a bit fat actually, the pathetic men who comment on such things online opined, but wasn't I a bit masculine with my muscles? Plenty of guys registered the opinion that they'd do both of us, a smaller number—trolls with unreasonably high standards—said neither of us would make the cut. I briefly considered having DON'T READ THE COMMENTS! tattooed on my hands.

For the thousands who watched the trial coverage, the worst moments of my life became a parlor game of speculation, a soap opera that people could tune in to and be scandalized and riveted by before going back to their normal lives. The country was in the deep end of the worst financial crisis since the Great Depression, and I imagined they looked at my family and thought, *We may be underwater on our mortgage but at least we're not these people.*

A parade of people Penny had deceived into thinking she was a dutiful mother who'd been deeply and despicably wronged by a negligent hospital and her evil family—the minor acquaintances, the rude aunties—reemerged for their moment in the spotlight. But there were also many people who testified bravely against her on Ava's behalf, participating in the awful, gruesome trial to do the right thing. The court-appointed special advocate who'd worked on Ava's previous case gave a thoughtful, convincing testimony about her experiences with Penny and Ava. Then there were the doctors from the SCAN team, nurses from Children's, the therapist who'd evaluated her for the original case. With no video evidence of Penny's misdeeds, the prosecution relied on the testimony of experts and on the massive, byzantine paper trail that detailed not only Ava's strange medical history and Penny's own, but other instances of fraud, including the fact—which my parents and I had only learned via the local paper's investigative reporting—that Penny wasn't actually qualified to work as a physician's assistant. This detail paled in comparison to her other crimes but was nonetheless dizzying. The lie had roots that went back the better part of a decade, and I could recall dozens of conversations with Penny about how hard she was working to get her master's. I'd been so proud of her for the achievement; I'd never questioned her. It was cold comfort to know that she'd been credible enough to convince actual medical professionals that she was qualified. One more piece of my sister turned to ash.

My testimony came late in the trial, weeks before the verdict. In addition to the doctor who'd been in the room with Penny when Ava coded and who had discovered a container of table salt in the bathroom off of her hospital room, and my mother, I was considered a star witness. People find sports celebrities credible, I was told, especially Olympians who'd stood on the medal stand, even if it wasn't a gold around their neck. Patriotism becomes a factor, and with a jury made up of red-blooded, red state Idahoans, this was key.

The prosecutors asked me questions about our family growing up, what Penny had been like, and how our relationship had been. They asked what I'd made of Penny's many health issues, and specifically of her previous "pregnancy," which we now knew for certain—given the medical records subpoenaed by the prosecution—had never existed. I answered as truthfully as possible and when asked if I had anything else to add, I spoke from the heart, my voice shaking. I was emotional, and saying this all in public, with the cameras and the jury and the onlookers, was more unnerving than I'd expected. I'd naively thought that my many interviews with sports journalists throughout the years would have prepared me.

"I just want everyone to understand that my sister has an illness," I said to the jury. "I don't know if she even understands what she's done. But my parents and I love her. We love you, Penny, we just want you to get help."

My sister—who had alternated between crying and an icy, blank affect throughout the trial—stared pointedly, angrily away from me, lips pursed.

Even then, even in that awful moment, when I was worn down by the battle fatigue of it all, I held on to some hope that there was, if not a happy ending—such a thing is forever negated by the death of a child—some reconciliation possible. I imagined Penny in a treatment center of some kind, where she would slowly be brought to the realization of what she'd done, where she would have to process the shock, the grief, the guilt, but we'd stay by her side. It was a fantasy that brought me relief, picturing the day when this trial was over, and some kind of healing could begin. It was the best outcome I could dream up, and still, it gutted me.

The defense's cross-examination was an entirely different experience from the prosecution's questioning. Penny had two defense attorneys: a young, fit man with a tight haircut who looked like a recruitment poster for the Navy, and a fiftysomething woman called Sheila Gregory who was broad shouldered and had the face and disposition of a mistreated bulldog. I was a big witness, so they used the big gun on me.

"Ms. Cleary," she said. "You're an elite ski racer, is that correct?"

"Yes." I'd been warned to keep my answers as short as possible when answering Sheila. She'd be on the lookout for chinks in my armor and would be ruthless once she found one. I'd already seen her bring a veteran ER doctor who'd treated Ava during a previous close call to tears on the stand.

"And how early does the career of a skier start?"

"Depends."

She gave me a chilling grin. I wondered for the hundredth time, what motivates a woman like this? Who takes on a case like Penny's? She seemed like a cartoon villain to me.

"Indeed. And when did yours begin, that is, at what age did skiing become a major focus for you?"

"Around five," I said.

"Five years old?" Sheila said. "That's very young, Ms. Cleary. You must have been extremely dedicated. And tell me, does it take a lot of resources to bolster the career of a young, potentially professional, Olympic-level ski champion?"

"Objection. Relevance?"

"Ms. Gregory," said the judge, who'd been looking increasingly exhausted as the trial wore on, "keep it moving or change tracks, please."

Sheila put her hands up.

"Is it true that in order to pay for your skiing, your parents deprived Penny of all but the most basic necessities? That she was forced to work outside the home from the time she was a teenager to help contribute to your family's dreams of having a gold-medal downhill skier?"

"Objection!"

"Ms. Gregory, I agree that I don't see the point of this line of questioning."

I wasn't so sure I wanted them to stop her. I wanted to answer, to defend my family. Maybe her hobbies hadn't been as costly as my skiing, but she hadn't been *deprived* of anything. Penny got a job waiting tables when she was sixteen to spend more money on makeup and clothes, not to pay for anything for me.

"I'm trying to establish that this is a particularly uneven family dynamic, one that set Penny Cleary up to be the screwup, the misfit, and one that affects her family's perspective on my client and her actions to this day. Penny Cleary grew up in the midst of extraordinary neglect in a home where she was forced to survive on the scraps of whatever was left over from her talented sister."

"That's not how it was!" I burst out. "My parents wanted me to succeed but never at the cost of Penny. Penny had jobs and I didn't, but that's only because skiing *was* my job and Penny didn't have a sport she loved or anything. My parents *never* deprived Penny, that's ridiculous! We weren't wealthy people. I moved to Sun Valley when I was fifteen, we had a team and patrons. It wasn't like they were taking anything from Penny so I could succeed."

Sheila smiled calmly.

"Indeed, Ms. Cleary, you moved away from home to Sun Valley to live with the Duncan family. Is that correct?"

"Yes."

"And at what age did that take place?"

"Fifteen."

"While your sister was still finishing high school, correct?"

"Yes." I legitimately had no idea where she was going with all of this.

"And your line of work since then, it involves a great deal of international travel, is that right?"

"Yes."

"So you haven't really been that close with your sister for what, a decade?"

"I wouldn't say that. I travel a lot but, I mean, we used to talk all the time, and I came to see her when I could. I was there when Ava was born, I was there for her first birthday party." My throat tightened—the pain of saying her name out loud was visceral. Earlier in the day, the prosecution had shown the most damning of Penny's many chilling Facebook posts featuring Ava. This one featured a selfie of a sobbing Penny, holding her lifeless child in her arms, moments after her death. *Heaven has a new angel today, my sweet daughter has journeyed on. There are no words for the pain of a mother who loses her child. My heart will never be whole again!* The prosecution used it to ask the jury what kind of sane mother does a thing like that. The defense argued that many overwhelmed mothers turn to social media in moments of grief and shock, to disseminate the news of a tragedy and get the support they need. It was easier than calling two hundred friends one by one. It may seem like bizarre behavior, and was perhaps not the most *appropriate* response, but who were we to judge a mother who has lost a child? Unsettling, sure. But not criminal. And inappropriate behavior wasn't so surprising, given Penny's "deprived" childhood and the constant stress of caring for a sick child.

"My point is," Sheila continued, "you were very focused on your career, as you should have been! You're a talented young woman, Ms. Cleary, and that kind of self-focus is normal for any twentysomething. But you'd allow that you were not directly involved with Penny and Ava during her short life?"

"No, I won't allow that. I really did everything I could to stay close.

We Skyped, Penny sent me pictures almost every day. I sent Ava presents. It was Penny who cut us off, not the other way around. I loved them so much." This last part came out meekly. Suddenly, it was all too much: the lights of the courtroom, the cameras, Sheila the bulldog.

"Would you please confirm some dates for me?" Sheila said. She proceeded to read off my partial tour schedule for the seasons that spanned Ava's short life, putting particular emphasis on the fanciest-sounding locales: *St. Moritz, Val d'Isère, Aspen.*

I confirmed that yes, I had competed in those locations.

"You didn't just compete, Ms. Cleary, you won a great deal of races."

I shrugged in response.

"Sounds very all-encompassing. Wouldn't leave much time for being an auntie, would it?"

"Objection!"

"Ms. Gregory, if you have a point to make, make it."

"My point is: Katie Cleary wasn't present throughout most of Ava's life, including a period of nearly two years when the sisters were completely estranged. The prosecution would like to paint her as the tight-knit auntie next door baking cookies and babysitting and leaving casseroles in the freezer, and I'm simply establishing that this is very far from the truth."

A sinkhole of guilt opened inside of me. What if I had been next door baking cookies? Could I have somehow prevented this?

"Let's move on, please," the judge said.

"One final question," Sheila said, a satisfied smirk passing over her face. "Ms. Cleary, you mentioned in your earlier testimony that your sister has an illness. Do you have any professional credentials or experience in the medical or mental health professions?"

"No, but—"

"No further questions."

ལᏚ

The press had a field day parsing my testimony. Many were critical of my defensiveness during Sheila's cross examination, while others accused me of being bamboozled by my nasty, power-hungry parents whose only aim had been to have a famous child. In their minds, I was just unwittingly complicit in their neglect of my sister. I wasn't sure what I could have possibly done differently, but I felt like I'd failed my family.

The next day, both sides presented their closing arguments. The prosecution's argument was straightforward. They focused on the preponderance of evidence—the metric ton of medical records that showed years of Ava's unexplained ailments, the parade of different doctors, the years of Penny's social media posts that exaggerated or lied about Ava and other parts of her life, the lies about her work, Penny's own bizarre medical history, including the fake pregnancy, the container of table salt discovered mere feet from the bedside where her daughter perished from sodium poisoning, the fact of the G-tube she'd so vehemently insisted on having surgically implanted in Ava's tiny stomach, giving Penny a means to poison her in an instant—as well as the testimony of the expert witnesses, psychologists, and the doctors and nurses who'd cared for Ava not only at the end of her life but also throughout it. There was only one possible explanation for Ava's death, they contended; Penny's disorder was the only thing that made any of it make sense. They mentioned my parents and me only briefly, knowing that Sheila's cross had lessened my impact.

"You've heard from many new acquaintances of Penny's, many folks who've known her less than a year and who have communicated with her mostly on Facebook. We ask you to take more seriously the impressions of those who've known and loved Penny her whole life, who have also lost a family member, a beloved grandchild and niece."

The defense's close was delivered not by the bulldog, but by her handsome young counterpart. He was chosen, I presume, for his big dark eyes and his buttery voice, his Clark Kent appeal to both genders.

"Penny Cleary-Granger was a neglected child, and this neglect caused her to sometimes seek attention in desperate and strange ways, but she nonetheless grew up to be a dedicated professional, a loving spouse, and a devoted mother. The prosecution has told you a terrifying horror story, but that's all it is, a story. They have not presented you with a smoking gun because no crime has been committed. A monumental tragedy has occurred; we ask you not to compound it by sending an innocent grieving mother to prison."

The jury deliberated for four days.

Penny was acquitted.

As the judge read the verdict, I saw my sister's expression transform from stoic to beatific relief. She smiled bravely and hugged superman and the bulldog. As I watched her, I realized that whomever I was seeing in that courtroom wasn't my sister anymore. Somewhere along the line, the Penny I loved had disappeared and was not coming back. I would not see my sister, or the monstrous doppelgänger who'd replaced her, again.

Stewart moved his wife to the Air Force base in Macon, Georgia, for a fresh start. Though their marriage did not survive—buckling under the weight of their loss and the stress of the trial—Penny remained in Georgia. The fact that she no longer lives nearby doesn't stop me from seeing Penny's face around every corner each time I'm home in Coeur d'Alene, nor does it stop me from seeing her in crowds hundreds of miles away from anywhere she's ever been. Penny is a ghost who is mine forever.

About a year later, another piece of news made its way back to us, joyful or horrifying depending on where you stood. Penny had met and married someone new after a six-month whirlwind courtship. They were expecting their first child.

⁂

During the year of the trial, I didn't qualify for the World Cup Tour and had an unimpressive run in a handful of NorAms, and I tried to get my bearings while Luke and Blair and all the rest of my friends did their normal run around the globe. I was demoted to Alpine C Team. Red Bull officially dropped me.

My therapist, Gena, told me I was suffering from PTSD, a diagnosis I couldn't wrap my head around; it felt somehow too dramatic, reserved for war veterans and refugees. At first, it was a bad night's sleep, then it was a bad day on the hill, then it was a shaky month on the hill. I couldn't sleep, couldn't stop crying. I began taking Ativan for the panic attacks and Klonopin to sleep, usually after several glasses of wine, sometimes a bottle. My focus was shit, my thoughts were consumed. Late in the season, not long after the verdict came down, I crashed out on a sloppy training run and shattered my tibia. Then the panic attacks got worse. Luke and I broke up. Everything I'd ever consciously lived for, every reason I'd had for getting out of bed in the morning, was gone.

And that's how Katie Cleary disappeared.

Liz Is Ready to Talk

TO SPARE myself, I ask Cali what she already knows about my sister. She recalls the broad strokes from the news coverage. The bizarre and horrifying story, the contentious, divisive acquittal.

"I remember feeling really bad for your family," she said. "For what it's worth, I believed you guys. I couldn't understand how she could just walk after all that. Obviously I'm not an expert or anything, but I just thought there was no way something wasn't seriously up with her."

Since everyone in my old life experienced it in real time, I've never actually sat down and told anyone the story from start to finish. Halfway through, sobs come up from my chest, and the familiar signs that I might dissolve into panic present themselves: the coldness in my throat, the tightness in my chest. Cali asks if I'm okay. Do I want to keep going? I don't need to if I don't want to. But suddenly I do want to. I need Cali to know. I can't hold the weight of it for another second. So Cali takes my hand and listens. I tell her about the breakup with Luke, the downfall of my skiing, and lastly, how I wandered into an airport and ended up here, with an alias and an apartment in San Telmo and an affair that's slowly devolving into a disaster.

"Oh, honey," she says, "exhale. That's a lot."

"I know." I tense up, realizing too late that perhaps this was too much to lay at the feet of any new friend, and I haven't even mentioned my pregnancy fear. "I'm sorry to just"—I mime a vomiting motion—"put that all out there."

"Not at all," she says. "I'm glad you felt like you could tell me." She squeezes my hand and smiles. "I sort of can't believe you're still walking upright after all that."

"Some days that's about all I can do."

"God," Cali says. "Liz, er, Katie. My friend, I am so, so sorry that you went through all of this. I don't even know what to say other than that I'm sorry for your pain."

"That's plenty, Cali, honestly." Her response is as close to the right one as exists. People had done many strange things when faced with this story, which—thanks to the news coverage—everyone in our lives had been. Some offered platitudes: *Whatever doesn't kill you . . .* or *The darkest hour . . .* Others parroted empty religious aphorisms about God's plans, and these especially rankled me. Where was God in this story? No god I could reconcile came anywhere near something like this. "I'm just glad you don't . . . I don't know. I'm glad you didn't run in the other direction."

"Why would I? It doesn't have anything to do with you, or I mean, it does, but none of it is your fault."

"I know that," I say. Do I? "Not everyone in my life back home reacted so well. Maybe things would have ended with Luke anyway, but it made it all so much worse."

"Well, that doesn't say much for him."

"He just wasn't up to it. We'd known each other since we were kids, and I'd always been one person—disciplined, positive, single-minded—and then this all happens, and I come unglued." It all sounds so familiar to me, I realize, because this is the voice in my head, the voice that berates me and exonerates Luke day after day. "I don't know, I just totally lost focus, I was crying all the time. I wasn't the same person. I wasn't what he signed up for anymore."

Cali thinks on this for a moment. "It's not that you weren't *you* though, you were just in a crisis. And when you love someone, you're supposed to be there for the bad as well as the good. I mean, you don't get to just take the easy parts of a relationship, that's not how it works."

I shake my head. Why do I always feel the need to make excuses for him? Maybe I'm just looking for a way to not hate someone I loved for so long. The cost of all this has already been too high. "I think a lot of people, not just Luke, had this feeling that I might be contagious. Like if they looked too closely at what was happening to me, they might have to accept that something like that could also happen to them. What was even worse was all the people who *blamed* us, me some, but my parents especially. And oh god, Cali, they deserve it least, they're the best people in the world." My voice catches as I think about my mom and dad in the eye of the storm. Of all the things I hold on to as truth—and some days, it doesn't feel like much—this I do know: my parents didn't fail Penny. I'm sure they made garden-variety parenting mistakes, but they were loving and kind and generous, and they did their best, which is all two humans can ever do.

Some of the trial watchers—the pathetic people who treated our misfortune as entertainment—speculated that I was deluded and didn't see the malevolence of my parents. But no one who *knew* the Clearys felt this way. People forget that I was the one who was there, following on her heels less than two years behind throughout the majority of her life. When it comes to Penny, I am the witness, the one and only. Once I started pulling on threads, there were a thousand tiny things she'd done: minor lies that had blossomed into major ones, her illness—such as it was—had been a progression.

I explain some of this to Cali now, how it happened slowly and then all at once. And while Luke had turned out to no longer even be up to the task of being a real friend, Blair's true nature had shined through, making him feel, by the end, like my last real friend on earth. He called me from every stop on the World Cup that year, occasionally badgering his brother, who'd not yet mustered the courage to break things off, to talk to me as well. He flew into town for barely twenty-four hours between races so that he could be there when I testified. He'd been the one in the hospital with my parents when I came out of surgery after my accident.

I'd repaid his loyalty by pulling away and now by fleeing the hemisphere without even telling him where I was going. I could only hope he'd forgive me. Knowing him, he would.

"Life is messy," Cali says now. "People fuck up, get sick, die, do insane things. You don't want anyone in your life who can't handle the hard stuff. Your story is obviously dramatic, but life comes for everyone eventually. Your boy Luke won't be charmed forever."

"I miss how it felt before I saw this side of him. I miss who I thought he was," I say.

"I get it," Cali says. "I was pretty crushed by how some of my friends in the orchestra acted when everything went down—just as you said, like I was contagious, like they were hedging their bets and not on me. But my family and my friends from childhood? One hundred percent on my side. I was barely able to stop my brothers from heading straight to New York and tearing him to pieces."

"As it should be," I say.

"Yeah, honey," she says, taking my hand. "As it should be. Look, people who are really driven, really competitive, some of them are good people—us obviously." She smiles. "But a lot of them are also narcissistic assholes who really and truly don't give a shit about any ends but their own. Sorry, but especially the men."

I nod.

Cali considers what she's said. "I take it back. Not sorry at all."

For a moment, we both look out into the slate-gray waters of the bay. Beyond us is the roughest sea on earth with its howling winds and unpredictable sky. Between Ushuaia and Antarctica are a smattering of islands, now mostly uninhabited. I remember from our cruise the day before the story of a tribe that once lived there. Despite the freezing climate, they wore almost no clothes and swam and fished in ocean waters so cold they would kill most people after a few minutes. We're built to survive, we humans.

"I'm assuming you're not in touch with Penny now?"

I shake my head.

"You know most people think that acquittal was nuts. I was on your side even before I met you. Not that it's much consolation."

I knew there were many people who thought the verdict was wrong, but of course, the outside world just moved forward while we were left forever in the blast zone. We'd had the option to try a civil case; the burden of proof was lower, and our lawyers told us we had a good shot. But to what end? We didn't want damages, not that Penny had any money. We didn't even really want her punished, even after everything. It was hard to pinpoint what justice even looked like; nothing could undo what had happened. And the idea of going through yet another trial felt unbearable. I just wanted Penny to get help, and I wanted her kept somewhere, safe from herself, away from children, and unable to procreate until she grew too old to have any more. I wanted her to accept and acknowledge what she'd done, to mourn with us, and ask our forgiveness so that we could give it to her. God, how I want to forgive her. I want to stop feeling like someone had blown a hole through the middle of my chest. I want to go back in time somehow to intervene. I want to stop feeling like Cassandra screaming into a void. I want to stop wanting the impossible.

"It *is* a consolation that you feel that way. That you believe me. That you know."

"Thank you for trusting me," she says. "I'm really glad we met."

"Yeah," I say, letting my head fall onto her shoulder as she puts her arm around me. "Me too. So the funny part is . . ." I continue, because for Christ's sake, if I'm going to tell her all of this, why would I not tell her everything? "This was not the bombshell I had in mind to share with you on this trip."

Cali cocks her head at me. "There's *more*?"

"Yes. I don't know. Maybe." I try to smile, but I suddenly start shaking. "I'm sorry, I'm sorry," I say. "This is all too much and you've been so good about everything. I just . . . never mind."

"Liz, oh my god, you're freaking me out. What?"

"I think I might be . . . that is, I haven't had my period in a while."

Cali's eyes get wide. "Have you taken a pregnancy test?"

I shake my head. The idea of going into a pharmacy alone and trying to explain, in Spanish, that I need a pregnancy test is too overwhelming to bear. But once the words are out of my mouth, it all just seems too ridiculous to be true. Besides which, I realize I'm feeling a familiar cramping, a distinct edginess. I must be just about to get my period.

"Well, that seems like a good first step," Cali says.

"I'm so nervous. I mean, I'm sure I'm not though, right?"

"You need to know for sure. I mean it's early so . . . sorry, that's insensitive, but you know what I mean."

Right, of course. There was always that. Theoretically, I had choices.

"Is it even legal here?"

"I don't think so," Cali says. "So I guess you'd have to go home."

"I'd go home anyway. Of all the things I'd like to experience abroad, that one's not really on the list. Not that I even . . . I'm sure I'm not."

The idea of being pregnant by Gianluca is horrific. I would end up another secret, cast away like his first little family and God knows how many others. But then, I also feel something completely unexpected; some unfathomable part of me *does* want to be pregnant, or is at least intrigued by the notion. Something is revived in the idea that my body isn't obsolete, that it has performed something miraculous. *Life* in the old girl yet.

"Come on," Cali says, "we're going to the pharmacy right now. You can wait outside. My Spanish is better."

Back in our creaky condo that smells of salt air, I take the test and sit with Cali for the longest three minutes of my life, waiting for the sign—plus or minus—to appear in the tiny window.

Pregnant.

Liz Has More to Lose

OUR FIRST night back in Buenos Aires, I go over to Edward's for dinner and right away spot Gemma by the pool. She looks especially pretty tonight with her soft features in profile in the crepuscular glow. I grab a bottle of red from the counter to go see if Gemma will have a glass with me—no more than the one I'm allowed, and besides, it might not matter. I don't realize until I'm out of the door that she's on the phone, holding it to the side of her head that faces away from me. I stop in my tracks, not meaning to eavesdrop but overhearing her nonetheless.

"Mummy loves you, she misses you terribly."

Mummy?

I step back to retreat inside but accidentally slam into the doorway and Gemma looks my way just as she's hanging up the phone. For a moment, her big round eyes widen and then she smiles broadly.

"Liz, darling!"

"Sorry, I was just coming to see if you wanted to have a glass of wine with me, but then I saw you were on the phone . . ."

"Well I'm off now, and *of course* I want a glass of wine, you goose." She motions me to join her where she's sitting.

"I was just on the phone with my little sister. She hasn't visited our

267

mother in ages, and somehow this has become my problem to solve from thousands of miles away."

"So your sister is speaking to you again then?" I ask.

"Oh, well, naturally! Once she needs my help with something." Gemma flutters her fingers. "How was your trip to the ends of the earth?"

For now, I've asked Cali to keep the many revelations of Ushuaia to herself. I've told her that Edward figured out who I was when I first arrived. She's as impressed as I am that he's kept it a secret. It's a relief that Cali knows, but however cathartic it was to tell her, it was exhausting too.

"It was great! We went on a lake tour, saw the penguins."

"Do they smell as horrid as I've heard?" Gemma asks, wrinkling her nose. We'd casually extended the invitation to her but were unsurprised when she demurred. Gemma has made it clear she's a city girl, not into outdoorsy adventures, which are the only reason to go to Ushuaia.

"They do not smell great, but it was a good trip. How are things here?"

Gemma shakes her head. "A bit of trouble with Anders, I'm afraid. He's not here tonight," she adds as I glance around us. "He's off pouting."

"I'm sorry to hear that. What's going on?"

"He just wants more from me than I expected him to. I mean, he's twenty-five, for god's sake, I didn't think he'd get so attached."

I smile. "You probably blow his mind."

Gemma grumbles, "I'm not sure he's accustomed to any resistance. I gather he was *quite* the golden boy back in Oslo, but I think this thing with his sister has just shattered him. I'm just not sure what he expects from a holiday romance."

"What are you going to do?" I ask.

"He says he needs me to *decide*," Gemma replies, taking the rest of her half-full wineglass down in one sip and gesturing to me to refill it.

"About what?"

"About him. I suppose you could say he's given me an ultimatum."

"Oh. Well, how do you feel about it? I mean, I know you care about him."

"I do, but it's more complicated than that. Besides, I'm probably just a midtwenties rebellion, something he needs to get out of his system. He'll tell his grandchildren about the old lady he had a scandalous romance with before he met their grandmother." She smiles.

"I don't think that's how he sees it." I consider the way Anders looks at Gemma—full of admiration and awe—and I feel a sudden flash of envy. "If anything, it seems like he's the one who's fallen for you. Like he's got more to lose."

"Oh, Liz," Gemma says, looking at me as though I'm a hundred years younger than she is, "women always have more to lose."

⁓

In my desperation to gain control over something in my life, I decide I need to break up with G now, before I get any more confused. I cannot make a decision about the pregnancy while I'm still enmeshed with him. The conversation we had the night before I left for Ushuaia has filled me with dread, and breaking it off for good seems the only way to kill it. His responses to my text messages since then have been frosty. My body without his goes into a kind of withdrawal, and the thought of never being with him again makes me panic, which is why I know it needs to end. I'm not in love, I'm chasing the dragon. Leaving him feels healthy and sensible, and I didn't know I had any self-protective instincts left. Though maybe it isn't myself I'm protecting.

I ask him to meet me at a café near his studio, a low-lit, quiet place that feels like it belongs anywhere but downtown. I wait for him for forty minutes in a small booth. He texts me that he's caught up in the studio but will be there soon. The more time passes, the more my resolve deepens. G is not any healthier than I am—between the secret family and the horrible history and god only knows what really happened in Saint-Tropez. What a pair we are!—and what we have is toxic. And I can feel him pulling away. Already it's reminiscent of Luke's breakup by attrition. Rather than leave me when he wanted to, he simply started calling less and less from the road, was suddenly never able to find a good enough Internet connection to Skype. When I called him on it, he claimed to be giving me some space to deal with everything. But space wasn't what I needed, it was what *he* needed. My grief repelled him. I was a drowning woman and he was not offering me rescue, he was swimming in the other direction.

When I told Luke it wasn't working, all I wanted was for him to fight for me, to tell me he loved me and needed me and would rise to the occasion of this disaster. But he said none of this, instead simply replying, "Yeah, I guess it's not." Was that all he had to say after all these years? After a lifetime of being a breath away from one another? "I'm sorry," he offered. "I'm sorry I'm not who you need right now. I'll move out. I'll keep paying rent until you can find a roommate or whatever." He said this like he was doing something gallant. There was a brotherly hug and a promise of friendship that I didn't ask for and wasn't given.

There'd be no need to find a roommate. Within three days, I'd have what became a career-ending crash. I might have recovered from the physical fallout, but losing my one outlet put my mental health over the edge. It wasn't just the crash, but the death, the trial, the acquittal, Luke, everything. The crash was *the* straw, but it was only a straw. Without my normal endorphin dose, my panic attacks soon became so debilitating that I went home to live with my parents.

The stakes with G are so much lower, I remind myself now, nursing my glass of wine. I plan it in my head so I won't forget once he's here, so that smelling him and feeling his touch won't shatter my resolve. I get clear on my own agenda: I will end this, but first, I will tell him what really happened to me. I just need him to know. He showed me his, I'm showing him mine. And then I will say, thanks for the memories. No more tango. Of any variety. I'm picturing sad smiles and a final kiss. A clean breakup for a relationship that never was, a proxy for the conversation I didn't get to have with Luke.

He comes in, and though he's not apologetic about being late, he looks unexpectedly happy to see me.

"Tiger," he says, pulling me out of my seat and into his arms, "I missed you." He kisses my neck just below my ear, which sends a spasm of desire through my stomach. He's not usually so affectionate in public. "Scoot over," he says and joins me on my side of the booth. He nods to the waiter for a glass of what I'm having.

It's hard being so close. I'd imagined this conversation with him sitting across from me, the table between us.

"How are you? How was Ushuaia?"

"It was good. Listen, I need to say something to you."

The waiter returns with lightning speed and sets down a glass of wine that G takes a sip of.

"Anything, sweetheart," he says, taking my hands in his. I'm unmoored. I'd imagined him surly and defensive, as though somehow the mood of this mercurial man would have remained entirely unchanged since he'd walked out my door five days before.

"I'm sorry I was being so pushy about things. I'm sorry I pried. The last time we saw each other . . . I had no right." *Even though*, I think, *I didn't ask you the half of what I'm wondering about: your children, for instance.*

G sighs and smiles. He runs his fingers over my scalp and gives me a fresh jolt of want. "It's my fault, Tiger. You didn't know. I shouldn't have gotten angry. I'm sensitive about it, well, obviously. But I know I can trust you, and I shouldn't have been such a jerk. Can you forgive me?"

I nod. The script in my head is torched.

"I just wish that you felt the same, like you could tell me anything. I wish you didn't shut me out. I wish I could know all of you." Now he gives me a deep kiss and I feel something come loose. When he pulls back from me, my eyes are brimming with tears.

The waiter comes back toward the table, but walks swiftly on when he sees the tears. I wonder if he sees a lot of tears in this dark little bar. I wonder if any bar in this beautiful, sad city doesn't.

"What is it?" G says, wiping away a fat tear that's rolled down my cheek.

"My sister," I begin.

"The one you don't speak to?"

I nod. He asks what happened and I find I'm still teetering, unsure if I'll tell him.

"She killed her daughter."

His eyes get wide, and it's oddly satisfying because now he sees. I'm damned by my family's sins just like him.

271

"Is she in prison?"

I shake my head.

"How?"

"It's complicated. Life isn't just." I smile sadly. "But you already knew that."

"God, my love, I'm so sorry." There is no shred of incredulity in his voice, no asking, as some others have: *But are you sure?* Their disbelief driving deeper the stake of the betrayal I feel *despite* my certainty. He grew up as the son of murderers and I am the sister of one. He knows what it is to care about someone evil, to buckle under the strain of holding such an unbearable love.

He pulls me close to him, and I'm quietly weeping. I'm not going anywhere.

Liz Can Explain

THAT FRIDAY, G meets me in the Plaza Dorrego. He no longer seems concerned about people seeing us together, about appearing taken. I imagine our connection is deeper now, now that we both know what the other is. At the café in the square, he pulls his chair close to mine and kisses me in public like we're teenagers, cutting me off in midsentence. I know the clock is ticking, and that everything has only become more complicated, but my talent for denial is well-developed. I reckon I'm too early in the pregnancy to feel anything, and so the fact of it remains abstract, surreal. Perhaps I'm not even really pregnant, or perhaps it will just resolve itself. Isn't it common to lose a pregnancy this early on?

We'll meet Cali at Red Door in a little while. Right now, a band is playing and people are dancing beneath some strung-up lights.

"Come on, Tiger, my star pupil. I want to show you off."

Here with him on this crisp, pleasant evening in my upside-down life as the days grow shorter rather than longer, wrapped in his competent arms, bound together by our monstrous ties, and maybe by something beautiful and new, it feels more than ever like love. But what happens when winter comes? Am I really going to stay here, be pregnant here? Have a child with this man?

273

G leads me off the dance floor, and I can see a hundred eyes clinging to us. I know I only looked so dazzling out there just now because of his expertise, but still. I feel purely happy in a way I haven't in years. Suddenly, it all feels possible.

Then, I see him. He's getting up from a chair in the courtyard where people sit drinking wine and eating empanadas, enjoying the mild evening and watching the dancers. I'm tempted to think he's nothing more than another ghost made material by my subconscious, the way I keep hearing Luke's laugh in crowded rooms or seeing Penny in the faces of every petite woman I see. But his eyes are locked solidly on mine, those warm familiar blues. I feel my mouth drop into an O. I tell G I'll meet him at Red Door in a little while. I'm walking away before he can react, my tether to him unspooling.

"Who is that?" G grasps at my hand, barely missing it. His jealousy might excite me a little any other time, but right now, I just want to get to him.

"A friend from home," I say. "Go, I'll be there soon." I feel him bristle at being told what to do, but I'm already moving away from him.

"Liz," G calls out as I get a couple of steps away. I turn around and he winks at me; I smile and roll my eyes.

"Blair," I whisper as I put my arms around his neck, melting into his arms, taking in his scent, which is of every good thing about home, everything I miss about my past. "What are you *doing* here?"

If the fact of his solid, lean body in my arms wasn't so certain, I wouldn't believe it was him. How long has he been here watching?

"What do you think I'm doing here, Bomber? Kjersti told me she ran into you. She e-mailed me and said you were living here. She knows I've been trying to track you down."

For a moment, I just stare at him, thunderstruck. "You came all the way down here to see me?"

He shrugs. "You weren't answering my e-mails."

"So you just figured you'd stake out the Plaza Dorrego until I appeared?"

"I had a few free days before I had to get to training camp, and what the hell else am I going to do with all the miles I've racked up on LAN? Besides, it worked, didn't it? I might have had a backup plan or two. Now, let's go get some dinner. Bomber, you've got some explaining to do." He throws one of his long arms around my shoulders.

Even though I've been hiding from him, I've overwhelmed by joy at seeing him. Seeing him *here* on these streets that we walked together before it all came crashing down, it's like we've managed to fold time in on itself. Is this what I've been hoping to do all along? "I know just the place," I tell him. "You'll never eat a better steak in your life."

We get a table at La Brigada and I can't get over the fact that he's here. He stares at me, and I wonder what he's thinking.

"You look great by the way," he says as we sit down.

I can't help myself: "I'm so out of shape."

He laughs. "I see you still haven't learned to accept a compliment. So," he says, tearing into the bread and dragging a piece through a dish of olive oil. Blair and Luke eat more or less nonstop, always have. "Do you want to start by explaining why Zorro out there called you Liz?"

I was hoping he'd disregard it. But of course G had done it on purpose, to stake a claim in the face of this stranger.

"I took my middle name and put it with my mom's maiden name."

"Clever." He nods. "Why all the cloak-and-dagger?"

"You know what it's been like back home. I wasn't sure how big the story had been here and there are a lot of expats . . ." Unlike Luke, Blair hadn't looked away when everything got messy. He'd kept calling me, kept coming to see me, put up with me when I was hysterical and when I was taciturn. Didn't ask me to recount any details when I didn't want to, and listened to every last gruesome one when I did. Part of the reason, maybe the *only* reason, I'd wanted to get away from Blair was because I was embarrassed about how much I'd leaned on him. Even seeing him now, I feel the sting of my own vulnerability.

"So you come to a place where no one knows you and you change your name so no one can find you." He reaches across the table to take my hand. "It's got flair, Katie."

"I also lead tours here, I have Americans in my group all the time. I've had people nearly recognize me. If the context wasn't so bizarre, they'd see right through me even without the name."

"Is it helping?" he asks. "Getting away?"

"As much as anything can help."

"I understand." He does and he doesn't, of course. The isolating, maddening thing is that as much as he wants to, he never quite will. I don't blame him, but I can't say I don't illogically resent it, and not just with him but also with everyone. Of course, *of course* I'm not that special in having been through a tragedy; my suffering isn't at all unique, but the circumstances are. There are no support groups for people whose family members have Munchausen syndrome by proxy, there are no gala fund-raisers for research, no 10K runs. There's no shared language of healing the way there is around other traumas. I've yet to find a single other refugee from this particular war.

Blair and I retreat into some small talk. I tell him about Cali, about Gemma and Edward with their upper-class drama and his magnificent house. Blair devours his *bife de chorizo* and goes into gratifying ecstasies over it. The waiters seem to find the speed at which Blair consumes his steak—not to mention an entire *provoleta*—marvelous. I tell him about my tango lessons. I don't want him to think I've been doing nothing here; I want him to see that I've accomplished something.

"Look at you, twinkle toes! That's an unexpected twist. Though I know you can do anything you throw yourself into. If you'd come down here and learned to be a brain surgeon, I wouldn't be half surprised."

"Gianluca is such a good teacher, he's amazing." I hear my own voice when I say his name and I'm a little embarrassed at the sound of it coming out of my mouth. It's as though somehow the moment I mention him, Blair will know I'm sleeping with him.

"That guy from the plaza?" Blair scrunches his nose. "He looks like a sleazebag."

I laugh. "Excuse me! You've never even met him, how can you tell?"

"Men can tell, trust me."

I roll my eyes. "You just don't understand tango, you heathen," I say, trying to wave him off. But I feel the heat in my cheeks, wondering if he only saw us dancing or if he saw us kissing too. Not that it's any of Blair's business who I'm kissing, or dancing, or sleeping with.

Blair shrugs. Is he jealous? My thoughts are scrambled. I still can't believe he's sitting in front of me. Then I think of G, who is expecting me to join them at Red Door. Since returning from Ushuaia, I've slipped back into an almost single-minded obsession, counting the minutes until I see him again, fiending for the physical rush of his touch.

"Will you come meet my friends?" I ask Blair as we're finishing up dinner. "We're having drinks at the bar where my friend Cali works."

"It's not like I have other plans, Cleary." He smiles. He's as easygoing as he's always been—so unlike his pigheaded brother.

When we arrive, Cali is leaning over the bar, chatting with Gemma, who sits with a glass of red wine in front of her. Unbeknownst to the two of them, they've become the focal point of the men in the bar: the beautiful bartender and the boisterous blonde. I call out a hello and feel the energy of the room taking Blair and me in. My arm is looped in his; I haven't wanted to let go of him since he arrived, as though he might disappear if I do.

"Blair, these are my friends Cali and Gemma, Cali, Gem, this is Blair."

Gemma startles and nearly knocks over her wineglass. "*Blair,* Blair?"

Cali cracks up. "Smooth."

"The one and only," I say, looking over at him as he shakes their hands.

"Been talking lots of trash about me, I see?" He glances back and winks at me.

"Oh, *so* much trash."

"Of course you're him," Gemma says. "My god, look at you, you Viking!"

"Nice to meet you. Glad you've been looking after . . . our girl." He catches himself before he says Katie. With him in the room, the alias feels preposterous.

"Tiger, there you are," Gianluca says in Spanish, appearing from nowhere, curling his arm around my neck, and kissing me on the cheek in a way that feels proprietary. "Who's this?" He nods his head at Blair.

"Blair," I say in English, trying and failing to ease myself out from under G's arm. "This is Gianluca, my friend and our tango instructor."

"*Mucho gusto,*" G says reaching out his free hand, which Blair regards and, I imagine, considers removing from his body before shaking. "And how do you know my dear *friend* Liz?"

"We go way back," he says simply.

"Blair's a skier too," I say, removing myself to grab the drink from the bar that Cali has set down for me, staking a more neutral territory between the two men. "An Olympic silver medalist, actually," I say, and barely meaning to, I reach over and squeeze his elbow. I'm so proud of him.

"Silver," G repeats, nodding. *Dick,* I think.

"If K . . . if Liz had been there, she would have gotten the gold," Blair says. "But next time."

I know he's trying to be encouraging, telling me he still believes in me, but it's like a knife to the gut, the mention of *next time.* I'll be thirty-four next time, a long shot even without everything else that's happened.

"Or maybe she stays here and becomes a tango champion," G says. "She's very talented. She's my favorite student," he adds in a way that seems designed to ensure that Blair knows we're sleeping together.

"You'll do anything you want," Blair says. "You deserve to."

Gemma gracefully inserts herself into the conversation and eases the tension, detailing the adventures we've had since I've arrived. I'm relieved to have Gemma in this moment with her levity and her talkativeness.

When Blair heads off to the bathroom, G wastes no time.

"So who is this guy? An ex-boyfriend?"

"He's one of my best friends from home. We've know each other since I was five. You're not jealous, are you?" I say the last part teasingly, but he takes immediate offense and laughs coldly.

"No, Liz, I've got nothing to be jealous of. Anyway, pardon me, I see a *friend* of mine over there, so." He leans in and gives me a swift kiss on the cheek. I watch him in disbelief. Angelina is near the pool tables with several of her girlfriends. I don't know when she arrived; I've been too distracted. Her face lights up when she sees him heading toward her. He takes her in a big showy hug, picking her up in his arms, twirling her around.

"You've got to be fucking kidding me," I say under my breath.

Gemma looks aghast. "*Really*?"

"Whatever," I say, feeling not *whatever* about it in the least. Blair comes back. "Let's get out of here," I tell him, and we say goodbye to Cali and Gemma.

Blair walks me back to my apartment. My mind is racing. Is G really this petty? Am I supposed to be flattered that he's jealous, that he's now trying to make *me* jealous? Am I jealous? (Yes.) All I want is to spend a little time with my friend, who's come all this way. I don't want to be thinking about G right now. I lean over and take Blair's arm. He smiles down at me, and suddenly I no longer am. Instead, I'm transported, walking with him through these same streets as though it's the first time. Is it only in retrospect that it felt like the beginning of something? Or not the beginning, because Blair has always been there, before that moment and after it and still. It was his voice on the phone; his face in the gallery; he was in the waiting room after my surgery; he told me in a thousand small ways that he would stand by me come what may. Not Luke. With Luke there were always conditions, I see that now; our love was based on a contract we'd signed when we were too young to know what life could be.

"Do you want to come see my place?" I say to Blair when we arrive at my door on Defensa.

"Of course." He follows me in through the lobby into the courtyard, and his eyes fill with wonder. "Wow," he says, ducking his head to clear the archway covered in ivy.

"This is the place," I say. We head into my tiny apartment. "Small, I know, but I love it."

"It's cozy," Blair says. We sit on the edge of the bed, which is really the only place *to* sit.

"So what do you think?"

"Of?"

I shrug. "I don't know, everything! My apartment, the steaks, my friends."

"Your place is great." He smiles. "The steak was the best I've ever had in my life. As for your friends, I stand by my opinion of Zorro. Gemma seems a bit nuts, but she's fun. I do like Cali," he says.

"Of course you do." I laugh. "Everyone is in love with her."

He shakes his head. "I don't mean it like that and you know it."

"What do I know?" I say, smiling. "She's awfully beautiful." Am I testing him? Surely not. Fuck, my head is a mess.

"You know," he says, turning to face me, "who I love."

I feel my jaw drop a little, and then he's kissing me. Blair, my oldest, dearest friend. For a moment, I'm lost in it all. And then I pull back.

"Oh Blair," I say, staring down into my lap with my fingertips to my lips. Suddenly, my heart—which I'd already thought was dust—fragments further. What have I lost by being with Luke? I had one chance to choose—but I never knew there was a choice! I always thought both of them were so far out of my league—and I blew it. Like I blew my shot at gold, like I've blown everything.

"I'm sorry, Bomber, was I out of line? I'd never want to . . ."

Oh, god, he thinks I didn't want him to kiss me, when, in fact, I have just realized that I did want him to—despite G, despite Luke, despite everything. Blair is someone I know I love, but in which way and how?

"Oh it's not that, Blair." I take his hand and I'm squeezing it so hard, my knuckles are white. "But we can't. You know we can't."

"Why?" he asks gently. "Why not?"

"Because of Luke, for one thing."

Blair sighs. I'm certain this was the answer he was expecting. In reality, of course, the issue of Luke is only for starters.

"That can't be the reason."

"Isn't there like, some bro code about this?" Everything changed when I got together with Luke, and changed again when we split up. But I'm holding on to the idea that there must be some way to have both of them in my life still. I wish I'd never been with Luke at all, I suddenly realize. People say they don't want to jeopardize a friendship for romance and it sounds like an excuse, but it isn't. The trade wasn't worth it.

"Bro code? What are we, sixteen?"

"You know what I mean, Blair. Don't pretend this isn't complicated."

He groans so heavily it nearly shakes the bed and buries his face in his hands for a moment. He turns back to look at me. "Do you want to know the truth, Katie?" I know he's serious because he never uses my first name. "Luke probably loved you as much as he could love anyone, but it's not half of what you deserve. I love my little brother to death, but he's the most selfish guy on the planet, and you know this. And anyway he's . . ." Blair catches himself, shakes his head.

"He's what?" I say, feeling my throat constrict, because I know. Even in the midst of all this, Blair is trying to protect me by not telling me.

"Never mind, it's not important."

"Go on," I say, "finish your sentence." I need to hear it. This thing with Luke is a defining feature of my life before—I need to kill it. If I have any lingering illusions about what I still mean to him, they need to go. I know what Blair's saying about Luke, about who he is, is true. A hot bubble of rage boils up from my stomach, and I realize that, despite what I've told myself, I haven't forgiven Luke for the way he handled everything: he should have either risen to the challenge or had the courage to leave me.

"He's seeing someone," I say. Blair's silence confirms it. I laugh, and it sounds like the beginning of a sob. "Well, I couldn't have expected anything else from the big man, especially with his new gold medals. Just tell me it isn't fucking Sarah."

Blair at last cracks a smile. "It's not Sarah," he says.

"Just dating every liftie and coed he can find or what? Making up for lost time?" Blair shakes his head but won't look at me. "No," I say, feeling hollow. "It's one person. It's serious."

"He's living with someone," Blair says quietly.

Luke slutting it up all over Park City would be one thing; his heart belonging to someone is something else entirely.

"Well," I say, my voice too loud, shrill, "he has the right to move on, doesn't he?"

Blair ignores the question. "You know what, Katie? I have to just say this. He was a goddamned idiot to let you go. He took you for granted, and he shouldn't have bailed on you."

"I wasn't what he signed up for anymore," I say, shaking my head.

"Don't make excuses for him. If that had been our family, you would have done anything to help him, and you know it. I know it. Luke will never have anyone in his life again who is one-*tenth* of the woman you are."

He looks down, then glances back up at me. It moves me to see him so vulnerable. I want to comfort him; I want to kiss him; I want to run away; I want to crawl into his lap and disappear there.

"Blair," I say finally.

"Katie."

"This is overwhelming. What you're saying, that you're *here.* Don't get me wrong," I say, grasping his hand. "I've never been happier to see anyone in my life, it's just . . . I don't even know who I am anymore."

"Well, I do," he says. "You're the bravest, most inspiring skier I've ever met. You're the best friend anyone could ask for. You're a kind, smart, beautiful woman who doesn't deserve what's happened to her."

I shake my head. He doesn't see how much I've deteriorated. How different Liz Sullivan is from Katie Cleary.

"Listen, my timing may not be awesome here, and I can wait as long as you need to. But the reason *cannot* be Luke. You do not owe him that, and neither do I."

"He'd lose his mind, Blair."

"I already told him," Blair says quietly.

"You told him *what?*" My heads spins.

"How I feel about you. This is not new for me, Katie. Do you really think I'd have come here like this if I hadn't? He's an idiot, but he's still my brother."

"What did he say?"

"He was pissed. He didn't talk to me for three weeks."

I wish I could say that it doesn't mean anything to me that Luke still cares, but it does.

"When he cooled down, we kept talking. If I could have just gotten over it, I would have a long time ago. Katie, you had to have known, at least a little."

And of course I had, but it had been too complicated to even look at. Sometimes, denial keeps us from seeing the good as effectively as it does from seeing the bad.

"I wouldn't exactly say he's given me his blessing, but he'll get over it eventually."

"Well, glad you two got that whole thing all sorted out."

"That's not what I mean and you know it."

The fact that Blair even felt he could broach the topic with Luke makes me realize something I've probably known on some level for a long time. Luke was checked out of our relationship long before he ended it, and if I think he was faithful all that time while he was traveling the world and I was home falling apart, I'm kidding myself. Maybe that was when he met her, the new girl, whoever she is.

"Just come home. I understand that you needed to get away. I know it's been hard, but you have a life back home, a career."

"Not anymore I don't."

"You could get it back if you wanted to. Everyone misses you."

I shake my head. "This shit with Penny, it broke my brain, it broke *me*."

"You have access to the best sports psychologists in the country, Bomber, if you want them. But look, if you don't want to go back to racing, then don't. There was always going to be an after. I'm going to be lucky if I have two more seasons, there's no way I'm making Sochi. We all have to move on at some point. Life's not over when skiing ends."

"What will you do? The school?"

Blair smiles. "My dad is already signed on as an investor."

"That's awesome, Blair, honestly."

"And I mean if you wanted to be part of it, I . . ."

"Blair." I can't let him project this impossible future onto me, it's too painful. "I'm pregnant."

For a moment; he's frozen in shock. "I . . . oh wow. Okay, um . . ." He rakes his hand through his hair.

"You met him."

"That guy?" He sounds appalled. "Are you guys even together?"

"It's complicated. I haven't told him. I haven't really decided what to do yet."

Blair goes quiet.

"It was an accident, obviously."

"So are you going to . . . like, move here?"

"I honestly have no idea. I feel pretty lost at the moment." As I say this my eyes well up, and before I know it a flood of tears comes pouring out.

"Come here," he says. What have I done to deserve him? "Look, Katie. Obviously I want you to come back. But if you stay here, I'll visit you every time I'm in the Southern Hemisphere, okay? Nothing is conditional with me, now or ever. If you come back as my friend, I'll be a lucky man. If you come back as something more . . . there isn't even a word for how lucky I'd be."

"But what if . . . I mean, what about . . ."

"I love you," he says, pulling back from me and moving my hair out of my face. "We'll figure it out."

Liz Is Not Liz

BLAIR LEAVES two days later and I say goodbye to him at the bus station, giving him a brief kiss and a long hug, promising to think about everything he said and call him soon. I ache watching him go.

I don't hear from G for a few days after Blair leaves. I text him a couple of times, but he's silent. He's punishing me.

"That guy is an emotional terrorist," Cali says when I tell her this. "Consider me officially Team Blair."

"We're not . . ." I say, "Blair and I . . . I mean, well . . ."

I feel my face get hot, and Cali laughs.

"Whatever you say, Blushy McBlusherson."

"It's just all so beyond fucked up, Cali. What? I'm just going to raise my love child with my ex-boyfriend's brother and live happily ever after?"

She shrugs. "Life is weird. I mean, do whatever's best for you and—"

"I haven't decided yet," I tell her before she can say *the baby*.

"What I'm saying is don't get caught up in appearances. Who cares? If there's any upside to being a pariah, it's that we no longer need to try to live up to anyone else's expectations."

❧

That night, we're lounging by the pool at Edward's, trying to figure out what to do with our evening, when Gemma convinces us to go into Puerto Madero. Anders is with us. I haven't had a chance to talk to Gemma about it, but I gather maybe she's decided to give him a real chance. Edward mentions that G said he'd try to stop by. I'm on edge hoping he'll come, dreading it too.

I haven't spent much time in the old port neighborhood, other than to take the occasional tour group through there. It spans the somewhat homely waterfront of the churning brown Rio de la Plata. It was once an actual port but never a terribly functional one, and it hasn't been used as such since the 1920s, when the new port was completed.

"You know I don't care for that place, Gem, it's a tourist trap. It's like being in Buenos Aires without being in Buenos Aires," Edward says, tipping the last of the bottle of Malbec into Cali's glass before immediately pulling another one from where he's kept it at his feet.

"There's a Hooters there," Anders says.

"And a TGI Fridays," I add.

"There is *not!*" Cali says, and we both nod. I cringe picturing the glaring neon lights of their signs refracted on the river. Seeing these sorts of American stains on beautiful foreign cities is so depressing.

"You're all being snobs! There are plenty of gorgeous places in Puerto Madero. Some of the best galleries in the city are there, and I can never get any of you to go with me." Gemma is pouting.

"Well, the galleries are closed right now, love," Anders says, taking her hand indulgently.

"But these girls haven't even been to the Faena yet!" she protests. "It's one of the most beautiful expressions of Philippe Starck in the world."

"Well, fine," Edward says, as though he alone gets to decide. "We'll go there for cocktails in the Library Lounge. I'm not in the mood for the precious food. Let's get a steak somewhere before we go."

"Speaking of precious," Gemma says.

Edward gives her a look. There's a strange vibe tonight that I can't quite put my finger on. I feel a bit like we shouldn't venture so far from our regular haunts tonight. Both Gemma and Edward seem like they're on a mission: what that mission is, I'm unsure.

"Fine," she continues. "Library Lounge is my favorite place there anyway."

⁓⁓

When we arrive at the Faena, I have to agree that it's worth seeing. The whole place is dimly lit and vampiric, and the moment we walk through the doors and down the long, narrow hallway with its bloodred carpet, it feels as if we're walking through the chambers of the city's literal heart. Gemma is visibly cheered by our awe and holds court as we walk around, telling us all about the architecture and the collaboration between the two iconic designers: Alan Faena and Philippe Starck.

"This," she says, taking us into the dining room, which is a stunningly all-white contrast to the deep, dark hues of the rest of the hotel, "this is pure Faena right here. He's known for never wearing anything but all white. I met him once in London, he's such a character."

I realize as Gemma continues to gush about the design—and even after we're seated in the cozy library bar with its eye-wateringly expensive cocktails—that every detail she mentions seems to tie back to some story of Gemma's old life. The other Faena Hotel and Art Basel, the gallery launch where she sat next to Philippe Starck in London. I realize we're here because Gemma is homesick.

We've scarcely been sitting ten minutes when Gemma runs into someone she knows.

"Gemma!" A tall brunette in an architectural-looking dress strides over to embrace her. Gemma is on her feet with a smile plastered to her face, trying to mask her alarm.

"Lucy!"

"Gem, my god, is this where you've been?" The woman's face, I notice, doesn't register the delighted surprise of someone who's unexpectedly run into a friend abroad. Her look is more shock and confusion.

Gemma dodges the question by turning to introduce us. I hear Edward muttering, "I knew it."

"Come meet my friends, Luce. Well, perhaps you know Edward already."

"I haven't had the pleasure, actually." Edward stands too, and soon the rest of us are awkwardly, uncertainly on our feet. Lucy looks utterly perplexed as Gemma introduces each one of us as simply "a dear friend," even Anders. As he leans forward to shake her hand, he puts his free hand on the small of Gemma's back possessively. He doesn't want to be introduced as a friend.

Lucy looks aghast. "Gemma, you haven't."

"Lucy, let's go chat for just a moment, hmm?" Gemma desperately ushers her away.

She hustles her off quickly but not so quickly that I don't hear Lucy mention "Thomas and the girls." And it becomes clear to me that I've always known Gemma was hiding something, and of course, we all have been, haven't we? Except, seemingly, the great bachelor of the ages, Edward.

Cali and I exchange bewildered glances—Edward is shaking his head and avoids looking at any of us. No one says a word until Gemma returns several minutes later looking distraught. She heads straight to Edward's side, and I feel a pang for Anders that she didn't come to him.

"Oh, Edward, Lucy won't say anything, do you think? She's a friend, she wouldn't."

"I don't know, Gemma. I don't know Lucy from a hole in the ground."

"Come on, love," Anders says, gently taking her arm. "Maybe we'd better leave."

"Yes," Edward says. "Let's go home. Gem, we'll talk about this later."

By the time we get back to Belgrano, despite Edward's pleas to her to drop it and Anders's increasing and obvious discomfort, Gemma is so shaken by seeing Lucy that she seems unable to let it go. Cali loses her patience before I do.

"Do you guys want us to leave? Because this is getting really awkward, so maybe Liz and I should go. Unless someone would like to explain to us what, in the general hell, is going on?"

Anders and Edward look expectantly at Gemma, as if to say: your call, throw your friends out or tell them the truth. Gemma turns to us and I can see her attempting to recover her sparkle a bit.

"Well, girls, as you're aware no one really knows I'm here, other than our darling Edward. But the thing is, Lucy runs in the same circles as my ex, Thomas, and so now we've got a bit of a problem on our hands."

"Why does it matter if Thomas knows where you are?" Cali asks. "I mean, it's none of his business, is it? He's your ex."

"Well, the divorce isn't . . . completely final."

Gemma buries her face in her hands.

"What does that mean, Gemma?" Anders asks.

My brain struggles to track this new information: the reason Gemma is hesitating about Anders is because she's still *married to someone else.*

"Did you know?" Anders takes a menacing step toward Edward.

"Of course not," Edward spits out. "Gemma! Dear god. Do you realize what you've done? He could take the girls away, permanently!"

Now both men are standing to one side of her and Gemma has collapsed into the Eames chaise by Edward's fireplace, prostrate, with her sobbing face buried in her forearms on the armrest.

The girls. Of course. There was Lucy's mention of them and the strange moment in the courtyard, *Mummy misses you and loves you very much.* I realize I've known it for a while: Gemma didn't only leave behind a maybe-not-so-ex-husband—she left behind her kids.

"So how old are they?" I ask. "Your kids?" My voice, as I hear it, sounds eerily calm. For a moment, there's a hush, and Gemma lifts her head and meets my eyes.

"Eight and six," she says. "My angels. My whole world!"

"Wait, wait, wait," Cali says, catching up now, not having the benefit of having heard the phone call, which it occurs to me now, Gemma lied about so swiftly, so seamlessly. "You left your kids?"

"I didn't *leave* them, for god's sake." Gemma's on the defense now. "I'm going back. I just need some time. You don't know what it's like! Thomas's family and mine, they're just going to think I'm some selfish harlot. I needed a moment to breathe, to strategize."

"You lied to us," Anders says.

"Don't be dramatic," she says. "Everyone here has a story. If I'd told you the truth from the outset, you'd have written me off!"

Not telling us she has kids seems not to constitute a lie of omission but a complex and detailed fabrication, of a variety that I'm far too familiar with. I feel something inside of me come loose, my mind racing ahead of me with a thousand tiny conspiracy theories.

Gemma switches again from angry to distraught, her eyes welling with tears. "I just wanted a chance to have some allies, to have some *friends* who don't look at me like I'm crazy. This has been the worst time in my life. And if you'd known I left my kids at home with their dad while I went gallivanting off, you'd think I was the worst mother in the world!"

It takes me a moment to realize why everyone has suddenly gone silent and is staring at me, their faces looking alarmed. I only hear myself belatedly, only realize after they do that the sound is coming from me: a horrible, hideous, mirthless laughter.

"The worst mother in the world!" I say. It's all erupting and I'm powerless to stop it. It's as though I'm watching myself at a distance. I feel Cali's hand on my arm, as a caution or as a comfort, I don't know, but I'm wild now and I want neither; I shrug her off. Suddenly, I'm on my feet. "You're right though. We're all liars. You know what? I'm not even Liz Sullivan," I continue. "I'm Katie Cleary."

Gemma looks helplessly to Edward, who won't make eye contact with her. I feel touched that he's obviously never told her; I'd wondered. She looks back at me, baffled.

"Honey," Cali says softly, sounding as though she's a hundred miles away. I keep staring at Gemma.

"One-time Alpine skiing champion? No? Nothing? Didn't make the news where you were, I guess. Well, I told you that I had to stop skiing because I got injured, and that's true. But I didn't tell you *why* I got injured, or why I decided not to just rehab and keep going, which believe me, I want more than anything in the world to do. But my mental game is shot, probably forever at this point. And that's because of something that happened nowhere near the mountain. Would you like to guess?" I ask, vaguely aware that I'm wildly overreacting but so filled with a righteous rage that I can't stop. Suddenly, all I can see are Gemma's lies, the charm, the manipulative veneer—I'm not talking to her anymore, I'm talking to Penny. She shakes her head. "My sister, Penny Cleary-Granger, is one of the most infamous women in America, Gemma. A year and a half ago, while I was on a flight home, she murdered her daughter. And what's more, she was acquitted. So I'm afraid *Worst Mother in the World* is a title that's already been claimed."

Liz Gets the Full Story

THE NEXT day, Cali asks me to meet her at Recoleta Cemetery. Amazingly, she's never been. We get large coffees to take with us, and for a while we quietly stroll and make small talk: commenting on the briskness of the day and the beauty of the extraordinary cemetery with its vast marble mausoleums built side by side like a small city, with narrow cobblestone corridors running in between. We pass Evita's grave, and though it's relatively nondescript, it's surrounded by a clutch of tourists snapping photos.

"Huh," Cali says, as we stand there for a minute before moving on. "It's kind of the *Mona Lisa* of this place. All hype."

"Come on, I'll show you one of my favorites," I say, and a few minutes later, we approach the family pantheon of Dorrego-Ortiz Basualdo.

"This is more like it," Cali says, taking in the ornate candelabra with the sculpted marble woman beside it. "This looks like a nice place to live, let alone be dead in."

For a moment, we're quiet.

"So . . ." Cali says. "Are we going to talk about last night or nah?"

I smile and shake my head. "Gemma."

"She was really upset after you left," Cali says. After my tirade, I'd stormed out and gone home alone with my righteous indignation.

"She hit a nerve. A few different nerves, actually."

"But you hadn't told her any of that, had you?"

I shake my head.

"God, I must have sounded deranged."

"Only a little." She smiles.

"I just . . . I guess I find it hard to be sympathetic to someone who's in a mess of her own making."

"Well, that's the other thing," Cali says. "You didn't really stick around for the whole story."

Cali fills me in. I'd known about Gemma's psychotic break, but what she'd been too ashamed to share was that, in a moment of the excruciating paranoia that had characterized her episodes, she'd packed her girls into the car and ended up nearly driving over a cliff with them. She'd come to with her children screaming from the backseat and the car teetering on the precipice of oblivion. Leaving London hadn't been self-indulgence; she'd been protecting them.

"And no one knew this?" I ask, feeling a pang of guilt. I'd conflated Gemma with my sister, but she was nothing like her. If only my sister had removed herself from her child.

"Edward knew most of it."

"Well, I feel like an asshole now."

"Nah. None of us had the full story. She'll understand."

We're quiet for a moment as we stroll among the crypts. The Recoleta Cemetery is eerie but peaceful too.

"Can I ask you something?"

"Anything."

"You and Edward?"

"Eh." Cali smiles. "We made out a couple of times. Nothing major. I find him kind of sexy, to be honest, even though he'd make a terrible boyfriend."

"Yeah, I suppose he would."

"Better as a friend. And actually, speaking of Edward, I have something to tell you."

"Oh, okay."

"I'm leaving Buenos Aires."

My heart drops through my stomach. The idea of being here without Cali is unfathomable, especially if I decide to stay.

"Are you going home?"

"Actually, I'm moving to Paris."

"Paris! Wow. Okay. Wait, what does Edward have to do with this? You said 'speaking of Edward.'"

"Oh, well, Edward knows one of the major donors to the Philharmonie de Paris. I know, la-di-da."

"Of course he does."

"Right? But, he said he can get me an audition, and I might as well take him up on it. I miss the cello too much, and I really can't go back to New York. Maybe someday. But I've loved living abroad, I'm not ready to be done with the adventure. It's been the silver lining of this whole thing. I probably never would have done it otherwise."

"Do you speak any French?"

She shook her head. "No, but I'll learn. I'm good with languages."

"You are. When do you leave?"

"Friday."

"Wow, Jesus that's fast. That's great, Cali. I mean it sucks, I'll miss you. But I'm really happy for you."

"Thanks, babe."

We stroll along one of the corridors of the cemetery. The skies are clouding a bit above us, and the shadows give even the most sparkling white tombs a sinister feel.

"You know," Cali says, "a lot of the people I met here, I don't know if I'd have been friends with them in real life. But you I would have."

I reach over to take her arm.

"Ditto. I hope your moving to Paris doesn't mean we're not friends anymore."

"Of course not!" she says, swatting me with her free hand. "I mean, shit, you can come with me if you want. Not that that's necessarily what I think you should do. Even though it *would* be a lot of fun."

"Oh," I say, smiling, my mind rushing forward. Did I want to go with Cali? Continue on with the adventure, without my little passenger? Though Cali wasn't going to be a bartender in Paris, she was going back to the thing she loved. "And what do you think I should do?"

"You really want to know?"

"I wouldn't ask otherwise."

"I think you should go back home, maybe do that ski school thing. I didn't tell you this, but once you told me your real name, I went and Googled the shit out of you. I watched a bunch of videos of your races. Girl, you're incredible, and I think you love it. And, since I'm telling you what to do with your life, I think you should see where things go with Blair. Because I think you love him, and I *know* he loves you. So there. You asked."

I'm quiet for a long moment.

"It's not that I don't want any of those things, it's just that when I came here, it seemed like the only way out was to get as far away as possible. But now, I don't know. I don't know what I'm doing here. But going back is complicated."

"Maybe," Cali says, squeezing my arm a bit more tightly in hers, "the only way out is back the way you came."

"And what about . . ."

"That I cannot help you with," Cali says. "I'm not sure if I ever want them, so I'm the wrong person to ask. You really do need to talk to Gianluca though, I think. For better or worse."

Katie Cleary Is Out of Here

Eᴅᴡᴀʀᴅ ʜᴏsᴛs a bacchanal that Thursday to send Cali off. I'd been feeling a bit queasy all week, and that day I wake and am so nauseated, the very thought of coffee makes me nearly retch. It's as though the tiny cells inside of me are asserting themselves, in case I'd thought I could forget them. I decide I'll go to the party early and leave early as well; I don't feel I can miss it. I've been texting with Gianluca—who's been hot and cold with me this week, in addition to being decidedly pouty about the fact that Cali is leaving. I know I need to talk to him, but when and how to do this I don't know. Once I know how he feels there will be no going back.

I realize I never pictured myself being pregnant. It wasn't that I specifically didn't want kids, but I always thought of them as a far-off abstract concept. And when I thought about kids, I thought about them as five-year-olds, old enough to run around with and teach to ski. But somehow I'd never really thought through what happens to a body when it's invaded by a microscopic being siphoning resources from its mother to create itself inside of her. In addition to the gnawing churn of my stomach, my breasts ache, and I'm so tired I feel I could sleep for a thousand years.

My focus on my body had always been on what it could do outwardly:

namely how fast I could hurtle it down a mountain, how sharply I could execute a turn, how close I could push it to the brink without destroying it. If I'd given any thought to how I would feel about being pregnant, I would have thought that I'd have hated it. But even though I feel physically awful, I marvel at the idea that the beginnings of life are stirring inside of me.

There's something else I hadn't properly examined until this moment: I assumed that it would be either hard or impossible for me to get pregnant. Even though I knew Penny had invented many of her pregnancy issues, the experiences had imprinted themselves on me nonetheless. When you believe something to be true in the moment, it's very hard to go back and edit that memory according to facts you've learned later. Rather than canceling each other out, those two truths—the one you felt and the one you later learned—simply live uncomfortably side by side. And so even though I know that Penny invented and engineered Ava's illnesses—that she likely caused her early entrance into this world as surely as she caused her early exit—the specter of the NICU and the ghostly, hellish corridors of Children's Hospital haunt me still. It has always seemed to me that the world was a hostile place for a child, one in which first your body and then their own could inexplicably turn on them. And this paranoia lived right alongside another one: that every mother of an ill child must automatically be a danger to that child. When I saw sickly looking children with their mothers, I immediately searched for signs of Penny—the eerie calm, the showy ministrations, the blank wash of the eyes. Even with the Madres de la Plaza, with their resolute but hollow eyes, I had the horrible thought that they were performing their grief. And then there was a third, even more potent fear: What if I held inside me some latent gene that would turn me into Penny once I became a mother?

These buried irrational fears, I realized, had been exerting their pull. If I kept the pregnancy, I would have to find a way to let them go.

I come to the party early and pass on the wine, citing stomach trouble.

"Is Gemma here?" I ask Edward.

"She's in the bedroom getting ready." He smiles. "Go on back."

297

I knock gingerly at the door.

"Come in!" I think Gemma won't be nearly so cheerful when she sees it's me. Sure enough, she catches sight of me in the mirror she's looking into and slowly lowers her mascara wand.

"Hello, Liz . . . er, Katie. What shall I call you now, darling?"

"Liz. Not everyone knows."

For a moment, we stand like that, her back to me, as we face one another's reflections.

"Gemma," I say, "I'm so sorry."

She turns around and comes swiftly toward me, taking me in her arms. "Oh no, *I'm* sorry. I feel like such an arsehole." She has tears in her eyes, and, just like that, I do too. Another side effect: I'm as emotional as can be.

We sit next to one another on the edge of the bed.

"You're not," I say. "I leapt to judgment without even hearing the whole story. I completely overreacted."

"Well, of course you did! I'd heard of the story, but I confess I brushed up on the details after the other night. My dear friend," she says, taking my hand. "I don't know what to say. Only that I'm so sorry for everything that you and your family went through. I don't know how you survived it."

"Some days, I'm not so sure I have."

"You're incredibly brave. For testifying. I admire you so much. I want you to know."

I smile weakly at her.

"And I should have just told you that I had kids. I feel so wretched about leaving them behind in England while I go walkabout. I just couldn't fathom that anyone would understand."

"I would have. I mean, I do understand. Cali filled me in. You're trying to protect your kids. You don't need to explain yourself."

"I'd like to, if it's all the same. If you wouldn't mind me bending your ear?"

"Happily."

"After the episode in the car, I was terrified. My doctor put me on lithium, but it zonked me out. I sought a second opinion, and my new psychiatrist—a more sensible lady doctor—prescribed an antidepressant and told me I needed to find a way to recuperate or I'd never get back on my feet. I tried to talk to my friends, tried to talk to my family, but they were no help. They didn't think I should leave Thomas, but he was cruel to me, albeit in a most subtle British way. For years, I'd felt like a piece of furniture. He belittled me and when I'd told him I thought I might be depressed—before the breakdown—he said I was being self-indulgent."

"Jesus."

"I just had to get away so I could regain my strength and stand up for myself. Otherwise, he'd steamroll me in a divorce. But now I fear I've made a mess of things, especially bringing Anders into all of this. I never meant to use him, I thought we were just having fun. I suppose the fact that he needed me so much should have been a tip-off. But if I'm honest that was part of the appeal."

No one wants to be the one who takes a fling too seriously, I think, as I suddenly realize that's exactly what I've done.

"I think you've done a brave thing coming here," I say. "If your friends don't understand, get new friends."

"Can I take you back to London with me?" She laughs.

"Nah, I think I need to go home. I need to face my real life too."

"Oh, Gianluca is going to lose it that we're all leaving him at once. Anders wants to come to London too."

I'm frozen for a moment, thinking about the infinite possibilities a new life brings with it. I've never asked them, of course, but I suddenly wonder if my parents regret having Penny. And do we wish she hadn't had Ava? There are no answers to these questions. Maybe life goes in a thousand directions and we never know which, and regret is always wasted on things we had no control of to begin with.

"Ooof sorry," I say. My stomach, which I'd thought was settled, flips over again, and I beeline for the toilet. When I'm finished retching, I come back to the bed and Gemma is smiling at me.

"Ugh. I've just had a terrible stomach bug all day." I sense I'm not fooling her.

Gemma nods. "For what it's worth, Liz. Whenever you decide to have kids, you'll make a great mom."

Before I can catch myself, I blurt out, "Do you think so?"

"I know so," she says. "Now, come on, we don't want to miss the party."

❧

Just like that, it's our last night together and it's bittersweet. Whatever I decide, I need to get in to see a doctor, and it really can't happen here. I'd looked at flights that afternoon; already I have one foot out the door.

I find Gianluca in the television room at the back of the house, curled up on the couch, talking so closely to Sandra that their foreheads are almost touching. They both startle when I walk in, making everything look that much worse. I know this isn't news you tell someone in the middle of a party, but I feel I can't live with it another moment.

"Hi, Liz," Sandra says. "G and I were just talking about you." I look at him askance. "With Cali leaving, Anders needs a new partner," Sandra adds. "And you're so tall! And your tango is pretty good."

Coming from her, this amounts to a compliment.

"Um, thanks." The thing I've been wanting; right at the moment, I no longer want it. "Gianluca, can I talk to you for a minute?"

"Off I go," Sandra says, bouncing up and gliding out the door on her long, storky legs.

"Hey, Tiger," G says, leaning over to kiss my cheek.

"You okay?" I ask. His face is wan, his eyes hooded.

"I'm sad about Cali. And Anders maybe now too, but I'm trying to convince him to stay."

I nod. "Yeah. I'll miss her too."

"Just don't you get any ideas." He says this casually, and I realize how certain he is that he's got me under his thumb. He gives me just enough line before pulling me back in each time, but he doesn't think it will be enough for me to leave him until *he* decides.

"I'm not sure how long I'll stay, to be honest," I say, sitting down on the armrest of the couch.

300

"What the hell, Liz. Are you being serious?" I've caught him by surprise.

"I was never planning to move here. You know? I've just been through a lot. I need to get my life back on track at some point." Ah, god, tears already. My hormones are making everything a nightmare. Horribly, G rolls his eyes.

"You know, you can't keep playing the victim forever, Liz. You need to grow up. Everyone goes through hard things, okay?"

I'm stunned by his vitriol. The moment I hint at the fact that I might leave, he starts acting like a cornered animal.

"Thanks a lot, G," I finally whisper. He looks regretful but says nothing. I stand to leave.

"Where are you going?" he asks, reaching up to take my arm and gently pull me back down next to him. "I thought you had something to tell me, or was that it? That you're leaving too."

I sit for a long moment as the options reel through my brain. Tell him, don't tell him. Stay. Go.

"Why didn't you ever mention that you have kids?"

He's taken aback, and for a moment, I think he's going to deny it.

"Because it doesn't have anything to do with you."

Tell him, I think, knowing I'm chickening out.

"Okay, but it's a big thing to leave out, you know?"

"It's not like I keep it a secret," he says. "But we've talked about this. I have to maintain a certain image for the studio."

"Were you married?"

He looks at me, annoyed, as though it's none of my business.

"For a while. She wanted children, and I thought giving them to her could make it work. It did not. The whole thing was a mistake. I'm not cut out to be a father, I should have known better."

"We saw you in Colonia. We were on a visa run," I say at last. "I've been wanting to ask you about it. You looked really sweet with them."

"Well, yes, I love them of course. And don't start thinking whatever it is you're thinking about me. I take care of them, I send them money every month. It straps me. Why do you think I live in that tiny flat?"

"But you wouldn't want . . . I mean you don't want to get married again or . . . ?"

He looks at me strangely. And then his face softens. "Oh, Tiger. You know I think you're an amazing woman but . . . I can't . . ."

He thinks I am asking him something I'm not, and yet he's answered my question all the same. I need to leave before I burst into tears. There is no good outcome to be found here.

"You know," I say, "I'm going to head home, I think."

"Yeah?"

"I'm not feeling so hot."

"Okay, well listen. I think Sandra is right, we should try you out with Anders. Why don't you come to team practice on Monday?"

All I can do is nod. By Monday, I'll be long gone. I hug Gianluca, and take one last deep breath of the skin on his neck.

"Goodbye, G," I say, my voice muffled.

"Goodbye," he says, "for now?" He pulls back and looks at me. Despite everything, I kiss him.

Epilogue

ONCE AGAIN I'm on a flight leaving Buenos Aires and what lies on the other side is uncertain. What I do know is that when I land this time, it will not be to the news of the worst thing that's ever happened. That moment has come and gone. All there is to do now is carry on and put years between me and it: to let those memories be crowded out by different ones, so that eventually they take up less of my soul.

My parents will be waiting for me on the other end. I don't know how they'll react to what I'm going to tell them, but I know that they'll support whatever I do next. We are all we have now. Or not quite all. I've e-mailed Blair to let him know I'm en route. He offered to be at the airport when I landed, but I asked if we could wait a day or two. I love Blair; I have always loved Blair, I realize now, having made it through to the other side of hell. But I need time to figure out what this means in my new life, time to be able to trust myself and my own decisions after this mess with G.

None of us get a happy ending because Buenos Aires wasn't the end of anything, but rather an interlude from which we all emerge, if not quite renewed, then altered in fundamental ways.

Cali goes back to playing the cello, first in Paris, then in Berlin, and then, at last, back in her beloved New York. Many years later, a wave of scandals sweeps up Cali's abuser and ends his career, with Cali bravely adding her voice to the chorus against him, a chorus which, for the first time in history, is listened to.

Gemma returns to London and, after a very difficult year, reaches an armistice with her ex-husband, and they become mutually respectful, if not exactly affectionate, coparents to their two little girls.

I learn all of this from the e-mails that the three of us periodically exchange long after we've left Buenos Aires for good. The happy ending is we all get another chance, another chapter.

For my part, people eventually forget the horrific headlines and I'm left to figure out the business of living a quieter, happier life. I love being a mother—and later a wife—more than I ever thought I would. I don't go back to racing, but I find my way back to the mountain and the peace it once brought me.

When my daughter is born, I am filled with such a fierce, protective love for her that I know not one shred of the monster that consumed Penny has been reproduced in me. The truth is I never stop missing my sister entirely. I wonder what's become of her second child, if she's had any more, if there will be a chance someday for my daughter to know her cousins. When the pain of that lands on me, I let it in, and then as with everything else, I put it to the side and carry on.

I never forgive Penny completely. But, in time, I don't think about her every day, I don't wake up soaked with sweat and crying in the night anymore. I know she may reappear in my life one day and that, like the changeling of a fairy tale, it's impossible to know what form she'll take, what her illness will make her into as time goes by. What I'm certain of is that the sister I grew up with, the sister I once loved, is gone. I mourn her death and, as I do, my memories of my own childhood become less toxic. By letting go of the hope that I'll get her back one day, I get a new hope: one for a happy life without her in it.

The happy ending is I do not become my sister.

The happy ending is life continues without her.

The happy ending is we all survive.

Acknowledgments

My deepest gratitude to my editor, Sarah Cantin, who was such a support to me as I navigated the fraught emotional territory of this book; I've been so lucky to work with you. And to my agent, Carly Watters, who has been there for me every step of the way these past few years. Thanks also to Taryn Fagerness and Dana Spector for all of your work on my behalf.

I have so much appreciation for the fabulous team at Atria Books, especially Rakesh Satyal for his support and guidance, as well as Ali Hinchcliffe, Loan Le, Albert Tang, Joanne O'Neill, and Shelly Perron.

Thank you, Crystal Patriarche, Taylor Brightwell, and the team at Booksparks, who have been instrumental in getting the word out about my books. I'm so grateful for all that you do. Thank you to Anna Katz for lending me your keen editorial eye on an early draft.

Brittney Muller and Leah Stroud educated me on the ins and outs of professional skiing and Breezy Johnson shared her perspective as an

Olympic and World Cup alpine skier; thank you so much for helping me bring those parts of the book to life.

I'd be lost without the company and counsel of writer friends like Geraldine DeRuiter, Caroline Kepnes, Taylor Jenkins Reid, and Laurie Frankel; your support and friendship mean the world to me. To my longtime mentor, Pat Geary, thank you for your feedback on an early draft of the book—to be able to call on you after all these years is a rare gift indeed.

To Natasha Minoso, Alyssa Hamilton, and all the other bloggers and bookstagrammers who have helped readers find my work, I'm eternally grateful for your passion and advocacy. Much love as well to all of the booksellers and librarians who have supported my career thus far.

Lastly, to Derek and Fiona. The happy ending is you.